D0875084

THE FORGOTTEN VOYAGE

OF THE

H.M.S. BACI

by

Robert Kline

Galaxy Books, Inc.
Post Office Box 1421
Orange Park, FL 32067 or
www.galaxybooksinc.com or
Email info@galaxybooksinc.com

First Edition
Publisher: Galaxy Books, Inc., Orange Park, Florida
Cover Design: Graphics Ink Design Studio, St. Augustine, Florida

ISBN 0-9652682-6-8

This compilation is dedicated to those who have sailed with me on Sir Edmund Robert's Forgotten Voyage. We have plied turbulent and calm waters together and for that I am grateful.

Robert Kline
St. Augustine, Florida

LET ME TELL YOU ABOUT THE NOTEBOOKS: At the cusp of 1831, unfettered by domestic bliss and flush with his most recent legacy, Sir Edmund Roberts, gentleman naturalist and inveterate adventurer chartered the H.M.S. Baci and left English waters on a voyage of discovery and intrigue.

Sir Edmund departed England still smarting from the cold reception his Catalogue of Faeries of the World's Forests, Mountains, Deserts, Valleys and Bogs had received and so sought solace by pursuing his old dream of finding and classifying the much mentioned but heretofore undocumented sea maiden fauna aswim in the seven seas. True, he published the faerie work almost twenty five years earlier, and also true, he filled the intervening years with service to the King in both the Royal Mounted Artillery, and then when things really heated up as Napoleon's armies devastated Europe like a child in a toy store, he became an officer in the 1st Life Guards; the preeminent fighting arm of King and country. And yet, whether campaigning France, Africa, Egypt or Russia, he suffered with the memory of his rejection by the learned community. So finally, he packed his kit (a very large kit), hired a reasonable vessel and embarked on his second expedition.

The naturalist kept two journals during his voyage; one of a scientific bent and intended for publication, the other more along the lines of a salacious diary detailing both the intimacies of various combinations of sea maiden and sea master courtship and couplings and the self-same waltzes of Sir Edmund and Captain Constance Daphne Fitzwillie, a woman who began the voyage as the Captain's wife and who because of her husband's mental unraveling ended up commanding the vessel for the bulk of the journey.

I came into possession of both journals while on vacation in Bermuda in 1997 at that glorious juncture of seasons when the air is fecund with fragrance as heady and alluring as a woman's vanity. One afternoon while putting about on our scooter, my wife and I found ourselves at an estate auction on one of the multitude of islands that flesh out Bermuda proper. And while the auction provided incredible antiques, it did so at prices in excess of what we were prepared to spend. Ever. Until at last the orphaned step-child of the auction came forth; to wit, a weather-worn roof ridge ornament; a rangy, terra cotta cat with an arched back and a broken tail and, simply put, a satanic smile.

Of course it interested only my wife and in the end we afforded an artifact of Miltonian appeal and questionable beauty at an attractive price.

We returned to Hamilton astride our scooter, my wife humming merrily as she stroked her cat, its weight and bulk unnoticed; she lost in the joy of her purchase and I busy navigating deep coral cuts and billowy tunnels of tropical blossoms. At last in town, we parked and beetled up the little hill to the Hog Penny Tavern where we shook sherry peppers into our soup and discussed how we would ship pussy home. Our feline statuary now stood by my chair menacing a sullen Brit one table away.

Overhearing our lament regarding sturdy packing materials and transfixed by our cat he remarked, "I've bloody well got more crates than you colonials have taste," (one of several utterances that put him at loggerheads with my wife) and then he continued, "I'll tell you what; set up a round and I'll send you to hell's own warehouse. I've got crates enough to box the crown jewels, the crown, the Queen herself (God save her), and bloody Buckingham Palace thrown in."

So we did (truly needing a crate and short on time before our return to the States). Tiny Bottoms was his name and he dunned three additional mugs of ale, got embarrassedly drunk and then sent us to a rubble stone warehouse beyond the cruise ship docks, but not before he had thoroughly insulted my wife and her nationality. As we rose to leave (read: *escape his surly, obnoxious presence*) he directed us to take our crate unopened, to forego emptying its contents onto the floor, to close the "bloody" door behind us when we left, and finally as he swayed at his table he extracted our easy promise to leave him alone; he was heartily sick of tourists in general and Americans in particular.

We left, my wife in a full-tilt rage, and wound our way to a building bathed in semi-darkness and so decrepit and lost in neglect and heaps of trash that the swirls of dust motes and sole-deep rat droppings hastened our exit from what to me was heaven and to my wife, less than. We found a right-sized crate (it had SIR EDMUND ROBERTS burned deeply into the wood and a panoply of worldly addresses stenciled on its sides) and lugged it out to the street where we hailed a reluctant cab and sent it to our hotel. That evening we pried it open and found, among other things, a crushed fore and aft hat, a lion marmoset skeleton wrapped in rotted sea togs, and Sir Edmund's illustrated notebooks ensconced in a bulky tarred canvas satchel.

I have buttered Sir Edmund Roberts' scientific musings and flights of erotic fancy with information gleaned by the historical research firm of Finder and Keepers Ltd., operating from London, England. They located not only letters and diaries of several of the H.M.S. Baci's crew, but also correspondence from Constance Daphne Fitzwillie to her sister Agnes, and three wonderfully childlike batches of letters from Daniel Cooperson (Gnarly Dan) to his wives in Australia, Britain and India. They also forwarded, along with an outrageous final bill, a slim volume entitled; A PIRATE'S LIFE IS THE LIFE FOR ME, an incredible little book of poems by none other than the loathsome pirate Naughty Nat, it including not only some respectable verse, but also a mention or two of his adventures on the main. More than a few times the H.M.S. Baci sails onto the pages.

All of this begs the question, of course; why was a voyage of such adventure and import forgotten? The answer is both convoluted and deceptively simple. Numerous parties were anxious for its obscurity. The scientific community, then and now is loath to treat the subject of sea maiden, for despite thousands of references and at least as many picture representations, hard evidence is missing. Sir Edmund noted after a rather gruesome dissection that their skeletons are in fact quite different from ours, they being, " . . .not so calcified, more pliable to be sure; perhaps consisting solely of cartilage." If that were the case, and there is little reason to doubt it, then skeletal remains would quickly have decomposed. No skeleton. No previous existence. Thus, sea maidens join Nessie, Sasquatch and the mythical Sober Irishman. Further, the British Admiralty had no inclination to revisit the Baci-Bounty-Bethia Affair, they being involved in her sale and absolutely rabid to turn the public's attention from mutinies and the deplorable conditions on board naval vessels. The United States Navy was also involved in an rather embarrassing manner. Losing the U.S.S. Constitution, however briefly, on her round the world farewell and goodwill cruise would have blighted that institution's heretofore-stellar record. And finally, Sir Edmund Roberts' relatives were most anxious to have him declared insane in an effort to access his incredible wealth. His journals were regarded by the court as ". . . lunatic ravings accompanying obscene art." In sum, it was "the mother of all conspiracies", successful to a fault until my wife and I stumbled upon Sir Edmund's notebooks.

What follows is a rounded out version of the journal entries and addenda previously published with the restored illustrations of solitary sea maidens and sea masters, sea couples and of course, sea babies. Finally, I have included "Manly Supplements" detailing the sea battles with the scourge of Sir Edmund Roberts' journey, the loathsome pirate, Naughty Nat.

THE FORGOTTEN VOYAGE

OF THE

H.M.S. BACI

Or

"*H*ow **Sir Edmund Roberts**, gentleman naturalist and **Sea Maiden** questor, unsung cataloguer of the world's mermaid population and champion of all battles save one with the loathsome pirate, **Naughty Nat**, circumnavigated the globe, fell in love with the recently svelte **Captain Constance Daphne Fitzwillie**, and still managed to leave this life cloaked in the cold blanket of obscurity."

A man unmoved by a sea maiden's dance
is naught a man at all.
—GNARLY DAN

And if, as you claim, I only imagined them, what
was the crime it that? They were so beautiful.
—SIR EDMUND ROBERTS

A BRIEF, TRUE ACCOUNT
OF ONE OF
NAVAL HISTORY'S
MOST REMARKABLE VESSELS

No one could have imagined the notoriety in store for the 220 ton merchant ship sent down the ways in 1784. Christened the H.M.S. Bethia, she enjoyed short-lived obscurity until bought by the Royal Navy in 1788 and fitted out as the armed transport H.M.S. Bounty. Her infamous voyage under Captain William Bligh ostensibly ended with her being torched by the mutineers in tropical waters, when in fact the story was a ruse concocted by Fletcher Christian and Lord Percival Frothingslosh and perpetuated by no less party that the Admiralty itself.

Renamed the H.M.S. Baci in deference to the lord's Italian and very oral mistress, she settled into a calm career until chartered in 1831 by the wealthy naturalist, Sir Edmund Roberts, for his circumnavigation in search of sea maidens.

Following two successful engagements with pirates in 1832, she was dramatically re-armed—this time by the soon to be feared, self-styled captain, Constance Daphne Fitzwillie. Flush with gold from her triumph over the ill-fated pirate, Fitzwillie set sail for Bermuda where she not only sent word to her agents to arrange for her purchase of the Baci, but also found willing sellers of a spate of heavy armament at the Royal Shipyard on the island.

There followed a series of running gun battles, the loathsome pirate, Naughty Nat commandeering ever larger vessels and dogging the H.M.S. Baci around the globe, intent on evening the score, culminating in one of the most dramatic and bravely fought encounters in the annals of fighting ships, resulting in the loss of the Baci.

Sir Edmund Roberts painted a striking watercolor of the vessel, noting he was " . . .taken by the Baci, her sails set to dry and ruffled by a rogue breeze." She was at anchor in Bermuda, Captain Constance Daphne Fitzwillie experimenting with cannon placement.

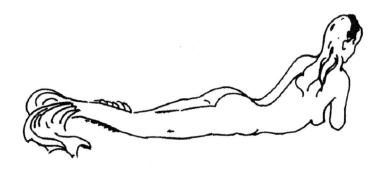

SIGHTING ONE

On a raw December morning in 1831, three disparate parties snaked through the streets and alleys of Portsmouth, England, each making their way to the waterfront. The first was led by Sir Edmund Roberts, gentleman naturalist and world traveler, who walked at the fore of an assortment of luggage bearers, footmen and servants. It was a large party, for Sir Edmund was not only wealthy but also determined to spare himself no luxury. Fourteen men lugged small and large trunks crammed full of books, notebooks, blotters, bits of furniture, bone china, collecting nets large and small, specimen jars, dissecting kits, bottles of the best gin, hunting rifles, fowling pieces, magnifiers, telescopes of various sizes, and a few trunks of fine clothing. Two men trailing the assemblage struggled with a massive and quite comfortable looking chair. At the fore and to Sir Edmund's immediate right a footman, crisscrossed by heavy bandoleers chock full of cartridges the size of a man's thumb, carried an inlaid box in whose velvet interior nestled a matched set of dueling pistols. Over his shoulder was slung a short-chamber Boxer Henry point-four-five caliber (the manufacturer's proto-prototype; a preproduction and highly experimental model whose availability to the military was decades away). It was a weapon of destructive power sufficient to stop a charging rhino dead in its tracks. In the sure grip of Sir Edmund it had done so on at least one occasion. To the naturalist's left walked two ill-fated water colorists of Sir Edmund's recent employ. What luck the artists collectively enjoyed either shunned travel or was shy of water for it would leave their company at the docks.

The second party was somewhat smaller, followed a different route, and could be heard bickering their way to the waterfront. Captain Fitzwillie, a slight man of diminished stature attempted to keep up with his wife, Constance Daphne, while pleading his case for the thousandth time: "The ship is too small, dearest, the voyage far too long. You'll surely be bored senseless; there is no fit company on board or abroad. The food will surely not be to your liking; our quarters are cramped and danger abounds. Please reconsider. Remember, your mother is not well. *My* mother is not well. Our home should not be left unattended for such an extended voyage."

And on and on he whined, his words pale feathers brushing against one of the largest women in London. Ignored and lonely in her earliest years, Constance Daphne made but three friends in her adolescence, they being breakfast, lunch and dinner. Beauty lay dormant in the doughy folds of her face and true adventure had only recently alighted her shoulder.

"Captain Fitzwillie," (she addressed her husband as such at all times) "you command a good ship; please extend that facility to your tongue. You will not escape me; I shall travel at last."

And that was that.

The third party was converging from the seedier section of the city. It was a small party but it was a party in the truest sense. At its heart was a sailor, an old salt, to be sure, grizzled, besotted, in the best of humor and accompanied by three ladies (loose examples thereof) and they too were sloppy drunk; their current celebration having run three days. He had been called "Gnarly Dan" for as long as anyone cared to remember and it is possible he was so-named in the cradle. He loved the sea in particular, life in general, and commitment in the abstract. Because he was a sailor he was superstitious, and three was his lucky number; thus his current companions, the number of his pet curs, the three lucky coins in his shoe, and his wives globally separated but as similar as peas in a pod.

He was good hearted and garrulous, filling all voids with words; they usually crafted to disseminate his boundless knowledge of all things nautical; real or imagined. He spoke at length and without pause of distant lands, whales, flying carpets, magnificent storms, strange peoples and fantastic animals. He was transitioning from ghost ships to elephants when all three groups of travelers intersected in the shadow of a tidy ship snugged to the dock at the port proper.

"That'd be 'er!" Gnarly Dan exclaimed as if finding a lost gold piece. "Ain't the ole Victory, but she's well found and as tight as a..."

Captain Fitzwillie was chagrined to find himself in such close quarters with one who served before the mast. Chagrined and then determined to spare his wife the conclusion of the old salt's analogy. "You there!" he interrupted. "Lend a hand with our dunnage and be quick about!"

Coincidentally, the captain spied Sir Edmund's entourage, recognized him instantly and regrettably as the charterer of his vessel and was doubly vexed when he noted the expanse of trunks and equipment to be stowed. The last straw was the large and comfortable chair in which Sir Edmund now rested as he surveyed the ship.

"Good God, man!" Captain Fitzwille exclaimed, "Surely this would be a joke; you can't possibly be thinking of bringing all that aboard. Why, it's all there but a coach and four."

The captain's tirade tipped toward irony in the shadow cast by his wife's assortment of trunks now being set to the dock. They were barely fewer than the naturalist's, and if one included the bulk of her person, would require more space.

Gnarly Dan, relieved to be out of his captain's thoughts and amused by the building storm, leaned onto the comfort of his hussies and listened, all the while providing a whispered commentary. "That'd be our cap' an' that gent must be a payin' customer by the looks a' things. They'd be steerin' 'ta shoal waters from the sound of it."

Sir Edmund settled back into his overstuffed chair and raised a haughty eyebrow. "I believe, sir, that I have paid in advance for this vessel. I further postulate that I chartered all of her, from her rudder to that pole-like apparatus in her nose. Please be so kind as to arrange for my equipment to be secured." Having ascertained that the captain's wife was accompanying her husband the naturalist came deadly close to an analogy regarding her and shifting cargo.

It was all too much for the captain, particularly since it was a confrontation taking place in the presence of his wife; his overbearing, eavesdropping and far too anxious wife *who was coming with him on a multi-year voyage of circumnavigation.* Captain Fitzwillie spun on his heel and began barking orders to any unfortunate sailor in his proximity.

"THAT MAN! LEND A HAND WITH THESE TRUNKS! AND YOU THERE, WHY ARE YOU STARING AT ME? HAVE THE MASTER RIG A BOSON'S CHAIR FOR MRS. FITZWILLIE! SHAKE A LEG NOW OR YOU'LL KISS THE GUNNER'S DAUGHTER BEFORE THE SUN SINKS THE YARDARM!"

The captain had a respectable voice for such a small man and it did indeed have the desired results: Every gob associated with the ship either leaped to help, settled into a dizzying myriad of obtuse and useless action, or dove below decks to warn his mates.

The ship was loaded, lines were cast off and Sir Edmund's voyage at last begun. Captain Fitzwillie commanded the quarterdeck, he now resplendent in his old Royal Navy uniform; a breach of taste if not the law, it being topped by his most coveted possession: his grandfather's fore and aft hat, the very same naval chapeau Lieutenant Chelmsly Fitzwillie used to shade Lord Nelson as he laying dieing on the Victory's deck at Trafalgar.

"AWAY ALL LINES! PREPARE TO SET THE FORE TOPS'L! SHEETS AND SETS! 'VAST HAULING! YOU THERE, LOOK LIVELY NOW! HELMSMAN, BRING HER UP A POINT!

Every syllable was for the benefit of Mrs. Fitzwillie, for the Bacis worked the good ship by rote, so often had they performed their tasks, so well did they know and love her that they anticipated her needs at least a well as her officers. And so the Baci moved smoothly from the dock, her yards a sea of competent sailors, her decks ordered motion as sheets were hauled and lines coiled.

It was a fine beginning. Mrs. Fitzwillie watched the flurry of activity, enamored already of Pretty Willie, now precariously balanced on the main yard. Appreciating a feminine audience and playing the fool for his mates, he capered until he lost his footing. He would have fallen to ignominy had Hans Larsen not reached out in time and given the falling fool a sure and powerful hand. Pretty Willie twisted in the air above the deck, his sole connection to the ship his handhold with Hans. Mrs. Fitzwillie put her hand to her mouth, uttered "Good heavens!" stepped back smartly, tripped, fell, and then lay exposed as a landed fish, her skirt up, her puffy legs thrashing.

Half of the crew watched as Pretty Willie hung useless and waited to be lifted back to the yard, and half stared at the captain's wife, who, unable to bend sufficiently at the waist to facilitate a recovery, now rocked from side to side so she might at least gain a hold with her hands and knees.

Less entertained was Captain Fitzwillie, for every sail now luffed as the unattended Baci fell off.

"YOU THERE! MIND YOUR HELM! BACK TO YOUR POSTS, YOU HAM-HANDED DOXIES!"

Pretty Willie gained his former position as Mrs. Fitzwillie, now on her hands and knees, eschewed the proffered hand of Sir Edmund Roberts.

Then a cacophony of shouts interrupted the recovery of the sailor, Constance Daphne and the Baci. Dead ahead was another ship just making weigh, her crew's attention drawn to the H.M.S. Baci as she bore down on them.

Her captain clutched a speaking trumpet and called out angrily,"AVAST YOU CLUMSY LUBBERS! YOU SHIP THERE! PORT YOU HELM! PORT YOUR HELM!"

Captain Fitzwillie joined the fray. "HELMSMAN! BY YOUR MOTHER'S GRAVE, HARD APORT! HARD APORT MAN, IF YOU VALUE THE HIDE ON YOUR BACK!"

Disaster was almost averted as both ships slowly turned from one another. They had achieved nearly parallel courses when the distance closed. Their hulls would clear, but rigging and yards were another matter. Mrs. Fitzwillie now sat and watched as the very yard on whose footropes Pretty Willie now stood tore into the starboard rigging of the other vessel. In a trice the Baci's stout timber ripped free of its entanglements, leaving the other ship with a handful of parted stays and at least one sailor thrashing in the narrow waters between the two.

It was a colossal embarrassment with minor repercussions. Understanding their ship's fault in the matter, the Bacis now fell to insulting the aggrieved party in the time-honored naval fashion. The wounded ship presented her stern to the Baci and there above the gilt name, H.M.S. Beagle, a knot of officers and lookers-on shook their fists and gestured impolitely. Embracing the spirit of naval brotherhood, Sir Edmund joined his captain and crew braying insults at those aboard the vessel they had fouled; Sir Edmund particularly pleased to call out to a young man that he was a scalawag and would amount to nothing; to which the young man responded, "And you sir are the son of an ape and it is your relatives I shall study!"

Of lesser clay is greatness sometimes modeled.

It was a sullen night aboard the H.M.S. Baci, followed by weeks of smart sailing and then a gale. The crew settled into their routines, Sir Edmund dining regularly with the captain and his wife, civility being served cold with each meal. And daily the naturalist waxed ecstatic about the certainty of spying sea maidens as he instructed the watercolorists he had brought aboard in the finer points of botanical illustration. A fair artist himself, Sir Edmund sketched incessantly while the two artists in his employ complained without end about the privations of life aboard a small ship.

"Was I any more seasick, I'd be dead," moaned Williams, green-faced and attempting to ignore his churning stomach. The other artist, nominally his assistant, was hale but at a loss for the girls he had left behind in Yorkshire and before that, Paris. "Mon Dieu, how I miss them!" Bistro lamented. "Oh, to hold just one!" He was speaking anatomically, his right hand cupped and lifting gently as his eyes rose. "Why did I ever go to sea?"

He'd roamed the ship from stem to stern and found little to assuage his longing. While she had a mysteriously pretty face, there was far too much of the captain's wife to be of sustained interest and so it was the only other woman aboard to whom he turned. Fortunately, Bistro was an accomplished wood carver, for his paramour was made of the same and mounted (more than once) at the head of the ship and below her bowsprit.

Whether the figurehead was of the vessel as the Bethia or a more recent addition of Bligh and the Bounty is uncertain, but she was handsome of face and duly attired as an equestrian mistress, complete with riding crop. Bistro discovered her early on, his artistic temperament and his unslaked lust moving him to visit the ship's carpenter, barter for a set of chisels and then steal nightly to his precarious perch beneath the figurehead and above the parting waves. He methodically and with great skill undressed her, a trail of wood chips floating in the Baci's creamy wake, until he revealed at last a buxom and beautiful woman poised with delicious menace, her crop awaiting something French, perhaps. Finally, he settled to refining her chest, his past conquests revisited until there were twin monuments to all that is soft and fulfilling; glorious, weighty mounds with nicely rounded sides, soft underbellies and perky, substantial nipples. He longed for the return of clear weather so he might further anoint his handiwork with tongue oil and bring her to a fine luster. Of late and in spite of his unease, Williams had come to joining his assistant in what Bistro would have preferred to be a solitary enterprise, and it was there, in the tail of the storm, their beautiful lady glistening and wet with spray, that they lost their grip in tandem and fell to be swept beneath the Baci's angry bow. They surfaced some twenty meters beyond the ship's stern, called out briefly and then disappeared for perpetuity,

Bistro's diary entries and a newly coveted figurehead the only traces they left behind.

The crew mourned briefly and well, for while they had known the two artists for a relatively short period, they thoroughly enjoyed the Frenchman's ceaseless lament regarding women; they too longed for female companionship (a few had already begun to notice Constance Daphne's mysterious allure, her size notwithstanding). And as for Williams, there breathes not a sailor who fails to find warm comfort in the sight of a landsman heartily seasick, particularly when that illness is protracted.

Sir Edmund redoubled his watercolor studies.

Onward they sailed, the good ship Baci making fine work of the broad Atlantic, the ocean doing her best to deny Sir Edmund the sight of his sea maidens, until at last they made landfall at the Cape Verde Islands in mid-February. The Bacis were thrilled to smell land once more and the naturalist was certain his search would soon be rewarded.

His scientific notebook records the first sea maiden sighting in Sir Edmund's unimaginative style:

Maidenus magnifica
"Amelia"
February 18, 1832
Cape Verde Islands

Seen on a moonlit night by a member of the watering crew who strayed in the company of a bottle of rum. He observed her for most of the night until he gathered sufficient sense to report to me. We watched her until the false dawn.

Medium height. Medium weight. Dark hair

Could not identify the object of her preoccupation. Exultant with our first sighting so early in the voyage.

Fortunately, the naturalist also speaks of the sighting in his personal journal. It seems it was Hundred Proof Hobbs who sighted the maiden, he in the company of the captain's cabin boy, Young Billy, and they in the company of much rum. The "watering party" Sir Edmund mentions was in actuality the two departing the larger group of sailors to relieve themselves. By their own account they staggered to the beach and whilst standing and admiring the moon, noticed what appeared to be a body washed ashore. "Could be one of the gentleman's artist types," Hobbs noted.

17

"Could be," Young Billy agreed, ever anxious to please. They continued standing, staring and contributing to the world's salt water supply until at last the sea maiden (for it was indeed a sea maiden) raised herself to her elbows, allowing man and youngster to note a fine womanly chest.

"Lord above," Hobbs whispered, "it appears I've died an' gone 'ta heaven."

"Thanks fer bringin' me along," Young Billy added.

Still the pair did not move, so fearful were they of being discovered and so clearly was the sea maiden visible in the cold blue light of the moon. A languorous movement of her chest accompanied every breath she took, her breasts swaying ever so slightly and with each subtle sway the sailors at the edge of the woods did sigh. Whether the two stood for a few moments of half the night is uncertain, but what is known is they were interrupted at last by Gnarly Dan, the oldest salt aboard the Baci and an absolute font of sea wisdom, obscurata and legend. He came crashing through the underbrush, startling the two sailors, for he too was in need of relief.

Yet, the sea maiden appeared not to notice. She continued prone on the beach, her elbows propped before her and she lost in reverie. Old Gnarly spied her immediately. "Now there'd be a sight;" he instructed with reverence, "and don't 'his honor' wish he was here ta see." The old salt was referring to Sir Edmund Roberts. Every sailor aboard the H.M.S. Baci knew of the naturalist's quest; knew of his quest and believed in his heart Sir Edmund would be unsuccessful. Not that they did not trust in the existence of sea maidens—to the very core of their hearts they did—but they were unimpressed with the scientific method. Look for something unusual and you will not find it. Attempt to study it and it will elude you. Sea maidens were magical; they swam through the dreams of every sailor and they were theirs alone. Sea maidens were not for landsmen such as the naturalist. Leave harlots and shrews and badgerers for landsman. Sailors, your common gob, adrift for years at a time, half starved, worked to within inches of death's door and lonely beyond description deserved sea maidens. Deserved their beauty. Deserved their magic and deserved their undeniable connection with the sea.

Had any sailor but Gnarly Dan shared the vision of a sea maiden on the shore, alerting Sir Edmund would never have entered his mind. But Old Gnarly was a different sort of sailor. He loved it all. Loved all life. Loved all who stumbled through it and loved most of all to accost them and then share his vast knowledge, their interest notwithstanding. He was attracted to the naturalist from the beginning for he too was different. Sir Edmund was unusual in that although he was a solitary soul, he still found time to talk to the common sailor, to corner him, question him regarding the mysteries of the sea, and most unheard of all, to then listen to his answers. And so after savoring the sea maiden for but a moment Gnarly Dan turned on his heel and went back to retrieve him.

When the two returned the tableau was as he left it. Young Billy and Hundred Proof on the shore staring, the sea maiden lost in reverie. "She'd be thinkin' 'a love," Gnarly Dan whispered to the naturalist as he moved forward stealthily, the two on their hands and knees.

"Shhh," the naturalist answered.

"They does that a lot," the old salt continued unabashed. "Ya see, yer sea maiden loves ta love, if yer catchin' the set 'a me sails."

Without question Gnarly Dan would have continued his monologue had Sir Edmund not taken the opportunity to place his face within inches of the old salt's and hiss, "My good man; I am grateful that you bought me hence. Science will forever remember your name. Scholars will revere your memory, making annual pilgrimages to the place of your birth. Great halls will carry your name." He paused and then came so close his nose brushed Gnarly's. "But if you have the temerity to open your mouth one more time I shall kill you dead. Here. Now. Not once, but twice. And the second time will be more painful than the first."

In his heart Gnarly Dan felt he'd been slighted, but he had not survived as long as he had by failing to recognize imminent danger when it crawled beside him on a moonlit beach.

They watched in silence through the remainder of the night until with the morning the maiden returned to the sea. Not one of the parties actually saw her move down the beach; to a man they claimed that one minute she was before them, the next, she was gone. In all likelihood they had dozed off as a group, but no one was willing to admit the possibility.

Once back at the ship Sir Edmund completed his first sea maiden painting. He also established a set of rules that he observed for the duration of the voyage: The sailor who first sighted a particular sea maiden was given the right to give her a common name. To Sir Edmund's chagrin, there followed a fool's carnival of monikers with mothers and prostitutes predominating. It should also be noted that in the face of all laws of probability the sailors named their sea maidens in alphabetical order, faring twice through the alphabet. The naturalist would provide the Latin title for each, naming both genus and species.

SIGHTING TWO

Sir Edmund Roberts' circumnavigation in pursuit of sea maidens continued with enhanced enthusiasm after the first sighting. Sadly, the voyage's misfortunes accumulated with at least as much vigor. Hundred Proof Hobbs, the crewman who had sighted the first sea maiden, predictably deserted to foster closer contact with her. Young Billy, the captain's cabin boy and reported to be enamored of Hobbs, also failed to sail with the departing ship.

To Captain Fitzwillie's chagrin, a quasi-giddiness infected the crew. Practical jokes increased so dramatically that he came to suspect tom-foolery with the rum casks. "Any more of this nonsense and I'll halve their rum rations!" he declared to Sir Edmund as they sat at dinner.

The naturalist defended the crew. "Why, surely it is a sort of 'sea maiden fever'. These men have been deprived the presence of attractive females for so long. . ." The withering stare of Constance Daphne stopped him from continuing his indiscretion. Abruptly he added, "What they need is a dramatic and significant gesture to enhance, not inhibit, their enthusiasm."

That evening while the men lolled about the ship listening to MacMurphy play his hornpipe, Sir Edmund strode into their midst, produced a large gold coin between his thumb and forefinger and declared, "The next man who sights a sea maiden shall be this much the richer!"

He had the men's and the captain's attention. Sir Edmund then pulled a rusty spike from his pocket and a small hammer from his belt. He turned to the main mast and to Captain Fitzwillie's horror, violated that pristine pole by hammering the gold coin into it. All accounts but Sir Edmund's relate that

Captain Fitzwillie trembled, and then reddened. Mrs. Fitzwillie muttered, "Oh dear," as the captain drew himself up to his full five feet, clutched Roberts by the throat, lifted him at least an inch from the deck and commanded in his foul weather voice that if any man every defaced his vessel again, he would have him flogged, keel hauled, thrashed and set adrift in an unprovisioned and leaking boat.

The following week a sea maiden was sighted, ending Sir Edmund's bout of cabin sulking.

His journal entry reads:

Wondrous news! We have identified our second sea maiden! Previous events were indeed the harbingers of good fortune. In a masterful stroke of enlightened manipulation I offered a reward for our next sighting. While Captain Fitzwillie managed to disguise his enthusiasm, I am certain he is merely reticent to appear over-zealous before his crew.

Without indulging in feminine pique, I must note our captain is disposed to melancholy. Could it be he regrets shipping Mrs. Fitzwillie, the infamous Constance Daphne, as his passage mate? The crew mocks all 30 stone of her. She blocks the passageway. Cleanliness is not her handmaiden.

Alas, perfection is but a myth. I am pleased with our voyage.

Maidenus splendidus
"Beatrice"
April 6, 1832
St. John's Rock

Another nocturnal sighting. Appeared 'mesmerized' and unaware of our observations. I begin to suspect 'female vapors' afflict sea maidens also.

Medium height. Medium weight. Dark hair.

The sailor, Gnarly Dan, insists, "she'd be lost in thoughts 'a love." I believe he has been at sea too long.

First letter of Captain Constance Daphne Fitzwillie to her sister Agnes.

April 10, 1832

Dearest Agnes,

This voyage is an unmitigated disaster. The Captain is preoccupied with his foolish ship and ignores my needs; I cannot imagine what I was thinking when I decided to go with the insensitive clod. We barely speak, except when we are taking our meals and even then he insists on discussing sails or the weather.

I must say, however, it is rather nice, if one is to be shunned by one's spouse, to be stranded on a ship loaded with men when it occurs. They are, as a rule, a rather coarse sampling, but there is an older gentleman; rather handsome, perhaps you remember him—Sir Edmund Roberts? Of London? Comes from an established, if somewhat eccentric family. You may recall his younger brother, Percival. He was a minister. Did some missionary work. Married Sarah Wordslessly. Moved to India and then Africa if I am not incorrect. You must have heard the story; a lion dragged her from their camp one night. All they found in the morning was her shoe. Ghastly color; she never was one for fashion. And big as a wheelbarrow.

And along those lines, dear sister, thank your stars daily you are in London. Being of capital size may be embarrassing in the city, but its disadvantages are manifold at sea. This ship is little more than a cork. The passageways are designed for children and goats, and the stairs—never mind! I must shun some weight. Were I slightly more fit, I think perhaps Sir Edmund might be persuaded to pay a bit more attention to me.

He and the Captain are already at odds; perhaps that is why I find him attractive. Oh yes, he is still obscenely wealthy and of course, titled.

Your sister,

C.D.

SIGHTING THREE

Through the winter of 1832 the H.M.S. Baci, ever vigilant for sea maidens, sailed southward into warmer waters, bad luck cruising in her wake. One gusty afternoon, Sir Edmund was on deck hoping to repair his abominable relations with the ship's captain. Noting the captain's ever-present hat, he called out, "I say, Captain Fitzwillie, I can't help but notice that is a singularly handsome hat you wear daily."

The crew, to a man, paused to watch the exchange.

Captain Fitzwillie glared at the naturalist for a moment, suspecting he was being mocked, and then grudgingly invited Sir Edmund onto his hallowed quarterdeck. Once joined by the naturalist he removed his hat with monumental reticence and passed it with menaced pride as he related, "That hat you hold belonged to my grandfather, Chelmsly Fitzwillie. He wore it with honor in Admiral Nelson's shadow at the Battle of the Nile."

Sir Edmund nodded appreciatively; as a former military man himself he was respectful of those who had known the smoke of battle.

Captain Fitzwillie continued with increased bravado, "And he continued to wear it when he served with the good Admiral at Trafalgar."

He waited for the naturalist to be duly impressed.

He was, noting, "Indeed, sir; you must wear it proudly."

Captain Fitzwillie beamed and went on, now lowering his voice as he administered the coupe de grace; "He was at Nelson's side when the Admiral was felled by a top man's bullet. Lieutenant Fitzwillie, my departed grandfather, kneeled to Admiral Nelson's side and in fact used this very hat to fan England's mortally wounded hero as he lay dying."

Sir Edmund was dumbstruck. It was indeed an extraordinary antique.

"This hat," Captain Fitzwillie confessed passionately and furtively, "is more dear to me than my wife."

It was as Sir Edmund struggled with that thought that he fell victim to the confluence of a gust of playful wind and the devilish masthead hail, "Sea maiden ho! Hard on the starboard bow!"

Every man jack aboard the good ship was instantly in on the joke. "THAR SHE BLOWS!" and, "AIN'T SHE A BEAUTY!" was followed by an excited, "THERE'D BE ANOTHER!" echoing through the rigging.

Sir Edmund dashed to the lee rail, neglected his grip and watched as the cherished hat wafted far out to sea before settling on a distant wave.

For three full days the Baci's crew rowed her boats and launches in ever widening circles around the bobbing and funereal ship, but to no avail. A fortnight later the third sea maiden was sighted by Sir Edmund himself.

His subsequent journal entries are aswirl with naiveté regarding Captain Fitzwillie:

We have crossed the equator and I have seen another sea maiden! Hove to at the small island of Fernando de Noronda off the coast of Brazil. Slept on shore and awoke to a glorious sea maiden illuminated by our guttering fire and within arm's reach. We stared at one another for at least an hour before she backed to the water and swam off. To assuage our captain, I have named her after his wife. Attempted to atone for that blasphemy with her Latin name.

> *Maidenus voluptuosus*
> *"Constance Daphne"*
> *May 27, 1832*
> *Fernando de Norondo*

Average height. Average weight. Dark hair.

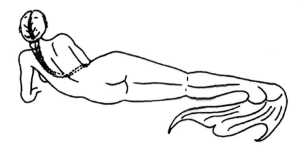

SIGHTING FOUR

The following week Captain Fitzwillie summoned Sir Edmund to his cabin. The naturalist was surprised to find two crew members standing to the left of the captain's desk, their heads lowered in servitude, their hands clasped behind their back.

"Sir Edmund," the captain began, "I've taken the liberty to choose two assistants to help with your 'fish-woman' quest." (Captain Fitzwillie still denied the existence of sea maidens and used every opportunity to belittle the naturalist's work.) "This chap here," he continued, pointing to a short oriental fellow, "hails from the Japan Isles. Calls himself 'Sushi' as near as I can ascertain. Most anxious to help in your quest. Most anxious. And this fine gentleman," he added now noting a massive African, "the crew refers to as Bones. Says as long as he has a friend, he fears no hunger. Perhaps you, sir, should be that friend."

Sir Edmund was wary. It was a magnificent gesture on the part of the captain. The naturalist had mentioned early in the voyage that should Captain Fitzwillie be able to spare a man, what with his two watercolorists gone, he, Sir Edmund, would most appreciate it. At that time Captain Fitzwillie fairly laughed at the idea.

"We're criminally short-handed as it is, sir," he'd answered obviously perturbed that the naturalist should suggest such a thing. "Seems you had two perfectly good chaps when we left England. Hardly my fault if you misplaced them already."

And yet, here was Captain Fitzwillie offering up a brace of stout fellows for his personal use.

Sir Edmund thanked the captain more than once, turned to leave and was somewhat mystified when the captain called after him as an afterthought, "Of course it will be your responsibility to see to their culinary needs!" and chuckled quietly.

Sir Edmund added to his journal:

> *Regret doubting Captain Fitzwillie's ability to forgive. Alas, it was but*
> *a hat!*

There followed what could be best described as The First Manly Adventure, for it was indeed an adventure, and manly to a fault; rife with big ships, cannons and courage. The second mate, Quill Drewson, sent a story regarding the event to the London Gazette, entitling it, "HOW SIR EDMUND ROBERTS, GENTLEMAN NATURALIST AND SEA MAIDEN QUESTOR SAVED THE DAY WITH BUT A SINGLE BALL!"

It seems the ill wind toying with the H.M.S. Baci blustered briefly off the coast of Patagonia. Sir Edmund was on deck for his sea maiden vigil. His assistants, Bones and Sushi were at his side, they anxiously investigating every wave trough and dolphin wake. Captain Fitzwillie, still miffed that Sir Edmund had lost his heirloom hat, was studying a strange ship astern and hull up on the horizon. Fitzwillie ordered more sail set and was savoring the comfort of increased speed when he was overcome by the need to boast of his ship's performance and the drama he was certain he had just averted.

"Sir Edmund!" he barked, "Come and enjoy a parting glimpse of the most feared pirate vessel afloat. Make a leg now; we're about to show her our heels." He offered his telescope to the naturalist. "See the black circle on her foresail? She's the Plunderer, captained by Naughty Nat—don't let the name fool you—he's a heartless scoundrel. She points fourteen cannon and is crammed to the gunnels with 150 drooling, snarling cutthroat vermin."

Sir Edmund looked from the distant ship to his captain. "Yet, you appear unconcerned. Jovial, even."

Captain Fitzwillie expanded proudly. "We are her sailing superior; out sailed her in '30, as we shall today."

Roberts studied the pirate ship for a long moment. "You don't find it odd she is increasing in size—a phenomenon, I believe, connoting decreased distance?"

Captain Fitzwillie snatched his telescope in disbelief. He focused on the Plunderer. He then looked to his own ship's sails; they were tight as drums and drawing well. As a last resort he examined the Baci's wake. It was true as an arrow. He glared at the helmsman anyway. Again the captain raised his telescope to the Plunderer and visibly started; she was dramatically closer. There was no vestige of bravado when he ordered the Baci's lone but powerful cannon brought up from the bowels of the hold and set up as a stern chaser. "MAKE A LEG NOW; HOIST THAT IRON FROM THE HOLD!" There followed a train of powder, tools, and the hastily assembled firing crew.

Sir Edmund's confidence deteriorated with each dropped cannon ball and was utterly ruined when the Bacis started lobbing random cannon balls into the wide ocean behind them. Meanwhile the Plunderer was returning accurate and deadly fire with her bow chasers. Holes appeared in the Baci's sails. Her rigging suffered. It was after the unfortunate captain of the gun crew took a ball full in the chest and became two halves of his former self that Sir Edmund addressed Captain Fitzwillie. "May I be of some assistance? Point your cannon, perhaps?"

Captain Fitzwillie barely noticed. Sir Edmund repeated his questions. At last the captain blubbered, "Yes, of course, do what you wish." By now the Plunderer's unruly mob of cutlass waving boarders could be clearly seen and faintly heard.

Sir Edmund stepped over the former gunner and began directing the helmsman. "Steady, there, my good man." He then coached the gun crew as they sponged out the cannon, pushed in a bag of powder and then hefted in a ball. "On the uproll," he directed.

Twice the Baci's stern stood high on the crest of a wave and twice the crew held its breath, but twice Sir Edmund muttered, "—not my style," and waited.

It was Captain Fitzwillie who exploded, "DAMN YOUR STYLE! HIT HER MASTS, MAN. HER MASTS SO WE CAN ESCAPE!"

Sir Edmund looked up from his cannon and asked coolly, "A particular mast, sir?"

"ANY MAST, YOU BLITHERING IDIOT!" Captain Fitzwillie screamed as he looked from the Plunderer to Sir Edmund and back again. "The main mast—the one in the middle!" he blurted. "Hit the main mast!"

"Just so," answered Sir Edmund quietly and laid his cheek along the warm cannon, closely studying the Plunderer. The stern of the Baci slowly rose with a wave, Sir Edmund squinting down the weapon to the pirate ship behind. At last the naturalist touched his cigar to the fuse and stepped away. The flame hissed along the fuse and then disappeared into the touchhole. Time dragged. Then the cannon jumped and there was a resounding boom. At first it appeared he had missed, for the ball could briefly be seen skipping ducks and drakes beyond the Plunderer. And then the top half of her main mast shifted as in a dream and fell and her sails and rigging went all ahoo.

The Baci's crew yelled and jumped and slapped one another, finally raising three cheers for Sir Edmund who stood humbly by, his attention directed to the Plunderer. Her captain had climbed onto his ship's rail and was presenting his fist in defiance. Sir Edmund squinted and then turned to Captain Fitzwillie who was sharing Sir Edmund's surprise. "I say, Captain Fitzwillie," he asked confidentially, "isn't that chap wearing your hat?"

(It is interesting to note that a poem concerning the brief sea battle appears in Naughty Nat's little book, A PIRATE'S LIFE IS THE LIFE FOR ME.)

Revenge

Me and me lads was sailing along, enjoying the bounding main,
When on the horizon appeared a small ship on whose booty we started to gain.
We was almost there; 'twas a prize so fair!
To a man we swore she was ours!
But it warn't to be, for don't you see, Lady Luck took one of her powders.
'Twas a lucky shot. That's what we got that scratched us from the race!
Our main mast come down with barely a sound;
An' me crew took a slap on the face!
Now I may be a pirate; that's what I do; I rape an' I pillage an' plunder.
But I ain't soon ta rest 'til they feels me best
An' them Baci scum hears me thunder!
I'll find her again. Though I ain't sure when; it may be today or tomorrow.
An' when I do them dogs'll feel blue, for I'm bringin' 'em shot-loads 'a sorrow.

Naughty Nat
The Pirate's Poet

The Bacis had but a moment to savor their victory, for their ship was sorely wounded and they knew they must work like heroes to mend her and put significant sea miles between themselves and the loathsome pirate, Naughty Nat. Back to the coast of Patagonia they limped so they might accomplish the more troublesome repairs. Captain Fitzwillie paced his quarterdeck and barked orders to his crew, he once more the little tyrant.

"YOU THERE! SHAKE A LEG WITH THAT SPLICE! THAT MAN! SEE TO THE MIZZEN TOPS'L SHROUDS!" (Captain Fitzwillie prided himself on his refusal to use the names of those who served before the mast. "Lubbers have names, sailors have work to do," was his mantra.)

Night found the good ship still plying the turbulent coastal waters, every man-jack of the crew scouring the coast for a sheltered inlet. Lightning flashed and St. Elmo's fire danced along the ship's yards. It was during an extended lightning display that Degas L'Amour, perched precariously at the tip of the bowsprit, spotted a sea maiden swimming earnestly to and fro before the Baci. At first he thought she too was in peril. "Sacre bleu!" he whispered, "Swim to safety, little fishy. Go where the water is deep and calm, my fair one!" His concern vanished when she rolled onto her back and beckoned the sailor and ship to follow, angry waves alternately washing over her and then exposing her glorious chest. L'Amour was instantly enamored and convinced succor was at hand. "CAPTAIN! CAPTAIN!" he cried above the din; "WE ARE SAVED!"

Captain Fitzwillie would have none of it. "She's a siren you idiot! And she's bent on our destruction!"

Sir Edmund laughed in the captain's face at that remark. "Pardon my saying so, sir, but even a fool knows sirens are but mythical confabulations. Sea maidens are recorded fact and benevolent by documentation." The naturalist looked over his shoulder to the lee shore now precariously close and imminently threatening. "Further, may I be so bold as to point out the proximity of those rocks on whose sharp edges we are about to crash? Don't you think debating if she'd be fish or fowl is cutting it a bit fine?"

Captain Fitzwillie relented muttering, "It's on your head, sir, if she leads us astray and we all end up in the knacker's yard."

So follow her they did that dark and story night, past towering rocks and barely visible reefs, and through a narrow cleft that broadened into a becalmed bay. The next morning repairs were hastily accomplished and when the storm at last abated the H.M.S. Baci rode the falling tide back into the open sea. But not before the captain called for L'Amour to be brought to his cabin. The sailor was interrupted stuffing his last togs into a sea bag and saying a tearful goodbye to his messmates. "It's true love at last, my friends. Adieu, for like a true Frenchman, I must follow my heart!"

Burly Smith grabbed the sobbing sailor and dragged him away.

"You sir," the captain informed him, "are under arrest."

"But my crime. . .what is my crime, my good captain?"

Captain Fitzwillie was in no mood for discussion. L'Amour had been so startled by Burly Smith's rough handling that he'd neglected to loose his grip on his sea bag. The captain pointed angrily and asked, "Is it your habit to carry your worldly possessions about with you? Weren't thinking of a hasty departure, now were you?"

29

L'Amour was put in irons, his plaintive wails carrying up from the bowels of the ship as the Baci made her way through the channel to the sea. Sir Edmund Roberts and old Gnarly Dan leaned on a rail and attempted to shut the Frenchman's entreaties from their minds.

"That'd be the saddest leg 'a this sorry 'venture," Gnarly Dan confided to the naturalist as he indicated their sea maiden now laying on a plateau of rock near the passage entrance, her back to the ship. "Her heart's broked," the old salt added and explained she was assuming the classic sea maiden pose for heartache and defiant refusal to let others witness her grief. Gnarly Dan allowed that she would remain there until her lover returned or perish doing so, "for a sea maiden loves but onst, and that be forever!"

Captain Fitzwille released L'Amour three days later and Sir Edmund encouraged the distraught sailor to not only give the sea maiden her common name but also provide the naturalist's description of her attributes—thus giving voice to the seaman's lament and also dampening the growing criticism that Sir Edmund's descriptions were repetitive and uninspired at best.

The naturalist's journal reads:

Maidenus forlornica
"Diane"

Then in L'Amour's hand:

The most beautiful sea maiden appeared like an angel from heaven in the midst of the worst storm ever. Her eyes were the color of the ocean after a spring rain, her lips the luscious pink of the setting sun. She was perfection in length and her breasts were fine and matched and topped by. . .

It isn't known if L'Amour succumbed to his grief and was unable to finish or if the pen was snatched from him, for the description, now in Sir Edmund's hand, concludes:

Medium height. Medium weight. Dark hair.

Sadly, Degas L'Amour and the captain's launch were lost in calm waters several nights later. Sir Edmund noted the crew's lack of remorse, commenting "an inappropriate joviality accompanied news of the tragedy."

"Bully for him!" was the most common reaction.

Second letter of Constance Daphne Fitzwillie to her sister:

Dearest Agnes,

At last we have excitement to break the monotony! A wonderful pirate (Nasty, or Naughty Ned or some such ridiculous name) pursued our little ship (the Baci) for half the day. I am told your pirate-sort pillage, plunder, eliminate the males and sell the females into sexual slavery in some distant land of sand and remote oases. (I have entertained worse options.) While the Captain was apoplectic, my handsome friend, Sir Edmund (though we have not really spoken yet), apparently has seen some service for the King; it turns out he really is quite the splendid man with a cannon (don't you just love a man with a large gun). It would seem he saved the day.

The Captain was absolutely useless. I'm beginning to see signs he is losing his grip once more.

Wish me luck.

Your sister,
C.D.

SIGHTING FIVE

Things never returned to normal following the sea battle with the loathsome pirate Naughty Nat. While he gloried in escaping the scoundrel, Captain Fitzwillie became moodier by the hour, his grandfather's hat in his thoughts all day and in his dreams at night. Initially the captain was merely grumpy, snapping at everyone who approached him, including his wife, Constance Daphne. Then he started to mumble to himself incessantly, at first regarding his grandfather's reaction if he looked down from heaven and noticed his grandson's lack of the coveted chapeau, and then toward the end it became a generalized and incoherent rambling. Captain Fitzwillie developed nervous ticks and began to stutter. He stayed in his bed for days.

Of course, his officers and the crew noticed. How could they not, for soon enough Captain Fitzwillie shunned clothing. And then came the mutiny. It was, however, neither the crew nor the officers who usurped command. It was his wife. One morning Constance Daphne struggled up the steps to the quarter deck, called for the crew to assemble, and made the announcement.

"OUR CAPTAIN IS INDISPOSED!" she began, her listeners immediately surprised by the power of her voice. "AND I AM TAKING COMMAND IN HIS STEAD." A grumbling rippled through the assemblage. "BY YOUR REMARKABLE BRAVERY WE HAVE ESCAPED A LOATHSOME PIRATE. WE POKED OUR COLLECTIVE THUMB IN THE EYE OF ONE OF THE MOST FEARED MEN AFLOAT!" The crew liked the sound of that. They now smiled and puffed out their chests. "BUT AS YOU KNOW, OUR CAPTAIN LOST HIS RIDICULOUS HAT! The crew chuckled audibly and nudged one another. "AND, SO IT WOULD APPEAR, HIS SANITY!" The crew now adopted a look of concerned indignation. "WE HAVE LOST OUR CAPTAIN, MEN! THE BRAVEST CREW TO EVER SAIL THE SEVEN SEAS HAS LOST ITS BELOVED CAPTAIN. ALL BECAUSE OF A PIRATE AND A HAT!" Now the crew got a bit nervous.

But Constance Daphne had a plan. She had a plan and she knew men. Knew their strengths and knew their multitudinous weaknesses. She delivered her coupe de grace: "THAT PIRATE'S NAME IS NAUGHTY NAT AND HE IS BY ALL ACCOUNTS THE MOST HEINOUS HUMAN BEING TO WALK THIS EARTH." She paused, and then delivered her finest stroke: "AND HE IS ALSO THE RICHEST. HE HAS PLUNDERED FOR TWENTY YEARS, ACCUMULATING MORE AND MORE AND MORE GOLD. GOLD ENOUGH TO MAKE EVERY MAN ON THIS SHIP WEALTHY BEYOND HIS FONDEST DREAMS! WEALTHY ENOUGH TO NEVER WORK AGAIN, TO DRINK RUM FROM MORNING TILL NIGHT. WEALTHY ENOUGH FOR HIM TO QUIT THE SEA. WHY, WEALTHY ENOUGH TO OWN HIS OWN PUB IF HE WISHES!"

Men wet their lips. They stood with their hands in their empty pockets and shifted from foot to foot while they thought of their poverty and their horrid existence. They adjusted the colorful bandanas worn as caps.

They wanted to hear her plan.

It was simple:

"I SAY WE PUT THE SHIP ABOUT AND SEEK OUT NAUGHTY NAT! I SAY WE GO GET THE CAPTAIN'S HAT!"

It had a wonderful ring to it and the men responded. Wave after wave of cheers washed over the ship. "THE HAT! THE CAPTAIN'S HAT!"

When at last they calmed down, Captain Constance Daphne Fitzwillie called out, "HELMSMAN, PERPARE TO PUT THIS SHIP ABOUT. PUSSER! AN EXTRA RATION OF RUM FOR THIS BRAVE CREW, FOR THEY ARE GOING TO SAIL INTO HISTORY!"

And it was done.

Constance Daphne's diatribe would have been picture perfect had Captain Fitzwillie not strolled onto the deck sans clothing and begun calling out in a timid voice to various sea birds. "You there, smarten up those feathers! And you, sir, get off the friggin' tops'l. That bird! We'll have no poop on the poop deck!"

There was, of course, a minor problem with the new captain's plan. The Baci's provisions were extremely low. It had been the previous captain's intention to revitual in the nearest port. But Captain Constance Daphne would have none of it. "Spare not a minute!" she proclaimed again and again. Plus, her control of the crew was far too tenuous, the situation still too fluid for her to

33

risk a port and its slew of authorities. At the base of it all was her realization that she had just stepped from behind a lifelong shadow. The mantle of responsibility, the joy of living, the ability to command her own destiny for the first time in her unhappy life, was hers. Authorities be damned. Food be damned. Why . . . she would diet!

So the good ship Baci came about, the crew went to half rations (even food becomes a luxury when stacked up against a pile of gold) and Captain Constance Daphne Fitzwillie diminished in girth as she gained in stature. The pounds fell from her like the days from the calender. Everyone noticed immediately. She went from 'the old sow' to 'not so bad' and before long she began to bump into such terms as 'a fair piece' and 'right nice lookin'.

Beauty was on the horizon.

North they sailed, Captain Constance Daphne having learned from various members of the crew that Naughty Nat was most feared in the Caribbean waters, and that he was rumored to have a treasure cave on Norman Island. The well-worn and half starved Bacis reached the Caribbean Sea in September of 1832 commanded by their newly svelte captain. To a man they were prepared to follow her anywhere.

Sir Edmund Roberts took the opportunity to broaden the scope of his sea maiden quest. It was on a reconnoitering mission at Tortola that the entire launch crew witnessed a sea maiden on a palm-lined beach. Caught by surprise, she struck what the omni-present sailor Gnarly Dan referred to as the classic sea maiden pose for embarrassment. She was facing the sea, poised as one sitting with feet tucked under, her head turned modestly to the side and looking down. Gnarly whispered to Sir Edmund, "They be as shy as they be beautiful; they was made that way."

Sir Edmund does not yet acknowledge in his journal entries Constance Daphne's bold seizing of power. His notebook reads:

Eight of the crew watched in awe as I sketched our most recent sea maiden with commendable rapidity. Since they all spotted the maiden coincidentally, some jostling later occurred as the men attempted a consensus on her common name. To my chagrin, "Eager Elizabeth" of Portsmouth popularity prevailed.

Maidenus timidus
"Elizabeth, Eager"
September 25, 1832
Brewers Bay, Tortola
Short of stature. Sandy blonde hair. Slight build. Handsome chest.

34

Very satisfied with our voyage on the whole, while some aspects are a bit unsettling. Captain's wife, Constance Daphne has become uncomfortably alluring while Captain Fitzwillie himself is now as crazy as a loon.

Third letter of Constance Daphne Fitzwillie to her sister:

September 30, 1832

Dearest Agnes,

Sister! So much has happened!

First, I am ravenous! I have not had a polite meal set before me in weeks; I would eat a horse, were he available and served on silver! We have just this side of nothing to eat on the entire ship; crew and officers, alike! (More about that later; it was my own doing!)

You absolutely would not believe the change that has come over me. The Captain has retreated to his childhood or perhaps an even earlier period. The man is ripe for Bedlam (you may recall his mother was never quite right; and his father was an embarrassment from the beginning). The long and short of it is that I am acting in the fool's stead until he finds some semblance of sanity. I fear I have absolutely no legal standing, but regardless, I have set myself up as commander of our ship. The men of the crew are really quite as soft as a kitten's underbelly; I promised wealth and fame and they were with me from the beginning (how wonderful it must be to be male and unfettered by reality!).

It may have started as a lark but I must confess I am rather settling into the role! And it is positively grand (impending starvation aside) to be losing so much weight! I wish I had our little sister's wardrobe with me. (Have you heard at all from her? I fear we will know no rapprochement!) As it is, I am availing myself of the Captain's old uniforms. Fortunately for me the little man has no use for them.

I will attempt to continue at another time; I have a ship and crew to attend to!

> *Your loving sister,*
> *C.D.*

Sir Edmund is becoming more pleasant by the day!

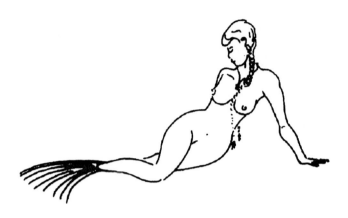

SIGHTING SIX

And so, as the deposed captain remained a mental invalid, his wife continued her plans to confront the fabled pirate and heartless cur; the loathsome Naughty Nat.

Immediately following Sir Edmund's sighting of his fifth sea maiden and his subsequent return to the anchored H.M.S. Baci, two crew members from a different reconnoitering party reported they had incredible news about their pirate foe.

"He's here! He's here!" stammered Hogshead Smith. "The Plunderer'd be hove to on t'other side 'a the island, but that dog's here!"

"Payin' a social visit to his ole mum, he is!" Big Bill added proudly. "Ain't got but a few 'a his scoundrels wif' 'im!"

Good news indeed! The loathsome pirate was planning to row around the island to visit his ailing, blind and partially comatose mother at her beach hut at Cane Garden Bay. With great haste Captain Constance Daphne Fitzwillie refined a plan. The Baci was brought to within a meter of a coral reef that extended from the edge of the bay. Their lone but powerful cannon was hoisted off of the deck and lowered onto a series of planks that allowed it to be manhandled to the beach and then to a point of excellent vantage where it could be easily camouflaged. Balls, powder and other implements of mayhem followed and the Bacis were ready. The first mate sailed off with the remainder of the crew in the ship, his instructions being to take her into the adjacent bay and then wait until he heard the cannon's roar, at which time he was to slip their cable and then sail for all he was worth to pick up the survivors.

The encounter is colorfully recounted in Sir Edmund Roberts, journal:

"Glorious events! We dashed the villain Naughty Nat once more, retrieved the captain's ridiculous cap, got a golden surprise and saw our sixth sea maiden!

As captain of the gun, I had it pointed, shotted and ready. Time dragged as we waited, Gnarly Dan mumbling non-stop about pirates, sea maidens and a plethora of drivel. At last we heard the pirates' raucous approach—they no doubt celebrating some obscure buccaneer holiday. I fear I commented too loudly, for Constance Daphne Fitzwillie, looking stunning, threatened to personally flog me if I made another sound—interesting proposition, that!

The pirates' launch rounded the corner of the bay, the entire bunch obviously besotted. The loathsome pirate, Naughty Nat, resplendent in our captain's lost hat roared to his crew, "A BIT LIVELIER AT THOSE OARS, YOU SONS 'A WORTHLESS LUBBERS! AND YOU, AWFUL BOB, YOU'D BE GRUMBLIN' TOO MUCH FOR ME TASTE!"

Awful Bob made the mistake of responding, "Me back aches an' me belly's growlin'; that's why I'd be grumblin'!"

In response to that remark Naughty Nat pulled out a huge pistol and shot the annoying pirate dead. He watched coldly as Awful Bob jerked about a time or two and then lay silent. "WELL, SHIVVER ME TIMBERS" *Naughty Nat roared,* "AIN'T OLE BOB QUIET NOW! THROW 'IM TO THE FISHES!"

The crew dumped the offending pirate's body over the side of the launch and resumed their journey. (I must say, I may have exchanged a glance or two too many with Gnarly Dan at that point; my own thoughts being with the efficiency of pirate justice when dealing with annoying human beings.)

The pirates got ever closer. At the propitious moment I redeemed myself by sending my first ball into the launch's tiny bowsprit, reducing it to splinters. I then blew off her rudder and finally halved her mast. Naughty Nat, ever observant, got my point and hastily departed his vessel as we reloaded. He was followed by his crew; a messy spectacle at best, those aquatically challenged proceeding to explore the sea bottom.

Taking advantage of the confusion, Constance Daphne took our boat and crew to retrieve her husband's hat, returning hastily with Naughty Nat's launch in tow. She wished us to leave our cannon, explaining with animation that Naughty Nat had been transporting two treasure chests—it seems the visit to his mother was a cruel and heartless ruse—his real intention being to bury the treasure; a large black x brought along to be left for future reference.

Two treasure chests, indeed! I confess my attention strayed as Constance Daphne stood gesticulating, drenched from masthead to keel, her clothing now diaphanous.

I trust to the confidence of my journal that I am smitten!

The H.M.S. Baci immediately sailed around the point like a hero, hauled up the chests and allowed our departure before Naughty Nat got his wits about him. It remains to be seen if we should have hunted the scoundrel down while we had him in our grasp.

Oh yes, we saw a sea maiden as we lay in ambush. Sensing us near, she struck what the increasingly irritating Gnarly Dan describes as the sea maiden pose of coy watchfulness: "Like their bodies, their hearts is wedded to the sea and so they loves only a sailor; himself being familiar-like. Naturally, when we was near and all salty she knowed it."

The gun crew, enjoying a fore view of her, voted to name her Fran, while the watch party, decidedly aft and much impressed, was mad for Fanny. Tossed coin—Fran prevailed.

Maidenus vigilante
"Fran"
September 28, 1832
Cane Garden Bay, Tortola

Long, multi-hued body. Strawberry hair. Admirable chest. Slightly worn tail.

Editor's note: *On a recent visit to Cane Garden Bay I searched out the Baci's place of ambush. There, in the tall weeds is the ship's rusty cannon pointing into the bay and half buried in sand. Looking across the lagoon I could imagine its thunder, smell the black powder and see Naughty Nat taste Constance Daphne's ire.*

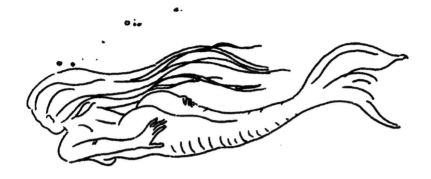

SIGHTING SEVEN

The H.M.S. Baci sailed north-northeast, the second part of Captain Constance Daphne's plan waiting at the other end of that leg of their voyage. They counted the pirate's gold three times, counted their good fortune at least once, and completed a fine passage to Bermuda. They sailed into Hamilton Harbor in October, the captain bent on using her share of the pirate's booty to fit-out her ship as a man-o-war. She had known from the beginning that the Baci's sole cannon was no match for Naughty Nat's might. She had depended on at least one bold move to weaken him, hopefully enhance her net worth, and then do exactly what she was doing now; give the good ship, H.M.S. Baci, some much needed teeth to hunt down the scoundrel, ship and all!

Captain Constance Daphne Fitzwillie took the opportunity to venture beyond her own accommodations and the hallowed quarterdeck. At first it was fantastically interesting for her to venture below decks and explore that part of the ship dedicated to housing the crew, and the remainder that was dedicated to stowage. The crew's quarters appalled her from the beginning. Sir Edmund and Gnarly Dan trailed, commenting when called upon to do so.

She addressed Gnarly Dan. "This area here is absolutely tiny. Don't you men go stir crazy in such an enclosed space?"

The old salt was embarrassed. "Beggin' yer pardon, Cap, but we ain't called on ta choose where we sleeps. She wouldn't be the worst I'se seed; but our Baci'd be a right small ship; she ain't the Victory; an', well, it's what we gobs deals with."

Constance Daphne ruminated while Sir Edmund piped in, "The men who work our good ship are a gallant lot, and they come from every borough, burg and country in the world. I do not wish to be callous, but it is their lot. There are no manors in their future, just hard work, enough food to keep from starving, and the joy of their camaraderie."

The captain added those remarks to her reverie. The three shipmates proceeded from the low-ceilinged crew's quarters to a lower deck. While the previous spaces had been dark and close and an assault on her olfactory senses, the presence of eighty-six men who seldom bathed leaving their mark, what she encountered now fairly took her breath away.

A putrescence arose that nauseated and then gagged her to the point of returning to the companionway she had descended and hurrying back to the deck and the fresh air of Bermuda.

"Good lord!" she expostulated, "are there stacks of the dead stowed below?"

Sir Edmund had no answer and Gnarly Dan seemed reticent to involve himself. Constance Daphne sensed his reluctance and pressed her previous question home.

"What is that smell?"

Gnarly Dan looked at his feet.

Constance Daphne was angering. "I asked you a direct question, Mr. Dan, and I expect a clear, immediate answer. I repeat: What is that smell?"

Gnarly Dan studied a tarred seam on the deck. There was a lone bubble of the viscous black raised from the heat of the sun. He teased it with the toe of his heavy, buckled shoe. He knew he was trapped. He knew he must answer her question, but he was uncertain how to begin without mightily offending her. At last he relented, speaking ever so softly.

"Our Baci'd be a very old ship, as we all knows. Close ta fifty years in the water by my reckoning. An' well, she's had a boatload a' men crammed below decks from the beginnin'." He was headed to shoal waters and he knew of no way to avoid them.

"Captain Constance, sir, ya knows, a' course that we afore the mast must use the head when we's inconvenienced, so ta speak. An' we're a capital lot for that, no hidin' behind the scuttle or lettin' go over the side for us. But Captain, sir, on dark stormy nights, with a rail in the water an' rain or sleet blowin' straight on, there ain't been a man aboard this ship in that many years what ain't make the choice ta steal down to the bilges an' find relief there. It ain't pretty, yer honor, that's the truth, but that's how she's done in the navy."

A huge silence answered his disgusting, startling information.

Sir Edmund coughed quietly. "Oh dear," he muttered. "That would explain the diseases we seem to carry, and at least as many vermin."

"Do you mean to tell me," Constance Daphne began, trying to remain controlled. "Do you mean to tell me," she repeated, this time not raising her voice higher with each word, "that this fine ship is, below decks, nothing more than a cesspool?"

How Gnarly Dan ached to be somewhere else. How he longed to be in the foremast tree, lounging in the fresh air. But there was no escape. "You could say that, mam," he whispered as embarrassed as if she had caught him squatting in the shadows, his trowsers at his knees.

Captain Constance Daphne Fitzwillie made no response at first. Then she summoned the ship's carpenter and the master. They met and haggled and argued for three hours. Then they went to the harbormaster and subsequently to a refitting yard. Further discussions. Further arguments. At last there was a plan:

At colossal expense, the H.M.S. Baci would go immediately into dry dock. Every item below decks would be removed. All of the rock ballast; the stinking, slime-coated (to be kind) ballast would be removed from the miasma and heaved into the vast harbor. Then both starboard and larboard strips of copper would be removed from the good ship's bottom, whereupon ages-old planking would we stripped away from an area sufficient to allow the good ship to first drain her odiferous muck, then provide a sluice for the tons of sea water that were to be pumped through the vessel's below deck space.

"Never heard of anything so ridiculous," the yardmaster huffed.

"Then to you, sir, I will give a gold piece if you will descend to the bilges with your dinner and there, partake."

He thought about that a moment.

"I take your point," was all he said.

So the vessel was stripped and cleansed, half of Hamilton Harbor passed through her carrying with it the effluent of the ages. With time and fresh air, the water became less offensive, until it at last was quite close to an unsullied condition after its journey through the good Baci. She was allowed to dry, the holes were closed, copper was reapplied, and new ballast was hefted below decks.

Ten canvas buckets, nicely tarred and long rope-handled were then established as an alternative for nocturnal sojourns to the depths of the ship.

"They will be emptied hourly, or the man who misses his trick will move his hammock to the bilges," she tartly admonished each officer. "And all access to the hold of this fine ship will be secured when we are at sea."

Then a deluge of white paint found its way below decks. And hatches were opened and sweet air found its way through the catacombs of the ship for the first time in fifty years.

Gnarly Dan allowed that the men would find it uncomfortable at first, but he felt certain they would grudgingly adjust; for they loved their captain. "It was all homey-like," he protested weakly, aware he was plying very rough seas.

His captain glowered.

Sir Edmund raised an eyebrow.

"We'd be men an' sailors," the old salt finally mumbled to himself as he walked away. "We likes how we smells."

The good ship was afloat once more and moved to the Royal Navy ordnance dock. And so while Constance Daphne toyed with carronades, cannons and swivel guns, the crew continued distributing its share of the gold equitably among the town's pubs and women. St. George knew their bounty also, as did just about every parish from Paget outward in both directions.

Sir Edmund Roberts, the gentleman naturalist and sea maiden questor now spent his time running down rumors of the islands' sea maiden population, the new gold neither here nor there to him. He explored the main island's natural caves, and the grottos and secluded beaches of its perimeter. He did find time to visit a few pubs himself, and it was in one of them that he heard a different sort of rumor that interested him immensely. He followed a convoluted series of trails, at last finding himself in a dark and malodorous warehouse in St. George.

After two hours of rearranging crates and barrels he came at last upon a huge item that would change the tenor of the remainder of the voyage. Somewhat the worse for wear, but still obviously serviceable, was an early version of Halley's (indeed, of Halley's Comet fame) diving bell. It was intact, the only explanation for its presence being that it had come from Africa years and years ago, its Laskar owners asking the warehouse personnel to sell it if they could.

"What price, might I ask?" Sir Edmund implored of the crook who had led him through the decrepit building.

"Oh sir, it's most valuable; priceless really," the goo-goo eyed scoundrel replied, "I hesitate to attempt a value on such short notice. Perhaps in a few weeks I'll have accomplished enough research to fairly appraise its worth

Sir Edmund pulled his gold purse from inside of his belt and doled out coins until he judged the thief would be unable to resist. And in a trice it was his. He produced an additional coin and had the wooden apparatus carted to a barrel-maker for refitting of the staves and thence to a harness shop where its various fittings, diaphragms and leathern hoses were either repaired or replaced.

By all accounts, Gnarly Dan had parted with his own gold earlier and was now the naturalist's unsolicited aid, companion and advisor.

"She don't look like much," he commented without end as the refurbished diving apparatus was finally moved to the bay, loaded onto a barge and then towed to various coastal reefs. Sir Edmund invested his days trusting his life to those who worked the clanking air pump while he sat in the submerged bell and observed the sea below through the bell's open bottom. Each time the apparatus was winched back to the surface Gnarly Dan barraged the naturalist with questions, his own reticence diminishing as he heard of the wonders of the deep. By his fifth submersion Sir Edmund was amused to find Gnarly Dan now willing to accompany him.

"Be there room for an old salt on yer next voyage?" Gnarly Dan implored with child-like innocence.

"I dare say, old chap," Sir Edmund taunted, "I thought you said you've spent your illustrious life *avoiding* sinking vessels."

Old Gnarly smiled quietly to himself and then allowed that perhaps he'd been over-cautious.

"I ain't a young swab, as yer honor knows, an' in many ways I ain't as smart as yer grace. But there'd be a parcel a' things I ain't see'd yet an' if I don' do 'er soon, could be she won't happen."

Sir Edmund was touched. He looked deeply into Gnarly's rheumy eyes and then smiled warmly. "Of course there's room enough, my good man. I'm told Halley designed it for a small crowd."

It was a high point in his relationship with the sailor. In the close quarters of Halley's patented diving apparatus, it resumed its downward spiral.

His notebook reads:

Fantastic news! Two weeks with Mr. Halley's diving machine and I have witnessed success—or more accurately, our seventh sea maiden!

I do not tire of the bell; do not mind the close and sometimes dark quarters; can tolerate the noxious smells (bodily, etc.) my pumping crew delights in sending down to me. (Though, I shall never again allow them to pack bean, egg and cheese sandwiches for themselves.) The undersea vistas the apparatus allows me are worth every discomfort.

And today! A heavenly creature fairly glided beneath me! Undulating slowly, she passed within inches. The grace of her movements—the ease with which she propelled herself—her flowing hair—her strong and responsive buttock muscles—why, I could have reached down and touched them.

Editor's note: *In Sir Edmund's manuscript the word 'touched' was apparently arrived at after a struggle; 'stroked' was initially crossed out, as was 'caressed', 'fondled', and finally, although scratched through with a vengeance, the word 'kissed' can be faintly discerned.)*

Oh, the Glory! It was a singularly brief sighting, but consequently and indelibly etched onto my heart. Her image is in my dreams! How I longed to slip into the water and join her! I must learn to swim with more skill!

My infatuation with our buxom and aloof captain is eclipsed.

Gnarly Dan (I hate him once more) claims I have seen a sea maiden at her happiest. Says he, "While yer sea maiden loves a sailor, it'd be the warm embrace of the sea what holds her heart."

How I long to embrace her . . .

Maidenus aquatica

Robert Kline

"Gail"
October 30, 1832
Horseshoe Bay, Bermuda

Medium height. Medium Weight. Strong and supple. Apparently healthy and content. Hair full length. Incredibly alluring. Sighted just prior to storm. (Thus her name.)

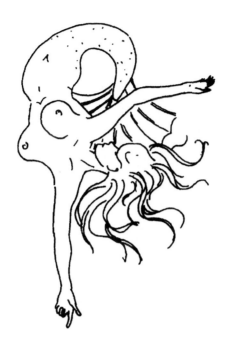

SIGHTING EIGHT

The H.M.S. Baci remained anchored in Hamilton Harbor into November. She was a beautiful sight, the vessel now fully armed with all the ordinance she could float, cannon barrels poking from rows of newly carpentered gun ports; swivel guns mounted every meter or so. Somewhat detracting from the image was her former captain installed in the foretop calling out to passing birds to join him for tea.

"YOU THERE! COME HERE AND BE QUICK ABOUT IT! THAT BIRD! YES, YOU SIR, WITH THE LONG FEATHERS AFT; SHAKE A LEG NOW! YOUR TEA IS ALREADY REMARKABLY COLD!"

On the quarter deck Captain Constance Daphne Fitzwillie stood proudly, her seething subservience shed coincidental to her epic loss of weight. With new confidence and a crew of slobbering sailors at her command, she savored a late, wondrous blossom of womanhood.

Enamored of pomp and emulating the Royal Navy, she turned out the crew in their best for a speech before departing Hamilton Harbor. The men wore blindingly white duck trousers and blue and white horizontally striped shirts accented with a bold red 'kerchief at their necks. The whole was topped with straw sennit hats sporting long red ribbons that caught the faintest breeze.

They stood respectfully and listened to her speech prior to weighing anchor. It was a rousing speech, relaying past glories (thumping Naughty Nat) and promising a glorious future. So well worded, so full of pithy prose and well turned phrases was it that speech-makers for the next hundred and fifty years would draw on her analogies and suckle from her intuitive knowledge of that which primes the human spirit. She opened with a dream she'd had of equality for all and an end to suffering. Then she lamented others "little noting nor long remembering" what she was about to say, implored the assembled crew to ask not what the good ship Baci could do for them, etc., etc., declared this their finest hour, lowered her voice confidentially and opined that while she had reduced the loathsome pirate, Naughty Nat, to penury, she was not a crook, then shifted obliquely but with mastery to men abed in England holding their manhood cheap (Prompting sly nods and bawdy gestures from her listeners; Old Seth the Lech going so far as to rudely grab himself and growl.) She raised her voice again and offered that England expected every man to do his duty even though they had not yet begun to fight; and further promised they would find a way or make one, confessing with a wink that she was the luckiest woman in the world.

Finally, Captain Constance Daphne Fitzwillie fairly whipped the men into frothy excitement spilling into mirth when she said that while "Baci" was Italian for "kiss", a kiss was just a kiss and theirs, indicating the rows of gleaming bronze cannons, came with tongues of fire. She encouraged the best gun captains by name (Itchy Ben, Einbear, Leaner) and urged the crew to shout their names in a chant heard from Salt Kettle to Paget Parish.

Yet it was more the drama than the words that inspired the men, for their beautiful captain had taken to wearing her husband's old Royal Navy uniform, gilt buttons and golden epaulets agleam, her ample bosom grudgingly entrapped in mightily straining blue fabric, her enthusiasm and deep-breathed delivery taking its toll mid-speech as buttons in descending succession succumbed. The first popped unnoticed but by the sailor who took it in the eye; the second soon sailed into a pack of startled crewmen, and with the third every man and boy was attentive.

When crescents of pale, up-thrust and bounteous bosom peeked forth, the crew believed en masse they were victims of their own active fantasies. But as further buttons sallied forth, intuitive cross-communication encouraged every passionate gesture of their new captain.

Pre-cut threads notwithstanding, Constance Daphne concluded with but a few chaste buttons denying the crew their final dark, ha'pennies of heaven. Amid roaring approval she raised her arms, bent proffered fingers into V's and shouted, "INTO GLORY WE STEER!"

Submerged in Halley's patented diving apparatus four meters below the ship, Sir Edmund Roberts, gentleman naturalist and sea maiden questor, heard only the faintest hum transmitted by the H.M.S. Baci's oaken hull. He sat rapt, watching a sea maiden perform slow, mute arabesques beneath his bell.

The Forgotten Voyage

His journal reads:

Fair sea maiden! How your silent dance entwined my heart! Oh, that I could slip these surly fetters and join you!
Maidenus bermudus
"Heather" (Bunches used to counter the bell's stale air.)
November 24, 1832
Hamilton Harbor, Bermuda

Well formed body. Powerful yet graceful swimmer. Supple. Healthy. Beautiful.

Gnarly Dan says, "A man unmoved by a sea maiden's dance is naught a man at all."

Sadly, Sir Edmund's stay in Bermuda was not without its trauma: In point of fact, one of the most disturbing events of the entire voyage occurred during the Bermuda refitting. Sir Edmund had finally figured out that Captain Fitzwillie's gesture, just prior to misplacing his sanity, of generously assigning the naturalist two assistants, was not one of magnificence, but was instead a cruel joke on the naïve scientist. The oriental fellow, Sushi, and his counterpart from deepest Africa, Bones, mentioned ad nauseum to Sir Edmund how anxious they were for the next sea maiden sighting. Further, the adjective, "tasty" had been bandied about once too often.

"Well, of course it was a joke, you nincompoop!" the new captain, Constance Daphne Fitzwillie, chided Sir Edmund. "My husband never did a kind thing in his life," she continued. "He disliked you when he met you; learned to detest you as time went on, and finally settled into viewing you as an absolute abomination put on this earth to torture him!"

It was doubly painful to the naturalist when he realized he had not only been put upon, but everyone else knew he'd been bested.

"Hardly the act of a gentleman," he muttered as he walked away from the beautiful Constance Daphne. "For all intents and purposes, the fiend assigned me two cannibals. If he were cogent today I'd have no choice but to call him out."

The naturalist brought with him to the H.M.S. Baci his cherished set of dueling pistols and while they were beautiful beyond definition, not one man, save Sir Edmund, had ever hefted one in anger and lived to tell of it. Sir Edmund Roberts could handle artillery. Cannon or pistol, he was a dangerous man. And his threat to the former Captain Fitzwillie was not breathed in jest.

That, however, was not the actual low point of the Bermuda stay. The naturalist and the old salt, Gnarly Dan, were exploring the main island, Halley's patented diving apparatus at the cooper's for minor repairs. Near Horseshoe Bay they walked the sheltered beaches, each scalloped inlet hidden from the next, the barnacle encrusted rocks a fascination for the naturalist. Unfortunately, the bays were all fouled by jetsam; trash from the island's busy harbor and its endless succession of visiting vessels was everywhere. It was late in the day, the sun low, the light mellow, when Gnarly Dan, rounding a rock outcrop ahead of the naturalist, stopped in his tracks and moaned, "Lord above. Ain't that the saddest thing ya' ever see'd."

Sir Edmund joined his companion and he too was overcome. There in the next inlet, sheltered from view by the surrounding cliffs, was a stricken sea maiden. She lay high on the pink sand, her body twisted, her hair askew. The two men walked slowly to her, both hushed, both saddened profoundly. They kneeled at her side and looked on in silence. She was beautiful even in death, her face serene, her body still caressed by the last vestige of its former health.

Sir Edmund spoke at last. "My good man, she appears too young to have succumbed to infirmity. And I see no abrasions or signs of injury."

He waited for Gnarly Dan's response.

The old salt swabbed a tear from his cheek and looked out to sea. He shook his head sadly. "Look around, yer honor. It's us what's done the harm. This here island ain't no different from everywhere else we touches. We dumps ever' item we don' needs. Where? Why into the sea, a' course. Yer sea maiden's pure in ever' sense an' when ya starts ta muck with the water she calls home, why, her balance is upset. Yer lookin' at how it ends.

Editor's note: *Ironically, Bermuda came to be where the naturalist returned to spend his final days. Following the public humiliation of a legal action initiated by his greedy relatives to establish his mental infirmity, and the public's absolute lack of interest in his manuscripts (the young Darwin chap hogging all headlines and notoriety) Sir Edmund left England and retired to the obscurity of the faraway island, spending his final days in a small cottage overlooking an obscure bay.*

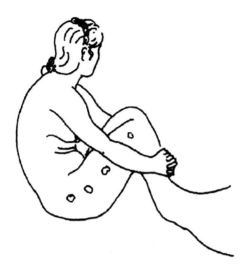

SIGHTING NINE

At sea again, the H.M.S. Baci and her charterer sailed southward into further high adventure and midrange romance. Several weeks out of port a mystery presented itself. At first casually and then with moderate concern the crew remarked the absence of their former captain from his masthead perch; his protracted infatuation with mental infirmity making that his favorite point of vantage while conversing with avian visitors and passers-by.

The beautiful Captain Constance Daphne Fitzwillie ignored the situation as long as she could, finally ordering a search for the man. He was reported unfound between bilge rat's belly and main mast cap. The accepted conclusion was he had been napping in one of the makeshift barges released for target practice—the odds thus being one in four he was on the only barge to have slipped into the distance unscathed.

With that explanation and upon further rumination, startling memories evolved: pitiful shrieks as cannon balls struck a raft, "It were awful mates! I heard our dear Cap's last words . . . and they warn't pretty!" Another saw blood in the water, "Spreadin' like a stuck whale he was; our departed Cap's vital juices mixin' in with the sea!" One imaginative cove swore he'd witnessed an arm and hand cart wheeling skyward in a graceful protracted arc after a direct hit on the second target. "It was wavin' mates! As plain as the nose on me face; our dear ole Cap was wavin' an' sayin' 'is last goodbye."

Fretting Willie piped in with his own ominous version: "He warn't wavin' lads; t'was a curse he was layin' on us for blowin' him up so bad and then leavin' him in little pieces for the fishes! He was shakin' his fist an' wishin' us on a cruise ta hell, he was!"

It was an unsettling proclamation for a gang adrift in a sea of superstition, prompting a series of curse-thwarting rituals: left ears tugged, lucky buttons rubbed, wood knocked, the ship's cat kicked and a barely heard litany of mutterings and oaths.

Morale on the good ship suffered as the men moved about in self-induced gloom. At last Captain Constance Daphne Fitzwillie would have no more of it. She called the crew to assemble before the mast at noon on the third day of their wake. She stood before them, resplendent in her naval tunic, all buttons replaced, many secured, her magnificent chest once more entrapped and struggling mightily for the light of day. Once she had the crew's undivided attention she stared off to the foretops'l as if she saw her departed husband sitting there one last time. She shipped a huge tear and then dramatically swabbed it away with her coat sleeve, said movement also lifting her breasts and allowing them respite from the enclosing darkness of her coat. She studied the sky. The crew tore itself away from their captain and studied the sky also. At last Captain Constance Daphne Fitzwillie ripped herself free of her nearly overwhelming show of grief and roared to the crew below her, ALL HANDS ALOFT AND ALOW TO SET EVERY STITCH OF CANVAS THE OLD GIRL CAN CARRY! IF WE CAN THUMP THE LOATHSOME PIRATE NAUGHTY NAT TWO TIMES; IF WE CAN TWEEK HIS NOSE AND MAKE HIM WISH HE'D NEVER HEARD OF BACIS, THEN WE CAN SURELY OUTRUN A CURSE!"

In a trice the rigging was aswarm with motivated men casting free gaskets and letting sail after sail fall and open to a fine Atlantic breeze. Sea chanties passed through groups of toiling sailors, the spirit of the brotherhood of the sea coursing madly through their veins. And so with a healthy wind dead astern the valiant ship caught the bone in her teeth and sailed south-southeast, pounding through rolling seas, breasting aside great sheets of white water. The marvelous figurehead the departed carver, Bistro, had freed from wooden clothes dipped again and again in the combing sea, her hair awash, her beautiful breasts glistening. Skysails, moonrakers, and studding sails burst forth above or beyond mains'ls, fores'ls and all of the other s'ls as the H.M.S. Baci showed off her full and impressive complement of sails. Captain Constance Fitzwillie paced the quarterdeck, every inch of canvas under her control and a source of deepest satisfaction. Oh, how she loved the power she wielded over the crew of the good ship; how comforting she found their respect, and how fulfilling was their love. What no man had brought to her in all of her previous years, eighty-six did now with wild abandon.

The Bacis responded so willingly because they did indeed adore their captain—craved her approval and longed for her smile. And it was not merely an emotional appeal; because they were men, physical attraction also reared its ugly head. The Bacis were extraordinarily adroit at securing nocturnal positions in the spars above her skylight, speaking in whispers to one another as they whiled away the night.

Surprisingly, Sir Edmund Roberts was the most dramatically smitten. He alternately attempted to impress her or ignore her, usually collapsing into unctuous courting of her favor. He lay awake at night and listened to her in the cabin next to his, the captain's quarters being spacious and situated at the absolute stern of the ship. The partitions between were wooden and light, designed to be "knocked down" and stored below along with all furnishings in the event the two powerful new cannons which shared her boudoir were needed for a hostile encounter. The crew practiced "clearing for action" often, Captain Constance Daphne Fitzwillie determined they would operate with lethal efficiency the next time they traded iron with the loathsome pirate, Naughty Nat.

It was after a night of tossing and turning as Sir Edmund imagined Captain Constance Daphne lying abed some inches from him that he hatched a rather intrusive plan. The next morning he made several mental calculations regarding what he knew of her cabin and its furnishings and then stared long and hard at the partition between. He chalked a small x on his side of the bulkhead and then moments before the crew struck the walls and sent them below he took out the auger he had borrowed from the carpenter. With speed, precision and a weather eye toward any interlopers he bore a small hole into the wall. Seconds later sailors appeared, knocked out braces and pins with wooden mallets and removed the wall. English Carl was on the captain's side and he did look momentarily at the tiny pile of sawdust on her floor, attributed it to a wayward termite or carpenter ant and went about his work.

The remainder of the day Sir Edmund alternately flogged himself for such an uncouth transgression, or, looking at his beautiful captain, dreamed of her preparing herself for the night. That evening, his heart in his mouth, Sir Edmund awaited his captain's return to her quarters. When at last she passed his door he went for the thousandth time to his augured portal. As he had hoped, he could just make out the top of her mirror below where his point of vantage intruded. Using a bit of psychology the naturalist conjectured that no woman would ever look above a mirror; not when her own visage was available to be inspected, scrutinized, criticized or complimented.

For what seemed like hours his beautiful captain padded about her quarters, first pulling off her heavy sea boots and then one by one, removing various articles of her uniform as she puttered at the stern windows; sat for a bit at her desk and dashed off a letter to her sister and finally called out to the steward to bring in hot water for her bath. She dragged out the large shallow basin in which she was to stand, removed the remainder of her clothing and slipped into a heavy robe before the naturalist had time to fully savor his good fortune. The water arrived and was installed, its steam looking nearly as inviting to Sir Edmund as it did to Captain Constance Daphne.

She combed out her hair at length, let the robe slip from her shoulders, and stood with her back to her voyeur. Because of the attention her chest commanded day after day; its proximity to fresh air and sunlight heightening its allure, its movement when she spoke reducing onlookers to tears, and its absolutely creamy softness (conjectured), no man on the good ship Baci had spent more than a fleeting moment speculating on the captain's other attributes. (Excepting Guido the Guinea, who spoke of nothing else.)

So there Sir Edmund Roberts stood on tiptoe, one eye glued to the smallest of holes recently penetrating the wall, staring at the most handsome, well formed posterior of which any man has yet to dream. It took his breath away, it stopped his heart; the captain's small waist, the sensual expansion of her hips and there, the capo de tutti capo; Captain Constance Daphne Fitzwillie's heretofore best kept secret. No longer would the naturalist sigh with disappointment when she turned from him.

"May Sir Isaac, Columbus and Marco Polo look down in unfeigned jealousy," he muttered softly; "for I have made the grandest discovery of them all."

The fates then toyed briefly with him, for he was called from his cabin by an enthusiatic gob banging at his door and proclaiming a sea maiden on the larboard bow. It turned out to be a dolphin and the excited sailor was doubly dashed when Sir Edmund scowled at him far beyond the anticipated level of disappointment they'd all seen him exhibit.

In his cabin once more he was loath to discover his pinhole was darker than his thoughts.

Of course, there was the following night, and the one after that, and the next, and the next. Sir Edmund justified his behavior in the name of artistic necessity—there being no other females available as models to advance his painting skills—except, of course, the very frequent sea maiden sightings!

A less forgiving mind would point out that he spent absolutely no time sketching fishes, though the crew pulled them onboard daily.

Sir Edmund Robert's journal records their next landfall and the ninth sea maiden sighting:

I am aswim! We made our landfall at St. Augustine, spied the light and entered the river, exchanged salutes with the massive Castillo de San Marcos and then anchored in the harbor proper. It is indeed a quaint little Spanish settlement, yet it disappointed immediately; the local women giving freely while the local men as openly take. Prices are outrageous and the heat, even in December, is oppressive. Mosquitoes tax the body's ability to replenish blood. And serpents of every shape and size slither about looking for an opportunity to plant a poisonous kiss. But most unsettling is the town's claim to be haunted from stem to stern, with at least as many ghosts as there are live inhabitants:

Indian spirits, soldiers' lost souls, and the vapory presences of bar maids, children, widows, spinsters and hermits wending the narrow streets at nightfall, loitering in the town's abundance of burial grounds and even mucking about outside of the fortress looking for jewelry. St. Augustine must sport the busiest afterlife this side of heaven. And yet the locals think it quaint, allowing it is "money in the bank if we can just get them to hang around for a hundred more years; nobody wants to see Aunt Maddie now; she was annoying enough in life, but give her a century and put her in a room full of people who don't know her, she's sure to scare them half to death or at least impress them," whatever that is supposed to mean!

I immediately tired of the walled city and took the opportunity to be ferried to the beaches along Anastasia Island. Within the day we sighted our ninth sea maiden!

Maidenous augustus
"Ingrid"
December 19, 1832
St. Augustine, Florida

Beautiful specimen! Hale, hardy, and quite long.

Saw her at sunset looking out to sea. Gnarly Dan interrupted my own reverie with his usual annoying observations, allowing, "She be in love it's certain. While a man's love is all spark and splash, yer sea maiden loves with the depth and breadth of the sea."

I am most anxious to return to the H.M.S. Baci, and my quarters before the captain retires. I find it bad manners to skulk in after she is abed.

Fourth letter of Constance Daphne Fitzwillie to her sister:

December 25, 1832
Dearest Agnes,

Happy Christmas!

Please forgive my silence! There is almost too much to relate and I know not where to begin. It is rumored the Captain is mort . . . (please remind me . . . am I supposed to entertain grief?) At any rate he is surely missing. I now weigh less than our little sister (any news?) though my bosoms are still very present (and noticed).

Sir Edmund is fascinating. His work is going splendidly as he is finding his heart's content of sea maidens (they really do exist!). He is quite the little boy with his diving machine.

Have you the inclination, I recommend you try some time as a ship's captain; it does wonders for your complexion, not to mention the benefits of a boatload of adoring men for whom you need not cook, clean or entertain! It rather puts one in mind of being Queen of a very small, mobile country. Though the food is dull at best (I have attempted the first meat that I believe could take a polish. Unbitten biscuits will depart the table of their own accord; weevils being their transport.). But for all that, I do not complain. The men find solace in their grog (watered rum) and cocoa (I have taken to the former on a nightly basis. I now sleep like a baby).

We have actually done a battle or two. There is something to be said for homicide as an arbiter. And it is one of the few things at which men excel (given adequate instruction).

Enough news of me. I hope all is well with you. How you would love to take tea on my quarterdeck!

Write soon.

Your loving sister,
Captain! C.D.

SIGHTING TEN

The H.M.S. Baci beat out of St. Augustine harbor and into the Atlantic Sea one year to the day of leaving England for a naturalist's circumnavigation. For all purposes it was a different ship that sank the land of North American than had done the same to Merry England. Not only had she swapped captains. . . and there breathed not a man aboard who did not welcome that change, but also the ship herself was like new. In the course of the voyage the rigging had been replaced, both standing and running. At least one new set of sails had been bent on; she had been repainted from stem to stern at least three times, and even to the casual viewer she looked different. The rows of gun ports were new, of course, and Captain Constance Daphne had them enhanced by a broad white stripe, Royal Navy style. Further, all the new armament threw her trim in a cock-a-bill, so below decks her ballast was lugged about until she once more lay level at her waterline. Finally, the captain had come to tinker with the rake of her masts in an attempt to recoup their former speed (tons and tons of bronze and iron on the gun deck slowed the good ship a might). So the H.M.S. Baci was quite the handsome and improved vessel as she headed for the horizon. For all the world she was a little ship to be reckoned with; her crew at least as sharp as she.

Daily the good ship was cleared for action. Hammocks were rolled tightly and brought up and lined in the netting atop the rails as makeshift protection from flying splinters and such. Bulkheads (the naturalist's offending wall included) were knocked down and stowed in the hold, as was every other item not directly involved in defending the good ship. The gun deck was thus cleared for the vessel's entire length, allowing crews to attend their neatly lined charges unobstructed. They could also move easily to the other side of the ship and that set of guns if need be; the Baci being less than a true man-a-war with its requisite number of sailors did not have enough men to fight both sides of the ship at once, necessitating crews move from starboard to larboard as the situation dictated.

Again and again the gun crews fired the big cannons, the smoke blowing back into the close quarters between decks. It happened so often and it conjured such powerful images of might that even their captain, Constance Daphne came to love the acrid smell.

"It is manly enough for me to find it arousing," she said to Babbling Bob, knowing the yammering gob would spread the word without haste. And so the crew now knew their captain not only loved exercising the guns, but that she too associated them with sex. Never again would she be able to run the flat of her hand softly along one of the cannon barrels without every man secretly praying she would not bid him step forward.

Days out of harbor Captain Fitzwillie mustered the men and complimented their manner. "YOU HAVE BECOME THE FINEST CREW AFLOAT!" she began, "AND OUR GOOD SHIP HAS NEVER BEEN IN MORE CAPABLE HANDS." She expanded the compliment: "YOU ARE IN THE RIGGING WITH GREAT SPEED, OUR SAILING ABILITY IS WITHOUT MATCH; AND BELOW DECKS YOU INSPIRE ME!"

The crew beamed unashamedly, nudging one another and smiling broadly. But compliments were soon to give way to innuendo and the men's dedication to their captain was about to achieve a new level.

"I HAVE NEVER KNOWN A MAN TO USE HIS CANNON WITH SUCH SKILL! YOU ARE WELL ARMED, MY FINE CREW! CHARGED WITH UNFLAGGING STAMINA AND A MATCH FOR ANY ENCOUNTER! ANY LOWLY GOB CAN GET OFF A DECENT ROUND, BUT YOU MEN RELOAD WITH ALACRITY! IT IS A PLEASURE TO SEE YOU HANDLE YOUR BALLS AND YOUR GUNS WITH SUCH SKILL! BELIEVE ME WHEN I TELL YOU THE THOUGHT OF MY CREW GLEAMING WITH HARD WON SWEAT AND MANHANDLING SO MUCH HEAVY IRON IS IN MY THOUGHTS AT NIGHT!"

For such an accomplished speaker, Captain Constance Daphne made the mistake of ending her speech too abruptly. With her last words the crew stood open mouthed in wonder and awesome imagination. She looked out to the assembled men, probably expecting a cheer or two, while they stood thunderstruck with revelation. Embarrassed smiles rippled through the group, as did quiet coughs. Silence hung like adolescent expectation.

The first to regain her wits was the captain when she hastily tacked a second closing to her speech. "YOU ARE MY MEN, ARE YOU NOT?"

As if awakened, the men roared.

They were her men.

Unfortunately the wind deserted the good ship the very next day. It was an unnatural calm, and coming so hard upon recently sinking land, it was particularly difficult for the crew, they being in the mood to crack on for a bit.

The Forgotten Voyage

The Baci rolled for days on oily swells, her masts lost in fog.

A consequent oppression gripped those who served before the mast. It had been a queer voyage thus far with a spate of deaths and desertions and while the captain's mental collapse was unsettling, his later reduction to a sort of sheperd's pie by the Baci's own cannon fire was too much. The crew's guilt returned stealthily and with each day becalmed it grew until they were convinced his ghost was now charting their cruise to hell, their present situation an interlude before they actively began that perilous voyage.

They heard their former captain stump across the quarter deck nightly (his leg lost by concensus). He mumbled curses from the ship's bowels and his malodorous presence tucked in every shadow. He followed the men into the rigging, jogging handholds and greasing spars. He whispered their names in deepest sleep.

They would have deserted to the man had it not been for their new captain, the ghost's widow. Her beauty was now as soft as a puppy's underbelly and she carried herself with regal abandon. So the crew remained, still jumping at every sound and ever anxious to tuck some wind into their sails and get under weigh once more to outrun their terrible curse.

Sir Edmund Roberts was not similarly affected (relative to the old captain's ghost). In the oppressive silence he became increasingly hermetic, spending his days quietly reviewing his notebooks, and savoring his evenings sketching Constance Daphne Fitzwillie; an activity of which she now feigned ignorance, although any woman watching her behavior would have known her subterfuge. But it was a ship of men and men savor little as much as they do the maternal comfort of their own ignorance. It is to them a warm blanket, a barrier against rejection. . . an opaque wall holding reality at bay.

And so as the beautiful Captain Constance Daphne stood before her mirror with nothing but a knowing smile, the naturalist sketched his heart out. When she raised her arms slowly, her magnificent chest rising also, he drew her thus. He drew her every way she chose to stand, walk, bend and move. And when she finally went to bed the naturalist added color to his sketches, her warmth still coursing through his veins.

Editor's note: Sir Edmund Roberts' paintings of his paramour are undoubtedly some of his best. His love for the woman permeates each stroke, the beauty of her body alive on the artist's paper. In addition to his sea maiden paintings, which fill one of his notebooks, Sir Edmund had another notebook, it being a more sensual portfolio that came to light at his mental competency hearing. Referred to as his "Blue Notebook", it contains not only static poses of Constance Daphne (a surprising number of posterior views: Degas-like images of the captain attending to her sponge bath), but also a series of accurate depictions of sea maidens and sea masters enjoying one another in various combinations and to the fullest. Further, there are included some fanciful images: Captain Constance Daphne in uniform, on the deck of the H.M.S. Baci, her glorious chest exposed for all the men to see. Captain Constance Daphne aswim beside the ship sans clothing (this may in point of fact have been an accurate depiction as it is recorded the captain daily had the good ship hove to, a large sail (usually the spritsail course) lowered over the side and flooded, thus keeping sniping sharks at bay while she stroked about langorously). Captain Fitzwillie lying seductively along the smooth barrel of one of the good ship's massive cannons. Etc. Etc.

So as the crew wrung its hands and whistled for wind, Sir Edmund expanded his notebooks and completed increasingly captivating portraits of his amour, the latest of which had her supine with her arms above her head, crossed at the wrists, her eyes closed.

And he saw another sea maiden.

His journal reads:

A year abroad and we have befallen ten sea maidens, each unique and equally captivating. I have learned much both by observation and by interviews with those of the crew who have additional knowledge. Unfortunately, a vast store of such information is Gnarly Dan, the most annoying of the lot. He spits tobacco at each pause and pontificates endlessly; I long to throttle him. I have learned: While sea maidens are often solitary, particularly on land (post aqua), they do migrate and do so in great numbers—at least they did historically, when they were more abundant, for they are on the decline; their environment increasingly spoiled by man's carelessness. Vast sluices of whale blood and uncounted rafts of jetsam have begun to render our delicate oceans poisonous.

So their numbers decrease—though they still migrate in small groups. Such groups are called 'pools'—somewhere between whale pods and fish schools. These pools travel great distances to the shelter of either pole (a matter to investigate) and as they do so they increase their body fat. Thus, a lithe maiden in equatorial climes will be corpulent as she frolics with penguins on ice islands. (Ha, ha! Perhaps our beautiful captain was in migration when we first met!)

While recently becalmed I have taken to employing my diving bell. I have seen but one sea maiden, she passing hourly beneath the bell's open bottom, face upward, her arms crossed above her head and locked at the wrists in what (who else?) Gnarly Dan refers to as the classic sea maiden manner of transmitting her status as unencumbered by love but ready to accept its servitude. Says he, "A sea maiden loses herself to love as easily as she slips into the sea, for she does both willingly and without regret."

The Forgotten Voyage

Maidenous servitudo
"Joannna"
December 30, 1832
Off the northern coast of Florida

Long, thin and beautiful. Curled blonde hair. Diminutive chest.

SIGHTING ELEVEN

The H.M.S. Baci finally picked up a wind, the crew ecstatic as cat's paws moved steadily past the good ship. They set sail once more and continued southward, New Year's Eve in a howling gale followed by weeks of high seas, blowing spindrift and ever-cooler temperatures. The Bacis seized every chance to repair their foul and cold weather gear. Only Sir Edmund, sea maiden questor, remained unprepared; no tar being available for waterproofing his long tarpaulin coat; it thus remaining brilliant white in a sea of black jackets.

Regardless, he spent much time on deck, scanning the endless horizon for a sea maiden while the crew kept a weather eye out for the loathsome pirate, Naughty Nat. Gnarly Dan, the omnipresent and always poised-to-speak common sailors' nautical expert lamented ceaselessly that the sea through which they were traveling should be thick with sea maidens, it being migration season ("southing" he called it) remarking, "Yer sea maiden should be southing in great pools, yer honor, making for the ice islands where they'll spend some time hobnobbing and laying about undisturbed by sailors and such." It was obvious Gnarly Dan was imagining them, for he wet his chapped lips, closed his eyes and continued, "Right lovely they'd be now, sir, and precious as gold dust; fatted up fer the cold water (he smiled to himself) and all healthy-like so's a man can get a grip and still have plenty ta lay into."

Sir Edmund attempted to dissuade further elaboration by feigning absolute disinterest, but Gnarly Dan was in the arms of his fantasy and unstoppable. "We sailors has a hard lot, sir, not that we complains, ourselves being used to it and all, but every hard workin' soul," he emphasized the word and repeated himself, "Every *hard* workin' soul takes 'is comfort where he finds it. It's like an unwrit law: the harder a man works the softer he likes his women. So yer bigger sea maiden is most pop'lar with a sailor."

Gnarly Dan collected himself and realizing he may have offended Sir Edmund, quickly added, "Beggin' yer pardon if yer missus is skinny, sir. Plenty o' sophisticated gents such as yerself likes 'em all sharp edges an' shiftin' bones. But not yer sailor."

There was, of course, no Mrs. Sir Edmund, sharp edges or no, to whom the naturalist could harken back. Just their current captain. Thin of ankle and long of leg, expansive, glorious hips, trim waist and then the twin gifts from heaven; firm, heavy, milky soft and beckoning. And a beautiful face.

The naturalist was in no mood to think of pudgy sea maidens.

Within a fortnight, on an unchartered island where they'd stopped to water the ship, Sir Edmund saw his eleventh sea maiden. She was robust as predicted and aloof and a sore temptation for Gnarly Dan to desert and join. But he knew her stay would be short lived and so he maintained allegiance to the ship.

Sir Edmund wrote in his journal:

Ah, most weighty discovery! A beautiful sea maiden in the bloom of migration! Sighted on an island we have named Succoro, she remained but briefly before returning to the sea. She studied the stars most diligently before departing, tracing odd figures and tangents into the hard sand. I now understand Gnarly Dan's preference even though my heart still belongs to our trim captain, Constance Daphne. (I do not discount her bounteous chest.)

Maidenous robustus

"Kathy"

Corpulent, yet agile. Dark hair, green glittering scales, strong but padded upper body

January 29, 1833

Succuro Island, South Atlantic Sea

SIGHTING TWELVE

Tempering the handful of victories the H.M.S. Baci savored during her extended and convoluted attempt at circumnavigation was a spate of humiliating failures. Notable was the setback the ship and company suffered when they made their first attempt on Cape Horn in 1833. Again and again, weeks of vexing winds, sudden squalls and blasting cold thwarted success. The good ship could not claw her way around the Horn and neither could she sneak by during the too brief windows of fine weather. At last, her rigging wounded, her mizzen mast a stump and her crew much reduced by the mountainous waves that swept her decks, the H.M.S. Baci turned tail and limped back up the South American coast seeking a harbor with naval stores to rebuild and repair, lick wounds and reconstitute the crew's fortitude.

The captain's resolve needed no such attention; in point of fact she had remained steadfastly defiant, nonplussed and a fair example right up to the moment Stumpy Pete's peg had come unshipped and sailed onto the captain's pate. She'd had herself lashed to the main mast so she could howl orders and wave her arms unconcerned for her own safety when the wooden missile knocked her senseless.

Half of the available crew untied and then hauled their captain to her cabin, willing hands buoying her ample bosoms and other tempting parts while the rest of the watch seized the opportunity to bring the floundering ship about and flee the Horn.

Sir Edmund Roberts acquitted himself quite well both in the attempt on the Horn and the subsequent coddling of the unconscious and much bathed captain. But words pale to describe the captain's reaction when she finally recovered her senses and learned they'd been beaten.

"Í BEG YOUR PARDON, SIR. . .YOU SAY WE ARE ON *WHICH* COAST?" she challenged as she raised herself from her bed. "WE DID NOT ROUND THE HORN? WE DID NOT ROUND THE HORN?" she asked in an incredibly forceful voice.

Sir Edmund remained composed. "While I do not know our good ship as well as you, my fair captain, we had only two of our three masts to work with and no captain for guidance. Were we to be in the same circumstances again, I dare say the choice would be the same. The crew performs in a manner best described as super-human when it finds itself at your command; as you well know. But with you down they feared greatly for your health and sought refuge immediately."

It did calm her down some. She slowed her breathing, flattened the sheets about her and studied the beams at her cabin roof. "Very well, then," she said, at last resigned. "Get us to port so we might refit and attempt once more. I believe that loathsome cur, Naughty Nat, has sailed before us and is now free to wreak his havoc in the broad Pacific."

Sir Edmund did as he was bid. They found a decent port, and the good ship Baci was first careened and then repaired. Sir Edmund had his diving apparatus roused from the bowels of the hold and moved to a small vessel he chartered to use while the H.M.S. Baci was being overhauled.

He sighted his twelfth sea maiden in the transparent depths of midday. She drifted slowly by the bell, seemingly transfixed, the most notable movement being that of her hair, at once ahoo and dancing seductively in the light currents. Sir Edmund studied the fair maiden, marveling at the perfection of her body; the counter forces of buoyancy and gravity ever so gently coaxing her beautiful breasts first this way and then that in a dance every bit as intoxicating as that of her hair. Gnarly Dan, accompanying Sir Edmund in the diving bell whispered that she was slumbering, carried forth with the slow tidal sweep. "Yer sea maiden dearly loves to sleep," he explained, "for it's there she dreams of her sailor."

Sir Edmund Roberts' journal reads:

Maidenus somnolentus

"Lisa"

Beautiful coloration.   Strong body.   Handsomely equipped for motherhood. Quiet smile.

February 27, 1833

Port Desire (how appropriate) Coast of South America.

SIGHTING THIRTEEN

Replete with a new mizzen mast, a recovered captain and a rested crew, the second attempt at rounding Cape Horn went as easily as "kiss my hand". And so in wonderous spirits the Bacis sailed into the vast Pacific Ocean and up the western coast of South America, fair weather and smooth sailing lofting morale to its newest peak.

There was, however, a new source of irritation for Captain Constance Daphne Fitzwillie. She was not sleeping well. At all. At first she attributed it to over-fatigue, and then the stress of the job, and then the lumpiness of her bed, but in the middle of one moonless night as she lay awake, she realized what was disturbing her sleep.

A low hum. A vibration that seemed to insinuate itself into her very soul. It was not relaxing; it was not soothing. It was incredibly, undeniably unsettling. She listened intently but could not imagine its source. She lay for hours, first stuffing her head beneath her pillow, then rising from bed and pacing her cabin. At last she pulled on her robe and went to her quarterdeck. But for the sounds of the rigging shifting and the sails straining, and the water hissing along the side of the fine ship, and the dark rustle of the sea all around them, it was tolerably quiet. There was no low hum.

Exhausted but full of hope she returned to her room, no sooner removing her robe when she heard it again. And so it was for the remainder of the night. With the false dawn she arose, exhausted and temperamental. Once again on her quarterdeck, frowsy and ill-tempered, and thinking the sound must be being produced by some working of the timbers of the ship, she had the ship's carpenter, Chips, sent to her. Captain Constance Daphne explained the noise and had him follow her to her room.

The noise was still audible and Chips listened intently, slowly moving to different portions of her quarters. At last he walked quickly to the row of stern windows. "As I figgered;" he said, "a followin' sea. Playin' 'Ole Harry' with the rudder." Then, seeing that his captain was not on the same course as his logic he explained in detail:

"A followin' sea creates strange swirls a' water aroun' our rudder. That soft wobblin' flows right through the cables to the wheel. A gob can feel her in the spokes. Sometimes she feels right nice. Other times, not." As he finished he went to the starboard side of the captain's room. He stooped to a low bench with a cushioned top and removed the panels from its top and from the side toward the center of her room, exposing a substantial rope, fully three inches in diameter, passing beneath its length. Sure enough, Captain Constance Daphne could see that it in addition to the movements transmitted from the man at the wheel to move the rudder, it was vibrating. Where it passed into the adjacent cabin it went through a block, and there it struck the wood, producing the low rattling hum.

Chips went back to the heavy rope and putting one leg over the rudder cable, straddled it, finally sitting and leaning to the block near the wall. He examined it carefully and then turned to his captain. "I can swab some grease on yonder block; should calm her some."

But the captain's interest was no longer with the annoying sound.

"It does that only with a following sea?" she enquired.

"Aye, Cap," he answered.

"And such a sea is common?"

"Depends on which way we's steerin' the good ship, Cap."

Constance Daphne got a faraway look and a hint of a smile.

"That will be all," she said, "return to the deck."

But when the carpenter went to replace the panels he'd removed, she added, "Leave them be; I rather like the sound now. A bit louder and more pleasant with the rope exposed."

With the carpenter gone Constance Daphne returned to stare at the stout rope. In her eyes was that for which women so quietly long, and men seek so actively without thinking.

It was a minor event, but as with so many things that appear inconsequential, it would help the fine captain weather some lonely nights.

They sailed on, the sense of goodwill and harmonious interdependence faltering and then failing completely with the sighting of the thirteenth sea maiden. No man could have dreamed of the trouble on the horizon, the discord around the corner, or the source of the most dastardly stroke of ill luck to affect the fine crew of the good ship, silently lurking in the deep.

It was not the loathsome pirate Naughty Nat.

It was another man.

Sir Edmund Roberts' journal entries best recount the series of events:

Curse of curses, most vile of luck! 13 indeed! Were I not the handmaiden of science I would fairly chuck the remainder of our voyage, strangle the crew, maroon our fickle captain (despite her beauty) and burn the good ship Baci to her waterline.

It began whilst I was sub-aquatic in Halley's patented diving bell, the H.M.S. Baci languishing in a snug and deserted bay, the crew replenishing supplies ashore. It seems a hunting party led by Sloshy George chanced upon a sunning sea maiden, befriended her with hand signs and proffered grog to the point of blind inebriation and beyond until the poor dear lost consciousness. Panic-laced argument discommoded her tempters, they having taken with them to that beach (along with copious amounts of rum), every shortcoming and act of cowardice known to round out the sea bag of man in general. "Whatever should we do?" they moaned. The options were few and despicable on the whole: abandon her on the sand and hope she recovered on her own; carry her to the ship and trust the ship's surgeon could practice a bit of veterinary medicine; or simply, wet her down some and see if that revived her. In the end they opted to float her, cold water being the sailors' proven tonic.

Big Bill hoisted the slack body over his shoulder and started wading through the surf. By all accounts the men were all frightened to immobility when a sea master appeared, cowed the crew with foul glances and prompted Big Bill to discard his load before he turned and ran back up the beach. The sea master gently gathered up the maiden, turned slowly and returned with her to the depths. It was shortly thereafter that he passed our diving apparatus, affording us the sight of their moving quite carefully to sea.

Nonplussed, Gnarly Dan, my bell mate remarked, "She's a beauty, ain't she? Appears besotted though, and that can't be good; it's that way with all women—they can handle a compliment much better'n a drink." Gnarly enjoyed the spectacle for another moment before he added, "That'd be Neptune, her king, doin' the rescue work."

And from these seeds grow our monumental fractiousness. The crew is divided as such: those angry with their mates for playing the fool with a sea maiden and rum; those ensnared in explaining away the sea master as Neptune and thus no threat to the romantic link between sea maidens and sailors; those remarking the sea master's lack of saintly beard and trident and advanced age as proof he is not Neptune and therefore suggesting a plethora of sea masters frolicking with our sea maidens; and finally, those jealous of Captain Constance Daphne's new interest in the diving bell and all detailed accounts of the sea master's physique and facial characteristics.

Consequently, the crew is doubly slighted and in no mood to brook quarter should the sea master reappear, some going so far as to randomly discard rope nets and loose cannon balls over the side. We are so near mutiny I go about with my notebooks and sketches on my person.

And so the H.M.S. Baci became an unhappy ship, their captain constantly belittling.

"MAKE A LEG, YOU LUBBER! CAN ANY MAN ABOARD THIS SHIP DO JUST ONE THING WITH SKILL? I BEGIN TO UNDERSTAND WHAT ACTUALLY DROVE MY DEPARTED HUSBAND TO MADNESS!"

Every ounce of sensitivity the woman had deserted her. She even turned against Sir Edmund saying "And you, you pompous, over-educated fool; why are you standing about staring? Is there not one useful thing you might find to employ your time?"

The naturalist's notebook provides but bare bones of the event and sighting:

Maidenous inebriatus

"Martha"

March 30, 1833

Average weight. Golden hair. Minimal alcohol tolerance.

Magnus neptunus

Hale. Strong. Defined musculature.

Both sighted in the protected harbor of San Carlos at the island of Chiloe'.

SIGHTING FOURTEEN

Mutiny! The injection of sea masters into the heady brew of men searching for women (albeit sea maidens) was predictably hypergolic. The timing could not have been worse; the euphoria of the crew after rounding Cape Horn being cruelly dashed by the first sea master sighting. The crew was then drubbed and slighted when their adored captain, Constance Daphne Fitzwillie, demonstrated instant devotion to making what she intimated would be very personal contact with the sea master should he reappear. Further, she allowed impatience and pettiness to dominate her relationship with the crew.

That slice of bitter bread was buttered with the devastating loss of the most loved of crewmen, the elder storyteller O'Brian—the gentlest of gentlemen gone; and so, no more swashbuckling tales, no more intrigue and love to supplement their meager rations and suppressed loneliness as they sat enthralled on starry nights, the fine barque working beneath them, the familiar constellations wheeling beyond the rigging above as he told the finest tales.

Sir Edmund Roberts' journal relates the ensuing events:

A pox on our captain, her overpowering beauty and its effect on otherwise temperate men! How I prayed we would spy no more sea masters—at least not right away—let the crew forget our first! But oh, those playful gods! Within a fortnight, our ship still embayed, we beheld another sea master; he quite certainly not the same as nor even cousin to the first.

We were readying the diving bell to be lowered. Constance Daphne was underfoot and overpowering the crew into the foulest of moods, some going so far as to roll cannon balls off the head in dumb show of their disdain for sea masters, Neptune or no. Then a remarkable specimen thereof fairly flew from the water off the starboard bow. He flipped nicely mid-aire and then reentered the water with nary a ripple. In the resultant cacophony of orders, curses, and accusations our aroused captain commanded at last, "Get this diving apparatus over the side, you bumbling idiots—I shall halve your rum rations for clumsiness!"

Clumsy indeed! She could not have been farther from the truth. They are a fine crew and as nimble as monkeys. Captain Constance Daphne erred thrice with her ejaculation: Firstly she allowed lust to overshadow judgement—surely a man's prerogative at best and no place for a woman to tarry! Secondly, she tampered with the crew's last pleasure—their daily allotment of rum, thus tempting riot, and finally, she allowed her anger to tax her normally crisp enunciation; the crew heard their captain declare she would have their rum ration, not halve it as she intended—and in fact only wished to threaten halving. But her mind was under the sea with the sea master and the damage was done—disaster awaited.

I must aver that I too erred, for I was aware of all and still had the temerity to enter Halley's patented diving apparatus with the captain and Gnarly Dan, leaving an incensed crew to lower us to the depths and look after our safety. Instead, they played "Old Harry" as we sat entombed for our sea master vigil. Our folly notwithstanding we saw our second sea master reappear (we in rapt appreciation) and effortlessly avoid the passing cannon balls and still remain visibly unimpressed by the deep angy boom of our ship's unshotted deck guns above. For all the world he seemed to be communicating that he was one of the lords of the water while we were the noisy and nosey fools.

Unfortunately, Gnarly Dan concurred. Says he as our captain sat squeezed between us, her face pressed to the thick glass of her steamed round window, "A gill a' grace'll float a woman's heart higher than a flood a' flash and thunder."

We in the bell were, however, most impressed when the Baci's anchor ascended rapidly by our window and the ship's long shadow passed across the ocean floor and away.

Maximus disdignare
April 12, 1833
Protected harbor of San Carlos, island of Chiloe'.
Average weight. Dark hair. Powerful yet graceful swimmer.

SIGHTING FIFTEEN

So once again the H.M.S. Baci strayed into troubled waters. Made jealous beyond endurance by their beautiful captain's fascination with sea masters, the slighted crew did the unthinkable and mutinied, leaving Constance Daphne, the old sage Gnarly Dan, and the voyage's underwriter, Sir Edmund Roberts, gentleman naturalist and sea maiden questor, stranded in Halley's patented diving apparatus beneath a ton of warm Pacific water.

The three sat in mute disbelief. The sea master who had been cavorting before them left. Time hung heavy for the three as each sat in silence and explored recent events. Old Gnarly Dan was the least affected by the mutiny itself; he was on the right side of maritime law since he was still with the ship's captain and he had uttered not a word of sedition (although they were probably the only words the garrulous old salt had not mouthed). But he also was entrapped, and so that is what initially directed the majority of his thoughts. Sir Edmund was also faultless relative to the mutiny. Of course he felt slighted by his captain; he had come to view her as far more (and considering the augured hole, he had come to view her far more easily and often), but so well bred was he that he would not have entertained any ideas of altering the hierarchy on which Britannia had risen to the world's most powerful nation. Instead, he turned his thoughts to the proximity of Constance Daphne. In point of fact, his thoughts alternated between the beautiful woman who sat not an arm's length away, and his increasing desire for Gnarly Dan to be spirited away from what otherwise could have presented a few interesting possibilities. Sir Edmund imagined the old salt simply not choosing to accompany them, he imagined the old salt somehow stepping to the sea bottom and being sucked into its depths by an unseen force. He even was intemperate enough to allow Old Gnarly Dan to suffer from an obtuse infirmity that immediately rendered him stone dead and absent any unfortunate heavings and releases the naturalist knew to accompany sudden death.

Captain Constance Daphne Fitzwillie (captain, though she now had no ship) sat as the huge inertia wheel of pent up anger began to slowly build speed. A fine end to a short career! An unthinkable termination of her late blooming of womanhood, independence, self-esteem and self-fulfillment! She seethed. On occasion she allowed herself covert glances at the two men who shared her immediate dilemma. She gave serious thought to throttling them both.

And then a brace of sea creatures swam forth. They were at once more attractive; their dance more subtle and sensual than any the bell mates had ever seen. At first the sea maiden moved in graceful arcs above the hovering sea master, continually getting closer, but skillfully avoiding touching him. Approach and denial, approach and denial; she came ever so close to the handsome sea master but did not touch him except perhaps with her trailing hair. Slowly she lowered her passes, now swimming in graceful circles around the master, each pass lower and closer to him, and again she did not touch him with her body. When she was at last beneath him, she circled there, at once oblivious to his presence and yet undeniably aware of him.

The three in Halley's patented diving apparatus quickened their breath. They shifted nervously. Pulses increased and clothing became an unfamiliar restraint. No one spoke.

Then the beautiful sea maiden cautiously swam from beneath the sea master, and as she glided upward, her body slowly brushed against his; tentatively at first, with the side of her cheek against his lower tail, and then her breasts flowed against him as she rose and her entire body softly moved along his. The sea master was rapt, his eyes closed, his arms behind his back, one hand locked onto the opposite wrist. He was as if bound, and she unfettered and dancing her provocation sensually against his strength of will.

She circled above him again and then went beneath and once more touched him as she swam upward, this time moving with more pressure against him, the side of her face pressing hard along his body, her chest moving to fill each contour of his, her thighs caressing his length, her own tail entwined with him. It was plainly visible that both participants were aroused; the maiden's breasts at once more full, her nipples hard and proud. And the poor sea master, required to remain unmoving strained against the encasing folds of his upper tail.

The three shipmates in the bell leaned forward and watched in awe, the sensuality before them palpable. Gnarly Dan whispered, "She'd be showin' that she captains their ship, don' ya' see. He must clamp ahold hisself and let her have her way. No clawin' an' fumblin' about like we men does."

They were silent again, watching the performance, until Gnarly Dan continued, "Yer sea master's all agog ta' learn her way. He may be strong as a Malay an' pleasin' ta' lay an eye on, but it's a lady's world down here. Yer sea maiden rules with her heart and their ain't a sea master afloat what cares ta' resist. She'd be doin' the choosin'. If she' decides he'd be worthy, why, things'll get right interestin' soon enough. All he can do now is be 'vailable an' hope she likes what she sees. 'Course he'd be payin' attention now; learnin' how she likes things. No guessin' by a mate down here. Why, she'll teach 'im ever way ta make herself feel like a queen. It ain't all confusin' like we has it," Gnarly Dan confided, with an eye on Constance Daphne. "We gobs'r inna dark most of the watch when it comes ta makin' a lass feel jus' right." He let the accusation set for a moment and went back to watching.

The dance progressed before them, a ritual of temptation, restraint and instruction as the sea master silently acquiesced. Coincidental to the lanquid performance, the bell's atmosphere was becoming progressively more cloying as temperature and humidity rose. Constance Daphne's light cotton shirt went from damp to soaked to transparency as she sat enthralled. At first with sly looks and then with full blown admiration both Gnarly Dan and Sir Edmund shifted their attention to their captain until finally, in what could only be seen as a mutual lapse of moral fortitude and decorum, Sir Edmund and Gnarly Dan nodded and then removed their own shirts, they then seemingly losing themselves in their attempts to staunch unseen leaks at the bell's bottom where it rested on the sea floor. At last Gnarly Dan winked at Sir Edmund and implored, "Could use a bit 'a cloth, Cap."

He said it quietly and with a show of humble honesty and the effect was, of course, what both men had hoped. Constance Daphne, still leaning to the newly steamed window, absently unbuttoned her wet blouse. Lower and lower her hands worked as the two men held their breath. She tugged one side and then another free of her pants and then removed her top, handing it without looking to Gnarly Dan.

As Sir Edmund already knew and Gnarly Dan had dreamed, her breasts were magnificent. Weighty and perfectly formed, they swayed as she leaned, glistening with perspiration, pale in the bell's subtle light and begging to be gently lifted and caressed. The old salt sat with his mouth open, his eyes agog, and slowly took the offered shirt.

Editor's note: *Sir Edmund's journal studiously avoids the occurrence while in his private diary, his "blue notebook", the incident was noted both in word and image. During Sir Edmund's waning years there was an unsavory attempt by his relatives to access his considerable wealth by having him declared mentally incompetent. The subsequent trial was the talk of London as everyone from chimney sweep to barrister followed its progress. A key and damning piece of evidence was the notebook containing his writings and sketches of sea maidens and sea masters cavorting in incredibly intimate combinations and situations. Included also were Sir Edmund's romantic musings regarding Captain Constance Daphne and a collection of watercolor drawings of her, which to speak conservatively, were of particular interest to the male jurors. Sadly, the more unsavory of the illustrations were reproduced as etchings and sold well in England and France. One glorious painting was of Constance Daphne bathed in the warm light of the diving bell's window, her pendulous breasts aglisten.*

And yet, for all of the prurient details and hoopla of the trial, and in spite of the small army of aunts, nieces and nephews proclaiming him ready for Bedlam, it was in the last hour of the last day of the trial that Sir Edmund, much reduced by the strain and notoriety, humiliated by the attacks on his sanity and made the fool for his steadfast belief in sea maidens and sea masters, slowly rose to his feet before a full courtroom and with a simple question brought the world back to his side. Leaning on the banister before him, he scanned every face of the jurors ready to pass judgement, and asked, "And if, as you claim, I only imagined them;" he paused, drew in a breath and continued, his eyes focused on a distant voyage, he no doubt on the rolling deck of the good ship, H.M.S. Baci, "what was the crime in that? They were so beautiful."

The last journal entries of that day read:

Maidenus commendare

"Nicole"

Average weight, dark hair, dark complexion, lithe and supple.

Magnus submissio

Average weight, tall, muscular, dark hair, dark complexion

April 12, 1833

Protected harbor of San Carlos, island of Chiloe'

SIGHTING SIXTEEN

The three, Captain Constance Daphne Fitzwillie, Gnarly Dan, and Sir Edmund Roberts, gentleman naturalist and sea maiden questor, remained trapped in their diving bell, the good ship H.M.S. Baci and her mutinous crew having sailed away. The fates did however have a third diversion in store (Constance Daphne's state of undress not withstanding) in the person of a sea maiden. The last pair were still in sight, though distant, their langorous dance at last approaching romantic fruition as the sea maiden finally allowed her sea master (an ironic naming) to use his body as he would. (Another painting in Sir Edmund's Blue Notebook Series.)

Constance Daphne Fitzwillie sat enthralled at the bell's window while Gnarly Dan and Sir Edmund's fascination lay in the crooked paths the beads of perspiration traced down their captain's exposed and lovely chest. One drop hung heavy from her right nipple, and each man tried mightily to control himself, though he could fairly taste its salty kiss on his tongue.

So at first no one was aware that a different sea maiden had hove into view, the invisible tidal pull moving her ever closer, her tail nearly motionless, her arms weaving a poetic ballet in the clear warm water. And of course, it was Gnarly Dan who first noticed and commented, "Lord above, ain't she asleep an' awash in dreams!"

Constance Daphne grudgingly shifted her attention to the maiden, her heart and body still involved with the distant coupling. Sir Edmund glanced several times from his captain's captivating body, each time with longer interludes, the singularly interesting drop of perspiration impossibly clinging to the captain's dark, lonely and beckoning nipple. But the sea maiden, drifting ever closer, was beautiful beyond words, her eyes softly closed and her body arched seductively.

It was now Gnarly Dan who leaned to the porthole, carefully nudging his captain aside, cautious to avoid contact with her bared upper body, though for all the world he wished to embrace her. He peered through the thick glass intently, gasped audibly, put his hand to his heart and murmured, "If I warn't sober as a judge, I'd swear she'd be me first wife, Olivia. I'd throw the other six away ta just see the ole girl one more time."

Both Constance Daphne and Sir Edmund looked to the old man to see if they had heard him correctly and if perhaps he were speaking in jest, but Gnarly Dan was far from humor. He had spent his life before the mast and each sea mile had left its mark. Murderous gales, pirates and privateers, hard rolls and bully beef had made him one with the tar and oak and iron. But all of that fell away as a profound sadness slathered with the remorse of lost love and squandered youth shone from his eyes and peeked forth from his ancient heart. "Warn't I the fool," he whispered and swabbed a tear from his cheek.

Uncomfortable with such bald emotion, Sir Edmund asked, "Now how can you be so certain she's dreaming? Perhaps her sleep is unencumbered."

Constance Daphne watched the exchange. Unconsciously she wiped the accumulated perspiration from her chest as she listened.

Heretofore it had always been the naturalist who was annoyed with the sailor, but now it was the old salt who replied with condescension, "And were ye born last night, Yer Honor? All them books don' tell all, now does they! A' course she'd be dreamin'; any gob can see that."

Sir Edmund let the assault on class-induced distance pass unremarked. Gnarly Dan shifted his tone to that of one addressing a child: "Can't ya see her arms, gov', how she's a-movin' 'em? Why when they sleeps, they dreams, and when they dreams they moves their arms about all graceful-like." As if to refute the old man, the sea maiden's arms hovered for a moment and coincidentally she began to slip slightly downward toward the ocean floor, whereupon that movement seemed to trigger her arms' silent weaving once more.

Sir Edmund catalogued it all with his naturalist's eye, had a burst of cause and effect logic and retorted, "Not dreams, my good man; negative buoyancy! She must move her arms, albeit slowly, or her tail for that matter, or she'll sink! Nothing to do with her mind, you old scoundrel!"

Gnarly Dan listened quietly with feigned respect but in the end would have none of it. In fact, his sad disdain grew. "You have the book larnin', sir, 'tis true enough; never met a gent so full a' thoughts a' t'others. But beggin' yer pardon, Sir Edmund, sir, but there be such a fish as a foolish one." He paused and watched the sea maiden's beautiful movements, lost once more in the memories of his youth and finally concluded with new patience, "Yer sea maiden ain't no different from us, cap'; for without dreams we all sink." He waited to see if Sir Edmund understood and when he saw no comprehension, added, "Though some don' know they's sinkin' an' t'others don' know what they's already sunk."

An apt remark for three submerged and stranded in Halley's patented diving apparatus. Captain Constance Daphne ended the subsequent silence by ordering the last cask of air upended, thus turning their thoughts to their current plight.

Sir Edmund's naturalist's notebook comments:

The bad luck of our inprisonment was mitigated by sea maiden and sea master sightings, but made worse by Gnarly Dan's prattle. How I wish he would drown. 'First wife', indeed! Dreaming sea maiden! Poppycock! However, our fifteenth sea maiden is glorious though slumbering.

Maidenus languidus
"Olivia"
Average weight, stunning coloration, beautiful orange tail, long dark hair.
April 12, 1833
Protected harbor of San Carlos (still!), island of Chiloe'

SIGHTING SEVENTEEN

And then, in the tepid waters off the western coast of South America, the extended ordeal in Halley's patented diving apparatus ended with a whimper. The three mariners had been submerged for the entire day, their ship sailed away and they stranded.

"Always know'd I'd die at sea," Gnarly Dan lamented, "but I never figured it ta be hot an' boring."

"It is a bit anti-climatic," Sir Edmund Roberts added looking with bald longing at their semi-clad and beautiful captain. "Pity."

The two men lapsed into quiet parley. Gnarly Dan, the old salt with a titanic store of obscure wisdom, and Sir Edmund, the sea maiden questor and gentleman naturalist at last concluding it was their manly duty to rescue their captain, Constance Daphne, from a watery and ignoble grave. "I say, we must step up to the mast and do our best," Sir Edmund commented. "Our Captain deserves our unflagging efforts to right this situation."

"Aye, warn't right fer them gobs ta leave us like this; I thought they was me mates," Gnarly sighed, "She ain't manly-like ta leave a lass ta die," he added.

With a show of aged and ineffectual bravado they lowered their feet to the soft sea bottom, braced their bare backs against the bell's oaken walls and heaved upward, the embarrassing result being that while the diving apparatus did not budge, the men succeeded after much huffing and tugging, in forcing themselves knee deep into the warm Pacific ooze.

Sir Edmund Roberts wiped his brow, caught his breath, and stole a glance at his captain's chest and then observed, "What we need is a firm bottom," to which Gnarly Dan, misunderstanding completely, apologetically nodded and said, "Beggin' yer pardon, Cap, but the gentleman may be right; might be we could use yer help."

Captain Fitzwillie, resplendent even in fatigue and perspiration, looked from man to man and then to the details of the bell's interior. It was some time before she responded, "In some things you remind me of my departed husband, your former captain, but in everything you remind me that you are men. Breathes there one of you with more insight than insensitivity? You pride yourselves on walking erect though your only advantage lay in you supine!" She warmed to her disdain as the naturalist and the old sailor exchanged uncomfortable looks. "I am mortified to admit I have spent these many hours with you abstensively trapped in a cramped, odorous underwater machine because I accepted your pronouncements of our helplessness.

She too now stood though she did not attempt lifting the bell. Instead she raised the base of her bench, exposing a rack of iron balls, which she began helfting out and dropping into the mire. Sir Edmund's face fell to humiliation even as he watched her moving chest when she exposed the row of ballast beneath his former bench and moved to empty it. (The bell was not normally raised by discarding weight; the ball's value sufficient to warrant using the muscle of those on the barge above to raise the apparatus following each dive, so the oversight was somewhat reasonable.) With each loosed ball the bell rose slightly from the sea bottom, until continued motion was apparent. The three quickly released a few more balls before they returned to their seats, their own weight slowing but not arresting the ascent.

In silence they drifted upward and in silence they saw their sixteenth sea maiden—a beautiful mother with a child riding on her back, the child's arms encircling her by the neck. Anger and embarrassment melted as the endearing pair circled the bell, both as curious as those within.

"I suppose the youth cannot yet swim," Sir Edmund noted, cloaking himself once more in his mantle of distant science and cold observation.

Captain Constance Daphne looked to Gnarly Dan to watch his reaction, knowing the naturalist was rarely correct in his assessment of sea maiden behavior. She was not disappointed.

"Lord above," Gnarly Dan huffed, "that child could swim to Merry England and back if she chose. She's just enjoyin' a ride an' lovin' her mum. We tends ta forget such things where we lives, but yer sea maiden don'. She gets her strength, and her love from her mum's heart. And she never forgets. They's like peas inna pod they whole life. I've see'd some right old sea maidens what turned out ta be mum an' daughter, jus' hobknobbin' an' havin' the time a' they lives. Their love don' get old an' it don' fade none. Chances are it grows with time, yer young 'un settlin' inta a real fine love as she gets older."

Sir Edmund's notebook recounts:

Intelligence will out: we analyzed an egress from Halley's bell and saw a sea maiden and her offspring.

Maidenus mater

"Pamela"

Average weight, blue tail, beautiful appearance.

Maidenus infans

"Ariana"

3-5 years approximately, slight build, beautiful appearance, scales higher on her body, blue tail such as her mother's.

The H.M.S. Baci is gone!

SIGHTING EIGHTEEN

The diving craft popped to the surface like a released cork, tumbled from side to side briefly and then settled inverted, its three occupants tossed about and then onto the old-roof-new-floor. It was as if they were in a flooded tub. Sir Edmund rose to the wall of the bell and peered about. They were not remarkably far from shore, the tide was on the make, and the sea calm. Except for the absence of their vessel, the good ship H.M.S. Baci, the situation was not particularly untenable.

Gnarly Dan now leaned against the opposite side of the bell-now-tub and brought his naval skills to bear. "Lay on a plank or two from our ole' bench and I wager we can paddle ta the beach afore the tide turns."

Which they did, but not before they spun the craft in circles for a few dizzying moments, Captain Constance Daphne, mortified to be in command of such an outrageous vessel. "Avast paddling, you nincompoops!" she ordered. "Let me free a plank and put it astern as a rudder." Which she did. The men learned to stroke in unison and propelled themselves to shore at last, Sir Edmund commenting to Gnarly Dan, "There is something to be said for a sharp captain to put things right. Bastion of civilization and all that!"

They reached the shore and were surprised to find the Baci's launch neatly beached, one of the Captain's trunks stowed carefully in it along with one of Sir Edmund's and the sea bag of Gnarly Dan. The mutineers were after all not without heart.

Once more presentable, the three attacked their future with aplomb.

And so, the beautiful and gloriously buxom Constance Daphne, intent on accessing sufficient funds to hire a ship and crew to hound the H.M.S. Baci and her mutineers to the ends of the earth, went north to Valdive and the Port of Valparaiso searching for an agent of her bank. Temporarily scuttled was her hunt for the notorious pirate, Naughty Nat.

Meanwhile, with fumbling self-sufficiency Sir Edmund Roberts, the gentleman naturalist, and Gnarly Dan, the pontificating old salt whose vessel of sea lore regularly plied the narrow but treacherous straits separating wisdom from absurdity, chartered a barge of sorts and manhandled Halley's patented diving bell back into the Gulf of Guytecas so Sir Edmund could continue his sea maiden observations.

Undermanned as they were, the pair divided the duties so that while Gnarly Dan remained at the surface with a handful of locals, Sir Edmund descended in his bell alone, there sighting the third sea master and sea maiden pair and immediately returned to the surface morose and stunned with grief. Once the bell was winched into the air beside the barge, Sir Edmund stepped from within, accomplished the barge and immediately sat.

Gnarly Dan was solitious and unrelenting. "What's afoot, sir? Why the sudden squall? Beggin' yer pardon, maybe I can help. Lay it on the deck and we'll nudge it about a bit."

Sir Edmund snuffled dryly and drew in several lungsful of air. At last he relented and spoke. "I am a naturalist, my good man, and death is as much a part of my work as the bloom of life—more so, often enough. Regardless, I have witnessed a sight to wound the heart of the hardest man: a handsome sea master 'in migration' apparently from Africa, has had his mate expire." Sir Edmund drew in more air. "She lay cradled in his powerful ebony arms, beautiful to the last and most serene in countenance. Oh, that I should die so content!"

Gnarly Dan frowned with the naturalist as he ruminated on what he had heard. Then ever so slowly, he perked up, as if awakening from the deepest, farthest thoughts. "Let me ask, yer honor, was her head back an' her arms a hangin' like twin anchor cables?"

Sir Edmund nodded and affirmed, "Indeed." Gnarly Dan brightened and continued, "An' tell me, sir, did she ever so lightly—like a ship's cat testin' wet tar—did she ever so lightly have just a corner a' his tail held between her thumb and finger?"

The naturalist consulted his sketchbook carefully. "She did."

Now Gnarly Dan smiled broadly and settled into mellow laughter. "Dead sir? That's a good un! Stow yer tears, squire, she's more likely dead tired! Gone ta heaven she has, but it warn't her at the pearly gates!"

For a man in the tropics, Sir Edmund's icy stare was commendable. At last Gnarly Dan relented and explained. "We've seen a pool of sea masters and sea maidens these last two days, am I right, sir? And they's been doin' their weddin' dance, if ya catches me meaning. A smart gent like yerself must have puzzled out by now that things is a sight different under the sea and what happens next is one of 'em. Ya see, when a sea master gets the nod from his mate, he's got ta prove he's worthy. An' sir, I'll not ask into the bedroom antics a' yerself an' Mrs. Edmund, but I'll give ya this—yer sea master don' just fire a shot acrost her bow and then retire. His job is to bend on every sail an' take her on the voyage of her life and never mind if it takes a watch an' a half ta do it! So he does. Light sails an' gentle breezes, then full gale an' batten down the hatches. Maybe even becalmed a bit an' then inta the breach onst more! Poundin' waves and spindrift, long swells and rough chop, broadsides and rollin' fire! No sir, the trip ain't over 'til yer sea maiden gets a kind a glommy look an' faints dead away! An' that's a fact!"

Gnarly Dan grinned like a stowaway startled by a fresh lantern. "They says little girls wants ta grow up an' be a sea maiden, but I tell ya what; big girls just wants ta spend some time at sea with a sea master. Ya see, like a good sailor, yer sea master knows; the longer the voyage, the sweeter the homecoming."

Sir Edmund was in shock. "You're saying she's alive. She's just passed out from. . ." The naturalist searched for the word. Such a concept as too much pleasure overwhelming a person was as foreign to him as spontaneous combustion or superiority of the female of the species, current captain excepted. "You're saying, my good fellow, that under the sea, the male brings to the female so much pleasure that she passes out?" Sir Edmund laughed. He thought long and hard. "My god, man, if that's the case, why we're obviously studying the wrong thing!"

His thoughts then strayed to Captain Constance Daphne Fitzwillie.

Gnarly Dan watched as Sir Edmund laughed softly at first, and then with heart. "My lord, man, science is a fickle handmaiden! She puts under our nose the keys to the universe! The answers to our deepest prayers! The path to happiness and fulfillment! And then she locks those secrets in the innermost hearts of creatures with whom we may never converse.

Sir Edmund's journal reads:

Sea maiden and sea master sighted near island of Quinlan (thus her name). He is magnificent, she beautiful but fatigued.

Maidenus mortis sublimis
Average weight, dark hair, dark skin, African, red tail.
"Quinlan"

Magnus erotis
Muscular, dark hair, dark skin, African, red tail.

April 13, 1833
Gulf of Guytecas, island of Quinlan

SIGHTING NINETEEN

May brought further reversals of fortune for Sir Edmund Roberts' extended voyage of circumnavigation and discovery. The naturalist had sufficient funds on his person (his belt of gold coins) to provide sustenance and shelter for the stranded trio. He and Gnarly Dan sought sea maidens by day and told tales by night, the two getting to know one another quite well.

For the first few days their conversation was mundane at best, neither individual anxious to allow the other more than pleasantries and minor lies and exaggerations, but by the third evening, an intimacy crept forth as they realized they were alone and thousands of miles from their homes. And marooned for all intents and purposes.

It was late one evening, after a modest meal of local fare, the two bedded for the night and exchanging questions in the darkness of their room, that Sir Edmund commented, "So you've been at sea your entire life?"

Gnarly Dan lay with his hands behind his head, his body swaying in the hammock he'd insisted on rigging beside his bed. "Aye, t'is true enough. Went ta' sea as a powder monkey in '82 on the ole Exeter. Survived the crash-up with the Frenchies in the East Indies though we was pounded ta matchwood an' lost our cap'n. Moved to the Superb an' then ta Howe on the Queen Charlotte."

Sir Edmund interrupted him, "My god, man, you were there, on the Glorious First of June?"

"So they tells me," Gnarly Dan continued. " I was just a little nipper, still, an' a powder monkey. Lost most a' me hearin' then. Helps ta be deaf when yer married. Always thankful ta have lost that an' not me pins." Gnarly

Dan moved the conversation away from himself. "An' yer honor served the Queen?"

"Before the 1st Life Guards I was in the Royal Mountain Artillery. Campaigned in every corner of the empire. With distinction. Learned to love a four-pounder and a mule. Either will back a man up to the last. More than I can say for most men and all women."

Gnarly Dan chuckled to himself and then objected, "I'd say our Cap is a good 'un. She'd back a man up when we's yardarm ta yardarm."

"Perhaps, my good fellow; that leaves to be seen," the naturalist countered softly. "Her husband, the former Captain Fitzwillie, rest his soul, was another matter. Grandfather's hat indeed! Shaded Nelson as he lay dying! Now there is your basic draught of bilge water!"

Gnarly Dan was strangely silent. Sir Edmund noticed and countered, "Surely, you don't believe that story, a wise old mariner such as yourself!"

"Well, sir, firstly I'd not speak ill a' the dead. Secondly, t'was true."

The naturalist would have none of it. "Come, come, my good man; you've heard the tale so often you've come to believe it! How droll! Positively droll!"

The old salt would not be denied. "He was on the quarterdeck, our dear 'Nellie', all decked out fer the Queen, a right smart target, he was. Took a ball from a Frenchie in the fightin' tops a' the ole Redoubtable. 'They've got me at last,' says he ta Hardy an' staggers. 'They've got me at last!' He fell there, 'bout early afternoon. Our ole Cap's Granpappy steps up with water, passes it ta Hardy an' stands above our dyin' Nellie. He was shadin' him alright, took his hat off an' stood above him till he was moved below deck. It warn't a lie, yer honor. The man was there, hat an' all."

"And you, sir?" Sir Edmund enquired with new respect.

"Aye, served before the mast on the Victory. Big ole sow she was. Full a' piss an' vinegar an' able ta' throw more iron than a 'hunnert' a' our dear Bacis."

It was incredible; beyond all odds and rational belief, but the naturalist had not a doubt as to the veracity of the old salt's tale.

"The Battle of the Nile?" Sir Edmund asked quietly.

"We was knocked about right soundly on the ole Bellerophon," Gnarly Dan answered. "Cap' Darby that would a ' been. L'Orient took our number, her 120 guns ta' our 74. We was busted up good. Dismasted, scuppers runnin' red with good men's blood. We fired the L'Orient though, an' then afterwards we drifted off, Alexander an' Swiftsure closed on her. Took over where we left off. Our Cap' fell. So'd most a' our officers. Never know'd we saved the ship. Bent on a scrap a' sail and moved outta the fight. Messed on the Foudroyant after that. That'd be afore Trafalgar a' course."

The naturalist was agog. If Gnarly Dan were speaking the truth, he had served on the principal ships involved in every major engagement of the last fifty years. And survived. A terrible omen for Captain Constance Daphne Fitzwillie, though, for the old salt appeared to be a "jonah". Not one of his former captains had survived the far side of a major dust-up. Sir Edmund lay in oppressive silence the remainder of the night and tried to sort out what he believed.

The following morning, Captain Constance Daphne returned tart and penniless, her hopes to access her new fortune (the feared pirate Naughty Nat's old fortune) dashed as no agent of her banking house could be found in either Valdive or the Port of Valparaiso. She moped about their rented room muttering, "Hounds of hell, man and institution both; nowhere to be found when needed and underfoot when not! Bugger the lot!"

It was later in the day, as she stood on their back porch looking out over the bay when an all too familiar ship appeared on the horizon, every sail bent on, a bone in her teeth, her dark bow smashing great bursts of white water along her sides. Captain Constance Daphne Fitzwillie snatched Sir Edmund's glass and brought the charging vessel into focus. "Does fortune play the hussy with me now?" she whispered, the color falling from her face. "It's my Baci! And if those fools don't pull some canvas off her soon they'll spring my masts!"

"Indeed," Sir Edmund added calmly. "I knew they would return."

And they had.

The great ship anchored and expectorated a timid delegation to seek out their captain and plead their case with a volley of conflicting versions of why they had sailed off in the first place: pursuit by pirates; a severely localized hurricano; dengue fever; and most amusing, seduction and abduction, ship and all, by a raft-load of giant women from the Amazon basin.

Constance Daphne's anger faded with each tale until at last she said, "Enough! Back to the ship and make ready to sail. I trust you did not drink all of our provisions. If you did, there'll be hell to pay and no tar hot!" All the while she silently remarked that Pretty Willey's knotted scarf looked for all the world like an intimate garment from her cabin.

Sir Edmund was much moved by the crew's return but implored the captain, "Could we not, Madame Captain, hover about for one more day. This bay has been copious in regards to sea maidens (he would not mention sea masters).

"Make it so," she answered tersely, herself intent on accompanying the naturalist; the crew and their weak-kneed prejudices be damned.

The next day during the last descent of Halley's patented underwater machine (before it was ferried to the H.M.S. Baci to be stowed), Sir Edmund spied a brace of sea babies cavorting in a galaxy of slowly rising bubbles. The naturalist was in the company of Gnarly Dan only, as Captain Fitzwillie had declined at the last moment, intent on readying the good ship for sea and deciding to not tempt or torment her crew. For such a short time without their captain, the crew (read: mutineers) had managed to put the old girl in major disaray, much to Constance Daphne's chagrin.

So while the Bacis worked like heathens to put their ship to rights, Gnarly Dan jostled Sir Edmund from the glass portal in the bell so that he might enjoy a better view of the sea babies, prompting the naturalist to object, testily, "Calm yourself, man; they are only infants," to which the old salt responded with venom and disbelief, "Any man what don' love a baby has forgot too much, learned too little, or ships a heart as cold as a broke cannon. Why, babies is the sweetest thing a gob can clamp his eyes on!"

Unmoved, Sir Edmund looked to the bell's open bottom to ascertain the source of bubbles but was unsuccessful. There was much ocean below them and though the water was remarkably clear, it did darken with depth. He turned to Gnarly Dan as he allowed him better access the bell's portal. "And what, my garrulous friend, is the source of said font of bubbles we observe?"

Gnarly Dan smiled to himself as he watched the babies play. He did not answer the naturalist, prompting Sir Edmund to again enquire, "You are not totally deaf, sir, though a cannon or two may have whispered in your ear. I repeat: what is the source of the plethora of bubbles in which said infants cavort?"

The old salt finally gave in and answered, though he stayed close to his viewing glass. "There'd be a klatch a' sea mums down there," he said, pointing to the depths, "sendin' 'em up ta the little 'uns ta keep um' close-like. Each bubble," he went on explaining with patience, "has mum's special scent; air so sweet an' fulla' love that yer sea baby takes to it like a treat."

He let Sir Edmund ponder that for a while, drained a pint of warm beer he'd brought down with him and concluded, "An' when yer sea maiden gets old and comes near ta scratchin' her name from the log, why, she'll journey to a special sea cave an' leave her dyin' breath in some dark notch in the roof; a quiet bubble that her sea babies'll return to when they's grow'd and sad, maybe, or just missin' their mum. They'll breathe in just a bit, to feel her love an' smell her scent again, always leavin' enough to last their own lifetime. And they's never wrong; they's always some of mum's love left 'til the time comes when they leaves bubbles of their own."

The old salt watched the babies quietly for a moment more, his visage full of longing and loneliness. "Ye see, cap, sea maidens values love like we does life."

Sir Edmund's journal reads:

Two sea babies observed in the depths off Quinlan. Scales remarkably higher on their torso than previously observed on adults. Postulate they recede with onset of puberty, revealing fair skin and heightening attraction and temptation.

Infans verde
Lively, playful, long hair, green tail.

Infans azure
Very young, playful, bald pate.

May 5, 1833
Gulf of Guytecas, island of Quinlan

SIGHTING TWENTY

The two adventurers returned to the ship at last, Gnarly Dan content to bother the cook for sweets while Sir Edmund supervised the stowing of the diving apparatus in the hold. It took but little interference from the scientist as the crew was anxious to win itself back into the good graces of those they had slighted by stranding.

On the morning of May 6, the H.M.S. Baci sailed into the open Pacific. Days of fair weather and fine sailing turned to weeks as the good ship cruised up the western coast of South America. All was forgiven by Captain Constance Daphne Fitzwillie as her once mutinous crew vied to please her; no order lingering unattended, no wish denied. Every man jack jumped to the rigging with alacrity while even the cranky cook hummed a sea chantey as he chased weevils from the flour and smothered slanderous beef in great vats of soup.

It turned out that Pretty Willey was not alone in borrowing from the captain's cabin while she was ashore. Had she moved to wear more than her departed husband's naval blouses and tight pants (he was a small man) she would have found those chests with her intimate apparel empty, for during the crew's shortlived flight they had maintained their unflagging attachment to her by fashioning scarves, head cloths and wrist bands from every stitch of fine silk she'd owned. Had these absconded and obvious items not been so coveted she would have called her sailors to task, but their motives were transparent, their behavior artless.

And while the crew was numerous (eighty-six men, to be exact), the good captain had once been a woman of large parts. When she retired her incompetent husband and gave chase to the feared and loathsome pirate, Naughty Nat with a partially provisioned ship, she left as many pounds as sea miles in her wake until the once bounteous woman was little more than beautiful legs, long arms, a captivating face and a magnificent bosom.

Only Sir Edmund Roberts and Gnarly Dan went without mementos, they content with their memories of the captain sharing their bell, she sharing her blouse.

Meanwhile, rumors blew like spindrift relative to the current whereabouts of the pirate Naughty Nat; the most substantive being that he now pursued the H.M.S. Baci, bent on reclaiming his treasure, flogging the crew to submission, hanging the ship's cat, ravaging Captain Constance Daphne Fitzwillie, forcing the charterer, Sir Edmund, to walk the plank, and finally dismantling the good ship Baci timber by timber leaving nothing but a sour memory of the enterprise that had tweeked his nose and sullied his reputation.

Totally nonplussed was Sir Edmund Roberts, whose forays in Halley's patented diving apparatus continued, his latest sea maiden sighting near the coast of Peru. They had hove to on a nearly windless day, the captain intent on taking a cleansing swim, the naturalist supervising the swaying out of the bell. The bowsprit course was lowered from its yard and allowed to fill with seawater, its belly fully twelve feet deep, thus making a shark-proof pool for the captain. Every man jack of the crew save those aiding Sir Edmund hurried to secure a position of vantage near the bow of the good ship. Never before had so much attention been paid to the fore yards and fore tops and fore sails, they now crowded beyond belief.

Feigning ignorance but savoring the attention, Constance Daphne stepped from her quarters wearing her departed husband's heavy Royal Navy robe, its hem just touching the deck as she walked forward, through the deserted waist and onto the fore deck and then the head. "ALL EYES AFT!" she commanded and waited a heartbeat before she continued. She stood poised above the figurehead, opened her robe and handed it back to Blind Samuel, whose extended hand took the burden, and whose secret smile went unnoticed. Her last command was obeyed to the man as she stood with her back to the ship, her shapely bottom beneath her diminutive waist. "Eyes aft," indeed!

Poised on the bowsprit, she stood with her arms at her side and felt the cool Pacific air caress her body. A wave of goosebumps flowed from her calves upward, pleasing as they went, delighting her nipples and then raising the very hackles on the back of her neck.

Life was very good, indeed, for Captain Constance Daphne Fitzwillie.

And her crew.

She raised her arms slowly, went to her toes and then dove, her arc wonderful, her sight a source of future daydreams, fantasies and night wonders for eighty-six men. She parted the water with narry a ripple at the center of the flooded sail, curved through the water and surfaced fifteen feet from where she had entered.

The men cheered heartily despite the fact that they were to have been looking to the rear of the ship and not the same of their captain. She splashed about for some time, delighted the crew with her backstroke, pleased them all with her breaststoke and even floated for a bit in the salty brine.

A god or two must have been watching also, for a chain of events was now in motion that would save the fair captain's life. Those working the blocks and tackle were clumsy at best, their attention with their captain. Again and again they jostled the bell, banging it against the side of the ship a time or two. Sir Edmund finally lost his temper.

"Stop you bumbling sods!" he called out to no avail, "Quit this moment, you imbeciles!" he taunted and it had no affect. He was about to shout, "Hold where you are!" when Gnarly Dan stepped to the side of the naturalist and bellowed, "'VAST HAULING, YOU LUBBERS!"

All activity concerning the bell ceased instantly. Sir Edmund looked to the old salt. Gnarly Dan produced a Cheshire smile and whispered confidentially, "We speaks naval aboard this slab-sided tub, Yer Honor."

Meanwhile, bored with its confinement, Constance Daphne had gained one of the sides of the protecting sail. She looked out at the inviting open sea, thought of sharks and called up to the foretopman, "How does it look to you, up there?"

To which the smitten sailor answered, "You looks just fine, Cap. Just fine!"

Rather than continue the banter in an effort at clarification Constance Daphne put her weight on the edge of the sail, submerged it, and pulled her body over its barrier. Out to sea she swam, the exercise glorious, the freedom sublime.

The crew got nervous. They alternately scanned the ocean surrounding their departing captain as she swam far from them. She was about to return at last, when the dreaded hale came from the maintop yard. "SHARKS! BY ALL THAT'S HOLY, SHARKS ABAFT THE STARBOARD BOW! AN' THEY'S SCHOOLIN'!"

As one, the crew begged and called and pointed, "SWIM, CAP, SWIM! THEY'S SHARKS NEAR! BACK TA' THE SHIP, CAP!"

The first mate ordered all boats into the water. "SWAY OUT THE PINNACE, THE LAUNCH, THE CAPTAIN'S BARGE AND THE CUTTER! BOATS AWAY! LIVELY NOW IF WE'RE TO HAVE ANY CHANCE TA' SAVE THE OLE GIRL!"

Sir Edmund hurried toward the bow of the ship while Gnarly Dan ran back to the naturalist's cabin. By the time Sir Edmund had achieved the bowsprit the old salt was racing across the waist and then the foredeck, the naturalist's short-chamber Boxer Henry point-four-five caliber and a bandoleer of heavy cartridges in his hand and across his shoulder.

A huge fin and then another was angling toward the captain, slicing through the wave tops with frightening speed. The pinnace was in and manned, the launch was halfway to the sea and the barge and cutter were being swayed over, a tangle of seamen struggling to accelerate the process.

Gnarly Dan reached Sir Edmund. The naturalist grabbed his rifle. "Capital thinking, my good man!" He shoved a thumb-sized cartridge into his weapon and snapped it to his trained shoulder. The fore shark was massive by all accounts and soon to be on their captain. The naturalist sighted slowly and then cursed. "Bloody hell! I'm too low; she'll skip as sure as the Queen loves her milk!" He looked about wildly, spied the foremast ratlines and hurried to them, his weapon now over his shoulder. Gnarly Dan slung the bandoleer over his own shoulder and followed. They climbed up the rigging like fools to access sufficient height for Sir Edmund's shots to penetrate the water.

Constance Daphne had rolled to her back to get a look at what the men aboard her fair ship were pointing to and screaming about. A huge white fin was almost upon her. She froze. She had neither knife nor club to delay what now seemed inevitable. She turned and looked back at her ship.

Sir Edmund could not risk the delay of climbing another foot. He steadied himself, wrapped an arm through the rigging and raised the Boxer Henry once more. He wet the fore sight with his thumb, drew a bead on the antagonist and simultaneously judged his height above the water, the motion of the ship beneath him, the distance to the fish, the angle of declension, and finally, the speed of the huge shark. He held his breath with the crew and squeezed off a round. He did not look to see if he had succeeded, rather he chambered another and squeezed off a second shot.

The great beast slammed into Captain Constance Daphne Fitzwillie, lifting her from the water as it rolled to the side, the water now red with blood. Sir Edmund chambered the third round and searched coldly for the next attacker. He had lost sight of it in the previous mayhem.

Gnarly Dan saw the naturalist anxiously scanning the sea. "WHERE, AWAY THE SECOND SHARK?" the old salt called to his mates.

"CAP'S PORT BOW!" came the reply and as quickly Sir Edmund picked up the fin and wake, this fish being impossibly larger than the first.

Constance Daphne splashed to the surface and then calmed herself immediately as she swiveled her head searching for her second antagonist. The naturalist fired low and to starboard, chambered the fourth round and fired again. A great chunk of shark meat blew to the side. The beast slewed to port, thrashed wildly, regained its bearings and attacked again. A fifth round home and Sir Edmund's Boxer Henry roared once more. Now the beast reacted as if clubbed by a giant mallet. It jerked and then rolled over and over itself, bloody water washing over the captain. The sixth round entered a corpse.

Two smaller sharks attacked the body of the first just as the pinnace reached the captain. She was pulled aboard in one motion and the boat was away and turned and nearly back to the good ship Baci before Gnarly Dan and Sir Edmund regained the deck.

By now shots barked from all over the H.M.S. Baci. Before it was over at least twelve sharks succumbed to the crew's retaliatory barrage. Captain Constance Daphne climbed weakly up the side and over the tumblehome, willing hands helping her, glaring eyes attacking the sailor who handed across a blanket.

She composed herself, wrapping the blanket about her body, still captain enough to leave the top third of her breasts exposed. When at last she caught her breath, Constance Daphne looked about her, "You are good men," she said at last. "You are good men," she repeated more softly, and every man within ten feet knew she was fighting back tears.

The crew averted their eyes and gave her a moment. At last she added, "Who is my marksman?" They turned to the bow of the good ship Baci where the naturalist now stood with Gnarly Dan. What a pair they made, the bandoliered salt looking like an outlaw from Old Mexico; Sir Edmund already cleaning the Boxer Henry as if it had been an afternoon shoot with quail.

Large quail. Very large quail. With numerous and very large teeth.

Constance Daphne led her entourage to the naturalist. When she reached him she stood very close and looked long and hard into his eyes. At last she raised her hands to his face, held it strongly and kissed him full on the mouth.

Cheers and huzzas went round the Baci as Sir Edmund stood dumb-struck and Gnarly Dan joked, "Looks like I shoulda done the shootin' meself."

That evening a triple ration of rum was served out and then it was 'Bobs-a-dyin' until dawn.

Except for the naturalist who was so discommoded by his captain's attention that he escaped to the depths of the sea. He was treated by the crew as a hero, Halley's patented diving bell handled carefully and well. Gnarly Dan descended with him, savoring the closeness he felt with Sir Edmund. They sighted another sea maiden and sea master couple, and as if Captain Constance Daphne's kiss weren't enough, the naturalist and the old salt beheld an undersea coupling.

The naturalist's journal, later damaged during overzealous scrutiny by his relatives while seeking evidence of his mental incompetence, speaks of the encounter and is reproduced in its entirety, below:

"Rebecca"
Amorous

SIGHTING TWENTY-ONE

The following day while the crew stumbled toward sobriety, Captain Constance Daphne watched the naturalist with renewed interest and Gnarly Dan told of the Sir Edmund's shooting skills for the eighty-fifth time.

They continued, the H.M.S. Baci cruising blithely up the Pacific coast of South America, her crew enraptured by two of man's greatest pleasures: the presence of a beautiful woman and the opportunity to make a lot of noise. Captain Fitzwillie was indeed attractive beyond words in both countenance and comportment, and it was she who ordered the daily exercising of the ship's complement of artillery, permitting the men to blast away in good form.

And so, each morning following breakfast, after the hammocks were stowed and the decks holystoned, the gun crews touched off their charges. Black powder erupted in billowous grandeur. Hot balls blew through the air and tons of cast iron bucked happily against constraining ropes as cannons recoiled.

The men laughed and swore and capered about, and each time without fail, the good Baci, crew and all, disappeared in a great cloud of self-congratulating smoke.

And while both men and captain reveled in the noteworthy speed and accuracy with which they splintered target rafts, flotsam, and shoreline details, both men and captain took their practice very seriously, indeed. Certainly they slapped one another's backs and played fools for a time (never mind the occasional crushed foot or singed face) but behind every laugh was the sure knowledge they were preparing for a rematch with the most feared pirate of all seas, a man whose name was only whispered and still brought a lump to the throat and a stomach plunging like a loosed anchor; the loathsome tyrant, Naughty Nat. (The same Naughty Nat who sold both his little brothers into Turkish slavery. The same Naughty Nat who shipped five logs every voyage to be whittled with a penknife into planks. Planks that were used, one at a time for out-of-favor crew members to take an enforced stroll into eternity—eternity most notably punctuated by roiling sharks. And yes, the self-named Naughty Nat who pledged fidelity and unending love to every woman he encountered—indeed, the same despicable Naughty Nat who respected no woman the night before, the morning after, or ever.)

This was the Naughty Nat Captain Constance Daphne Fitzwillie wished to reengage, ordering the brave Bacis to crack on with as much canvas spread as the old ship could handle, the lookouts searching the horizon for the ship with the ominous black ball on her foresail. (Naughty Nat's calling card and warning.)

In point of fact the H.M.S. Baci was now leap-frogging with the pirate, both vessels unaware of the proximity of the other, sometimes passing in the night, sometimes sailing just out of sight on parallel courses.

Sir Edmund still insisted on an hour every day for his research, Halley's patented diving apparatus being lowered into the depths. It was after a rather grating day that he and his bellmate, the surly and garrulous old salt, Gnarly Dan, spied a sea maiden quite apparently pregnant. For all the world she appeared to be posing for her voyeurs, throwing out her stout tummy and planting her hands on her hips as if to say, "How nice this is!"

Gnarly Dan watched and then commented, "They does that, you know, Gov."

Sir Edmund adopted a demeanor of unflagging disinterest.

The old salt was relentless. "Cause they be all proud-like. Ya' see, onst yer sea maiden has a young 'un stowed away she's right special. Ain't another sea maiden nor master what ain't certain she be at her most beauteous. An' lookee at her fine white hair, Yer Honor; like a new sail bent on inna midday sun! An' white it'll be from beginnin' ta' end! Goes back ta natural onst her little 'un ships out. Proud as punch she be. Posin' ever chanst she gits!"

Which she did for the better part of an hour, arching her back, her hands occasionally sliding slowly forward to caress her fine belly.

Sir Edmund's journal reads:

Sighted gravid sea maiden.

Maidenus praegnantus
"Sue"
Very large. Very proud. Purple tail. White hair.

Sighted off the coast of Peru.
April, 1833

SIGHTING TWENTY-TWO

T here was another dust-up with the fabled pirate, and another story in the London Gazette:

The second MANLY ADVENTURE: a story PREGNANT with DASTARDLY PIRATES, heavy cannons and BRAVE sailors or, How the FAIR SEX proved to be a FINE INSPIRATION in a TIGHT CORNER.

Off the coast of Peru the H.M.S. Baci scudded happily before high winds. She carried enough canvas to cheer her crew and keep the good ship breasting aside huge seas, the flying spray reaching the mizzen topsail. Stumpy Pete had the wheel, the spokes humming heavily in his hands, and Deadeye Dick was in the mainmast trees riding the huge mast in broad ellipses watching for foreign sails. At nine bells he spied a ship already hull up and on a parallel course burst out of a squall line near the horizon. "SAIL HO!" he called. "IT'S HIM!" Within seconds, every man jack aloft and alow knew that once again they were going to trade balls with the most feared pirate of the seven rolling seas; the heartless cur, Naughty Nat.

Every glass on board the H.M.S. Baci was instantly trained on the distant ship and every straining sailor could see she was altering course just as they were, putting the two greyhounds on converging courses; both ships racing to the apex of a triangle where villainous pirates and the stout men of the good ship Baci would meet; where hot cannons and cold steel would surely decide the day.

"Pipe the men to an early dinner," Captain Constance Daphne Fitzwillie ordered, "while I go below to dress for the occasion." And dress she did, donning, as the crew knew she would, her departed husband's best Royal Navy uniform. She took their breath away when she returned in his very handsome white pants and an appropriately named and buxomly challenged double-breasted jacket, the bottom buttons of which strained to maintain closure.

The gun crews of the Baci had named their cannon with the port side pointing Donner, Dasher, Dancer, etc., and the starboard side picking up with Blixen, et al., while old Gnarly Dan broke ranks with Wide Mary and Thundering Thelma chalked on the sides of his weapons. Shot and powder were brought up, and the entire crew held their breath as the two ships moved ever closer. At a range too distant to pose a hazard to the Baci the pirate ship (Slow Death was in point of fact her name) veered to starboard, presented half of her complement of cannon, and disappeared briefly in a cloud of smoke as she let go a broadside followed by rolling thunder.

Sir Edmund Roberts, sea maiden questor and gentleman naturalist, stood beside his captain on her quarterdeck, silently counted, and remarked, "I believe, Captain, she throws something like twice the metal we do. Our friend, Mr. Nat seems to have procured a larger vessel and outdone himself in over-arming her, much as we gave our fine Baci more teeth."

Captain Constance Daphne Fitzwillie lowered her glass and turned to the naturalist. "And you fear that?"

"Good heavens, Captain," he returned calmly, "would he had one ten thousand the men now abed in England I would not fear him. We are a fine crew in a fine ship," his eyes were drawn to Captain Constance Daphne, "with an ample captain. We are enough to do him loss."

The ships drew to lethal range and began to trade iron in earnest. Hot balls, huge splinters, chain shot, pieces of rigging and shredded sail flew through the air. Both ships suffered dreadfully as they traded shot for shot. Broadside followed broadside, punctuated by rolling fire. Sailors in the fighting tops of both ships peppered away with small arms. Men screamed and fell and it began to appear both ships would be pounded to oblivion before either could grapple and send over borders.

A squall line chased the ships, threatening to subsume them in its midst. Sir Edmund called out to Gnarly Dan, "QUICKLY MAN; A LAST GOOD SHOT! A GOLD PIECE IF YOU CAN REDUCE THAT POMPOUS CUR TO JAM!"

Naughty Nat again stood on his rail and raised his fist in defiance. A diminutive figure in a fore and aft hat stood beside him, his fist raised also.

Sir Edmund and Captain Constance Daphne took up their glasses. Sir Edmund spoke first. "I say, Captain, isn't that your departed husband's hat your departed husband wears?"

"It is both," she answered focusing her glass, "and truth be known, I never cared much for either." Her last word was lost in the roar of Gnarly Dan's carronade as both ships were engulfed in blinding rain.

Big Bill, Stumpy Pete, Sleepy, Sushi, Pretty Willey, Dopey—their names hung like black crepe over the stout hearts of the surviving Bacis. As shipmates they had done battle with the villainous pirate, Naughty Nat, made good account of themselves and then were denied victory when Mother Nature parted the two quarreling ships and masked them in her fury.

Those Bacis who had not joined the fishes now limped about, heroes of an empty war. They moaned as they sorted and tended tangled rigging and some sobbed quietly when they came upon one part or another of a departed shipmate. "That'd be Bill," or "Sleepy won' be usin' that no more," was heard, as was, "Pass the parts bucket mate; ole Sushi's addin' up!"

And no one had escaped untouched. Sir Edmund discovered his right ear lobe to be history and old Gnarly Dan lost an index finger and a broad rag of scalp. He told everyone, regardless of interest, "Seems me hair's a bit thinner, though I can't put a finger on where!"

Captain Constance Daphne was the exception until about an hour after the last shot was fired, the squall past at last, the horizon now clear. A block hanging by a thread from the mizzen top broke loose and landed squarely on her left foot, breaking more bones, big and small, than it had any right to do. So she hobbled about blaspheming her rediscovered husband and cursing his hat. The crew, to a man, now remarked they'd "know'd all along" he was in the undamaged target raft, and weren't they a shipful a' lubbers to have whined so regarding his spirit. "Captain's ghost, me big ole arse," was bandied to and fro in the rigging and below decks.

So back to the Peruvian coast they dragged, ever watchful for Naughty Nat as they repaired the good ship Baci and wagered on the effectiveness of Gnarly Dan's last shot with Thundering Thelma. "She don' often miss," was the old salt's contribution.

Halley's patented diving bell, though well below decks at the time of the recent battle, was unfortunately in the path of one of Naughty Nat's balls when it hulled the ship, splintering fully a quarter of the bell's staves. Consequently, while the ship's carpenters Chips n' Small Beer repaired the apparatus, Sir Edmund spent his sea maiden vigils either from a masthead, or once they achieved landfall, on the beach hiding in the underbrush. He had his 22nd sighting while in the company of Gnarly Dan, he now more cantankerous and impossibly talkative since the shoot-up. They watched from their place of hiding as a sea maiden sat with her hands to her hair.

Sir Edmund whispered, "I believe she's in the process of grooming; tending her hair, as it were."

To which the impatient Gnarly Dan swatted his thousandth mosquito and responded, "I ain't educated like you, sir; an' I ain't done a lotta larnin' from books an' such. But I do know sea maidens an' sailors, an' both of 'em 'preciates beauty." He paused and continued, "She's just enjoyin' hers—gloryin' in not wearin' clothes like we does—her beauty out in the open, an' all. Ya see, they likes their beauty ta show. It's natural-like if yer readin' me chart. An' she ain't ashamed, neither. It's as soothin' ta' her as summer rain."

Sir Edmund thought about this and inquired, "Are all sea maidens so beautiful? It seems we've encountered uncommon beauty at every turn. There must be some plain ones—in fact, I recall hearing the crew speak at a tavern of some unattractive ones. Hideous—like sea cows."

Gnarly Dan hesitated before he responded, apparently reluctant to trust Sir Edmund with what he was about to say. At last he relented. "Sir," he began, "yer not a sailor, there'd be no arguin' with that. But you've proved a good sort—fir a gentleman—so I'll share a secret. No sailor wants every lubber ta know about yer sea maidens' beauty. We're real protective-like, 'cause often enough, they's all we got fer years on end. Wouldn't do ta have ta share with a pacel a' smelly lubbers. So we lies; says they's ugly. Yer average sailor will draw a sea maiden so she looks like a cow's hind side. Make her all scarey lookin' and nothin' a gob'd wish ta look at twice.

"Why there's one lives in the Gulf a' Mexico off Florida near Maria Island. Most beautiful creature you ever see'd. Body what would make ya' cry ta see again. Know what they calls her? Sea hagg. Ugly? Best kept secret a sailor ever had. Lubbers what lives inna town nearby got no idea she's there. She collects what stuff falls off'n ships or washes up onna beach an' trades with the sailors what stops by. They stops mainly just ta' lay their eyes on her; she's that comely. Captain won't stop, why a sailor or two'll jump ship just ta hobnob a bit and feast they eyes. Onst a captain thought he'd be clever-like. He sends a party ahead a' the ship with some right mean gobs. Ordered 'em ta lure her onna beach with some rum, tie her up all gentle-like an' keep her outta sight till the ship sails by. No problem, 'cept one—them gobs what fetched her an' tied her up never returned. Seems they give her a tot a rum ta settle her down afore they set her loose, an' well, one thing led to 'nother an' they ended up spendin' the rest a' they life on the beach lookin' at her an' hobknobbin'—lived on coconuts an' fish. Cut their boat in halfs, upended 'em an' made two cunnin' homes. Died ole men. Happy ole men! Ugly sea maidens! Sea haggs! Ha!"

Sir Edmund listened, fascinated. He knew the loneliness of life at sea and could not imagine it without sea maidens. Or Captain Constance Daphne Fitzwillie. He still felt her kiss. Every night as he peered through the hole augered into her wall he remembered it. When he lay abed he remembered it. When he shaved. When he dined. When he lolled about the ship or walked a beach or stared at the stars. He remembered it.

His journal reads:

Sighted a lovely sea maiden savoring her significant beauty as she sat on the beach.

Maidenus proudus
"Teresa"
Long dark hair, beautiful torso, fine, perky chest, healthy.
June 24, 1833
Central Peruvian coast.

SIGHTING TWENTY-THREE

A new problem confronted Sir Edmund. It seemed everyone on the good ship Baci, save himself, was ready to forsake his voyage in search of sea maidens. Bickering and maneuvering, lecturing and cajoling dominated every waking moment as sailors begged they hasten to the nearest port and further arm the already gun laden H.M.S. Baci. And to what end? Why to strike out again and confront that loathsome cur of a pirate, Naughty Nat; to dot his eye, to pepper his ship, to board him, crush him and avenge the lost Bacis. And why augment the Baci's armor? Why, because Naughty Nat's latest vessel was so much larger than the good Baci and sported so many more cannon, each of which was more powerful than any of the Baci's. The pirate kept upgrading his ship-of-the-month. And he had oceans from which to procure a better vessel. All he had to do was seize it. And that was easier than it might appear. Every ship eventually took to port and the crews became sloppy drunk, thus presenting fine ships with challenged crews. Or more exactly, crews soon to become skeletons after Naughty Nat and his despicable cohorts dealt with them.

Sir Edmund's opposition was simple, his argument succinct; "I chartered this ship in good faith with good money to search for sea maidens. Had I wished to dither with guns and make war I would have joined the Royal Navy." There was no question of fortitude, for Sir Edmund had acquitted himself well in battle. It was he who, with balls whipping about like insects and the deck a sluice of blood and parts had declared, "We have not yet begun to fight." (Gnarly Dan's muttered, "We oughta start real soon," not withstanding). Then later, when the full weight of Naughty Nat's iron took a viscious toll on the H.M.S. Baci, the Torpeydro brothers, Vincent and Guido the Guinea struggling at the helm, petitioned their captain to luff the mainsail to allow a brief respite before reengaging their foe. The valiant Sir Edmund would have none of it. "Damn the Torpeydros," he cried, "full speed ahead!"

Unfortunately, many were incapable of understanding his scientific resolve. "Blast your charter and your sea maidens, this is now my ship," Constance Daphne Fitzwillie reminded him.

And so it went. Day after day, until one evening Sir Edmund strode into the captain's cabin to pursue his case. She stood soaked in the blue glow of the moon shining through the stern lights, and although Sir Edmund's mouth launched into his practiced diatribe, his eyes absorbed the captain; the translucency of her shirt, the soft curves of the sides of her breasts outlined . . . no they were not merely outlined, for she wore the thinnest of silks; clearly her night wear, best described as transparent, a gossamer separation between her beautiful body and the naturalist. And when she drew her breath Sir Edmund's heart stopped. He could no longer help himself. He took a step toward her and then another until the days and months of proximity, the hints of perfume in a sea of musk, the glimpses of her smile, the knowledge that she bathed and dressed and slept a mere few meters from his own room was too much (as a gentleman, he forced the augured hole from his mind).

Their violent first embrace played counterpoint to the crew's gentle silence as they peered over the skylight's rim. Bets were won and lost as whispered oaths drifted through tarred rigging toward the stars, chiding an awestruck crew to further elevate their beloved captain and the brave, quirky naturalist they considered a friend.

"Looks like ole Cap finally's gettin' the wind she deserves," Softy Barthelemew whispered to Runny Jake. "Aye, an' Sir Edmund's finally makin' port," was Jake's quiet reply. "Lucky dog."

The sun rose on a contented ship. Captain Constance Daphne Fitzwillie coveted her morning tea and quietly ordered a new course set, "West-southwest, Burly Vincent," she directed, "Steer this good ship for the Galapagos Islands."

"Aye, aye, Cap," the helmsman replied, "west-sou'west it is."

And yet, when the naturalist came on the deck exhausted and bedraggled from his night of wrestling with the fair captain, he was first confused then wholly dashed when her indifference turned this side of cruel. And with the fullness of day she totally ignored him, speaking to virtually every member of the crew, but pointedly refusing to direct a comment to the sulking Sir Edmund.

That night he stewed in his cabin until at last he marshaled his courage and once more invaded the sanctity of her quarters. He was confounded when she strode angrily across the room to him, her lips tight with resolve. And then as she neared she transitioned effortlessly to passion, her arms reaching and then fully encircling him, her mouth searching for his, her body melding into his startled presence, her right hand moving to the back of his neck as she forced his lips hard onto hers.

"My god, how I have missed you," she whispered into his ear.

Such was their relationship for some time; stormy days and lovely nights. Sir Edmund tried, but he could not follow its logic. Confused and nearly angry he confided to Gnarly Dan, "I do not understand women."

To which the old salt responded, "Mark me well, sir; any man what says he does'd be either a fool or a liar." Of course the need to elaborate built like a distant wave until he continued, "Ya see, Yer Honor, a woman's heart is like this here ship. Why, it's a big thing, as full a' cubbies an' cabins an' secret places as you'd never guess. An' onst a woman gets a notion, why she'll steer the whole thing ta China an' back if she chooses. But don' expect she'll take the simple route! Ain't no quessin' how she'll plot her course!"

He let the naturalist absorb that before he continued, "Not at all like yer man. No, a man's heart is a simple thing, more like a log than a ship. He drifts about an' he's happy wherever wind and tide takes him." Gnarly Dan smiled, scratched his crotch briefly and added, "So don' go getting' yer sails inna bunch an' yer sheets all tangled worryin' it. Jus' lay back an' enjoy yer log, Yer Honor; the voyage'll likely be shorter than ya wish."

A week later, while ensconced in Halley's patented diving apparatus, Sir Edmund witnessed a sea maiden cavorting with a dolphin. The friendly connection between the two was readily apparent, their games mutually satisfying. The naturalist commented softly, "They certainly seem to enjoy one another's company. It's almost as if they're related in some obtuse fashion."

Gnarly Dan struggled with Sir Edmund's message, finally answering, "Aye, Squire, they mostly gets along down here. They's nought a creature yer sea maiden don' respect an' love."

They watched the playful encounter for nearly an hour before the sea maiden and friend swam away and disappeared into the distant water. Gnarly Dan sighed and added, "We could larn a bit if we paid attention."

Sir Edmund's journal reads:

Sighted a dolphin and sea maiden frolicking for some time in the intimacy of the warm sea.

Maidenus delphinus

"Una"

Strong swimmer. Accompanied by dolphin, she the more interesting to watch. Beautiful body. Long brown hair. Red tail.

June 2. 1833

WSW of Peruvian coast.

SIGHTING TWENTY-FOUR

There is a moment in the life of every lucky man when all that can go well does, when the wind is abaft the beam and steady and warm and the ocean a bathe in sensuality. At such a time, with a good ship working beneath him the strength and sanctuary of true love may cradle his very soul and buoy him beyond all that is tedious and common. Such was the case for Sir Edmund Roberts, gentleman naturalist and sea maiden questor when late in life he fell into a relationship with the beautiful Captain Constance Daphne Fitzwillie. Old Gnarly Dan was moved to observe that, "While she ain't often enough much of a cruise we's signed on for, onst in a while we gets a good leg. An' when a gob does, he'd best enjoy 'er; they's dregs what will follow soon enough."

Sir Edmund thrived in a fog of glorious grace as he and Constance Daphne drifted from their respective wharves of self-absorbed solitude. Every night her heart and body were his and every day she and the naturalist were captain and charterer once more. There was no familiarity on the hallowed quarterdeck, for Sir Edmund dared to neither cross her stern nor bow until the captain was in her quarters, the mantle of responsibility slipped from her shoulders, past her magnificent chest and onto the floor (followed immediately by less magisterial articles of clothing). And there, for a time, the two feasted in the privacy (if a skylight and an enraptured crew could be allowed to expand that definition) of their nocturnal adventures.

But as Gnarley Dan predicted, the dregs did follow; brought on by a damsel in distress.

"Old Bubo" was the first to sight her bobbing just at the horizon in a launch, a ragged sail flapping idly and she being chased around the small vessel by another castaway. By the time the Baci closed the distance and scrutiny was allowed, a different drama was seen unfolding. It now appeared she, semi-clad, was chasing a uniformed gent; she armed with a belaying pin and he in a panic to avoid her wild swings. At last within hailing range the pursued fellow turned toward the approaching ship and called out, "PREPARE!" or BEWARE!" or some such ejaculation, whereupon, before he could elaborate, he hesitated and she smote him squarely on the head. He staggered a step or two, swerved to the side and tumbled across the gunwhales and into the drink.

Posttraumatic interrogation was made academic when a triangular fin raced to the floating form, dined vigorously, and then cruised by the Baci's bow, a protruding ankle and boot giving the sated fish the unsettling appearance of a man savoring his pipe following a good meal. The damsel was recovered and her story of abduction believed in reverse of the listener's mastery of logic over lust, for her account was from top to bottom, bilge.

"Such a terrible man took me by force; our ship sank and we managed to get to the only boat that survived the blow" (it was a hurricane that appeared from nowhere, she explained). In fact, the damsel allowed, he was a villainous pirate and she the wife of a very wealthy Boston merchant. He, the pirate, took a fancy to their captain's uniform and managed to slip into it minutes after he killed the man mightily, and before the huge winds blew the unfortunate ship on her beam ends, drowning all but the two. "Oh dear! Such a strong wind it was! I thought we would all die right there!"

Sir Edmund Roberts was moved. "Why the cad!" he expostulated. "And what abominable luck to be set back by a terrible storm!" he added, clearly moved by the poor dear's story.

Old Bubo exchange looks with Gnarly Dan and whispered, "Looks like his honor's takin' to her tale!"

Gnarly Dan chuckled confidentially. "He's takin' to 'er tail, alright, an' I can't say's I blames him!" A few moments later he asked, "Well, mate, what's yer bet?"

Gnarly Dan was the first to ask the question and he was not the last. For almost immediately the entire crew, save the officers, asked themselves: "Would she be 'Nasty' or 'Naughty,' for she was clearly either the pirate vixen, Naughty Natalie or her lethal twin, Nasty Natalie, that distinction separating the amorously accomplished and insatiable from one similarly inclined but who preferred torture as an appetizer and homicide as an aperitif.

Both were beautiful beyond words; identical twins, with long dark tresses, longer legs, handsome sterns and often promising and seldom disappointing pirates' chests. They had been at sea since birth, an unspeakably sad event separating them from their natural parents, and passed from one pirate ship to another; first kept as good luck tokens, and then with puberty and stunning beauty, they became welcome members of various crews. Then, in their late teens they graduated beyond attractive chattel, they both being able to fend for themselves with pistol, musket, rifle, cannon or when need be, dagger, sword, cutlass, dirk, knife or club. They were both incredibly bright and cunning, the only real difference in their personalities becoming apparent with early adulthood. Nasty Natalie was bitter with a vengeance. How anyone could have allowed her to suffer the outrageous events delivered by the slings and arrows of fate was beyond her. *If this is what the world has to offer, then I shall respond in kind,* was her motto (Captured schoolmasters, scientists and gentlemen and women schooled both girls aboard sundry ships; it being to the pirates' advantage to use the twins as ladies-in-distress). Nasty Natalie learned well, doing so with a vengeance, for she had also taken the initiative to acquire every dark art and torture her pirate companions could teach her.

Naughty Natalie was a different story. Nature versus nurture was at odds with her development. She obviously shared the same gene pool as her twin, and had exactly the same experiences, but a portion of bitterness was never stirred into her mix. Certainly, she also had mastered every weapon in the 19th century arsenal, but she reserved them for self-defense, (Although, she did on occasion allow herself the luxury of employing offensively those skills; unkind lovers sometimes found themselves at the wrong end of a midnight prick from the sharp, thin knife she kept about her at all times.) All of which does not mean she shied from a fight; quite the contrary; both twins loved a good mix-up, preferring cannon smoke to perfume and an exhilarating swing from one ship to another, cutlass in hand and teeth clenched firmly on a dagger, to a calm afternoon with a book. They were, after all, pirates.

So there was the rub on the good ship Baci: which of the twins had they rescued?

It might seem odd that the crew made no attempt to inform the officers of the vessel. But those who served before the mast respected the rights of the educated and the upper class to extricate themselves unassisted from any situation in which they found themselves as a result of unbridled, unforgivable ignorance. "Gonna be mighty interestin' ta see how the Cap deals with this 'un," Old Bubo muttered.

Understandably, the most powerful and most often employed weapon in the twins' inventory was their sexuality. Trained in the gentle arts by masters from sundry cultures, they had refined information gathering by providing pleasure to fair-thee-well. And the twins' preferences were not gender specific. Scholars of their predilections have speculated that the absence of companion

109

women in their normal society encouraged in the pirate vixens that same longing shared by companies of deprived men. So not only was the crew at risk, so was Captain Constance Daphne Fitzwillie.

No student of the pirate twins, Nasty and Naughty Natalie, has failed to see that while the two used sexuality to accomplish their means, they did so far too often and far too well; especially when there could be no possible advantage, save personal pleasure. The academic community concurs; they were a lusty pair.

So, Naughty (Nasty?) Natalie was brought back to the H.M.S. Baci. (No relation to the similarly named pirate, but for the fact that upon reaching maturity the twins found themselves aboard the Plunderer, serving Naughty Nat. As a matter of convenience and in a bald bid to flatter the loathsome cur, they adopted Natalie as their common name, using Nasty or Naughty as a distinguishing moniker.)

The crew fairly fell upon her, anxious to provide shirts and trowsers as replacements for her strategically rent dress. Man after man received a demure and provocative 'thank you' from the damsel until at last Captain Constance Daphne made her presence felt at the perimeter of the impromptu gathering.

"Make way for the Cap'," riffled through the group. "Move aside there, ya clumsy dog; our Cap's comin' through!"

And indeed she did. When at last face-to-face, the two surprised women stared long and hard. Until at last a comely smile crossed Nasty (Naughty?) Natalie's face.

"My, oh my! I have *never* seen a more beautiful woman! And the captain of this fine ship! I must get to know you better, my dear," she cooed in a Southern drawl and looked deeply into Constance Daphne's eyes. The captain was equal parts flattered and wary, until the vixen continued, her eyes covering Constance Daphne, "And my word, that is the most delicious figure a woman could ever dream of! There isn't a woman alive who wouldn't kill to have that body, dearest!"

The crew winced at her use of 'kill', but they were pleased the woman shared their opinion of their beautiful captain.

Captain Constance Daphne was attired in her normal fashion; tight white trowsers, and a naval jacket accenting her uplifted, bountiful and half exposed chest. Natalie took it all in and added, "Why you could command a fleet with those! What man wouldn't dream of laying his head on such glorious pillows!" She then gave the captain an impromptu hug, placed her lips sensually close to Constance Daphne's ear and whispered to her.

What she said, intimated or suggested is unknown, but the captain's reaction was noted: She flushed, smiled, whispered something back and then, as if remembering the attending crew, pulled away and ordered, "Enough idleness! Show this woman to my quarters!"

And while the pirate vixen's presence provided endless hours of speculation below decks and in the rigging, Sir Edmund took advantage of a weatherly calm to continue his search for sea maidens. In the company of the foretopman, Big Berlinni, and the old salt, Gnarly Dan, the naturalist sighted his 22nd sea maiden. She was clearly pregnant as she drifted silently by Halley's patented diving bell. "It'd be the birth a' Venus!" Berlinni exclaimed, he being a bit premature in descriptive powers, while Gnarly Dan drew in a long breath to repeat his own previous lecture on pregnancy under the sea.

Sir Edmund was preemptive, interrupting, "Yes, yes, my good man; her hair has lost its color with her impregnation. And of course, as you noted, it will return to its natural state after she gives birth. And yes, she will no doubt spend the duration of her pregnancy savoring said state and looking most beautiful for, 'They believes, under the sea that she be at her most beauteous,' etc. etc. etc. Now be a good sort and shut up while we enjoy the view in peace."

The naturalist's timing could not have been worse, for Gnarly Dan had been feeling particularly vexed that he had not warned his friend concerning the potentially lethal attributes of the new passenger aboard the ship. Not only had Naughty (Nasty?) Natalie befriended their captain (and if nocturnal moans were an indication; *pleased* their captain), she was also spending considerable time with Sir Edmund.

"How positively fascinating!" was heard again and again as he explained to her his theories of sea maidens, faeries and other little known creatures as naturalist and vixen strolled the ship's waist, she fairly hanging on his arm, a firm breast teasing his side, as he droned on and on. "However could such a handsome individual know so very many *interesting* things?" she queried to no one in particular. Sir Edmund, always a man, found nothing remarkable in her fascination with all he said, thought and intimated, other than believing her to be one of the brightest, most interesting women he had yet encountered.

He did, however, find his nocturnal visits to the captain on hold; a disappointment partially offset by the startling nightly engagements he viewed through his augured peek-hole. (Yes, unfortunately, those encounters found their way to his drawing pad and, later, to the courtroom in London for his mental competency hearing. The male jurors did indeed mutter sanctimoniously, "A bit unnatural, if you ask me, not healthy at all! Tut! Tut!" Then, to the man, after prematurely passing the painting to the next juror, each hastily amended, "I say, good fellow, could I see that last sketch a second time?")

Following Sir Edmund's tart comments to Gnarly Dan, the old salt decided to "let such a smart gent learn a thing or two on his own!"

The three sat in the submerged bell in heavy silence and watched the sea maiden drift past.

Sir Edmund's journal reads:

Picked up a stranded damsel. Alluring woman. Quite bright. Popular with our captain; making astonishing inroads in the friendship department.

Becalmed, we lowered Halley's apparatus and also saw our second pregnant sea maiden.

Maidenus pregnantis
"Venus"
Long, beautiful white hair.   *Comely body.*   *Bright green tail.*
Apparently healthy.
July 10, 1833
At sea, off the coast of Peru.

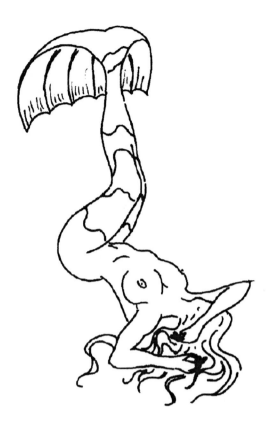

SIGHTING TWENTY-FIVE

It wasn't long before Naughty (Nasty?) Natalie had spent considerable time in the company of all aboard the good ship H.M.S. Baci. She learned much of the ship's wealth, strengths and destination. She also planted multitudinous seeds of discontent.

Where Captain Constance Daphne Fitzwillie had tempted the crew with Naughty Nat's wealth, Nasty (Naughty?) Natalie offered up golden treasure beyond the crew's imagination. And what treasure would that be? Why none other than the fabled mountains of gold belonging to the Incas. Gold plates, gold cups, necklaces and objects of art, all of whose location Naughty (Nasty?) Natalie held the secret.

Which she shared with unabashed regularity. "Surely, a traveled man such as yourself has heard of the riches of El Dorado?" she asked again and again. And who hadn't? She went on instructing, using a sudden Spanish accent, "It means 'golden man', for that is what he is. The Inca Indians gave countless sacrifices to their sun god. Do you know what they did?" (Every man questioned nodded guiltily here, ashamed of his ignorance.) "Why, they took human sacrifices, covered them with sticky resin . . . (she said this part in a manner that sounded appealing to the listener, he imagining the pirate vixen coated in sticky resin, honey perhaps, and he willing to release her from its grasp using only his tongue.) Every time she got to this point she lost her listener and had to repeat, "They covered him in sticky resin . . . and then coated him in gold dust!"

It was an intriguing image: a golden man or woman!

She continued, "Then they loaded the golden person onto a barge with piles and piles of other golden objects, paddled it all with great ceremony to the center of a lake, and with the first rays of the rising sun, they dumped the whole lot into the inky depths. Year after year after year. For hundreds of years. Thousands, even!"

It was a captivating story. And since the men had heard of the legend of El Dorado previously, it was not a new tale. They also knew of the great Spanish treasure fleets of hundreds of years earlier that had returned to Spain with mountains of gold.

There were two more parts to her story: First, having sufficiently awakened the listener's interest in riches, she added, "And I know exactly where the lake is located."

No one doubted that she did.

Then she challenged, "And do you know why it is still at the bottom of that deep lake?"

They didn't.

"Because those who know of the vast treasure, do not know how they can descend in such deep, dark water and retrieve the mounds of gold and the golden bodies."

At this point, every listener, every time, thought for a moment, and then, depending on the state of his alertness, a glorious, golden idea hatched whole in his head. For some it was the first new idea in a long, long, time and took a while to break out of its shell. For others it occurred as Natalie was finishing; before she finished, even! And each time, regardless of gestation period, the victim then glanced covertly to wherever Sir Edmund Roberts was standing at that moment.

Halley's patented diving apparatus!

Indeed.

Even Sir Edmund was pulled in. "My dear," he exclaimed, "I have just the machine!" Then he soured briefly. "Unfortunately, I have no need for gold, mountains thereof or small piles; I am well situated in life and most desire to continue my sea maiden quest. Perhaps another time on another voyage," he concluded. "Perhaps," he amended, "the two of us might take an extended voyage together. Seek your treasure if you wish; see the world; get to know one another better."

Nasty (Naughty?) Natalie did not answer at first. In fact, she acted as if entertaining the idea. "That would be a true pleasure," she said warmly and brushed her fingers lightly over the back of his hand. "But I thought you would wish to see the fresh-water maidens that populate the lake."

There was a stunned silence. And then, "Fresh-water maidens?" the naturalist begged, pouncing at last on this incredible piece of information.

"Fresh-water maidens, you say? Where? What lake? How do we get there?" he implored. "Fresh-water maidens! Why I'll be famous!"

"Not that it matters," she concluded, "but they are said to be the most beautiful of all of the sea maidens. Although it is also said they are more timid by nature; subservient, even."

And so the H.M.S. Baci, crew and all, came about and scudded happily back to the South American shore; the mountains of Gran Columbia and the volcanic Lake Guatavita their destination. North-northwest they sailed until they reached the appointed coast and disembarked.

Even Captain Constance Daphne Fitzwillie was enthralled. Sucked into the vortex of greed she dreamed again and again of using her share of the treasure to outfit more ships, find additional treasure troves (Naughty, Nasty? Natalie had a list as long as your arm.) and become the wealthiest woman in the world.

Never mind the Andes Mountains towering between shore and lake. Forget the unwieldy bulk of Halley's patented diving apparatus and then ignore completely the questionable hospitality of a people who had been ravaged for three hundred years by fair-skinned interlopers. Pass over also the inconvenient fact that two of its geographical entities had just sheered off for political independence.

Golden men were worth the risk.

While proper guides, donkeys, llamas and locals were arranged, and while the diving bell was dismantled and packed for the trek, Sir Edmund's sea maiden quest was addressed from the beach. Midafternoon of his first day ashore he was rewarded with the sight of a glorious sea maiden resting, her tail raised and lolling above in a lazy attempt to shield the sun's radiance from her eyes while she enjoyed a light breeze. She had the stunning and unusual tail patterning and coloration of a clown fish, and her chest was simply beyond words; its weight succumbing to gravity, its perfection taking the viewers' breath from them.

When at last he could speak, Gnarly Dan explained she was savoring the open air. "Yer sea maiden likes her time outta water; herself being proud-like a' her looks an' pleased to be seen. She's doin' that fer us."

It was apparent she knew she was being watched, for she slowly moved her hands along her body, caressing her hips, then her narrow waist, then her breasts, finally idly combing out her long hair onto the sand, all the while slowly waving her tail over her head so she was alternately in and then out of the sun. It was a performance as alluring as any the men had ever witnessed.

Sir Edmund's journal reads:

Beautiful sea maiden. Handsome, bountiful chest. Content. Medium hair. Coloration of tropical clown fish. Orange, white and black. Apparently healthy.

> *Maidenus pomacentidae*
> *"Wendy"*
> *August 4, 1833*
> *Gran Columbia, South America*

SIGHTING TWENTY-SIX

Sir Edmund's quest for sea maidens headed inland. Halley's patented diving apparatus was distributed across a drove of taciturn llamas, as was the captain's and crew's gear, articles for trading, and an assortment of weapons. The H.M.S. Baci's old swivel guns (formerly of her days as the H.M.S. Bounty) were added to the mix, Woody, the ship's assistant, assistant carpenter having fashioned several cunning little carriages to accept the four-foot cannons now stowed aboard several of the mules also making the journey into the Andes.

Captain Constance Daphne was stunningly attired, as was Naughty (Nasty?) Natalie, each upping the stakes for the crew's attention, the captain's approach being more buxomly uplifted than the pirate vixen's, she being smaller of chest but rather more wanton in comportment and astonishingly revealing with each breath.

The procession was a humorous sight from the beginning as it meandered into the foothills, the Bacis without their land legs wobbling beside the pack animals. Sir Edmund strode ahead, he rather miffed that a succession of llamas had demonstrated their penchant for spitting in the eye of their beholder, naturalist or not. The captain and the pirate vixen strolled together as schoolgirls, chattering incessantly and laughing at unheard jokes, the two often holding swinging hands as they progressed.

Days of walking turned to weeks as they hiked beyond the foothills and then ever higher into the mountains, across impossible suspension bridges, the adventurers entertaining themselves with wild speculation regarding the Inca treasure in Lake Guatavita while they clung like heroes to the thick ropes of the swaying bridges and refused to look down. The locals were sullen at best, it being apparent to them they were in the company of their most recent pillagers.

The glory of the volcanic lake opened to the Bacis on September 2nd when they crested the last ridge and looked into the circular valley and the huge body of water below. They descended easily to the lake shore and Sir Edmund's diving bell was hastily assembled as llamas and donkeys were unloaded. A camp was established and fortified after the swivel guns were mounted, loaded and primed. A large raft was fashioned to ferry Halley's diving apparatus and the requisite crew out onto the lake. As they paddled away from the shore Gnarly Dan repeated what he had learned from the laborers and guides regarding fresh-water sea maidens, he being initially mortified by his ignorance of their existence.

At last he was able to expound with easy authority. "Unlike yer normal sea maidens and sea masters, these here'd be more forward in nature. Yer sea master rules; is rough-like in disposition, spending his leisure playin' in the gold, romancin' sea maidens and tusslin' with other sea masters. We should be on double-watch when we's below; some sea master what feels his hawser's been crossed could swim 'neath yer bell, grab an ankle an' yank a gob inna the drink, if ya catches me meaning!"

So they were cautious, diving day after day at different locations and at greater and greater depths. They saw no treasure but within the week spied a brace of sea creatures communing. Sir Edmund, Captain Constance Daphne Fitzwillie and Gnarly Dan were in the diving bell, Nasty (Naughty?) Natalie insisting she feared water and would be quite content to remain on shore for the duration.

Gnarly Dan watched the pair embracing and said, "Any gob can see he's at the helm a' their ship." He smiled and continued, "An' she ain't close ta mutiny, that's fer sure!"

Sir Edmund's journal reads:

Great and glorious news! Fresh-water maidens and masters exist! What a magnificent discovery! Finding the company of Natalie most invigorating.

Maidenus enraptus

"Xenia"
Magnus enraptus
"Inca"
Handsome couple. He dominant. She submissive. Strong physiques.
Healthy. Preoccupied.
September 5, 1833
Lake Guatavita, Andes Mountains, Gran Columbia

SIGHTING TWENTY-SEVEN

Gold, gold and more gold. At last the treasure came to light. It began when Sir Edmund spied a spectacular golden mask shining beneath the submerged bell, and that was followed by the discovery of plates, sun god images, small figures, and then necklaces, bracelets, cups and calendars. Again and again Sir Edmund took Halley's patented diving apparatus into the deep waters of Lake Guatavita and each time he reached the lake's sloping sides he saw more treasure. The men on the barge became giddy as more and more gold was sent up to them, and those on shore, once they learned of the finds were increasingly celebratory, Captain Constance Daphne virtually overflowing with excitement (her double-breasted Royal Navy jacket opening past virtue), while Nasty, (Naughty?) Natalie was at first pleased and then ominously preoccupied.

Sir Edmund studied and marveled at the craftsmanship of the pieces but was unmoved by their worth. He was, however, most anxious to spy additional Lake Maidens and Masters (he deciding that title more appropriate than sea maidens and sea masters . . . a naturalist's prerogative).

On the shore, fortifications were reinforced and the growing pile of booty was monitored by concentric rings of guards watching guards watching guards who were themselves nervously surveying the surrounding jungle, where they observed with concern the mounting agitation of the Indian guides and laborers.

The golden treasure accumulated while Sir Edmund's quest to classify additional lake maidens went unsatisfied for nearly a week until on September 10th he and Gnarly Dan encountered their second pair of lake maidens and masters. She was wrapped tightly about her master, her arms clutching him, also.

"Ain't they a sight," Gnarly Dan whispered as the couple drifted up from the depths. Sir Edmund and the sailor watched in new silence. At last the old salt continued, "Yer fresh-water maiden is all clingy-like, Cap; unlike yer maiden from the sea, what is all in charge an' ready ta captain her ship an' his too, as like as not." He sighed and then finished softly, "No, yer lake maiden is quiet-like an' shy. Why she's content ta just let him have his way when he wants." He thought about that a moment and added, smiling to himself, "Know'd a girl like that onst. Should a' married her when I had the chanst."

They watched the couple pass silently by the bell. Gnarly Dan confided, "Appears they's both becalmed 'bout now." Then he added, returning from his reverie, "I guess we'd a had a sight had they hove inna view sooner!"

Sir Edmunds journal reads:

Saw a handsome couple in a resting state. She quite taken with her mate. No question of her submitting to his will.

Maidenous volcanus
"Yvette"
Magnus volcanus
Striking couple. He darker than she. Becalmed.
September 10, 1833
Lake Guatavita, Gran Columbia, South America

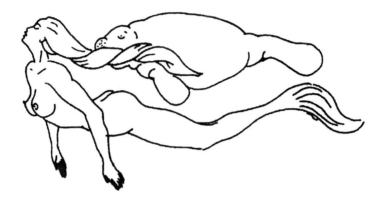

SIGHTING TWENTY-EIGHT

Sir Edmund Roberts' adventures high in the Andes Mountains met with continued success. With the crew of the H.M.S. Baci, the beautiful Captain Constance Daphne Fitzwillie, the wantonly mysterious Nasty (Naughty?) Natalie, and with the grumbling aid of a diminutive army of Indian laborers, llama and mule drivers and guides, they not only sighted five fresh-water (hence, 'lake') maidens and masters, but also gathered more gold artifacts than anyone could have imagined. The fabled treasure of El Dorado (although the actual 'golden man' eluded them so far) lay in a hut-sized mound at their fortified lakeside encampment. Nearly a month of successful descents in Halley's patented diving machine had finally ceased yielding results. Again and again the sun set on days with neither lake maiden nor master sightings, and without new additions to their golden trove.

Those on shore and guarding the loot were developing nervous twitches as they bickered among themselves, while the Indians (Inca relatives, surely) grumbled and glowered, speculating endlessly on whose family had lost the most to foreign intruders. All of the Europeans, save Naughty (Nasty?) Natalie and Sir Edmund Roberts, wished to immediately load the gold onto the llamas and mules and transport it down from the volcanic lake, out of the mountains and into the comforting security of the hold of their good ship, the H.M.S. Baci.

But Sir Edmund, compulsive as always, and Nasty (Naughty?) Natalie, acting as if the last piece of her own personal puzzle of intrigue and subterfuge was not yet in place, were insistent on their remaining a bit longer. "Just one more day," the two chanted. Until at last Captain Fitzwillie, nearly mad with calculating her share of the booty and the number of ships she would outfit and command as a result, ordered her crew to begin loading the treasure onto the pack animals and break camp. Sir Edmund insisted on a last dive, and so the naturalist, Captain Constance Daphne, and the old salt, Gnarly Dan accompanied the diving bell as it was barged out past the center of the lake for a final dive into the cold, dark waters of Lake Guatavita.

A triple surprise was in the offing: First, and almost immediately, a glorious lake maiden glided by the diving bell. Sir Edmund was impressed. "Why, she is surely the most beautiful ever!" he proclaimed. Constance Daphne was uncomfortably moved by her sensual demeanor and Gnarly Dan, ever garrulous noted she was "Right happy just to be swimmin' about," to which the captain commented, "The last time I was that happy I was twenty years younger and in the arms of the Admiral."

Sir Edmund looked with surprise to the captain and said, "Really, Madame Captain, I never realized your husband attained flag rank, however briefly." She immediately corrected him. "If you think I'm referring to that little twit who commanded our ship you're sadly mistaken."

Gnarly Dan, ignoring the two bickerers, smiled and continued, "Ya see, yer sea maiden an' lake maiden is a sight different from what we be. They takes their pleasure where they finds it, if yer steerin' me course. Now, her swimmin' all quiet-like through cool water, it touchin' her right-gentle as it flows down her tummy an' acrost her tail, can please yer maiden better'n any gob all clumsy an' anxious ta maybe fire a broadside an' board."

Captain Constance Daphne reflected on that description and thought perhaps it was time for her to take a swim.

Gnarly Dan would surely have continued had he not caught sight of the second of the day's surprises when an errant ray of sunshine penetrated the depths and shone on an object that stopped the hearts of all of those in the bell. On the sloping side of the volcanic wall just below them was a full-sized golden statue.

"El Dorado!" the captain whispered and drew in her breath.

"Not quite," Sir Edmund amended, for the statue was of no man.

"She'd be the most beautiful woman, ever," Gnarly Dan breathed as the light played off of her golden chest. He expertly lowered a weighted loop of rope to her raised hand. "Reminds me of me second wife," he said as the rope encircled her wrist.

Ever so gently the three raised and brought their find into the bell, and ever so carefully they examined her, oblivious to the muffled retorts of the swivel guns at the distant lake encampment, regardless of their increasing frequency.

It was not until the barge crew above began a hasty and not so gentle raising of the bell that the three did note the apparent battle being waged at the fortified encampment.

That was to be the bell-mates' third surprise, for while they were submerged, the Indians surrounding the crew and treasure launched a fierce attack. The stout men of the H.M.S. Baci gave as good as they got, their swivel guns barking again and again, throwing mawsful of grapeshot into the charging Indians whose fallen number began to accumulate with gruesome rapidity.

Much noted was Nasty (Naughty?) Natalie's failure to participate in the mayhem., and it tended to slake the good men's ardor.

Then, impossibly, pirates began to appear amongst the attacking Indians, they waving cutlasses and firing off muskets and heavy pistols into the defending Bacis, quickly reducing their number. Their fierce visages; eye patched and often toothless, further cooled the Bacis' fighting spirit. Then, as tiny cannons were wheeled into sight and prepared to fire, an apparition in a half-set of Conquistador armor took the remaining wind from the dispirited Bacis' sails. It was Nasty (Naughty?) Natalie in the flesh (much revealed), she being their own Naughty (Nasty?) Natalie's evil twin sister, now before them with an ancient and raised sword. She waited until a lull in the fighting and shouted a defiant and tempting command. "SURRENDER, GOOD BACIS, AND WE WILL SHARE THE TREASURE!"

Outnumbered and without either their brave captain or beloved naturalist to inspire and rally them, and immediately abandoned by their own lustful Nasty (Naughty?) Natalie; she now slipped across to the attackers, the good Bacis hesitated. But when the departed pirate vixen, now half-naked also and armed with unassailable logic, shouted back to them, "YOU MAY FIGHT AND DIE ON THIS LONELY MOUNTAIN TOP OR SURRENDER AS WEALTHY MEN AND LIVE TO DRINK GREAT QUANTITIES OF RUM!" the Bacis succumbed to reason and lay down their weapons.

By the time the bell was raised and Sir Edmund Roberts, Captain Constance Daphne and Gnarly Dan were on the barge with the diving apparatus secured, the fighting at the distant camp had stopped.

"By jove, they're scurrying about like ants in an upset nest," the naturalist observed with concern in his voice. "Drat! I wish I had my glass! I can't tell if we've won or lost!" he lamented.

Gnarly Dan did not comment; he was once more in the awkward position of being separated from the men whose number most readily accepted him. The naturalist and the captain were quick to distance themselves unconsciously from Gnarly Dan and the crew of the barge, both in actions and in spoken word.

"They do tend toward the actions of rabble," Captain Constance Daphne muttered when it became apparent that the mules and llamas were being lead off, sailors in the midst of the Indian guides and laborers. (They were still too distant for the presence of pirates to be noted.) By the time the barge was near enough to distinguish personalities as well as clothing, the encampment was empty. Until two pale females appeared, shouted indistinguishable insults at them and then turned and bared their backsides as a final insult.

Constance Daphne was fit to be tied. "Low heathens, one and all!" she proclaimed. Then she realized the presented mystery. "One of those harlots is without a doubt, our Natalie," she hissed. "I never did trust her! But who is that beside her?"

Sir Edmund, always the naturalist answered, "Well-formed posteriors, I must say. No idea with whom our Natalie is comporting."

Gnarly Dan delivered the news quietly. "That'd be her twin, Natalie. You're beholden Nasty and Naughty, though I can't tell ya which is which."

Constance Daphne and Sir Edmund frowned with confusion as they alternately studied those on shore and then the old salt. The barge crew continued admiring the now-disappearing backsides.

By the time they had crossed the broad lake and accomplished the shore all that remained in the camp were smoldering campfires and a handful of llamas and mules that had apparently run off with the initial fusillade and then later returned. A broad and trampled path indicated the fate of the defenders, attackers, and the loot.

Sir Edmund's notebook reads:

Most vexing day! We recovered a blindingly beautiful golden maiden, sighted an equally enchanting lake maiden, and lost our crew, treasure, guides and equipment in one stroke. I fear the loathsome pirate is somehow behind this mischief. Two pirate vixens aided the scoundrel. We have been made the fool.

Our golden statue is fully life-sized, attractive beyond description, and may in fact have a sacrificed maiden entombed. (They suffered the loss of much beauty by their pagan act.) Finely shaped legs. Well-formed posterior. Alluring chest. Elegant facial features of a young Inca female. Long hair.

Sighted a lake maiden as she glided past our bell. Gnarly Dan (never silent) allows she was at peace with the water (aqua-erotic).

Lake maiden:
Maidenous goldus
"Zena"
Long golden hair. Shapely body. Healthy. Orange tail. Bemused. Sated.
September 26th, 1833
Lake Guatavita, Gran Columbia

125

Editors note: *Sir Edmund's illustration of the lake maiden is one of the more vexing of his series. The maiden herself is as he described her in regards to coloration, attitude and movement. However, there is a disturbing omission in his narrative as there is no mention of the manatee we see swimming at her side. There is absolutely no scientific substantiation of the presence of manatees in land-locked, high altitude, fresh-water lakes. Further, having sent the painting to the art restoration firm of A Closer Look, Inc., in Miami, Florida, they report the animal was added some time after the original painting was finished; perhaps as much as a year or two later.*

It is difficult to believe that Sir Edmund became uncomfortable with what his companion Gnarly Dan claimed the lake maiden was experiencing. (Later paintings of Captain Constance Daphne Fitzwillie present in his 'blue notebook series' put to rest any fears that the naturalist avoided sensitive subject matter, one painting in particular showing his paramour, the captain, entertaining herself in an unquestionably ribald manner.)

So the manatee remains a mystery.

Sir Edmund did also complete several stunning images of the golden statue, one of which has found its way to a most prestigious museum in London.

SIGHTING TWENTY-NINE

Confusion and mayhem, the handmaidens of Sir Edmund Roberts, made an unscheduled appearance high in the Andes Mountains of Gran Columbia. As usual, it was left for Sir Edmund to recover with his own devices, which he did. Key to his success was the remarkable beauty of the golden maiden he had brought up from the cold depths of Lake Guatavita. Remarkable beauty and her haunting resemblance first to Captain Constance Daphne Fitzwillie; for she shared her glorious figure, thus inspiring the remaining crew. But most impressively, she had facial characteristics uncomfortably and closely related to one of the Indian guides who had returned to the naturalist's camp after Nasty and Naughty Natalie, the pirates, the crew of the good ship Baci and the bulk of the Indian guides and laborers had departed with the lake's golden treasure. But the golden statue was in the possession of the naturalist's party and the Columbians fairly fell to their knees when they saw her.

After a lengthly but halting translation it came to be known she was El Maideno Revierdo de Muy Bueno Fortunato, or some such thing. 'The revered maiden; the lucky one'; the last sacrifice of the doomed Inca civilization before they fully succumbed to the treachery and avarice of the invading Spaniards. She was the most beautiful of the land, the daughter of the greatest chief and every bit as sacred to the survivors of that proud race as the sun god himself.

And where less than fifty Indians had helped the Bacis into the lofty mountains originally, word spread instantly and now hundreds upon hundreds flocked to view their lost princess.

Sir Edmund had polished her himself and stood her in the middle of their old campsite. He made no effort to keep the Indians from approaching her. As yet there had been no discussion of her current ownership.

Captain Constance Daphne felt the dilemma more strongly than the naturalist. "My god, man, she's priceless. I certainly hope these heathens don't take it into their minds to abscond with her much as our pirate friends did with the fair mountain of gold we'd accumulated!" She got a faraway look and continued, "You have no idea what I could have done with that treasure!"

Sir Edmund, wealthy beyond description all of his life, was unmoved. "A bit of gold here and there has never altered the taste of my dinner," he taunted gently.

"And that would be because your first was from a silver spoon," she retorted and glowered.

"Well said, fair captain," he rejoined with an impish grin. "Yet, I cannot help but believe wealth to be over-rated."

Gnarly Dan was fairly chewing on his own tongue. He gritted his teeth; he tried to look away. He attempted to ignore the exchange. But he couldn't. "Beggin' yer pardon, Sir Edmund; a spell or two before the mast'll likely put the glitter back in yer gold. Chase a weevil outta yer roll or get a letter from yer misses sayin' another nipper was lost inna cruel winter an' you're sure ta hold that fat purse a bit closer."

The naturalist could not help but finger the leather belt stuffed with gold coins he wore about his person. He looked long and hard at the sincere old salt. He cleared his throat. He saddened. "I take your point," was all he allowed himself.

He turned from Gnarly Dan and asked his captain, "And would you willingly die for said golden statue? More accurately; are you willing to risk your life for it by alienating those who would help us return to our ship? Assuming the good Baci is still there when we arrive and not in the clutches of one Nat or another, Nasty or Naughty. Are you willing to risk untold hardship, perhaps lose a digit or two in the process?"

Gnarly Dan now unconsciously teased the stump of his missing finger.

At last they relented in the face of Sir Edmund's logic, although there was not yet any indication of in whose ownership the statue remained. It did become apparent that the Inca's relatives wished for her remains to be liberated from her gilt sarcophagus; which Sir Edmund accomplished with great and wise fanfare. She was buried with solemn reverence, an attitude that gave way to celebration after her interment.

Then, Sir Edmund, Captain Constance Daphne, and Gnarly Dan and the remaining crew were fairly spirited by the throng from the high mountains to the coast once more.

All were astounded at the rapidity of their return to the sea until they deduced their original ascent had been circuitous in the extreme; the guides leading the explorers in cruel circles, traversing the highest and most dangerous peaks. But now, steeped in gratitude they took the old Inca highway through the passes and valleys, returning to the ship well in advance of the pirates and treasure; early enough to prepare a surprise!

The good ship Baci was warped into the bay, a broadside prepared by the skeleton crew, the boarding nets rigged and cutlasses and pikes sharpened and belaying pins secreted along with knives and other implements of defense. But a battle was not to be, for it was only the lost Bacis, depressed, defeated and hang dog who finally stumbled out of the jungle. It seems they had attempted an attack on the pirates but were soundly drubbed, unable to retake the treasure and lucky to keep their own skins intact. All they brought was the sad news that the pirates had turned inland and due west, bent on a rendezvous at the Oronoco River.

And so, reunited, the Bacis revitualed, licked their wounds and set sail once more, finally and truly intent on carrying Sir Edmund to the Galapagos Islands. Most satisfying had been the Indians' continued gratitude, reaching a peak when they carefully carried the hollow golden likeness to the beach and then after a ceremonial good-bye, hefted it to their shoulders and walked it solemnly to the long boat.

"ALOFT AND UNFURL!" Captain Constance Daphne commanded. "LET'S GET THE OLD GIRL OUT TO SEA AND LET HER HAVE HER WAY!"

And they did.

The crew recovered quickly from their ordeal, and Captain Constance Daphne Fitzwillie was captivated by the golden princess who now shared her quarters. Nightly the brave captain buffed the sarcophagus to a brilliant luster, and every morning she greeted her with a warm, "Good morning!"

En route the H.M.S. Baci was becalmed briefly. Sir Edmund had his diving bell rousted from the hold and lowered into the salty depths once more. He and Gnarly Dan were talking quietly when the 27th maiden was sighted.

His journal reads:

Most awesome sight! We spied a healthy specimen drifting by the bell, stretching and preening for what seemed like hours. While a bit padded here and there, a glorious balance was maintained by the most magnificent chest I have yet to encounter. She does indeed make our endowed captain appear the preadolescent schoolgirl. Gnarly Dan noted (who could stop him?) that her excessive and obvious lung capacity allowed her prolonged time sub-aqua. Says he, "Any maid what has a chest like that ain't in no hurry; anything she wants'll likely come her way if she be patient."
Indeed.

Maidenous buxomous
"Anna"
Stunning body. Long dark hair. A bit fleshy. Magnificent attributes, fore and aft. Magenta tail.
October 30, 1833
Pacific Ocean, east of Gran Columbia

Editor's note: *This is the only maiden sighting that the naturalist celebrated with two paintings, one remarking a full frontal view, the other from behind. It is obvious Sir Edmund was most impressed with her figure as there is also a sheaf of unfinished sketches of her.*

SIGHTING THIRTY

Fair wind. Becalmed. Fair wind. Becalmed. Thus did the good ship H.M.S. Baci stutter toward the Galapagos Islands. Twice in the vicinity of the American whaling vessel, Pequod, they saw their once pristine ocean flow with a river of whale blood and viscera. It was after one such encounter that Sir Edmund Roberts, gentleman naturalist and sea maiden questor, sought solace in the deep.

Over the side and submerged in Halley's patented diving machine, in the company of Gnarly Dan, the ever-verbal old salt, and the beautiful Captain Constance Daphne Fitzwillie, Sir Edmund watched in silence as a massive sea turtle appeared out of the distant darkness accompanied by three cunning sea babies.

"Chelonia mydas," he quoted, stirring Gnarly Dan from his reverie (no doubt involving at least one of his three current wives and probably including more recent interests, for he alternately smiled and frowned).

The old salt squinted and remarked, "I'd call 'em sea babies an' a whoppin' big turtle an' skip the mumbo jumbo me self, though talking in tongues does seem ta please Yer Honor."

Captain Constance Daphne smiled to herself at the mention of tongues, her own reminiscences straying to the attractive side of their past guest (Nasty or Naughty?) Natalie. She leaned to the window. In the wake of the sea turtle three babies did indeed appear from the gloom, lanquidly following.

"They appear to be making sport with other sea fauna," Sir Edmund observed in an attempt to wrest the flow of conversation from the others, in particular, Gnarly Dan, who, ignoring the naturalist's unspoken wishes, corrected him.

"Ya does recall, yer honor, that not three cables back we passed a pacel a' whale blood an' guts foulin' the sea?"

"I could not have missed it had I tried," the naturalist answered, curious in spite of himself.

"An a' course, ya recollects yer sea babies an' they mums keeps track by mum's sweet air bubbles bein' blowed up from the deep; the young 'uns playin' in 'em an' never strayin' far?" Gnarly Dan waited and when Sir Edmund restrained from answering he concluded, "Well that lake 'a whale scud has thrown 'em off. Why them sea babies is as lost as a blind man inna gale. They's lost, sure enough; an' Ole Mrs. Turtle's leadin' 'em back ta mum."

Clearly, Sir Edmund was grudgingly impressed. "They do that? Sea turtles are capable? Consistently?"

Gnarly Dan slowly rubbed his grey stubble, nipped a fleck of liquid from the side of his mouth and confided, "'Course they does. It's natural-like. All yer sea creatures takes care 'a one another; lest they's eatin'. That sea turtle'll get 'em back as sure as the mornin' breeze. They'll be a sorta homecomin' an' she'll get a hug or two from the sea mums an' then off she'll go as sure as kiss my hand.

"Might be a little sad, what with the whale bein' defeated. Be a pity if she has young 'uns." The old salt ruminated and then added, "Know'd a sea cow what adopted a whale baby or two. It happens."

Slowly, the foursome swam past the bell, one sea baby looking in through the viewing window, nearly breaking Constance Daphne's heart with his smile. She reflected as long as she dared on her own childless state, wiped a slow tear and then looked away. The sea baby realized his cohorts were swimming off and raced to join them, finally disappearing into the gloom.

Gnarly Dan cleared his throat and concluded, "Bad enough how we mucks things up on shore. Don't seem right we brings our shortcomin's inta' the sea."

Sir Edmund's journal reads:

Sighted more sea babies. Different colored tails. Little hair. One bald. Infans Four, Five, Six
Near the Galapagos Islands.
November 14, 1833

SIGHTING THIRTY-ONE

Sailing blithely over the bounding main once more, Sir Edmund Roberts, sea maiden questor and adventurer, at last reached the Islands of the Galapagos without further incident. Weeks of exploring ashore befuddled the naturalist completely, he at a loss to explain the profound diversity of fauna inhabiting or merely using as a breeding grounds each of the distinct islands. "Most unusual!" he exclaimed again and again as he pointed out the differences to Gnarly Dan who alternately walked with and then stooped near the naturalist. "Completely different animal from the ones we saw on the last island! A conundrum, to be sure," he chided both the old salt and their beautiful Captain Constance Daphne Fitzwillie who was charmed by the lack of fear demonstrated by the island creatures. For a change it was the naturalist who came near to being throttled for his nonstop babbling.

At last, Gnarly Dan took the naturalist to the side and confided, "Yer a smart enough gent, Yer Honor, we all knows that. But yer drivin' our Cap' a bit daft with yer moanin' 'bout diff'rent bugs 'n birds 'n such as we been seein'. My advice is clamp aholt a' yer yammerin' fer a bit an' then just stew fer a while becalmed. Some sorta idear or theory'll likely grab ya soon enough. All quiet-like it's sure ta worm inta yer head an' just evolve."

Sir Edmund stared at the old sailor for a moment, wondering at his erratic vocabulary. *'Evolve' indeed,* he thought to himself, pleased with the word but unsettled by something on which he could not place his finger. At last he pushed it from his mind, the naturalist priding himself on his ability to keep his thoughts swept clear of useless information and obtuse observations.

That afternoon the three came upon their twenty-eight sea maiden, she perched on a ledge near the sea, morose and apparently bemused.

Gnarly Dan studied her briefly and, of course, had an explanation: "Look in 'er hand, yer honor; it's as plain as . . ." His eyes were drawn to Constance Daphne's open naval tunic and her uplifted and magnificent chest, tanned deep brown to where the cloth began and thereafter hints, stark white and beckoning, "Come look at me!" Her nipples further stressed the already challenged fabric. The old salt collected himself. "It's as plain as melons shiftin' in a too-small bag." He smiled to himself and continued, "Why she's gotta make a decision what will chart her course fer the rest a' her voyage. That there necklace she's got aholt of was made by a sea master an' give ta her. He fashioned it outa bits an' pieces he foun' on a beach an' in the sea, an' maybe even aboard some wrecked ship. (God save her crew; may they rest in peace.) An' he's give that necklace what he made ta missey there, most likely. Now it'd be more'n just a trinket ta her. Why if she 'cepts it—an' the decision's all hers—under sea folk bein' ruled by they women an' all (unlike yer fresh-water maids)—if she puts it 'roun' her neck, then she's givin' him the chanst ta please her the rest a' they lives. That ain't somethin' she takes lightly.

"We jumps inna marriage easy enough," Gnarly Dan continued, thinking of his three current entanglements; fortunately separated geographically but hopelessly entwined in his crusty heart, "but yer sea maiden don' just jump on the first handsome gob what pays attention to her. He's gotta be perfect: strong body, sharp mind, sensitive-like, good fer a laugh an' helpful inna storm, an a' course he's gotta please her again an' again. An' not the same ever' time. She won' tolerate no pirates' tricks a' ram an' board. No, she's lookin' fer him ta bring gentle breezes an' poundin' waves onst she's inna mood, if ya catches me drift. So she'd be ponderin' a bit. Don' look too pleased if ya asks me. Prob'ly finds him a little weak in the 'gentle breeze department'. I got it on good authority most us men is like that."

Contstance Daphne Fitzwillie stood nearby and listened carefully. She did, however, reserve comment.

Sir Edmund's notebook reads:

Sighted our 28ᵗʰ sea maiden, she, according to our font of worthless information, in the throes of a matrimonial dilemma.
Maidenous dilemmas matrimonus
"Barbara"
November 24, 1833
Galapagos Islands

SIGHTING THIRTY-TWO

Sir Edmund Roberts, gentleman naturalist and sea maiden questor, left the Galapagos Islands in a haze of confusion and doubt, and sailed south-southwest through the unforgiving main. Captain Constance Daphne was at the height of her beauty, her body that of a glorious and mature woman, her confidence soaring as she was truly master of the vessel she commanded; it being the H.M.S. Baci. Her sexual proclivities were being handsomely addressed once more by Sir Edmund Roberts, gentleman naturalist. Still she did not acknowledge their nocturnal meetings, and still, she was somewhat aloof during the day, but not nearly to the degree of the previous years with him. They had come to trust one another and enjoy the time shared. It was remarkably satisfying for the crew to watch, they caring more than a little for the pair.

Through the seemingly endless ocean they plowed until they came to the Easter Islands. In the busom of the Rapa Nui culture Sir Edmund continued his sea maiden exploration in earnest. The massive statues slanting across the island hillsides fascinated him, of course, and as expected, Gnarly Dan, the vessel of endless obscurata and font of homey wisdom, had his theory regarding the huge carved heads tilting everywhere.

"Any fool can see they's giants' toys; Jack an' his Beanstalk, an such as that. This musta been home afore they went wanderin' ta Merry England an' the land a' the Frenchies."

To his credit, Sir Edmund neither bothered to refute nor acknowledge the old salt, he being drawn more to the birdman petroglyphs and then, amazingly, to a lone petroglyph of a sea maiden.

"By jove, they're here! he exclaimed. "And by the looks of this carving, they've been about for eons and eons." He then went about finding one. It was the following morning in the glow of a beautiful dawn that he spied his 29th sea maiden, she reclining on the beach with her back to the naturalist and his companion, Gnarly Dan. Sir Edmund watched and pondered and sketched, at last whispering, "You needn't tell me; I remember well enough from the 4th sea maiden we sighted; Diane I believe it was. She's grieving over a lost love and she won't move until the piker returns."

Gnarly Dan smiled a small smile and then chuckled. "Well, Yer Honor,'tis an honest mistake, sure enough, and it does have ta do with there bein' no lover near 'bouts." He paused as if he expected the naturalist to ascertain where he was guiding him. But Sir Edmund was unable to follow, he still staring blankly at the old salt. Gnarly Dan continued, "I'd be a might becalmed here, Squire, not knowin' the polite way ta sort this out for ya, an' yourself havin' your own way a' explainin' things. The long an' short of it bein' she's no doubt dreamin' a' bein' in the arms of another." He waited to see if Sir Edmund finally understood. When the naturalist remained obviously chagrinned, Gnarly Dan huffed, "Her other han'! Her other han'! Fer an educated gent you sure does miss what's nailed to the main mast!"

Sir Edmund did at last understand and he was embarrassed to the core with that knowledge. He was about to turn and leave when Gnarly Dan amended his current theory. He was studying the sea maiden's attributes when he added at last, "Ya know, sir, there may be another explanation."

Sir Edmund wanted no more of it. He ignored the old salt.

"Yes, sir, there could be another reason."

Sir Edmund remained silent.

Gnarly Dan pushed on, regardless. "When ya look at that beautiful lass, there'd be but one thing what catches yer notice, right off quick."

Sir Edmund said nothing but covertly examined the sea maiden. The breath of a smile crossed his visage.

"Yer right, yer honor!" old Gnarly exclaimed as if the naturalist had just shouted out a response. "That would be the most handsome stern what a gob has ever see'd! I can tell from these years you'd be more impressed with a treasure chest, sure enough, but yer true sailor loves an honest stern." He looked longingly at the sea maiden's posterior and expanded, "An' that'd be the best lookin' one ever. Why it's easy ta see she'b be designed fer the water. It'd flow past her waist with uncommon ease, and then, quick as you please, it'd move beyond, an' then down her tail. Nothin' but smooth lines an' glorious curves. More like a French hull than the slab-sided doxies we builds in Merry England."

The naturalist had to concur. He didn't wish to. In fact, he was loath to lend credence to anything the old salt proposed. But there, before him, was the best looking, most alluring, begging to be touched, hiney to be bared for a lucky man. Sir Edmund took her in, felt his hands twitch and his mouth begin to pucker and proclaimed, "Yes, my good man, in this you are correct. Though a well turned chest will make me smile, I am sorely tempted to become a stern man myself; it is indeed the best ever."

Sir Edmund's journal reads:

Sighted our 29th sea maiden, either entertaining herself or showing off her attributes.
    Maidenous plus belle posterus (or fantasia)
    "Cathy"
    Beautiful body. Derriere extraordinaire! Green tail.
    January 8, 1834
    Easter Island

SIGHTING THIRTY-THREE

Editor's note: *As an inveterate explorer and sea maiden questor, Sir Edmund Roberts continued his voyage aboard the H.M.S. Baci. It must be remarked, however, that as stated from the beginning, the primary sources of information regarding the journey are the naturalist's journals, and those documents do on occasion demonstrate colossal vaults of logic; or as in this case, inconsistencies regarding the flow of time. To wit: Sea Maiden 29 was sighted reclining on a beach at Easter Island, the preceding sightings having occurred in logical sequence considering our globe, its oceans, and the ship's initial departure from England. Yet, the sighting of sea maiden 30 and her companion, sea maiden 31, occurred thousands of nautical miles distant from Easter Island in spite of the fact that the sketches and journal entries are impossibly dated within a month of that exploration. Simply put, the H.M.S.*

Baci was in the right place for these sightings (Sir Edmund's topographical descriptions are accurate) at the wrong time.

Perhaps the wisest course is to observe old Gnarly Dan's admonition, "Spend enough time with yer nose draggin' the deck an' yer sure ta miss an adventure."

Sir Edmund's journal reads:

Glorious sailing and fine exploration! We roused Halley's patented diving machine this morning and lowered ourselves into the placid Aegean waters. Gnarly Dan and this naturalist continued our sea maiden quest, sub-aqua. Mid-day we spied a most glorious sight! A brace of sea maidens drifted by the bell whilst performing the most intimate dance I have witnessed. Gentle touch played counterpoint to a series of slow arabesques, both maidens monuments of serenity. I remarked their perfection to be sibling by nature but Gnarly Dan would have none of it. Says he, "Why Cap, it's beauteous that'd be sure, but they'd not be sisters." His smile was melancholy when he continued, "I'd not expect an educated bloke such as yerself ta understand, yer honor, but ever' sailor knows that though a man an' a woman fits natural-like, if yer steerin' me course, often enough there'd be a rasp to it; kinda like a peck a' wet sand in yer shoe, or a sailor ashore too long. Sometimes it just ain't right.

"That page may be blank in yer chart book, Squire, but some of us knows the way. Why them two sea maidens belongs together like moonlight on a calm sea."

> *Maidenous languorous*
> *"Dawn"*
> *Maidenous serenus*
> *"Elaine"*
> *Off the Island of Lesbos, Greece*
> *February 20, 1834*

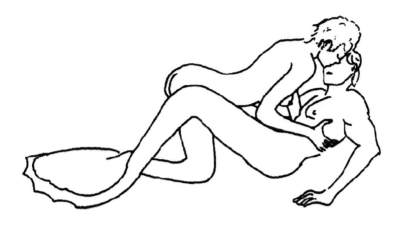

SIGHTING THIRTY-FOUR

Just prior to departing the Easter Island complex the naturalist, Sir Edmund Roberts, in the company of Gnarly Dan, spied his 32nd sea maiden and 8th sea master. Gnarly Dan, the source of sea maiden lore, and the producer of more words than the average individual hears in ten lifetimes, explained the situation, though much affected by the drama before them. He swabbed a salty tear from his bristled cheek, snuffled loudly and whispered, "This'd be better luck than the time me second wife's three sisters needed consolin' when they favorite cat was trampled by a coach an' four. Warn't one of 'em much ta look at, squashed cat included, but they tears turned ta huggin' an' such, an' well, afore I know'd it, we was sailin' fer heaven in a crowded boat."

Sir Edmund glared heavily toward the old salt and hissed, "I do not give a hang about any of your multitudinous wives, sisters, pets (pussy or otherwise), or predilections for unsavory unions. If you have information regarding the couple before us, do tell; otherwise, please keep that ever moving mouth of yours shut before I throttle you."

Old Gnarly Dan feigned a deep psychological wound and then continued, "As I was a sayin' afore Yer Honor got testy: That'd be wondrous good luck we'd be spyin'. Firstly, a sea master finds hisself alyin' on the beach fer but one reason, an' that'd be if he's give up on findin' his love. Secondly, yer sea maiden saws off her hair when she's grievin' fer a lost love. Onst she does that, she rips the page involvin' love from her chart book. She'll nary love again. Think a' the chance a what we sees happenin'."

He turned to Sir Edmund, triumphant.

The naturalist shook his head in an attempt to clear his consternation. "My good fellow, you make absolutely no sense."

Gnarly Dan passed a sigh of taxed patience and began again. "Yer sea master there obviously got lost somehow; maybe a storm; a typhoon, perhaps, blowed him far away. He's struggled back after a powerful lot a' swimmin' Now, yer sea maiden was his girl, if ya catch me drift. She musta thought he copped it; drown or got eat by a giant squid, 'cause she chopped her hair clean off, an' yer sea maiden won' do nothin' that capital lest she be powerful sad."

Sir Edmund did finally understand, and when he went to acknowledge Gnarly Dan's wisdom, he stopped, for the old salt was again lost in reverie. "Gave that cat a right nice send off. Headstone an' all. Was that grateful."

Sir Edmund's notebook reads:

Maidenous gratitudus
"Fanny"
Maximus surrendus
Sighted in the throes of a homecoming.
March 1, 1834
Near Easter Island

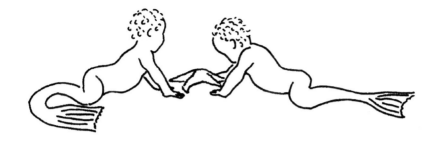

SIGHTINGS THIRTY-FIVE, THIRTY-SIX, & THIRTY-SEVEN

Again the forgotten voyage of the H.M.S. Baci made the London Gazette:

THE THIRD MANLY ADVENTURE
OR
How the **Loathsome Pirate, Naughty Nat**, was denied **Revenge**.

The long and short of the article was: The journey of the H.M.S. Baci continued with intrigue and action; Sir Edmund Roberts' sea maiden quest once more flavored with a run-in with the loathsome pirate, Naughty Nat. One evening after the crew had turned out for their ration of grog, a dense bank of fog appeared on the horizon. With a following wind there was no avoiding it, but as the mist approached the wind steadily lessened until with its last puff crew and ship entered the hazy obscurity. As near as they could tell they were making no way, but the density of the fog measurably increased until not a man could see the hand in front of his face. Those on the rigging moved carefully, every step as if in a dream. A hush fell over the ship, the men speaking in the smallest of whispers, even Gnarly Dan strangely subdued.

And then they began to hear other sounds. Faint. Perhaps only imagined. Tiny voices. Muted groans from another ship. The Bacis listened, their hearts in their throats. To a man (and if one included their beautiful captain; to a man and a woman) their thoughts were the same:

Naughty Nat.

Naughty Nat in his newest, most heavily armed vessel. Naughty Nat with hundreds of rabid vermin at scores of double-shotted cannons. The scum of the earth with cutlasses and a decided lack of conscience.

And just when the crew of the good ship Baci believed it could get no worse, the other voices became distinct: "It'd be another ship I hears, Cutthroat Will, mark me word!"

Then an answer, "Let's fire a few broadsides, Deadly, we're bound ta hurt somethin'!"

"How I longs ta muck about in a good fight!"

Bravery deserted the Bacis. Even their captain, the beautiful Constance Daphne Fitzwillie, was quiet. And then as if by a minor miracle, both ships passed into a hole in the fog, each traveling in the opposite direction, each within an arm's length of touching. Man and pirate looked in stunned silence as their foe glided silently by. Not a Baci had the temerity to so much as make an unfriendly gesture, and not one pirate, though he may absently wipe a gob of drool from the side of his mouth, had the presence to lift a pistol or fire one of the multitude of primed cannons. On the quarterdeck, the loathsome pirate Naughty Nat stood open mouthed, a fat cigar smoking at his feet. The stunning Captain Constance Daphne Fitzwillie, astride her quarter deck, her magnificent bosoms half escaping her tight Royal Navy jacket, also stared blankly. Her husband, the former Captain Fitzwillie, was at the despicable pirate's right hand, he, too, befuddled. And there also, as apparitions from a particularly bad, albeit erotic, dream, were the tempestuous twins, Naughty and Nasty Natalie, they fairly dripping with gold necklaces, pendants, amulets and bric-a-bracs.

And as quickly, the ships ghosted into the fog once more. And both crews came to life. "FIRE THAT STERN CHASER, YOU MISERABLE SON OF A WORTHLESS DOG!" (Obviously Naughty Nat speaking.) There followed a cacophony of small arms fire, a mighty cannon barking in its midst. The good Bacis answered in kind, their own stern chaser quickly readied and fired. But no matter how either ship turned to reengage their tormenter, it was to no avail. In the thick fog the sounds became more distant until each was shrouded in silence once more.

Morning dawned on a clear horizon. The H.M.S. Baci continued, her crew intact but for Clumsy Samuel, who failed to appear for the morning muster. He was last seen on the yard of the fore skyscraper, a pistol in each hand and he firing into the fog. "He was a good 'un," his mates said as an epitaph as his ditty bag was divided between mourning friends.

Later, invited onto Captain Constance Daphne's hallowed quarterdeck, the naturalist, Sir Edmund Roberts, was quizzed by his captain. "And what, Sir Edmund, have you to say of our last meeting with that despicable cur of a pirate, Naughty Nat?" she inquired.

Sir Edmund had obviously given the matter much thought, for he answered without hesitation. "My first reaction was to the sheer size of his latest vessel. It was significantly larger than the old 'Plunderer', and noticeably larger than his last vessel, 'Slow Death'." He warmed to his subject. "Obviously, the wretch is consistently upgrading his ships, appearing in ever-larger craft. Further, the magnitude of each vessel is further enhanced by the fact that I count an increase in the number and mass of the artillery he commands. That last ship, 'Your Nightmare', I believe I read on her stern, floated eighteen pounders on her gun deck and twelve pounders above. I confess I was unable to ascertain the number of each, but needless to say, they far outnumbered in addition to outweighing our own rather modest complement of six and four pound cannon. We were hopelessly outgunned, though I still would not count the intervening fog a blessing; our good crew spoiling for a fight. Further, the rabble aboard 'Your Nightmare' outnumbered us three to one, and those I saw appeared fit, angry, and dare I say 'genetically challenged.'"

Sir Edmund paused to ruminate and further refine his subsequent comments. At last he continued, "On the whole, I would speculate the verminous dog is not only stalking us (much as we are him) but also actively intent on trumping the good ship Baci in floating might. Finally, though he was as startled into inaction as we, once in motion his crew worked their guns commendably, getting off a round every four minutes with his larger pieces. I must conclude we face a formidable foe." He pondered a moment and then concluded, "And finally, the dog is obviously connected to that wretched woman, Natalie. It would seem that with her help he has reconstituted his lost treasure with our recently stolen gold." (The naturalist had still not come to terms with the existence of the pirate vixen's twin.)

Sir Edmund now stood in silence, his hands clasped behind his back. Captain Constance Daphne mimicked his posture, the effect different considering her bounteous chest, now thrust forward and teasing the naturalist to remain focused on guns and ships. She began to pace her quarterdeck pensively and the naturalist followed. It was obvious that she was going to speak, and that what she was to say would be important.

"Sir Edmund," she began. "I hold many of your skills in the highest esteem, though that was not the case in the beginning. I agree one hundred percent with your appraisal of Naughty Nat's floating might. I must admit I was a bit stymied to see his ship's name as 'Yon Nightingale'. I believe your reading more accurate, although, that is neither here nor there. The point is; if we are going to trump that audacious, drooling rascal, we cannot depend on iron alone. Even closing and grabbling immediately is not a wise option. Though the good Bacis will fight like heroes, we are sorely outnumbered."

She let all of this lie for a moment; she had relayed nothing the naturalist had not already mentioned. At last she stopped, turned full to Sir Edmund, and said, "We are in need of a brilliant idea. We must have at least one outrageously clever weapon up our sleeve if we are to not only survive our next meeting, but triumph. I am determined to send that detestable, abhorrent, odious fiend to the bottom of the sea. And my cowardly worm of a husband with him."

Sir Edmund did not choose to respond so fresh on the heels of Constance Daphne's mention of her husband. Worm or no, he was still her husband, a man whose previous death amounted to naught and whose wedding vows were therefore still intact. The naturalist was bedding his wife . . . nightly, now . . . and so a wave of discomfort washed briefly over the man.

Constance Daphne, ever observant, commented tartly, "Produce the proper court and I will divorce the slug."

Sir Edmund ignored that rejoinder, also. The sun then broke from behind a cloud, bathing the captain in its light. At last Sir Edmund answered, "My fair captain, I have already turned my mind to matters of military tactics and equipage. The problem is complex, in that the good ship Baci is also an old ship. A very old ship. According to our carpenter, she is not only fifty years old, hogging at the keel, sprung at the knees and rife with both dry and wet rot, but she is also already over-armed and a sore challenge for her ballast to keep her upright. I am cautioned that in her present condition every broadside she fires is potentially more damaging to her own timbers than those of her foe. You will recall the Royal George, at only twenty five years in the water, sank in Portsmouth harbor with all hands lost because her bottom fell out.

"So we cannot, it would seem, rely on merely stuffing more artillery into the old girl. Fortunately, I have followed the experiments of a fellow named Congreve, and he may have just the thing. Further, there have been advances in other sciences of which we may avail ourselves. I have a few projects anticipated, but my hope is that you will be so kind as to allow me the time to formulate more definitive plans before I lay them before you."

'Lay them before you' made both captain and naturalist secretly smile. When they resumed their pacing of her quarterdeck, they spoke of more intimate matters, the captain leaning to the naturalist and whispering, "That thing you did with you hands last night; you know, just before . . . when you were so gentle . . . it was magnificent! I was thinking . . . perhaps . . ." And then she lowered her voice further, whispering more quietly than even an omniscient narrator could hear.

That night, neither Captain Constance Daphne Fitzwillie, nor Sir Edmund Roberts, nor the crew above the captain's skylight was disappointed.

There followed a melancholy day of clear sailing, and then a week of the same until the H.M.S. Baci came upon a remarkable little spit of an island. Laughing Phillip was the mainmast lookout, he in the trucks with a leg wrapped around the skinny pole. He was chuckling to himself when he spied the island.."HA, HA! LAND HO! HARD ON THE STARBOARD BOW! AND AIN'T IT A' COVERED WITH SEA BABIES! HA, HA!"

The news roared through the ship like a pistol ball through butter. "Get His Honor!" "Find Sir Edmund!" "Tell him we gots sea babies on the horizon!"

The naturalist was beside himself when they finally reached the island, lowered a boat and rowed to explore. Hundreds of sea babies of every make and model cavorted on the broad sand. Old Gnarly Dan tugged at the thatch of hair escaping his ear and provided colorful commentary as Sir Edmund looked and listened, pointing here, there and everywhere at the wriggling, crawling and cooing assemblage.

"They be right happy now!" Gnarly Dan instructed. "They mums comes here but onst a year."

Sir Edmund was confused. "My good man, I see no mothers. Why, these babies are unattended. Perhaps disaster has struck!"

Gnarly Dan scoffed at the naturalist's ignorance. "Why 'a course they ain't right here!" He then turned and pointed to an area beyond the Baci. While the ocean was calm, the area the old salt indicated roiled gently, bubbles breaking the surface to and fro. "They mum's 'd be out there. They's hobnobbin' an' catchin' up on sea maiden news. They all meets here, then leaves the young 'uns on the island an' slips off for a watch or two ta just be together an' chat."

Sir Edmund was adrift. "Why would they do such a thing?" he inquired, obviously at a loss.

Gnarly Dan looked at the naturalist as if he'd been born that morning. "Has His Honor ever been in close quarters with a little 'un day after day after day?"

Sir Edmund shook his head and answered, "My good man, I have no children."

The old salt squinted at the naturalist. "Well, mark me word, Gov'ner, them mums needs ta get away or they'll go daft. At last count I got 'bout a dozen little nippers me self an' a good three year voyage is a nice break. It's why I goes ta sea."

The first of three separate journal entries reads:

Wondrous sighting! Sea babies everywhere! The first two we studied were enraptured by a starfish!

Sea Babies 7 and 8
Sex indeterminate
Infans curious
Diminished height. Light of weight. Short, curly hair.
Multi-colored tails.
Sighted on an uncharted island.
May 4, 1834

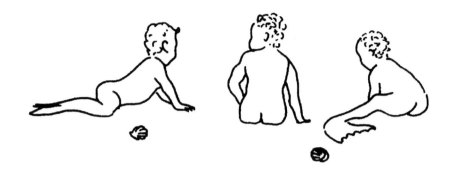

Then the subsequent entry:

Again we studied the sea baby colony! The little buggers are everywhere. Appear to have no fear of humans and are remarkably well behaved.

Sea Babies 9, 10, and 11
Sex indeterminate.
Infans curious
Diminished height. Light of weight. Short curly hair.
Multi-colored tails.
Sighted on an uncharted island.
May 5, 1834

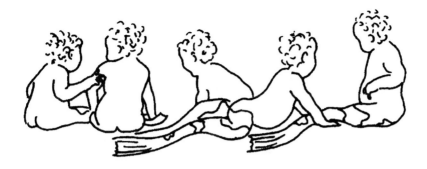

And the next day's entry:

The third group we studied was to all appearances holding some sort of sea baby conference! Gnarly Dan claims their distinct coloration assures nothing more than a distant relationship. Says he, "They could be five mums what calls 'em hers, or as few as one. All them tails tells a gob is that they comes from the same place on the chart. Could be they's never laid eyes on one another 'til this watch. You can be sure they mums's fast friends by now. Nothin' opens yer sea maiden's heart like a child. They feels they ain't had but half a life 'til they gets a little nipper or two ta round things out."

How droll.

Sea Babies 12, 13, 14, 15, and 16
Sex indeterminate. Light of weight. Short, curly hair.
Tails of clown fish.
Sighted on uncharted island.
May 7, 1834

The despicable cur, Naughty Nat, addressed the earlier misty encounter in poetry:

The second Naughty Nat poem:

A pirate must do what a pirate must do;
There's never a choice in the matter.
So when I find that I'm dogged like a fox
Someone's head should be served on a platter!

We was gliding through fog, not a care in the world,
What we couldn't see hardly our worry.
When them Baci fools ghosted beside my fine crew
Like they hadn't the first cause to hurry!

They bested me twice, and it looks like a third

147

Time they've managed to keep their heads anchored.
Once more I'm the fool; my luck's been most cruel!
So I'm drowning my glum by the tankard.

But tomorrow will come, and the day after that,
And a night and a morning and so on,
Until them damp scum feels the heat of our guns
And that crew's cooked—domestic and foreign!

You Bacis beware, there's no need to prepare,
Beyond writing your loved ones and neighbors.
Say your goodbyes; there won't be dry eyes
When they find out we made you dead sailors!

On the seas you've been tossed, but this pirate you've crossed,
And past storms will soon seem a trifle.
For Naughty Nat knows that wherever you goes,
His vengeance is nothing you'll stifle.

Editor's note: *Unfortunately, the loathsome pirate Naughty Nat was also the unforgivably verbose pirate Naughty Nat; he being apparently so consumed by his humiliation and anger that this particular poem goes on for some forty-two pages, the rhymes more forced and the whole thing finally deteriorating into a ridiculous list of off-hand threats and adolescent challenges interspersed with some pretty macabre allusions (eyeball hors d'oeuvres, pancreas sandwiches and such). In the interest of brevity I have included just enough to give the reader a sense of his preoccupation. The full text is available in the library of the Tortola Museum of Pirates and Buccaneers (open weekdays, 3:35 p.m. through 4:05 p.m., closed weekends and holidays, September through November) under Naughty Nat's less known moniker: Nathan Pinkwater.*

SIGHTING THIRTY-EIGHT

At last they weighed anchor and sailed off, Sir Edmund absolutely and heartily sick of sea baby children underfoot. "How can anyone put up with their incessant mewing?" he asked everyone who would listen.

Gnarly Dan lowered his estimation of the naturalist. "So it'd be all books an' quiet, fer Yer Honor?" he asked.

"That sounds wonderful," Sir Edmund rejoined. "Absolutely wonderful."

All the while, the unease growing in Captain Constance Daphne Fitzwillie went unnoticed. She studied the sea babies with her telescope. She dreamed of them at night. And on occasion, as she stood alone on her quarterdeck, she found her right hand idly rubbing her flat stomach.

The evening before they were to leave, she and Sir Edmund were leaning on the taffrail. A blue moon glowed above them. To the number the sea babies had exited the island and rejoined their mothers. Gnarly Dan explained they'd be off to other places now, perhaps meeting up with their sea master fathers and visiting a ship wreck or two as a kind of pleasant diversion.

A quiet enveloped the naturalist and the captain.

At last she spoke. "I miss them already," she sighed.

Sir Edmund had a rare spark of insight and remained silent.

She noticed, and continued, regardless. "My first husband (that vile worm) did not care for children. So I have none."

They stared back at the deserted island.

Constance Daphne then looked long at Sir Edmund and spoke again. "For all of your aloofness and regard for your quiet time, I believe you would be an adequate father. You are intelligent and fair," she concluded, wishing she could add, 'and sensitive'.

Sir Edmund explored her comment, thinking of a real companionship with the beautiful woman beside him. He placed her in his country home and thought of awakening with her; of walking through the moors with her at his side. He imagined them at the ruins of his ancestral castle (a smallish one, to be sure, but adequately crenellated and sufficiently steeped in history to provide interest).

An accomplished equestrian, the naturalist asked, "Do you sit a horse well?"

At first at a loss, the captain at last decided that in some oblique way the naturalist was still on the same topic as she.

"I'm told I do," she answered.

Now Sir Edmund had them on horseback galloping down wide wooded trails and over rolling countryside. They stopped for a picnic. They studied plants. They lay on their backs on a tartan blanket and looked at shapely, distant cumulous clouds. "That would be a pirate!" he pointed out to her.

"I remember the cur, well," she responded, remembering the villain of her middle age. "And that would be our old, beloved Baci," she added, pointing to a complex cloud that did indeed look like the good ship, bow-on.

The naturalist savored his fantasy. He was only able to force a child into it with magnificent difficulty. It was a little boy—no, a little girl. She accompanied him into the woods as he sought faeries. She actually hugged him once. She had a high voice and laughed easily.

The naturalist smiled. He did not do that often.

Meanwhile, Constance Daphne was tangentially occupied, also. To all appearances she was struggling with an inner dilemma. At last she interrupted the naturalist's thoughts. "May I tell you something in strictest confidence?" she implored.

Sir Edmund laughed quietly. "And with whom do you fear I would share your secret? Our good friend, Mr. Dan?"

Not ten feet away and secreted in the reefed sail on the spanker boom above them, Gnarly Dan frowned with wounded feelings.

The captain continued. "These many months since my husband's departure, I have refrained from violating the sanctity of his personal possessions, save his old uniforms. Only recently have I looked into his journal and official papers. What I found was at first rather a shock."

Sir Edmund pinched his lips together in thought. He could not imagine what her husband, their former captain, could possibly have written that would so discommode Constance Daphne.

She told him.

"That little worm researched and verified a captain's legal right to not only perform marriages at sea, but to also initiate divorce action under said circumstances; to wit: both parties being at sea. Further, the scoundrel drew up the documents and had the audacity to add his signature where required. With a flourish!"

"The cad," Sir Edmund answered because he felt a response was expected, when in fact, his mind was racing ahead with other possibilities. "And so . . . " he began.

"They were wanting only my signature," the captain continued, a tone of expectation in her voice.

"And since he, our former, duly appointed captain, drew up the papers and in effect, executed them, then . . . " Sir Edmund was again interrupted.

"Then, my own rather timid legal status as captain of our fine ship is irrelevant," she finished.

A long silence ensued.

"Sign them!" the naturalist exclaimed with unfeigned excitement.

Captain Constance Daphne Fitzwillie looked long and hard into the naturalist's eyes, seeing, she believed, into the depths of his distant, scientific soul. Apparently satisfied, she smiled and whispered, "I already did."

It was, without any hint of a doubt, the finest news the naturalist had received since his nomination for the British Society of Very Honored Naturalists and Explorers (he was subsequently drummed from its ranks for his treatise concerning the existence of faeries and goblins, but that in no way diminished his memory of his earlier excitement).

The need to pull his captain to him and hold her close was nearly overwhelming for Sir Edmund. But they were after all, on her quarterdeck, on her ship, surrounded, quite literally, by eighty-some members of her crew, and she was wearing the (her *former* husband's, actually) uniform of a captain in the Royal Navy; her half-liberated bosom notwithstanding. Sir Edmund restrained himself mightily.

They both felt the tremendous pull as their bodies ached and their minds raced. Then Sir Edmund asked the unimaginable:

"Do you believe you have the authority to perform a marriage?"

It was out. It was said. There could be no retraction and no doubt as to the true implication of his query. A warm wind came over the starboard quarter of the Baci and caressed them. The good ship heeled over an additional strake. With that movement a shadow passed from the couple and rested at their feet. The sun shone on them.

"I do," the beautiful captain whispered.

It was answered.

They both smiled and stood toe to toe.

"Well, I'll be a salty ole dog," floated down from deep in the folds of the furled sail on the spanker boom above.

The remainder of the day Sir Edmund thought of matrimony at last, and of companionship, and on occasion, of a child; a true heir, and of many things domestic and uncomplicated. Because he had always been unmarried, he was able to view such matters without the encumbrances of prior experience.

He thought of warm tea in the morning and of pleasant conversations. He imagined other voyages to faraway lands, his wife at his side and excited for his recent discoveries and impressed with his undeniable skills of observation. "You have such a clever way with words, Sir Edmund," he heard her say again and again. "Well, my dearest," he answered "she is, 'of average height and average weight'. There can be no better way to describe her!"

"How wonderfully true!" Constance Daphne Fitzwillie responded as she held his arm against the side of her soft chest.

And on and on.

A child playing. Children upright in stern chairs, respectfully silent, awaiting something wise from their father. Constance Daphne ensconced in a warm bed in a cool room with a dancing fire at the hearth, heavy covers pulled half way over her chest, her pale bare shoulders declaring the state of her undress, while he, Sir Edmund Roberts, himself unclothed but for a pair of polished riding boots and impatient beyond words, could wait no more and so clomped heavily to their bed, to his love, to her now open arms. A tangle, as blankets and sheets were thrown to the side.

"Beggin' yer pardon, Squire."

The declaration confused Sir Edmund. Constance Daphne now lay fully naked on their bed. Every cover was on the floor. The light from the fire bathed her willing body, highlighting her breasts and casting orange shadows on her soft, beckoning tummy and below.

"Beggin' yer pardon, Squire."

Who in hell's kitchen was in the room with them? Constance Daphne also heard and futilely tried to shield her body with too few hands.

"The Captain says ta tell His Honor that they's land sighted hard on the larboard bow. We should make landfall afore night."

Embarrassed to dyspepsia, the naturalist hid in sudden anger. "Sir! Be so good as to knock before you enter my quarters! Good manners are a gentleman's only comfort at sea. I was deep in thought. An incredibly complex problem was about to be solved! Now I've lost it entirely, you ill-bred nincompoop!"

The diatribe was lost on the sailor standing in Sir Edmund's door. He stared dully at the rows of leather-bound books and then at the stuffed bodies of rare birds and small mammals hovering near his dinner plate, rabid to eat after so many dusty years. The naturalist waved the sailor away and tried to return his thoughts to Constance Daphne Fitzwillie until he recalled what the sailor had said. He pushed back his chair and rose to join his captain on deck.

Captain Constance Daphne Fitzwillie was as the naturalist had been remembering her, except that she was mostly clothed and pacing her quarterdeck. "We have sighted land, my dearest" (the first time she had knowlingly employed a term of endearment within earshot of others).

Gnarly Dan called up from the waist of the ship, "It's Pitcairn Island, Yer Honor! The ole girl's come home at last!" And indeed she had; the H.M.S. Baci, launched as the H.M.S. Bethia, bought out later by the Royal Navy and then renamed the H.M.S. Bounty, in whose command she suffered the ignominy of a villainous captain and a mutinous crew. To Pitcairn Island they'd sailed and there, moments before she'd been burned to the waterline she was rescued by Lord Frothingslosh of the Admiralty, renamed the Baci for the Italian mistress with whom he'd been vacationing in the heretofore solitude and secrecy of Pitcairn.

The island was a tropical, albeit poorly harbored paradise. As the Baci approached, scores of blonde natives waved and beckoned both from its shores and from the outrigger canoes speeding to greet them. Dark-skinned women of glorious beauty waved and called out, their lack of clothing no impedance to their friendliness.

Gnarly Dan waved back in big anxious arcs. The crew manned the sides and the ship's rigging; laughing and beckoning the greeters to come closer. "Bout time we reached paradise!" the Bacis called to one another. "Been a sore temptation; what with our naturalist-cove gettin' the only woman!"

First one and then another and another of the Bacis who could swim dove to the warm waters and swam toward the women in the canoes, they exuding the Polynesians' measure of innocence and the Europeans' bald seductive allure.

While it was Captain Constance Daphne's intention to water the ship and revitual, it would be a brief stay indeed; for although the H.M.S. Baci was a warm sight to those islanders who knew their history, the Union Jack she flew was an ancestral enemy. So while preparations were made to replenish stores, Sir Edmund had his diving apparatus roused from the hold and lowered into the clear depths. Gnarly Dan accompanied the naturalist, his aquatic skills unfinished, and his taste for dark women visually quenched.

"I should think a woman's man such as yourself would be drinking in those native beauties, Mr. Dan!"

The old salt shook his head sagely. "There'd be a sight more than I could handle," he explained, "an' my own experience bein' that a pacel a' fine pieces such as we's see'd might could lead ta trouble onst more. Warn't that long ago what ole Cap Bligh an' the Bounty coulda larned that lesson."

Sir Edmund looked carefully at the ancient sailor. He studied every line on his face, each salt and pepper whisker and the tobacco stains at the corners of his parched lips. But as usual, it was the old salt's eyes that told the tale. They were far away, seeing a distant voyage and a time when he was very, very young. "Tell me about it," the naturalist asked with care.

Gnarly Dan looked at his companion. They were seated opposite from one another in Halley's patented bell as it was being slowly lowered. He smiled a small, sad smile. "Was the Bounty's ship's boy, I was. The ole man'd passed on from the bottle the winter afore, an' my Ma, she didn't have a chanst with all us kids. I just up an' left. Ole Bligh, he warn't half bad at first, till things kinda came unshipped. Fletcher Christian, he was a capital sort; treated me square. But then, really, so'd Bligh. Warn't much fer small talk or a favor, no Cap'n is; so I stay'd outta his way. Reminded me a' ole Da. Blimey, if he didn't. Likely why I chose ta stay with him.

"An' educated cove such as yerself likely knows the story; a long, long trip inna little cocked-hat of a boat. But we made it. Bligh, he know'd his stars, an' lord above, he could sail a boat. Warn't much fun, it bein' my first passage an' all, but I expect others see'd worst.

"The ole Bounty, she ain't changed much, 'ceptin' her name an' Cap Daphne's deck full a' cannon. Bad luck ta change a ship's name. The ole girl came down the ways the Bethia, an' that's what she shoulda stayed. Bad luck ta change a ship's name."

It was at that moment that their thirty-third sea maiden swam beneath them, her dark hair trailing, her broad tail making long, powerful thrusts. As quickly as she appeared, she was gone.

Sir Edmund blinked as if he'd missed something. "I say, she was in a bit of a rush. Late for dinner, perhaps?" It was his attempt at humor.

Gnarly Dan, happy to be back to the present, shook his head. "Ain't likely. It'd be a right smarter bet ta be lookin' out fer a sea master. Likely, he's back there all lonely-like, wishin' fer some companionship."

"And she flees him?" Sir Edmund asked, his interest undeniable.

"Ain't so much a case a 'fleein'; more like she ain't inna mood."

"So he should swim by presently?"

Gnarly Dan looked disgusted. "Does Yer Honor unnerstand we's discussin' sea maidens? Not women. Sea maidens. They ain't no sea master what'd be so bold as ta chase a sea maiden. Worst thing a gob could do. Against all they laws an' customs. He just likely made the mistake a' bein' a little too forward with a look or somethin'. An' she's decided they's somewhere's else she'd rather be. Simple as that. He's out there, sure enough. Waitin'. That's what yer sea master does. He waits. When she gives him the nod, well that'll be different."

The two sat in silence for a moment. Finally the old salt added, "Can't speak for Yer Honor, but as I recalls, most ever' problem I had with a woman was 'cause I shoulda waited a might longer. We could learn from yer sea master."

Sir Edmund's journal reads:

Fantastic day! The good ship, Baci has returned to Pitcairn Island. Incredible population of Euro-Polynesians; most beautiful women; men seem to be reticent to approach a British ship.

Saw a stunning sea maiden (our 33rd) swim by the bell, she apparently moving with haste!

Maidenus urgensus
"Gloria"
Dark long hair. Well-formed body. Medium height. Medium weight.
Sighted embayed at Pitcairn Island
July 18, 1834

Editor's note: *Most unfortunately, the remaining original watercolors of Sir Edmund Roberts suffered an extended immersion in seawater as a result of the great hurricane and subsequent flood that overtook Bermuda in 1874. According to the art restoration team of Lost and Found, LTD., the packing crate containing the naturalist's papers and paintings sat in three inches of water for at least a week. The principals of that same firm assure the author that with time (and copious quantities of money) the paintings will be brought back to near-pristine condition; until then the reader is asked to please be content with Sir Edmund's written descriptions.*

SIGHTING THIRTY-NINE

The trouble Gnarly Dan anticipated at Pitcairn Island was at least manageable. Many of the men were enraptured with the native women, they being of remarkable beauty. And consequently some of the crew wished to remain behind with their new loves. Captain Constance Daphne Fitzwillie had the good sense to handle the matter in a rather off-hand fashion.

She called the men to muster and stood before them a full ten minutes before she spoke. "Some of the crew of our fine vessel have let it be known they would prefer to remain behind with a new-found mate. It is their wish to in such a way avoid months more of our fine food and our luxurious accommodations." A light chuckle passed through the assembled men. "They do not long to be sent aloft in the middle of the night, a fierce hurricano in their teeth threatening to broach the good ship Baci and send us one and all into the cold depths. They do not care to sleep in narrow hammocks in the dark confines of their quarters."

She paused and looked at each of the attentive faces. "So be it;" she concluded, "the fewer men, the greater share of honor.

"We shall continue without those who remain behind. We shall sail from this splendid bay with first light and a willing tide, and once more prepare ourselves for our next encounter with that loathsome cur, the despicable pirate, Naughty Nat."

(They had forgotten about him.)

"Those of us who continue with the good ship, H.M.S. Baci, shall stand shoulder to shoulder when we find and once more thump that villainous rascal. He still has our golden treasure from the lake. And he no doubt still has untold chests of booty from untold years of pillage. God willing, we shall seize them, too. Those who continue will once more hear our thunder and know our will. We are a ship of proud men with whom no wise man would trifle. We have cold steel and hot balls for that cur. We have gunpowder and boarding axes and service muskets to serve him out as he deserves.

"He among you who has no stomach for our fight, let him depart; we would not share his company. We few, we happy few; we band of brothers shall stand with shoulders back and heads held high. And we shall prevail.

"And in the distant future, word will come back to this beautiful island paradise, of our deeds. While some lay in huts on the beach sipping from coconuts and watching the unnumbered waves roll onto the shore, we Bacis will have done our work. You who stay behind may tell your children; 'I knew those proud men. I once stood with them. I once fought at their brave side. I once looked the most heinous of evil men dead in the eye and said, *I shall not fall. But if I do, my brother who stands beside me will not. Nor will he'— "* Captain Constance Daphne was now pointing to individual sailors in the assemblage—*"nor he—nor he!"*

It worked. Not a man chose to remain behind, although there were a rare few who grumbled. Most notable was Jack Scratch, a big man with an oily pigtail and a black bandana whose game was trouble. He had joined the ship recently and would not settle in. His arms were solid tattoos, and each of them was a variation of the themes of death or torture, the more lurid involving puppies and kittens. It was apparent from the beginning that he was a rough customer with other motives. And while his presence unsettled most of the men, it was old Gnarly Dan who had his number from the start. The next morning, just prior to weighing anchor a small group was still below decks rolling their hammocks. At their center was Jack Scratch, trying to gain a following.

"They's beautiful women here what knows how ta treat a man. Ain't right we has ta go with the ship."

Simple Bob disagreed, "But Cap says we can stay. I heard her with me own ear (Simple Bob had lost one of the pair in the last altercation with Naughty Nat)."

Jack looked with menace at Simple Bob. "Then yer a one-eared fool. I say we's been had onst more. I say, we take this foul tub a' tar an' start a pirate's life."

One man gasped audibly. Another man stepped slowly back. But one man strode forward from the shadows. It was Gnarly Dan. "I knows trouble when she's hull-up, mate, an' you'd be yer own travelin' squall. Cap says ya can leave if ya wants an' I knows ya heard her. So leave or stow yer squawkin'. It'd be that easy."

Jack Scratch spun round. There was death in his eyes. "You worthless old pile a' sea bones an' spittle; I'll shut yer gob onst an' fer all!" He was actually feeling for his knife as he spoke, his back to the main mast, that stout timber extending between decks, her base below them, another deck down, her flat heel on a broad slab of wood that rested on the spine of the ship. Jack Scratch had the mast's width full to his back—the defensive posture of a man prepared to fight. He had his hand wrapped around the handle of his pirate's blade and was quickly pulling it from its scabbard when Gnarly Dan had his own blade out, balanced reversed on his open palm, aimed, and then hurled across the narrow space before anyone knew he had moved.

Jack Scratch shrieked with pain as he dropped his knife. Gnarly Dan's blade had found its mark, and that mark was Jack's starboard ear, now pinned to the main mast's hard wood by cold quivering steel. In a trice Gnarly had produced an additional blade and stood nose to nose with the pirate. "Ye may leave our fine ship if ya wishes; our Cap tole ya as much. But if ya chooses ta stay, know right well I'll be watchin' ya close. If I hears more a' yer blabberin', why she won' be pretty. I'd be too ole' with too many sea miles under me deck ta tolerate such muck as you."

The old salt pulled his blade from the wood and slowly wiped it on Scratch's shirt. "This 'worthless pile a' sea bones an' spittle' knows a trick 'er two hisself, mate; an' I ain't no puppy an' I sure as thunder ain't no kitten." With that said, he turned and walked to the aft companionway where he slowly climbed to the bright morning air.

Jack Scratch cupped his split ear and muttered, "See if ole Jack Scratch don' spit in yer beer afore we's finished."

On deck laughing men were already aloft and alow, scrambling to prepare the good ship Baci for sea. Captain Constance Daphne stood on her deck, the morning sun bringing a glow to her countenance. Sir Edmund Roberts had joined her; he quietly preoccupied with children and matrimony and still tired from an active night.

Gaskets were loosened and the yards filled with men leaning over their length, prepared to let free the good ship Baci's full set of sails.

"UP AND DOWN, CAP!" was chanted from the larboard catshead and then echoed aft as the anchor cable was pulled taut. The men at the capstan picked up a chanty as they walked the barrel-sized winch in circles. Then, "ANCHOR'S AWEIGH!" was shouted as the massive iron broke the surface at the ship's side, water and weeds dripping from its length.

"PREPARE TO SET THE MAINS'L" Constance Daphne bellowed at last, her fine chest rising handsomely with each intake of breath. "ALOFT AND LOOSE TOPS'LS AND COURSES! LIVELY THERE, ON THE MIZZEN, SIMPLE BOB! YOU THERE, MR. SCRATCH! MOVE OUT OF THAT MAN'S WAY! SHAKE A LEG IF YOU PLEASE!"

The sailor with the bandaged ear moved with an outward show of lugubrious concern, but once in the shadow of the fores'l, covertly glared at his captain. On the foretop yard Gnarly Dan looked over his shoulder and caught the sailor's eye and watched until he quickened his pace.

The good ship Baci came around, stuffed the free wind into her straining sails and left Bounty Bay in her foamy wake. They were at sea once more and charting a course for Papeete and the Society Islands where another bevy of beautiful women and more adventure awaited them.

Jack Scratch avoided Gnarly Dan for the most part and he was relatively quiet, but he had identified Sir Edmund Roberts as the old salt's friend and a particularly weak link in the ship's complement of fighting men. Twice he bumped heavily into the naturalist and then the third time he actually knocked the naturalist's glass from his hands as he studied a distant wave.

"My god, man, steady there!" Sir Edmund snapped, more concerned with the condition of his telescope than the actual affront he'd suffered.

Jack Scratch looked about to be certain none of the ship's officers were near and then laughed openly. "A smart cove such as Yer Highness oughts to stay outta a workin' tar's way." He glared defiantly at Sir Edmund who was only now realizing it had not been an accident.

"My good man," he began slowly, "were we ashore I fear I would demand satisfaction."

"An' you'd have much ta be a'feared!" Jack Scratch hissed, puffing out his chest and stepping up to Sir Edmund.

"We are crowded aboard a very small ship, sir; there is little enough room for a quarrel with pistols or swords."

The pirate laughed with hearty derision. "How I know'd you'd fold at the knees, mate! Too bad the Cap'n ain't about ta fight yer battle!"

Sir Edmund was at first overwhelmed by the magnitude of the sailor's pluck, but slowly he gathered his wits and pulled himself back a step and then coldly looked the stocky sailor over from his bare calloused feet to his black bandana.

"You, sir," Sir Edmund said levelly, "are an ill-bred clod. Were we on land, I would part your hair from fifty paces or run you through a time or two at closer quarters. We are, however, at sea (though you may not have noticed) and so all that is left for me is to ask you if I might have the pleasure of teaching you some manners by way of a sound drubbing . . . I hope you understand the term . . . to put it more succinctly; let us have at it like men . . . with our bare hands."

Jack Scratch could not have been happier. He immediately imagined his thumbs in the naturalist's eyes, and a litany of other low tricks.

A small crowd had now gathered, Gnarly Dan among them. He spoke quietly to the naturalist, "Could be this ain't yer best idea, Yer Honor; what with it bein' a fight an' all."

Sir Edmund answered, he too speaking quietly, "Your concern is appreciated and duly noted, my good Mr. Gnarly. There has, however, been an affront and I intend to make things right."

And so it was arranged; hand to hand tussling after the evening ration of grog, the event taking place with the captain's permission on the foredeck.

Captain Constance Daphne Fitzwillie was not amused but she did assent. "Will you men never tire of mocking your maturity?" She looked long at Sir Edmund, her paramour, the man whose hands could please her, and instructed. "Do what you will, Sir Edmund; I shall not recommend you use care for I have learned enough of you to suspect you do not stray where you have not already tread often."

That evening, grog (a double ration!) was served out to a buzzing, anxious crew. Wagers swept through the good ship Baci, Jack Scratch being the favorite hands down, his own notoriety expanding greatly with the event.

"'Bout time we teach some manners aft a' the mast," he bragged, massaging his rough hands and glaring at those who surrounded him. He pretended to tear the poor naturalist limb from limb, knocked his beaten body to the deck, kicked him a time or two and then spit in his thumb-swollen eyes.

To no one's surprise, Captain Constance Daphne Fitzwillie was present when the gathering was accomplished; she of course dressed handsomely for the occasion. Sir Edmund waited patiently for the rough sailor to appear. The naturalist wore rather tight trowsers, had removed his shirt, and did a series of odd exercises, obviously foreign in origin. He was a tall man, but hardly big. He was muscled lightly, his upper body pale to the early evening sun.

At last a crowd jostled up from below decks, Jack Scratch in its midst and then at its fore. For all of his evil, he was impressive in physique. He had stripped off his shirt, an encyclopedia of horrendous illustrations covering his entire upper body (not visible were his favorites: two interlocking hearts on his right and left heavily muscled, hairy buttocks with Nasty Natalie on the larboard cheek and Naughty Natalie on its twin). As he moved and flexed his muscles a panoply of dragons and villains did battle on his body.

Sir Edmund, of course, had no visible tattoos, though there was an unsettling array of ragged scars and puncture wounds on his chest.

The two men faced off, a wide ring of sailors surrounding them. Captain Constance Daphne actually started the event. "Have you men yet reached an agreement?" she asked.

"His Honor has agreed to be hurt bad!" Jack Scratch answered with surly superiority and looked around with a broad grin of anticipation.

Sir Edmund responded simply, "It appears words only deepen his dilemma and amplify his risk."

With Captain Constance Daphne's assent the fight began. Sir Edmund stood as upright as the good Baci's main mast, while the pirate crouched low and warily began a slow circle around the naturalist. Then he bellowed and charged, his countenance so fierce the ship's boy actually averted his eyes. Constance Daphne narrowed hers, her concern masked.

It appeared Sir Edmund was about to be plowed through when the naturalist took a deft half-step forward and caught the villain early with the fastest cross-right blow to the chin the crew had ever seen (more accurately, *wished* they had seen) and in a trice the formerly threatening, charging, foul-mouthed Jack Scratch was on his back and as silent as the broad pennant at the foremast truck. He had been knocked cleanly off his feet and rendered doubly unconscious; first by Sir Edmund's blow and second, when the back of his head anticipated and then cushioned his fall to the deck.

The crew stood for a moment in stunned silence. They could only believe the pirate had slipped, but then they noticed Sir Edmund carefully examining and blowing on his right hand, finally shaking it gently.

"I would rather have stuck a cannon ball," he mused. "I believe iron would be a bit more giving."

Gnarly Dan was relieved beyond description.

Captain Constance Daphne smiled broadly, anticipating a just reward for her gentleman.

One of the two stepped to the naturalist and to everyone's surprise, hugged him.

Sir Edmund struggled to free himself. "Please, Mr. Dan, control your elation."

Not a soul so much as bent to Jack Scratch's outstretched body. And so he lay unmoving on the fore deck for half of the evening. Morning found him in his hammock. He was shunned henceforth as a bad omen, those who had bet on him so much the sorrier. Behind his back he was now referred to as 'Jack Scratched', his defeat by Sir Edmund and his encounter with Gnarly Dan's knife a burden he carried silently as he planned his sweet revenge.

Fair weather, then foul, then fair again accompanied the H.M.S. Baci as she plowed through the warm Pacific toward her next island stop. At last the masthead hail, "LAND HO! THREE POINTS TO LARBOARD!" greeted the crew one clear afternoon.

It was make-and-mend day, so the crew was already disposed to rouse out their best outfits, they by consensus establishing white trowsers, red and white horizontally striped shirts and red beribboned hats as their unofficial uniform.

Palm lined atolls and islands hove into view and then the usual small-breasted tan native women swam out to the Baci as she backed her sails smartly, lost most of her weigh and then let loose her starboard anchor. The good ship settled slowly back onto her heavy cable as the smiling natives hurried up its length. Sir Edmund was the first to notice the unusually forward friendliness the women possessed, they seemingly extraordinarily content.

Their good nature only compounded the naturalist's difficulty in bribing sufficient crew members to help him prepare Halley's patented diving apparatus for his first descent, so many of the ship's boats already in the process of being readied for the short pull to the white sand beach. He did in time manage to start his first in a series of dives. But for nearly a week he had no success in sighting sea maidens, their population apparently shunning the good ship Baci; and while that was tedious in and of itself, again and again the naturalist heard the native population call out to him something that sounded like, "shooney bwego, shooney bwego" as they pointed to the water around them. It was of course left for Gnarly Dan to find a way to interpret the words. After two days ashore the old salt returned, apparently sated in all respects and puffed up with his new knowledge. He did however wait until the captain was safely out of earshot before he confided in the naturalist. "Bad news, Yer Honor; 'shooney bwego' means 'handsome sea god', and the women-folk here 'bouts are powerful pleased ta have him visit. Seems there'd be a certain stinginess concernin' the availability a' sea maidens in these waters this time a' year (they's at a sea maiden meetin' a' some sort) an' it appears yer unattached sea master is a bit on the lonely side. Seems he spends more'n a little time pleasin' the local lasses (they comes down to the beach at night, wades in a ways an' he takes his pick). An' there ain't a complaint ta be heard. The men-folk consider him powerful good luck an' so they's happy ta lend him a wife 'er two. He sends 'em back in better shape than he gets 'em, so I'm told."

The old salt stole a look back to where Captain Constance Daphne Fitzwillie now paced her quarterdeck. "If you recalls, Squire, the last time our Cap took an interest in yer sea masters, the crew mutinied an' left us ta fend fer ourselves. Won't do ta push 'em again. I say we weigh anchor an' tell her they's better pickens a few weeks north a' here."

Sir Edmund was entirely discommoded. It had been his intention to formally request the Captain's hand within the week and it wouldn't bode well to have the remainder of her glorious body preoccupied.

As he thought of her 'preoccupation', his imagination strayed to the thought of her stealing to the beach on a moonlit night for a rendez-vous with the undersea king of romance. Stopping the pirate Jack Scratch required only a deftly delivered right hook. But Sir Edmund was wise enough to know the sea master was not to be so easily deterred. And then, if what Gnarly Dan suggested were true, and a meeting of captain and sea master took place, the naturalist would have the remainder of his life to know he was forever being compared to a certain balmy night in the arms of an accomplished sea master.

The whole thing was nearly beyond endurance. Sir Edmund was in some ways a typical man; unsure of his prowess and uninterested in improving himself in that department. "If a charge at full gallop did the trick for Wellington at Waterloo, well then!"

All he could say to Gnarly Dan was, "Let me give this some thought, my good man. Surely we don't wish to compromise our captain. Nor should we jeopardize the remainder of our voyage. Perhaps there is a solution. I shall sleep on it."

Oh, that life could be so easy for the naturalist. Not fifteen minutes later the incredibly handsome sea master in question leaped from the sea less that a stone's toss from Captain Constance Daphne Fitzwillie. And in the moment before he reentered the water, he caught her eye. No man who saw the twinkle in the sea master's eye, or caught the broad grin on his face had any doubt as to its effect on Captain Constance Daphne.

She flushed. She smiled. She felt herself gloriously naked and yet intolerably clothed. Her hands sought her—they seemed lost, unable to reach their intended destination and so they settled onto her hips. They stayed but momentarily.

She crossed her arms across her magnificent chest and then finally, she raised a fist to her mouth and bit her thumb as she looked to the spreading ripples and smiled. "Sir Edmund," she called out softly at last, "please be so good as to rouse out Mr. Halley's patented diving apparatus. I have a need to enter the sea."

Sir Edmund was dumbstruck. He walked as a man in a stupor, absently giving orders to those associated with his submersible bell. Surprisingly, old Gnarly Dan would have none of remaining on the surface.

"I remembers what you said at ole Bermuda Harbour, Cap: 'Inna the breach onst more!'" The old salt fairly beamed with his ability to remember something so distant. "So lively there, you slab-sided tars, what we got ta get our Cap unner the sea again!"

Fortune denied a sighting that afternoon, and the next. However, reports from the locals were that the sea master was about, quite active at night, and not a woman had a complaint, save Captain Constance Daphne Fitzwillie. And while Sir Edmund did not suspect she had heard of the sea master's nocturnal forays, it did seem a bit odd that she strolled the beaches ashore before returning to the ship each night.

There was one night for which there is no report, affirmative or otherwise, and then the following day Sir Edmund, old Gnarly Dan, and Captain Constance Daphne Fitzwillie descended in Halley's patented diving bell and saw the elusive sea master once more. He glided beneath them as if he knew more than he was letting on. Then he swam beside the bell and hovered at its perimeter. He feigned disinterest but it was obvious the show was for those encapsulated.

Gnarly Dan slowly took in his breath. He scratched the stubble at his chin, squinted through one bleary eye and whispered, "There'd be no doubtin' why them local gals is pleased by His Honor."

Without thinking, Captain Constance Daphne added, "I know."

Sir Edmund attempted to persuade himself he had not heard. He fidgeted nervously. At last he said, "The bell's bottom is open. Perhaps the captain would prefer other company."

He did not intend to sound as angry and offended as he was. He had, in fact, thought of his remark as a reasonable suggestion. Constance Daphne eyed him coldly.

"It is small wonder," she sighed, "that men undervalue performance so remarkably. You are not unlike a child discounting the next town as far less attractive than their own."

At that moment and for a few after, Sir Edmund Roberts, gentleman naturalist and sea maiden questor, would have traded the company of his captain for that of someone as undesired as Jack Scratch.

Finally the sea master glided off into the gloom and the three in the bell sat in cold silence for an eternity before Gnarly Dan muttered something about 'the calm afore the storm'.

They signaled to the surface for the apparatus to be raised. It was, and the three separated as if avoiding a pox.

Sir Edmund's journal reads:

Another sighting. Sea master. He quite unremarkable in my eyes, though others may disagree.

Magnus mediocratus

Medium height.   Forgettable hair.   Insignificant weight.   Average swimmer.
Sighted neat Papeete of the Society Islands.
September 5, 1834
Sea Master number nine

SIGHTING FORTY

There followed a series of arguments and uncomfortably long periods of pique, the captain walking nightly on the beach, Sir Edmund retreating to his work, his little oil lamp burning late as he reviewed his notes and organized his observations, all the while attempting to ignore the significance of the absence of his captain. There were no more sea maiden or sea master sightings (by the naturalist) at the Society Islands and when the good ship Baci at last sailed from her waters the two principals of the ship were once more figuratively alone with one another. The solitude of the sea, its vast stretches of water and open skies may either facilitate forgiveness or foment deeply buried wounds. For the naturalist and the captain, it was an arbiter; they were once again quite intimate; though Sir Edmund had not as yet returned to the subject of matrimony. The Sandwich Islands (Hawaii, etc.) lay ahead; the stories of her bounty, beautiful women and balmy climate an elixir for the most tedious work. Jack Scratch was meanwhile laying low, his only comments being those made to his small coterie of hangers-on, and they no less the dregs of the ship than those which scurried aboard along the mooring lines at every port.

None of this in any way intimates that Captain Constance Daphne Fitzwillie did not in reality have an encounter with the fabled sea master. In fact, her last evening before the Baci's morning departure did find her alone, walking a long and lonely stretch of beach. While her mind was not directly on the sea master; if one were to consider an oblique bank shot of fantasy, the good fellow would have been seen swimming just a bit to the port side of the corner pocket. The moon was rising and full and the sea was as tranquil as a millpond. Long gentle rollers washed softly up the beach and streaks of iridescence danced on the breaking waves. Constance Daphne was awash in melancholy, her life at last satisfactory but her past still an unpleasant burden. Sir Edmund Roberts was on her mind; his gentlemanly characteristics, his good manners and his aloof yet boyishly intimate way of standing in her presence pleasing to recall. It was as she toyed with the thought of marrying him that an errant reflection caught her eye. There, beyond the first row of breakers the moonlight played on the shining hair of her sea master.

He was watching her intently, it apparent he had been doing so for some time. She stopped short, making no attempt to disguise that she too was now aware of the other. She turned full to him, her breath already coming more deeply. They stood for some time studying one another across the distance, the whispering of the settling waves the only sound. At last the captain, entirely captivated and, feeling ridiculous to be standing clothed in the night air, began to walk carefully to the water's edge, a ragged trail of her garments marking her path as they fell.

Robert Kline

By the time her feet entered the warm water she was unencumbered and with no fear as to that which she wished to do. The sea caressed her ankles and then her calves, her knees and at last her pale thighs as she moved forward. All the while the sea master glided carefully toward her, his interest enigmatic and immediately intoxicating.

And while we can describe in some detail that which followed, we are inclined to inform the voyeur that what took place does not allow itself to be included in what is conventionally refered to as a 'sexual union'; have no fear that anything tawdry or ill-considered might wend its way into our narration.

Captain Constance Daphne Fitzwillie was simply taken on a very private journey. Where she went was beyond all of her previous experiences, past that which she ever imagined and beyond her ability to adequately recall. Much later, when she found herself once more on the sandy beach it was to her as the morning after the finest dream—the sort of dream that takes a person back to glorious childhood or pleasant memories so laden with good feelings and steeped in joy that we sadly curse the morning and our wakefulness.

She waded past the combers that night, the heat of the water immediately embracing her. Before she knew it she was to her waist and her sea master before her. He was neither old nor young; he was simply a man. His features were strong yet gentle and he was assured. He reached a hand to the captain and waited patiently for her to take it. When at last she did he held it and allowed her to become familiar with his touch. When she could no longer tell where her fingers ended and his began he carefully opened his own, the barely curved plain of his hand toward her. He waited, looking at her face, absorbing her features as well as her mood and her silent needs. Unbidden and for a reason she did not understand, she knew what her sea master wished for her to do next. She took his hand and first raised it to her cheek and brushed down the side of her face. From there, and after she had felt him warm her skin, she placed his hand on her neck and then she moved it tenderly to the beginnings of the valley above her rising breasts. Again he waited. She knew he was sensing her preliminary softness and yet it was as if he were already holding her; cupping her fully in his tentatively outstretched hand.

His other hand was to her now and it was at her waist, firmly molding itself and then entreating her to lean to him, to come to him, to banish the water from between them.

Constance Daphne now felt his strong chest counter to the vulnerability of her own. He brought her to him and she felt the charge of his presence flow through her as a warm dawning of a summer day. And then she knew he was on his back slightly inclined but swimming backward, bringing her to him and propelling them past the nearness of the shore, out to the realm that was truly his.

Surely, Constance Daphne closed her eyes now. She moved her lips to the salty wetness of his upper shoulder and cradled her head to him. She sensed the broad powerful sweeps of his tail as he moved them out of the bay and into the sea. She could not imagine how he could have been more than against her but she knew he was—knew they were moving together in that which was not merely swimming.

And yet the sea master was not taking her as anyone who had not had such an experience could explain. It was more that he was giving her. He was giving the captain her beauty, her love, her sensitivity; giving to her a sense of self, the likes of which she had never dared to dream. He was offering up to her his knowledge of that which should have been hers to give. Constance Daphne suckled the new confidence of knowing herself and the refreshing fulfillment of loving what was recently discovered in her own heart.

Even the open sea was calm that night. The moon set silently and the sharp stars pierced the water around them. The sea master moved with increased determination and Constance Daphne felt his mouth at her neck and then moving below. She clung to him, wrapping her arms across his back. Gradually she felt his back broaden as their relative positions changed. His head was flat against her stomach while he carefully held her from the water. The hot sea moved past them, roiling as it eddied at the sides of her neck. Then for a moment she felt he was not with them; that he had swum away, for he was no longer sharing the night air with her.

She realized at last he was still there, though under the sea. Carefully she felt herself being turned so she was now parting the water with her own back. He was beneath her—but holding her as they swept through the waves and the darkness. She felt herself being raised gently from the water, she now nearly flying above it. And then the seas increased and it was as if they were in a storm, the waters wild and beckoning. Giant waves careened past them, breaking and crashing to their sides. The wind would have howled had it a voice. It was then as the sea tossed about them that she became truly aware of his strength as he protected her in its midst.

And then it was calm once more. Constance Daphne opened her eyes to the night sky. Constellations wheeled silently above them. Shooting stars gradually accomplished one horizon and then another.

Later, they turned again and his dark hair pushed the water aside to flow past his glistening shoulders. They embraced and she could sense that the beach was once more near. She wished to sleep then, to silently weep, to be allowed to drift to the shore of her own accord. But he did not allow her that release. Instead they moved parallel to the breakers, just outside of where they rose before they leaned to reach for the land. And now the captain and her sea master looked at one other; not with curiosity or even satisfaction. It was that they knew. He knew her heart and her loneliness and she now knew his and in that sharing she realized he would be with her forever. He brought her to him a last time as they moved with the swell of the breakers and he held her above them and with the retreating sea left her lying on the beach.

The wave returned and Captain Constance Daphne Fitzwillie did not attempt to see if her sea master had paused to look back. Because it was a warm night she moved higher on the beach and allowed herself to dry.

When she was back to her ship and in her own quarters she did not permit herself to remember their night. Instead she thought of her quirky naturalist and smiled sadly and finally went to sleep as the good ship Baci rocked beneath them all.

Captain Constance Daphne wished desperately to remain in her quarters that morning, for her bed held her closely. But the Baci was destined to sail. The crew was aloft and alow, drinking in the beginning of their next adventure and anxious for their captain to appear and pace her sacred quarterdeck. When at last she did they were relieved, one and all; none more so than Sir Edmund Roberts, gentleman naturalist and sea maiden questor.

The Baci departed her anchorage under low scudding clouds as the first of the weeks of rain they were to endure swept over them. Sails were loosed into sheets of the warm spray. The men in the foretop squinted back into it and saw that it was going to be more than a squall. Those working on the deck welcomed its cooling effect as the tar between the seams finally cooled and hardened. The crew was at first entertained by their drenching, and some even capered about as fools, but as they continued preparing the ship for the next leg of her journey it began to be felt as a nuisance. Soaked bandanas were wrung out and then stuffed into leather belts. By the third day every man-jack among them was praying for the sun.

On and on they sailed through weeks of wet weather. When at last it was rumored they should be hailing land soon nervousness infected the crew. It had been too long since they had heard of the whereabouts of that loathsome cur, Naughty Nat. Added to that was the fresh smugness of Jack Scratch. There was no question he was expecting a change in his fortunes soon, so much so that his attitude attracted the attention of Gnarly Dan.

Though he had never done so before, the old salt went to Sir Edmund with his concerns. "It warn't that I'd be sure, Yer Honor; but somethin' ain't right, an' that dog Scratch is likely at the bottom of it an'up ta no good. If I had ta lay me pay against it I'd wager our ole friend Naughty Nat is somewheres abouts preparin' ta pay us a visit."

It was, of course, an unsettling proposition. The Sandwich Islands were the perfect haunt for the likes of the despicable pirate, with plenty of places for him to make his plans and spring his trap. Sir Edmund had been able to accomplish little regarding his work toward secret weapons and such things, so he fell back to stealth and surprise. For days he studied the charts, attempting to think as the loathsome pirate might. At last it was far too obvious for him. He informed Captain Constance Daphne.

"That cur is here now or soon to be, my beloved captain. And I am sure he is afloat in a vessel more threatening than his previous dreadnaughts. I have a plan and if you approve I believe a bold move on our part could save the day."

Constance Daphne studied the naturalist's assumptions and ideas as the two looked at the charts spread before them. At last the captain acquiesced. "It is an incredible idea with untold risks and I am not entirely pleased with the danger into which you are placing yourself. Multiple assumptions and untried scientific calculations are at the crux of this; I trust you truly have faith in the theories you are espousing."

Sir Edmund was quiet for a moment before he answered. Captain Constance Daphne had an unsettling beauty, the kind that when wed with intelligence is totally disconcerting. Consequently there was a part of the man that wished he could remove the two of them from their current dilemma without the injection of further risk; for the first time in his life he longed for the respite of domestic bliss.

He abandoned those hopes, pursed his lips briefly and then answered, "We need a broad hull, an artillery piece of heroic proportions, much sailcloth, and more than a little tar. Plus ballast, a capstan and sufficient heavy rope."

Captain Constance Daphne smiled grimly. "I believe, sir, we can satisfy your needs."

Sir Edmund countered in half-jest, "Oh, that yours were so easily addressed!"

The enterprise actually eclipsed the naturalist's sea maiden quest as he further refined his knowledge of buoyancy.

The fair Baci reached the outlying islands of the chain within the week and Captain Constance Daphne set about satisfying her part of the equation. First, a derelict intra-island brig was rescued from some rather unscrupulous traders. Then a capital 32 pound (the weight of her shot; it being roughly the size of a grapefruit) cannon was blackmailed from an ancient fortified outpost on the biggest of the islands. (As a point of reference, the largest cannon the Baci could safely carry and fire from her decks was a mosquito compared to the huge iron artillery piece now stowed dangerously in the Baci's hold.) With nearly everything he had requested available, the good ship then surreptitiously slipped beyond the prying eyes of those about the islands.

They located a remote embayed beach and set to work. The long and short of it was that within a week the hull of the brig was reinforced, the masts removed and then decked over flush. The whole of the vessel was then tarred heavily, making her as watertight as a waxed cork. She was then pulled out to the Baci, and as she bobbed at the ship's side the huge cannon was swayed out from the hold and assembled and lowered onto the little craft's waiting deck. As the tiny hull took the cannon's weight she settled lower and lower into the water. By the time the huge gun rested firmly on her decks the craft was, as Sir Edmund had hoped, close to being awash. The gun was then secured between the stout rails Sir Edmund hoped would help to control its recoil. Because the brig was beamy and relatively long there was a reasonable amount of stability to the whole affair.

It was, as Sir Edmund explained it, ready to be sunk. As with many brilliant plans, its strength was in its simplicity: The naturalist intended to tow the weapon to the channel between two islands, attach it to an incredibly heavy mound of ballast, and then pull the whole thing, cannon and brig, under water and secure it to the sea bottom. If Naughty Nat sailed past as hoped, cables would be released at the propitious moment and the weapon would pop to the surface in the pirate's wake; whereupon miraculously appearing gunners would quickly man and fire it at close range into the pirate vessel's vulnerable stern, causing such immediate and devastating damage that the craft would, to Naughty Nat's chagrin, sink from under him like a rock in a bucket.

The devil, of course, was in the details: The cannon would have to be loaded and then waterproofed. Sufficient manpower would have to secret itself in an adjacent attached diving apparatus. And there could be positively no leaks in either.

And then the matter of timing:

It all hinged on where the loathsome pirate was currently and how soon he could be lured into a trap. Gnarly Dan, apprised of the naturalist's plan, felt the answer was already aboard the Baci.

"That vermin eatin' scum, Jack Scratch'd have an idea 'er two concerning the whereabouts 'a our friend, Mr. Nat. An' I believes I got a way ta persuade the rat inta discussin' with us a bit."

Sir Edmund was interested. "My good fellow, Mr. Scratch is rather tight with his information, wouldn't you agree?"

Gnarly Dan rubbed the scruffle of whiskers on his chin and grinned. "Does Yer Honor happen ta recall the matter 'a Mr. Scratch an' his recent tumble inna the drink?"

Of course Sir Edmund did. Who could forget the pathetic spectacle? As sometimes happens, a sailor lost his footing and his grip together while balanced at the yardarm tip, some distance above the sea; and while some sailors can remain afloat in their unnatural element, content as clams in muck, others cannot. And a rare few positively panic when wet. Such a man was Jack Scratch. From his pitiful wailing and pleading as he thrashed about, one would assume he had never been damp in his life.

"I do indeed remember that performance," Sir Edmund admitted.

"Well, Squire," Gnarly Dan whispered in confidence, "what say we moisten the pirate a bit an' see if it don't loosen his tongue!"

Having served the King on many occasions, the naturalist was not averse to blurring the line between a question or two and bald-faced torture.

The partnership between the old salt and the naturalist had matured to the point that they readily agreed upon a plan. As luck would have it, Jack Scratch was asleep in his hammock that very moment, his rumbling, phlegm-laden snores signaling his state. With the help of a handful of trusty swabs, Sir Edmund and Gnarly Dan had the pirate blindfolded, gagged and trussed tightly in his hammock before he could awaken and attempt to protect himself. Next his hammock was cut from its moorings and that cocoon was carried to the deck where a rope was attached to the struggling man's ankles. His gag was removed and he was hoisted aloft and swayed out over the side of the good ship. By now Jack Scratch was aware of his predicament and also suspicious of what was about to happen.

It was a relatively calm night, with the Baci swaying gently at her anchorage. The myriad of sounds produced by the idle ship did not mask the equally complex tune of the ocean.

Profound concern embraced the pirate. "Not the sea, mates!" Jack entreated. He felt his body lowered. "I'd be a sorry lubber for all I've done," he begged. Panic began to wend its way into his countenance. He whipped his bound body about like an inchworm stuck in sap. "Anything but the sea!" he moaned. "I'd threaten ta kill ya, but I'm sure-certain it wouldn't have no effect!" he cried. Once again he was lowered. "I can't drown! It wouldn't be right! Don't put me with the fishes! Not the fishes!"

And then, after an errant wave drenched his head, the sly, cruel, sadistic, over-bearing pirate became unhinged.

"Oh please," he blubbered. "I swear on me mother's broken heart I'll do anything—just raise me back to the deck. Don't dunk me again!" Before long his body fairly convulsed with his sobbing. Rare words and phrases escaped him. "Forgive. No good. Worthless. One chanst!" And then he totally lost control, even his very intake of breath plaintive and pleading.

So far, no one but the pirate had spoken. At last Sir Edmund began. "You sir, are a curse to our fine crew and a blight on our ship. Since you have repeatedly demonstrated you are not with us; I can only assume you are against us." To accentuate his last statement the naturalist had Jack Scratch dipped to his shoulders. After the pirate ceased crying Sir Edmund continued. "And if you are against us I further assume you are with that scoundrel —"

The naturalist did not need to finish his sentence for Jack Scratch did it for him. "Naughty Nat! Naughty Nat! I been with Naughty Nat these many years. He raised me from a baby. Me Da left us and me Ma was 'et by gypsies. I got no goodness left in me. Nat beat it outta me." Now the pirate lost control again, crying and whimpering, "No more water! Please! Don't do 'er! I ain't truly bad. I just never had no chanst ta really be good." Then he said the most remarkable thing: "I wanted ta be good, an' more 'n anything afloat I just wished an' wished ever' night I had a puppy or a kitty like a reg'lar kid. Nat always beat me when I tole him that. That's why I got all them bad tattoos; Naughty Nat made me get 'em; said nobody was afeared a' no soft body."

The sad pirate swung quietly for a moment as Sir Edmund, Gnarly Dan and the other sailors helping them absorbed what they had just learned. At last Sir Edmund had Jack Scratch raised and swung back over the Baci's deck. He lowered the pirate until he was at eye level, though inverted. Sir Edmund reached to him and carefully undid his blindfold. Jack Scratch's eyes were red and swollen. His hair dripped saltwater.

"Mr. Scratch," Sir Edmund began, his skills as a master interrogator immediately apparent, "you have before you, for the first time in your wretchedly long life, an opportunity to do something honorable; something good for your fellow man for which you may feel justly proud. And I do inform you, as one honorable man to another, Mr. Scratch, that if you do what I ask you will find yourself on the right side of life. You need never again sneer nor pretend to hate that which you desire with such passion. Do what we ask you, Mr. Scratch; help us, and by the power vested in me as an English gentleman by birth, I promise, I pledge, I do guarantee that I personally will procure for you, for your own, to care for and take full responsibility and guardianship of, a soft, cuddly puppy and if you wish, a warm and most likely snuggly kitten. You may name said animals and you may encourage them to share your hammock."

As the naturalist paused and drew in his breath he noticed the pirate's hammock was sodden. "And you'll get a nice dry hammock, too, sir."

Since time immemorial, there were never gifts so well received.

The one-time pirate, Jack William Scratch, was a changed man from that moment forth. He immediately and fully divulged that Naughty Nat was only days behind them, that Jack was to slip away within the fortnight and inform the "miserable dog" (Jack's own words) where the good Baci could be found so Naughty Nat could bring his newest ship into action. She was, as Sir Edmund had feared, a larger vessel with even more pirates and larger guns. She was called the Last 'a Kiss, so-named because of Naughty Nat's obsession with destroying the H.M.S, Baci.

At first Sir Edmund thought the name was bad Italian, but he quickly came to realize Nat was implying his latest ship would see to the last *of* Kiss (Baci)!

Gnarly Dan added his own cleverness to the intrigue by pointing out to Jack Scratch that the ship's cat had given birth just the week before and he could immediately choose a kitten for his own if he wished, adding levelly, "Though ye may pick 'er out, mate; we'll keep 'er all safe-like till ya returns."

Sir Edmund, although he remained stone faced, covertly smiled at the old salt's wisdom.

So the secret was out and the suspicions confirmed. Now it only wanted the naturalist to set the trap.

Scratch was sent off in a dingy to begin his subterfuge. The cannon and its brig were towed to the previously designated channel between two islands. Mountains of rocks were loaded into an old sail and lowered at the correct spot, heavy ropes attached to the mound to be used to winch down the brig, etc. A small version of Halley's patented diving apparatus was assembled and readied (it was decided Sir Edmund Roberts and Gnarly Dan would be just adequate to aim the craft and fire the cannon when necessary.)

All that was left to do was wait. And wait. And wait.

The final refinement was that the Baci would anchor at the opposite end of the channel, plainly visible and a sore temptation for that loathsome cur, Naughty Nat to proceed without regard for caution.

Days passed and all that happened was Sir Edmund Roberts came close to strangling Gnarly Dan. Once Sir Edmund actually stood up in the little punt in which they were bobbing about. His intention was to grasp the old salt and wrestle him into the surrounding sea, but instead he lost his balance and nearly fell overboard. Gnarly Dan quickly grabbed and steadied Sir Edmund, admonishing, "Calm there, Squire, wouldn't do ta have ya fall in an' drown afore we gets ta thump ole Mr. Nat!"

The naturalist was humbled sufficiently to be able to endure two more days of his companion's non-stop chatter, learning grudgingly about the old salt's three current wives, his twelve children, his long and actually quite distinguished naval career, enough superstitious clap to last him a lifetime, and finally, that the crew was indeed anxious for Sir Edmund and Captain Constance Daphne to formalize their apparent union with a ceremony ("Yer common gob dearly loves ta be in on somethin' official-like! Ain't often we gets ta do more'n hear the music from a respectful distance," he added with a misty sound to his voice).

And then at last, on a sunny afternoon, Naughty Nat made his appearance. As anticipated he sailed directly from the Big Island where he was supposed to rendez-vous with Jack Scratch. And as expected, Last a' Kiss was larger than his previous vessel. One by one her huge sails popped up at the horizon, and when at last she was hull-up, it was apparent she could requite herself quite well against a ship twice the size of the poor Baci.

Sir Edmund and Gnarly Dan accessed their small diving bell, set free their tiny boat to be carried away by the tidal current and then waited until Naughty Nat was within an hour of passing through the channel and the trap before they released the attached casks of air, allowing them to sink slowly to the top of the submerged brig and cannon. Tar had been slathered around the business end of the cannon, and then a canvas mitten applied, it then also smothered in tar for waterproofing. As noted earlier, the powder bag had been thoroughly waxed before insertion, and the touchhole on the gun similarly protected. In a word, the big weapon should by all accounts be ready to fire once raised.

The little bell rested, as planned, aft of the gun. Sir Edmund and the old salt had an abundance of air, as a trail of bubbles was escaping from the ship beneath them and into the bell.

ESCAPING FROM THE SHIP BENEATH THEM!

Both men immediately understood its threat. "My good man," Sir Edmund whispered (unnecessarily), "there now exists the possibility sufficient air has already escaped and our weapon will fail to rise when necessary, putting the good Baci and our fine captain and crew in grave danger."

Gnarly Dan often used sarcasm when he was particularly worried. "Thought a' that yerself did ya, Yer Honor?" he answered to the naturalist's withering stare.

The gravity of their discovery was significant enough that Sir Edmund restrained himself from countering the old salt's jibe. "The question before us is if we should immediately release the ballast and see if we still have a weapon available, and if so, thence maneuver said weapon in a semi-circle and do battle bow-on with that rascal."

They both pondered that possibility briefly. Bowshots were liable to glance from the curved stem of the approaching ship, defeating their advantage (the flat stern of the ship accepted round shot willingly, the ball then passing unhampered through the remainder of the vessel). Neither occupant of the bell gave a thought to their own danger as the Last a' Kiss would no doubt subsequently ram them, all the while allowing its crew to practice small and large arms gunnery on the hapless two.

Gnarly Dan voiced their best option. "I say we waits an' tries ta pop up just as she's overhead. Should surface by the time she's past."

It was agreed, although both knew timing was now critical, the big ship certainly silent when she passed overhead. No sooner did they mention that when dull thuds were heard.

"That'd be Baci's broadside," Gnarly Dan exclaimed.

Unbeknownst to them, Captain Constance Daphne had altered her own plans. She did not intend, as she put it, "to let those two madmen have all the fun!" She had a stern anchor rigged placing the Baci side-on a half mile beyond the channel, thus allowing full use of 50 percent of her meager armament. She had commenced firing long before the Last a' Kiss was within their range, her intention to keep the loathsome pirate's attention from the casks and small boat that had inexplicably returned to where they were released, for all the world marking Sir Edmund's and Gnarly Dan's whereabouts.

Unfortunately, Naughty Nat's bow chasers were far more powerful than the Baci's peashooters. They came within range and began punishing their nemesis. The pirates' second shot took the head off the Baci's beautiful figurehead, leaving her luscious body otherwise intact. (It would later be remarked by more than one sailor that she was now the ideal woman.)

The situation deteriorated further rather quickly. Number four-gun crew was nearly eliminated when a ball from the pirate struck and upended their cannon. Then the mizzen top was hit and came down with half of its rigging. The rudder was holed as was much of the Baci's side above the waterline. Captain Constance Daphne stood on her quarterdeck fully exposed to the pirate's wrath, her bounteous chest also vulnerable as much of it had worked free of her constraining Royal Navy coat. But the men bent to their weapons and again and again they sent forth the Baci's iron, it at last reaching the Last a' Kiss, though it did little more than bounce from her stout sides or dishevel her rigging.

The pirate ship was almost to where the naturalist and the old salt were submerged, they nearly insane from waiting. The sounds of the battle tortured them as they stood poised to release all of the ballast from gun, ship and bell. At last they could stand no more. "I can wait not a second longer!" Sir Edmund barked as he released his lines.

"Time fer us ta do battle!" Gnarly Dan whooped as he too freed his lines.

But nothing happened. The bell was now secured to the brig deck and so it could not rise on its own; and the boat beneath them was going nowhere. Naturalist and sailor looked to one another in the guttering lamplight.

And then they felt movement under their feet as the brig sucked free of the ocean bottom. Up and up they went, finally popping to the surface.

A meter before the oncoming Last a' Kiss.

The naturalist and the old salt released and tipped the big diving barrel to the side, the bright mid-day sun then blinding them to their peril. Naughty Nat's huge ship slammed to the side of the brig and cannon, starting it spinning as the Last a' Kiss passed. Sir Edmund was nearly thrown from the side of the cannon, as was Gnarly Dan. The pirates' bow chaser fired directly over their heads deafening them. Again their craft bounced against the side of the ship, its tumblehome still masking them from those above. And then the ship passed, but not without sucking the now slowly spinning brig into its wake. The turbulence was such that while it arrested their revolutions, it also kept them snugged to the pirate ship's stern, it now towering above them, the huge wooden rudder post barely two arms' lengths away.

Sir Edmund quickly gathered his wits and hastily tore the strip of tarred cloth from over the cannon's touchhole. He produced his water-tight match holder from his pants, uncorked it and pulled out a large stick match. "I do indeed love these things!" he said grinning at Gnarly Dan. The water hissed along the side of the brig, its black, tarred deck sometimes awash. They were almost through the channel. Gnarly Dan shouted, "We'd best make some noise; they'll present a broadside soon's they can! May spit us outta their wake!" As he spoke he produced a waterproofed fuse from his own baggy pants and stuffed it into the touchhole of the cannon, careful to pierce the bag of gunpowder within.

Shouts came from high above them.

"LOOKEE THERE, BELOW!"

"AVAST THERE, YA POND SCUM!"

"SWEET MOTHER A' NAT, THEY GOTS A BLOODY BIG GUN WITH 'EM!"

"KILL 'EM QUICK 'AFORE THEY SHOOTS THAT CANNON!"

Unbelievably, that loathsome cur, Naughty Nat leaned over the taffrail and down at the two men below. His eyes widened (actually only one eye widened, for he had taken to wearing a black eye patch for effect. So infectious was it that as a fashion trend it swept through the pirate ship, man and boy now sporting them. Even Naughty and Nasty Natalie did the same, ever-humorous Naughty Natalie sporting one over her left bosom also). "You'll both die unnatural painful deaths fer that trick!" he taunted as he reached to his waistband for one of his pistols.

Neither Sir Edmund nor Gnarly Dan had time for self-defense. They were out of the channel and desperate to accomplish their task.

Naughty Nat looked over his shoulder and called, "PREPARE TA COME ABOUT, YA SONS A' THE DEVIL!" Then, "READY ABOUT!" followed by, "BRING THAT WHEEL FULL OVER NOW, YA VERMINOUS MAGGOT!"

175

The naturalist and the old salt saw the big rudder pivot. Once the Last a' Kiss completed her turn she would loose a full and horribly massive broadside into the sputtering Baci, sinking her immediately or at least turning her into matchwood, her scuppers awash in blood from the brave Bacis. It would be over very soon if Sir Edmund and Gnarly Dan were not successful.

In the moment it took for that wretched hound Naughty Nat to bark his orders, the naturalist struck a large match and touched it to the fuse. Above them, a little man in a fore and aft naval hat leaned over and shouted down to them as he recognized Sir Edmund, "I NEVER SHOULD HAVE ACCEPTED YOUR CHARTER, YOU PANSY-FACED SCIENTIFIC WORM! MY LIFE WAS JUST FINE BEFORE YOU STROLLED INTO IT!"

His last words were drown in the unbelievable roar of the massive weapon below him.

Many, many things happened coincidentally or in succession: Fortunately, the thirty-two pound iron ball cleared the barrel of the cannon first. Then the force of the recoil transmitted itself into the brig. It shot backward, hopping as it flew over the water, Sir Edmund and Gnarly Dan holding on for all they were worth.

The Last a' Kiss began its turn.

The ball smashed through her stern timbers as if they were taffy. Being just above the waterline it roared down the lower gun deck, taking the pins from pirate after pirate until near the bow it struck beneath a gun barrel with a loud clang and deflected downward sharply, still sufficiently charged to pass through the gun deck flooring and then out of the outer hull just abaft of the bowsprit and five feet below the surface of the water. Last a' Kiss now had a gapping hole through which tons of the warm seawater quickly filled the whole of the below-decks area of the ship. It was flooded so rapidly that it began to tilt as it sped forward, further worsening Naughty Nat's precarious hold on sea worthiness.

Still at the stern and attempting to draw a bead on Sir Edmund he found it impossible to compensate for the tilting deck and the speedily retreating brig. The final insult was the water he felt sloshing about at his ankles. Calves. Knees.

The Last a' Kiss bade a hasty farewell to the world above the surface of the sea and sank precipitously just beyond the mouth of the channel. Waterlogged pirates thrashed in the tossing waves or attempted to climb the descending masts and ratlines ahead of the rising sea. Naughty Nat and the former Captain Fitzwillie were washed into a tangled mass of spars and rigging along with Naughty and Nasty Natalie. They clung eagerly to the floating mess, each jostling with the other to accomplish a higher perch.

Meanwhile, the cannon-laden brig at last dug her retreating stern into a rogue wave and flipped backwards, the naturalist and sailor flying through the now-quiet afternoon air. Miraculously they landed in the water just to the starboard of their little punt. They clambered aboard, stepped her mast, popped up a virtual handkerchief of a sail and sped hastily toward the H.M.S. Baci, she sorely wounded but manned by a jubilant crew and an amazed captain.

Pirate after pirate floated to shore, discarded his soggy eye patch and went in search of Naughty Nat, he now the dampest, maddest villain in the seven seas.

"NOW I'D BE REALLY ANGRY!" he shouted again and again. The former Captain Fitzwillie drained a gallon of water from his cherished hat and glared at the distant H.M.S. Baci. At last he turned stern-to, lowered his drawers and saluted the cheering sailors who now lined the Baci's rail, waving and taunting and calling mute insults.

"Why did I ever marry?" the former captain moaned as he hitched his pants back to his waist.

Sir Edmund and Gnarly Dan joined the bedraggled but happy Bacis and were hastened aboard. Already the crew was clearing damaged rigging, discarding pieces of wounded spar and tattered sailcloth and gently stacking like cordwood those who predeceased the celebration.

"Welcome back, gentlemen!" Captain Constance Daphne exclaimed as she hugged first the old salt, Gnarly Dan, and then Sir Edmund, she all the while oblivious to the fact that her Royal Navy jacket had earlier parted company with all of its buttons, her embrace thus doubly satisfying to naturalist and sailor who momentarily blocked that cherished view from the good crew of the Baci.

It was hardly considered prudent to go back and attack the pirates, particularly when the old Plunderer hove into view at the horizon.

"Lord above, he's still gots that ole tub!" Gnarly Dan mumbled.

And while the channel was pretty well blocked, Constance Daphne was not prepared for another set-to so soon. She had the Bacis slip their anchor cables and readied the good ship for a hasty retreat.

"EVERY ABLE MAN ALOFT!" she called, her jacket blowing back in the breeze, an alluring perkiness now added to her demeanor. "SET EVERY SAIL THE OLD GIRL CAN SAFELY CARRY!" she commanded the master and crew alike. "LET'S PUT SOME DISTANCE DOWN BEFORE DARK! BOSON! SWAY TEN KEGS OF RUM UP TO THE MAIN DECK; I FEEL A POWERFUL THIRST APPROACHING AND I WON'T SLAKE IT ALONE! I WISH TO DRINK WITH HEROES TONIGHT!"

Cheers rolled through the rigging as gaskets were released and sail after sail fell to catch the triumphant afternoon breeze.

And so, once again blessed by good luck, the H.M.S. Baci sailed out of harm's way, repairing and celebrating as they passed. Of course numerous bodies were also committed to the deep with dignity, but as the Baci became more warlike in her accumulated experiences, the crew grew increasingly stoic.

About the second day out, a party brewing on deck, Sir Edmund Roberts and Gnarly Dan sought the comfort and camaraderie of Halley's patented diving apparatus. In the quiet depths they spied a sea maiden and a sea master in a long, soulful embrace. Gnarly Dan was humbled as they witnessed the bald display of love. "Ain't they a happy bunch," he whispered to the naturalist. "That'd be why they lives so long;" he added and then continued, "the more ya kiss an' hug, the longer ya lives! It'd be as good as writ," he said as the happy couple drifted by

All the old salt's references to embracing were making the naturalist increasingly uncomfortable in the close confines of Halley's patented diving apparatus, good friendship notwithstanding.

"Control yourself, old man," he muttered in defense.

His journal reads:

Sighted sea couple eight in the warm embrace of the sea. Handsome male. Beautiful female.
Sea Maiden 34
Maidenus cupidus
"Heidi"
Sea Master 10
Maximus tenderus

Both apparently healthy and content.
October 2nd 1834
Hawaii

A competition to repair the decapitated figurehead was launched. Of the twenty-three participants, all but one attempted a likeness of their fair captain. (Jack Scratch thought a kitten's head would do just fine.) Burly Vincent was the clear winner, Captain Constance Daphne Fitzwillie's likeness captured to perfection.

The ship's company was briefly entertained by a Hawaian gentleman who nightly serenaded the good ship, apparently as a gesture of good will. Kawakawiwo'ole was his name, and he was filled to overflowing with the gifts of song, friendliness and the love of life. He was a big, happy, handsome man indeed, with a voice so sweet and clear and moving that more than once it brought the homesick Bacis to tears.

SIGHTING FORTY-ONE

With the Sandwich Islands now far astern and the loathsome pirate Naughty Nat back aboard the Plunderer and contemplating his next act of attempted revenge, the H.M.S. Baci set a course for her subsequent destination, that being north to the Aleutian Islands. There was an uncomfortable sense aboard that they were fleeing the loathsome scoundrel, Naughty Nat, but Sir Edmund and Captain Constance Daphne assured the men they were prudently buying time to come up with their next plan.

Cold weather dogged them, along with gales and squalls. A date was set for the betrothal of the naturalist and the captain, they all but sharing her cabin now. In a perverse twist, Sir Edmund rather regretted the prospect of losing his augured peephole; it remaining a bewitching source of erotic visions and fodder for an unending series of fantasies, the good captain cognizant and contributing in a wonderfully alluring fashion.

The H.M.S. Baci was worked back to fighting trim, although the crew now recognized themselves as more the terrier than the bull. Few, if any, underestimated the despicable dog Naughty Nat's fierce determination to find them again. A standing joke was that he would appear on the horizon in a ship of the line, a first rate, no doubt. More than a few nightmares were generated. Unasked but on every sailor's mind was whether 'our naturalist cove' would come up with a new idea to extricate them once more from the maw of danger.

Old Jack Scratch joined them in a stolen skiff late in their last battle, he all anxious and beside himself to get to his new kitten. "Did me part!" he exclaimed, his eyes searching the deck for his furry reward. Surveying the damage a horrible thought crossed his simple mind. "She didn't . . ." he began and stopped short, unable to utter the unthinkable. Gnarly Dan hove to about then, the little fuzz ball in his arms. He offered her up to the reformed pirate saying, "We been lookin' sharp fer a puppy—don' think we ain't!"

And although Scratch's ear still displayed a nasty slice, he had long ago forgiven and forgotten that episode. "Thanks, mate," he answered and held the tiny kitten to the side of his scruffy face, "I know'd ya would."

So all were content as they snuggled into the Baci's close company of friends and plowed through the cold Pacific swells. One crisp Sunday Sir Edmund Roberts and Captain Constance Daphne Fitzwillie repeated their vows and became an official unit, the crew decked out and proud as fathers of the bride and comrades of the groom. Even old Gnarly Dan shaved close for the occasion, his face pink and bright. To a man the crew was at its best, 'kerchiefs neatly tied, buckled shoes polished, pants and shirts freshly washed and visages scrubbed. They were a happy lot, content in the knowledge that the naturalist and the captain had found the happiness that seemed forever just over the horizon for themselves.

Sir Edmund was resplendent in his old military uniform, he going so far as to wear his cuirass; a steel and silver breast plate, the gilt sunburst nearly covering it, the Arms of Hanover with the battle honours 'Waterloo' and 'Peninsula' scrolled above. ('Waterloo' brought fawning respect from every sailor who could read. "His honor was there when they thumped Old Nappy," whispered knowingly to those who could not.) Sir Edmund's sword hung at his side, the golden sash nearly as bright as the braided epaulettes bedecking the blue tunic above, its high gold collar impressive, accenting the former soldier's proud bearing. He wore the tight white pants well, his over-the-knee black cavalry boots gleaming like thunder, the silver spurs jingling as he walked. But most impressive was his headgear; a silver, rounded cap with a gilt edged visor, the sunburst motif repeated, its fittings and chin strap scales also gilt, all agleam but dwarfed by the huge crescent of the black bearskin plume that curved from the base of the helmet to its apex and then above, adding another foot and a half to the naturalist's height.

Sir Edmund wore the beautiful uniform easily, it being apparent that though it shone awesomely, it had seen much service, brave grooves and dents and scars polished but easily detected on the front of his cuirass. Its effect was to overwhelm the supercilious attitude the naturalist sometimes bore and replace it with that of a handsome, powerful and decorated (the Order of Bath predominating) officer of the King and Country.

Captain Constance Daphne Fitzwillie was stunning beyond words. Her dress was silk and white but somehow managed a military bearing, the bodice tight and uplifting, her glorious bosom celebrating quite above and nearly free from the rest.

The ceremony was long enough to please the bride but of sufficient brevity to keep the crew's attention. It was followed by much drinking, a speech or two, and the happy couple retiring at last to the captain's quarters.

Sir Edmund's dilemma regarding his augured peephole was addressed when Constance Daphne suggested he keep his former quarters as a retreat where he might "access his papers, organize his scientific musings, and indulge any gentlemanly thoughts he might wish to entertain in the privacy of his study."

They both, naturalist and captain, knew of what she was alluding.

Gnarly Dan assured Sir Edmund that multitudinous sea maidens should be in the offing, it being the season for (of course) their 'northing', as he put it.

"And they will be 'all healthy-like' and rotund?" the naturalist teased.

Gnarly Dan missed the humor, he now lost in the vision of soft sea maidens. "Right nice ta have yerself a first rate woman," he sighed and closed his eyes. " Me second wife, the lass in India; she'd be soft as yer puppy," he informed the totally disinterested naturalist. "When she lays back onna bed, a gob can be sure he's gonna roll right to 'er; inna dark, even!"

Sir Edmund looked away in an attempt to block out the encroaching vision of Gnarly Dan and a substantial bride. No sooner did he accomplish that when a score of rotund children sailed into view clamoring for their father.

At last it was "LAND HO!" and they were amongst the Aleutians, their spare, rocky coasts as uninviting as any the naturalist had encountered. That is, on the rare occasions they actually could see them, for it was fog, morning, noon and night and consequently, slow going; Captain Fitzwillie anxious for her ship, the rocky bottom waiting to tear the poor Baci wide open. Unalaska Island lay before them, and near Cape Aiak the Baci anchored. On Christmas Day the captain's launch went in with a small party to explore the area and hopefully sight a sea maiden or two. Aleuts greeted the sailors, they bedecked in sea-fur garments and poor beyond description, their existence under the iron thumb of the Czar of Russia little better than servitude. They did know of several areas where sea maidens could be found and were willing to lead Sir Edmund and the others to them. It was on a treacherous stretch of coast near Cape Izigan that the naturalist saw hundreds of sea lions, and scores of sea otters. As they watched and Gnarly Dan provided a running commentary on the attributes of sea otter fur and the variety of subjects he'd seen scrimshawed on sea lion tusks, a sea maiden pulled herself onto a rocky outcrop nearby and turned to face an unusual show of sunlight.

She was substantial, pleasing Gnarly Dan to the point of breathlessness.

"Lord help a poor gob," he gasped, "ain't she uncommon beautiful!"

Sir Edmund agreed politely, reserving his first thoughts.

"Yes, my friend Mr. Dan, she is 'uncommon beautiful'; life has denied her few opportunities to feast, it would appear."

Gnarly Dan ran his tongue over his chapped lips and then raised the arm of his sea coat and wiped away the moisture. "I knows you'd be a true gent, Yer Honor," he began, "an' I know we talked afore 'bout yer bigger sea maidens. But ya got ta know, Squire, a man ain't truly enjoyed a woman till he lays into yer softer sort. Nary a bone ta scape agin an' it'd be all 'thank ya sir' from beginnin' ta the end a' the voyage."

Sir Edmund knew the old salt was unstoppable, but still he tried. "Yes, yes, I've heard it all before."

But, of course, it was to no avail.

"Ya see, sir, yer bigger woman (or sea maiden fer that matter) is all comferble-like, so's ever'one's happy. She ain't gonna be all squashed er stoved in by a bloke like yer skinny woman. An' a gob ain't gonna hear no 'Ow!' er, 'Careful there!' No, she'll jest lie back an' savor the trip, if ya catches me drift."

At this point Gnarly Dan realized the naturalist had lowered himself and was now crawling off toward the sea maiden, attempting to keep his profile as low as possible.

"So you'd be a sneakin' up on her, would ya?" the old salt called out through cupped hands. Sir Edmund glared over his shoulder at Gnarly Dan, whereupon the sailor strode right up to and then by the naturalist, clambering awkwardly over boulders as he did, making absolutely no attempt to conceal his presence. At last the sea maiden turned, saw the old salt and smiled coyly.

Sir Edmund sat upright and watched, his mouth open.

Gnarly Dan at last gained the same rock as the sea maiden and then walked to her and sat, as boldly as 'kiss my hand'! They seemed to chat for some time, although the old salt never would explain what was communicated or how it was accomplished, allowing Sir Edmund only the simple statement, "I believes I'll be seein' her later."

In point of fact Gnarly Dan chose to spend the night on the island, the Christmas celebration on the Baci notwithstanding. "I'll have a small party a' me own, later," he informed the naturalist as he once again wet his lips. He produced a bright trinket from his pocket and admired it briefly. "Ain't a woman alive what don' 'preciate a gift!" he added and turned and walked away, humming as he departed.

Captain Fitzwillie sent a boat to retrieve the old salt the following morning.

"You must have frozen last night!" Sir Edmund exclaimed as Gnarly Dan stepped onto the deck.

The old salt smiled warmly. "Squire, ya ain't been warm till ya lies in the arms a' yer bigger woman. They loves an' they loves, and they true enough knows how ta please a man." He thought a moment, smiling dreamily and added, "An' most 'portant, they *wants* ta please they man. That'd be the best gift ever!"

They did not depart the cold northern waters without a last adventure. A week out they spied a Russian whaling vessel in the distance; it hove to with all boats lowered and away. As the Baci got nearer it became clear the Russians were pursuing a leviathan, it having been harpooned and prodded more than a few times and currently towing three whaleboats at speed back and forth across the broad ocean. At last the proud whale broached and shook the irritants from its body. He then turned on the whaleboats, smashed through two of them, sounded and came up under the third, tossing it high. Whalers, harpoons and lines flew into the cold air. Unfortunately for the good Baci, while so doing, Mr. Whale spotted their ship and erroneously identified it as the mother of its current woes. Forgetting the Russian whaler, he turned on the H.M.S. Baci and ploughed through the Pacific swells.

"WHALE HO!" came from the foretop, followed by the traditional, "THAR SHE BLOWS, HARD ON THE LARBOARD, TWO POINTS OFF THE STEM, AND AHEADIN' THIS WAY, CAP!" While the Bacis easily sent their hot iron after that horrendous rat, Naughty Nat, they did not generalize their angst. No man moved to direct harm in the direction of their broad, grey, charging foe. Captain Constance Daphne Fitzwillie watched the advancing mammal through her glass and when it became apparent a collision was imminent she shouted orders to the helmsman, Runny Jake, "HARD OVER TO STARBOARD, MR JAKE!" And then to the master, "COMING ABOUT,

NOW, SIR!" Followed in quick succession with, "PREPARE TO COME ABOUT! COMING ABOUT! TACKS AND SHEETS! LIVELY THERE! HAUL AWAY, YOU BACIS!"

But it was too late. The fair old ship was just answering her helm when the beast slammed its broad head into the Baci's weary timbers. The ship shook from stem to stern, the motion transmitted to her very tops. And then the whale came around again for another run, raised its huge head from the water, and finally, as if realizing its mistake, sounded and disappeared with barely a wave, its tail flipping lazily as if to say, "Sorry about that," before it too slipped beneath the surface.

The ship's carpenter, Chips, along with Constance Daphne surveyed the damage before they proceded south; a handful of planks started and at least three of her knees cracked badly. "The old girl can't take much more beatin', Cap. We oughts ta haul her out one a' these days."

Captain Constance Daphne Fitzwillie had come to love the Baci as a dear member of her family. She listened sadly and then looked the ship over slowly, appreciating her beauty, her strength and her heart. "We shall do what we can," was all she could promise, knowing full well they were far from any respectable port and farther still from a major shipyard. At last she amended, "The old girl will hold out; I believe she loves us as much as we do her."

Simply said, it was what they all knew. The H.M.S. Baci would do that which she was called on to do, and more. She always had and she always would. She was not iron and steel and rivets and fire. She was a marriage of wood and canvas and the heart of the wind. She was among the last of the best and she would deliver all that her soul allowed her.

Captain Constance Daphne could ask no more, and every man jack of her crew would help her in every way possible. And so they sailed onward, aware they were a dying breed and their fair ship was one with them.

Sir Edmund's notebook reads:

Sighted our 35th sea maiden, she rather rotund but content. Gnarly Dan affected some sort of communication although I cannot ascertain its method or message. Also had set-to with leviathan.

Maidenus rotundus

"Isabel"

Beautiuful sea maiden. Large body. Long dark hair. Pale complexion.

December 25, 1834

Happy Christmas

SIGHTING FORTY-TWO

The good ship H.M.S. Baci sailed along the Aleutian chain of islands for several weeks, but the crew failed to sight another sea maiden, much to Gnarly Dan's chagrin. Further, it was apparent his heart was still at Unalaska, for the old salt spent all of his spare moments at the ship's rail looking back to where he had left his love.

"Shoulda married, her," he muttered sadly to anyone who would listen. "A gob can't have too many wives."

At last Captain Constance Daphne Fitzwillie ordered a new course set and they turned southward and set sail for another chain of islands, these being midway across the broad Pacific, significantly warmer and home to a species of bird Sir Edmund longed to study.

So by February it was Midway Island and Sir Edmund had his chance to spy the Gooney Bird, the world's most accomplished flier but less adept at rejoining terra firma. Again and again the naturalist and crew watched as the big birds drifted in to land, lowered their webbed feet and then tumbled topsail over copper.

And there was a sea maiden, she with her child and it at her breast. Captain Constance Daphne Fitzwillie, Gnarly Dan and Sir Edmund Roberts were near the beach at the time, they enjoying a quiet evening stroll and discussing repairs to the good old Baci.

Gnarly Dan was the first to spy her. "Warn't that the most sweetest thing," he whispered as he lowered himself to a half-couch and pointed out the pair to the naturalist and the captain. They were at the shore, the mother cradling her baby and looking off to sea, the most serene look on her face. The baby suckled and cooed from time to time, finally nestling closer and apparently falling asleep.

Constance Daphne became wistful, a tiny smile and a teary look accompanying her as she held her arms to her own chest and slowly rocked from side to side as if holding a child.

Gnarly Dan was also moved. "There ain't no denyin' the beauty of a cannon or a well-found ship; but yer sea mum an' child . . . that'd be about the best they is."

Captain Constance Daphne turned away momentarily, dabbed at her eye and then looked long and hard at Sir Edmund. He was watching the mother and child intently and when he finally looked back to Constance Daphne it was as if he were imagining a different scene. He thought a moment and then said, "While I am an older gentleman, as you are well aware, we shall eventually return to England. There are only about thirty extra rooms in our ancestral home; I dare say at least one could be made into a proper nursery."

They sat and watched quietly until the sun set, Captain Constance Daphne leaning heavily onto Sir Edmund, Gnarly Dan a little in front of the two and muttering without end about sea babies, babies proper, nursing mothers, sugar treats and assorted other bits of conventional wisdom. So perfect was the evening that at one point the naturalist entertained the thought of inviting the old salt to visit them once ashore for good. He actually toyed with offering employment.

Years in the future he would look back on that day and evening as one of the finest in his life.

His journal reads:

Most content of afternoons. Whilst in the company of my recent bride, the beautiful Constance Daphne, we spied our 36th sea maiden, she a mother with child. Endearing spectacle. Pleased to have viewed it in the presence of the captain.

Maidenus leche
"Jane"
Healthy mother. Long hair. Medium build.
Infantus contentus
Healthy child. Short, curly hair. A bit pudgey.
Sighted on Midway Island
February 15, 1835

SIGHTING FORTY-THREE

And finally, to the Japan Isles and the Orient! Spring was glorious for all of its patent reasons and more. Sir Edmund and the captain lounged in marital satisfaction, the missing ingredient of secrecy more than offset by the intimacy they shared on demand. And of course Sir Edmund still spent the early portion of his evenings in his old quarters (his new 'study') where he could savor the privacy he coveted and continue his nightly invasion of the captain's own privacy through his augured vista. Such was their relationship that she too found it titillating, her nightly performances in many ways more arousing than those she had provided before he was aware that his secret was not. More than a few times the naturalist visited his interest on Constance Daphne before the final curtain, and those times she laughed well and often at his inability to practice patience.

At one of the outlying islands Captain Constance Daphne brought the ship in so a watering party could be sent ashore. Sir Edmund and Gnarly Dan accompanied the sailors, the former bent on exploring and anxious to access the sea maiden population of the Far East, postulating that their features would surely have at least a minimum reflection of the oriental.

Their first encounter however was not with the sea maiden fauna. At a remote beach they came upon what they first considered a straw and thatch hut, its apparent owner at the door and deep in meditation. At the respectful approach of the two Westerners he rose slowly and bowed, offering hospitality. After much gesticulating it became apparent that he was a samurai (and a very tall one at that!) and no longer needed by any warlords because of his age. Invited inside, their shoes at the door (to Sir Edmund's deep embarrassment, for his socks were sorely in need of repair), they found themselves in the antithesis of Western clutter. Never had the naturalist or the old salt been in a lodging as spare and immaculately clean as the minka (country house) in which they sat. Cross-legged on the straw tatami mats they talked, Gnarly Dan wonderfully conversant (for once!) in Japanese, he explaining in an aside to Sir Edmund that he had been shipwrecked on an outlying island years and years earlier. At the naturalist's urging Toshiro the samurai unpacked and displayed his *o yoroi*; the finest suit of armor Sir Edmund had ever seen. Much of it was constructed of small individual scales of leather and iron that were laced together in horizontal rows by brilliant silk cords, the iron breastplate laquered and displaying fierce bas-relief gilt dragons entwined with chrysanthemums and long legged cranes. The duck-billed helmet was most impressive, a fine golden dragon mounting the crest, the scaled skirt of the *kawari kabuto* flairing at the helmet's base to a point halfway to the extremes of the wearer's shoulders, the whole lending the wearer an other-worldly ferocity.

At last, Gnarly Dan allowed that perhaps the gentleman might enjoy seeing Sir Edmund's uniform (he and the rest of the crew being smitten with it at Sir Edmund's wedding). So off the old salt went and returned some hours later with two crewmembers lugging the naturalist's campaign chest. The samurai seemed to enjoy the bright colors, the sturdy cuirass, the insignias and the polished metal helmet with its gilt sunburst and black plume above. It was with unmasked reverence that he handled the naturalist's medals, particularly the Order of Bath. Toshiro then brought out his blades, and allowed Gnarly Dan and Sir Edmund to marvel at their quality and the keenness of their edges, both absolutely amazed when a silk scarf falling lightly on them was effortlessly sundered. This was of course followed by the display of Sir Edmund's boxed set of dueling pistols, the two perfectly balanced and tooled in silver.

And so the afternoon passed, the men exchanging pidgin tales of past battles accompanied by much knee slapping and camaraderie. With the setting sun each of the noble warriors, much moved by the other's sincerity, offered up his own ancient uniform as a gift. There was no doubt the naturalist was getting more than the samurai, though that aging gentleman was more interested in the naturalist's blue high-collared tunic than anything else. And so when they parted, most of the Oriental's armor tied atop Sir Edmund's campaign chest, it was with wonderfully felt goodwill and newfound affection.

Additionally, the samurai informed the naturalist of a nearby cove where a coy and definitively Eastern sea maiden appeared with the first rays of the morning sun. So Sir Edmund and Gnarly Dan returned to the Baci, spread the armor out on naturalist's day bed and agreed to seek the sea maiden with the new day.

The beach was as the samurai described it, and as predicted the first rays of the sun illuminated a glorious, dark-haired sea maiden. She was diminutive, remarkably light skinned (almost pure white . . alabaster!) with a colorful tail. Naturalist and sailor watched her for some time, Sir Edmund surprised that the old salt made no moves to join the sea maiden as he had months before at the Aleutian Islands.

"You don't seem disposed to strike up a friendship with this lass," he quietly taunted the sailor.

Gnarly Dan looked with disgust at the naturalist. "Ya know, sir," he began, "there ain't but one gob inna fleetful what has the sense ta know when a woman actually fancies him." He stared at Sir Edmund, communicating that the naturalist was obviously not that one. "Most of ya simply busts in with yer fine words er fast hands. It would help ya boatloads ta unnerstan' that yer female ain't lookin' ta be taked. Most often she'd like ta do a little captainin' her ownself." He was quiet for an unusual moment and concluded confidentially, "Ya might keep that in mind when yer settin' a course fer our Cap."

Sir Edmund's journal reads:

Encountered a brave old warrior. He directed us to our 37th sea maiden. She was most definitely of Eastern influence in stature, features and coloration.

Maidenus orientus
"Kim"
Short stature. Black hair. White complexion.
Sighted on Kuchino Shima Island
April 1, 1835

SIGHTING FORTY-FOUR

The good ship H.M.S. Baci breasted aside long rolling swells as she sailed from the Japan Isles north along the Kuril Islands to the Russian mainland, the Kamchatka Peninsula her goal. Sailing north in the spring was a heartbreak to captain and crew alike. As they put aside their lighter clothing tempers were tested. The temperature sank, the evenings and nights the worst. The only sailor who didn't seem to notice was Jack Scratch, his kitten and new puppy snuggled into his hammock every time he was not on watch. He had named them, taking the Captain's heart when he began calling the fuzzy kitten Connie, and further moving the old salt Gnarly Dan when he scratched the puppy's little neck and called him Danny. (Sir Edmund did huff a time or two, his last comment being, "Edmund would have been a fine hound's name.")

The naturalist finally roused out his diving bell from the hold once more, first repairing several damaged staves and cracked leathern hoses before it was swayed out and lowered. The waters were remarkably free of aquatic life for some time, Sir Edmund confused and concerned. It was just before they sailed to the mainland proper that they sighted their ninth sea maiden and sea master couple, they, of course, embracing.

"One would think they have nothing better to occupy their time," the naturalist noted, to which Gnarly Dan, for the first time in years, held his tongue, simply shaking his head in sad disbelief. He did finally mutter something about a 'silver spoon', but Sir Edmund, if he heard, did not comment.

The couple drifted by the bell, each moving languorously, awash in affection and oblivious to those in Halley's patented diving apparatus.

Sir Edmund's journal reads:

Another couple! They were in the throes of enjoying one another. Not a particularly productive species. No undersea factories, that much is certain. Must query how they would fare if the purity of their environment were spoiled.

Maidenus leisurus
"Leslie"
Maximus leisurus
Both remarkably fit. Handsome. Precoccupied.
June 11, 1835

SIGHTING FORTY-FIVE

Sir Edmund relented. As fed up with the increasing cold as the rest of the Bacis, he petitioned their fair captain, his wife, to put the good ship about and pursue warmer climes. Captain Constance Daphne's answer was immediate: "PREPARE TO COME ABOUT! READY ABOUT THERE, BIG BILL! PUT THE OLD GIRL'S HELM DOWN, MY FRIEND!" She called it out to the crew in general, all the while smiling secretly to her husband the naturalist. "You do sometimes make very good sense, sir," she added for his benefit.

Cold flying spray, shouted orders and laughter in the rigging was the response. The good ship Baci turned her stern to the north and leaned toward warmer waters and further adventure. To a man they knew they were off to the land of the Chinaman now, and more of the Orient and its mysteries. Everyone aboard was once more in the best of humor, MacMurphy's hornpipe out in the evening and every chanty and song in general bandied from the mainmast forward. There are few things in life quite so innocently happy as hard working men, steeped in friendship, sailing merrily along.

The sea miles rolled past the good ship's bow and lay in a straight line in her wake. Days came and went, the sun rose and fell and the stark, timeless constellations wheeled overhead. China was before them, the last month a respite from the tedium and the danger they had known in the past.

Big junks sailed by, their crews foreign and mysterious. The fair Baci sailed along the Chinese coast, Canton the only port open to them, and so Sir Edmund bit his tongue and waited, his naturalist's lust unslaked as the land of Pandas and mysterious plants slid by. Shanghai, Sangmen, Fuzhou, Xiamen, Shatou all closed to foreigners, an international incident in the offing at each. At last they reached the huge bay and the river referred to as the Pearl, sailed deep into it, past hundreds of junks and other craft, and then accomplished Canton, its bustle nearly overwhelming. Sir Edmund was certain his chances of adding to his sea maiden sightings were better in downtown London. They remained on the good Baci until the Hoppo made his official visit, he aswirl in his silk robe. With great officiousness he measured the ship's length and breadth and announced the tariff. It was of course outrageous, but neither captain nor naturalist objected, a certain closeness inexplicably forming with the Chinaman. Sir Edmund invited the great gentleman to view some of his sea maiden sketches, which he did with wonderful glee, his aloofness falling away with the first sea maiden. Hengshang was his name and he would allow no respite until Sir Edmund had dragged out every painting, including those in progress. Once more insightful, the naturalist then allowed Hengshang a tempting glance at those illustrations in his 'blue notebook' series. It was as if opening a chest of fine jewels, for the Chinaman stepped back as if struck by their rare beauty.

It should be noted that Constance Daphne was similarly overwhelmed (as mentioned in one of her letters to her sister, Agnes) for she had no idea of the erotic paintings' existence. Most interesting to official and captain alike were the images Sir Edmund painted with the aid of his augured point of vantage, Constance Daphne blushing noticeably (possibly for the first time in her life) at the cunning details displayed, while Hengshang looked slyly too her and then quickly snatched the top drawing from the pile, fairly devouring it with his eyes. At last he grinned from ear to ear, his appreciation of the captain's more subtle attributes fairly beaming from his face.

Sir Edmund stole a glance to his wife, concerned he had perhaps sailed a sea mile too far, but when she murmured, "You do have a way with the brush, sir," his concern vanished. When Hengshang at last came to feel he was possibly straying past decorum and went to place the drawing back on the pile, Captain Constance Daphne reached out and gently stayed his hand, making it clear the painting was his to keep and appreciate.

A fine tariff indeed!

Editor's note: *The exact image the official received is currently unclear, although this office is in the process of contacting those associated with various Chinese museums and private (!) collections in an effort to clear up that particular mystery. From the sequential gap in the extant drawings, it is probable Constance Daphne was captured in a most private moment.*

Hengshang smiled and bowed deeply. The three spent fairly half of the day with Sir Edmund's drawings and paintings, and then they turned their attention to other matters. Not only did representatives of the H.M.S. Baci have free reign of the European quarter normally open to visitors; in an unheard of gesture, Hengsheng offered to accompany the naturalist and captain inland to the great bamboo forests where they might enjoy viewing the most unusual of bears.

Editor's note: *That journey was to take place later in their stay and was chock full of little adventures of its own; they in all likelihood too oblique to be of interest to the reader. The subject will possibly be treated in a subsequent expansion of this volume. Please allow the summary that they journeyed together to the mountains and saw and were much taken by the Hengsheng's big, black and white bears.*

After the official departed with a promise to return in a few days, Sir Edmund and the captain made preparations to pursue their own immediate interests. Toward evening, while Captain Constance Daphne, the ship's master and a handful of crewmen wandered the shops open to them, the naturalist cajoled Gnarly Dan into joining him in a foray in the very harbor. Halley's patented diving bell was lowered, hundreds of prying eyes at once alert. In the depths the two sat and discussed the tragedy of isolation.

Their first day's dive was unsuccessful. As was the second's. But the third was an unmasked success, a sea maiden drifting past the bell in the twilight of the day. Gnarly Dan whistled softly as she hove into view. "There'd be a beauty," he whispered and then sighed loudly. "Does ya think, Yer Honor, they's any connection 'tween yer sea maiden an' her sister on shore? Hard ta 'magine they ain't somehow related. That lass looks purebred Chinawoman ta me."

And she did; straight black hair once more, almond shaped eyes, modest in stature. Dainty even. Sir Edmund frowned and thought. "And how would an old salt such as yourself be able to identify the characteristics of an Oriental woman?"

The old salt snuffled loudly. "Ya does believe don't ye, mate, that all yer smarts must come outta books! I been sailin' this little world long afore yer wet nurse turned her back on ya, sir. Nearly married one Chinawoman or t'other twice't that I can recollect."

Sir Edmund smirked and rejoinded, "And why, my discerning friend, did you fail to do so? I do not recall much standing in the way between you and matrimony." He waited a moment and continued, "I would be inclined to ask if there is some currently undiscovered upper limit to the number of women you feel you may safely wed, or do you hold that as long as there are new ports there exist new possibilities?"

The old salt was cut to the quick. He looked down at his shoes a moment before he responded. "Yer Honor, we been sailin' these many years while ya seeks out yer own version a' lady; be she sea maiden or otherwise; an' we ain't made so much as one complaint 'er suggestion. By yer way a thinkin', Yer Highness oughta been satisfied long ago with what he's already see'd." He let that rest a moment and then concluded, "Ta my way a steerin' a boat, they ain't no two women alike in the whole world. Seems only a fool'd be content ta dock in just one port, long as his ship still sails."

Both individuals decided simultaneously that further discussion was moot.

The next day two related occurrences steered Sir Edmund's military plans in a new direction. Apparently, there was a celebration of a sort inland for the sky was bedecked with giant silk kites and then that evening fireworks lit up the night. The naturalist went on his own trading expedition the following morning, taking with him a retinue of sailors to help cart his purchases back to the good Baci.

The markets were a cacophony of noises and colors, all vying for the naturalist's attention. He at last found the wares he sought at several disparate locations and returned to the ship in good time. That evening at dinner with the captain he alluded to one of his plans.

"Mythology, as you know is rife with mention of men and their attempts at flight. I do recall reading in an obscure journal that more than a few fellows did indeed achieve ascension in a larger version of the flying machines we witnessed the other day."

Constance Daphne tentatively tasted the saki set before her. "Kites, you mean," she amended. She smiled at the warmth felt with her first swallow. She looked at her glass and asked, "Japan Isles, am I not correct?"

Sir Edmund waved off her interruption. "Yes, yes, they are much taken with it; rice wine. Our friend Toshiro consumed great quantities." He paused. "As I was saying, before the good captain's thoughts strayed to beverage; I shall attempt to soar with the birds in a 'kite' of sufficient magnitude to support my weight. The advantages are manifold. From great height we may ascertain Mr. Nat's approach long before he is aware of ours."

Constance Daphne was actually listening carefully by now. She quickly interrupted again. "Your belief being that that heinous hound Naughty Nat will find a soaring kite viewed mid-ocean to be a normal occurrence?"

"Well of course he won't!" Sir Edmund answered, embarrassed by his mistake. "But he won't know it's us!" he countered weakly, crestfallen and sorry he had brought the whole thing to her attention. (Breathes there a man who has not had brilliant ideas dashed over dinner? As the ever-sage Hottentots aver, 'Show me a man with a new idea and I will show you a woman in the shadows saying he is wrong.') The naturalist went on quickly, "The point is, he will necessarily lose the element of surprise. At any rate, this is remarkable saki, please pass the bottle; I have recently developed a considerable thirst."

Then when he was silent Constance Daphne asked, "And what are your other plans? You alluded to more than one."

To which the naturalist shrugged and muttered, "I'm sure they wouldn't interest you. Not sufficiently logical."

A slow storm built as Captain Constance Daphne toyed with the two possible references in his last statement. Sir Edmund smiled thinly and excused himself from the table.

His journal reads:

China is at least as fascinating as Mr. Polo writes! Met a fine gentleman, offered up an interesting portrait of our captain as a gift. Ha! Ha! And we sighted our 39th sea maiden.

Maidenus orientalus
"Mary"

Long dark hair. Short stature. Fine features. Handsome tail.
August 3, 1835
Canton Harbor, Pearl River, China

Sir Edmund's early experiments with his giant kite were, to be kind, amusing. The naturalist learned with much difficulty the importance of an adequate tail for his flying apparatus. Three times in succession he had a very long rope secured from the anchored Baci to his apparatus and then had his kite and his person rowed far downwind. Holding tightly to several loops of rope he then stood at the stern of the vessel and presented the kite's full height to the brisk breeze. He was immediately and wonderfully airborne, unfortunately achieving respectable height each time before his apparatus took it upon itself to spin in decreasing circles, the tightest of which always managed to toss the naturalist into the air far from the kite. The only good fortune was that although the harbor was crowded with all manner of boats and ships for each demonstration, Sir Edmund managed to consistently avoid crashing onto one of them, he instead falling into the water.

At last he decided, *Far too many prying eyes here*, and allowed that he would wait until they were in a less public arena before he continued his experiments.

A further unfortunate incident took place the last evening before they sailed from Chinese waters. Hengshang arranged a large dinner for the foreign captains and officers currently in the harbor, he obviously doing so as an excuse to see the woman of his painting one last time. At that dinner Sir Edmund Roberts had the misfortune to be seated across from a rather brash and ill-mannered America captain by the name of Alan Smithers who became progressively inebriated and, consequently, more rude as the evening matured.

Time and again his humor was at the naturalist's expense, the final straw breaking with his allusion to Sir Edmund's flying display.

"I'd think if I was thrashed soundly by a country as big as the United States, not once, but twice, I'd surely keep my head a little lower when I was around one of her representatives," he slurred.

"And represent her appropriately, you do sir," the naturalist rejoined.

The young captain pushed his chair back precipitously, it tipping to the floor, and then leaned across to Sir Edmund, upsetting a glass as he did. "I take that as an insult!" he brayed.

"And well you should," Sir Edmund answered quietly. "That would be the first evidence of perception I have noted from you this entire evening. Perhaps, sir, you should be escorted back to your vessel before you find yourself in deep water."

And of course at the mention of water the captain snatched a nearby glass and flung its contents onto the naturalist.

All was deathly quiet for a moment, Sir Edmund at last allowing, "Tomorrow morning when you are sober I will accept your apology, sir, or settle this in the presence of your second; there is no excuse for bad manners. Be informed I already forgive you your ignorance."

The fellow was just sober enough to know he would not currently requite himself well against the dead-steady Sir Edmund. The party wound down quickly, and the following morning on the deck of the Baci the American appeared with a small party, he now recovered from the effects of drink but still bearing the heavy burden of poor judgment. The young captain made it apparent there would be no rapprochement.

Sir Edmund turned to old Gnarly Dan who stood proudly by with the naturalist's inlaid box harboring his matched set of dueling pistols. Their quality did temporarily give Alan Smithers pause, but he bulled ahead regardless. Twenty paces were decided, the naturalist asked a last time for an apology, noting, "You are a young man, sir; perhaps you would appreciate a few more years to search for wisdom."

The captain desired no such thing.

The long and short of it was that after waiting out the captain's misplaced shot, Sir Edmund coolly parted the young man's hair. When even that did not appear to be adequate for the bully, the pistols were reloaded, the American trembling with a lethal mixture of rage and new-found concern.

Twenty paces again, the captain's ball going wide before Sir Edmund slowly raised his own balanced pistol. "An apology, sir," the naturalist magnanimously called out.

It was answered by a derisive comment regarding Sir Edmund's departed mother, who, it should be noted, the young captain soon joined. (Whether he was more differential toward her upon their acquaintance is not yet known.)

Sir Edmund's notebook is magnificently obtuse regarding the entire encounter, mentioning only, *On August 5, found both dueling pistols to be working well. Must cast four new balls.*

Captain Constance Daphne Fitzwillie was at the periphery of the dispute from its genesis, she apparently the only one who understood the international implications of the encounter. She had no doubt the incident would echo in Whitehall and Washington equally, and that neither government would now treat them kindly. A hasty departure was in order.

SIGHTING FORTY-SIX

So it was goodbye to the Orient as the good Baci weighed anchor, spun on her heels and escaped down the Pearl River in a rush for the open sea. Then past Hong Kong to their larboard and with every bit of cloth the old girl would carry, off to the southwest they sailed, every man jack of the crew moving with great speed but differential to their quirky naturalist, he having once more impressed them with his manly skills.

Gnarly Dan must have cleaned and polished the naturalist's matched dueling pistols five times a day for the first week, Sir Edmund finally remonstrating, "Good lord, man, you've handled them more than I since I received them as a gift from the King of Spain fifteen years hence. Be so kind as to return them to my campaign chest. Should I have use for them once more you may see to them then." He smiled a menacing smile and added, "Unless of course we have a falling out, in which case I shall clean them myself."

It was all bravado and the old salt knew it was, for Sir Edmund had vacillated between profound depression and melancholy since the incident, his only allusion to it being, "The coin of youth is too often ill-spent. Oh, that it were not squandered in a fell swoop on something as foolish as braggadocio."

Constance Daphne gave the naturalist physical space and time in which to work through his sadness, he standing alone at the lee rail by day and retiring nightly to the solitude of the little bed in his study.

"Perhaps another adventure in your diving apparatus?" she asked one day. "The charts show an island near; it is marked as Tungsha Tao." Sir Edmund agreed, feeling the need for a diversion. And what a diversion it was. They hove to off the island's shore, the naturalist insisting on descending alone. He saw no sea maidens; not immediately or later. What he did see was gloriously astonishing. Beneath the bell's open bottom he spied a huge vessel. The more he studied it the clearer it became that it was an enormous barge. He signaled for the bell to be lowered farther, it at last coming to rest on the ancient deck. There before him, as well as he could see from the bell's little window, were row upon row of Oriental soldiers, they sitting grasping their oars, their uniforms intact, their clothing perfect. The naturalist was curious as to how the soldiers remained so pristine, but upon closer scrutiny Sir Edmund could see the craft was resting in the middle of an undersea channel, the water's movement keeping it cleared of silt.

He signaled for Halley's patented diving apparatus to be raised several feet, stripped himself down to his pants and undershirt, took a deep breath and departed the bell. He needed touch only one of the oarsman to confirm his first impression; it being that they were statues, each and every one, full-sized terra cotta representations! He returned to the bell, dried off and pondered that which lay below. At last he decided he had found a royal burial barge; the final resting place of one of the Ming emperors, the first, perhaps, and no doubt full of priceless objects of art and antiquity. He began a series of free dives to the vessel, gaining its interior and the first of a series of cabin-like chambers. Jade carvings and golden images abounded and these he hefted back to the interior of the bell.

He was preparing for another dive when he felt the diving bell being hoisted hurriedly to the surface. He was greeted by Gnarly Dan who admonished, "We's got a bit a' company, Squire," his sentence interrupted by the masthead hail, "MORE SAILS TA' LEWARD, FIVE POINTS OFF THE BOW AND BEARIN' DOWN! PIRATE JUNKS, CAPTAIN! THERE'D BE FOUR!"

And there were indeed. Four handsome examples of the Chinese answer to naval design; two of them rather large and two smaller, all approaching, the former approximately the size of the Baci with half again the armament, the smaller being two-thirds her length and each a fair match. They were classic craft with huge curved and battened sails and an angry eye painted on both sides of each ship's prow.

"SHAKE A LEG THERE, MEN, GET THIS SHIP UNDER WEIGH AND THEN SWAY UP OUR ARMAMENT FROM THE HOLD AND BE QUICK ABOUT IT! AND DON'T MAKE A GRAND SHOW! THE LONGER IT TAKES FOR THEM TO REALIZE WE HAVE TEETH, THE BETTER OUR CHANCES!"

She did not elaborate, for their chances were slim at best. Each of the pirate vessels was a challenge, and en masse they were close to certain death for their ship. Fortunately, all the ship's armament had been secreted in the hold during their visit to Canton. For all the world she still looked like an unarmed merchant vessel. With efficiency and determination the good crew of the Baci roused their firepower and prepared cannon after cannon behind the closed gun ports. In a trice the lower gun deck was prepared, the deadly rows of armament double-shotted and ready. The artillery on the upper deck took a bit longer as everyone was careful to avoid too obvious a bustle, the fear being the pirates would discern their subterfuge. Finally, the stubby carronades (Gnarly Dan's 'smashers') were in place, the decks at last spread with sand to soak up errant blood and provide a gritty surface in the heat of the coming action.

Huge wads of tangled rope were lowered into the water at the stern of the Baci and dragged behind, slowing the ship to the point that she appeared to be a clumsy, overloaded merchant vessel. A quick meal was served followed by a double ration of grog and all was ready, the Bacis crouched behind their guns waiting for the approaching junks. They were about to be set upon by four ships crammed full of no less than two hundred cannons and upwards of six hundred scurrilous Chinese, the Baci's only real advantage being surprise, for hopefully the pirate lord was deceived into believing he was bearing down on a sluggish, undermanned cargo vessel.

A half hour before the battle, Captain Constance Daphne Fitzwillie, resplendent in her Royal Navy jacket, tight white pants and riding boots gathered the entire crew in the waist of the Baci. Her demeanor was without fear and even her bounteous chest struggled mightily to free itself for the coming fight.

"MEN," she began and then elaborated, "FOR YOU ARE INDEED MEN! FINE! BRAVE! HANDSOME! (the first time such a word had been set at the feet of more than a few of the rugged Bacis) FEARLESS MEN!" She looked ahead and over the rail at the approaching junks. "BELIEVE ME WHEN I SAY THAT IN THE ENTIRE HISTORY OF THIS FINE SHIP, NEVER BEFORE HAS SO MUCH DEPENDED ON SO FEW! MORE POWERFUL THAN THEIR CANNON IS YOUR COURAGE! MORE DEADLY THAN YOUR IRON BALLS IS YOUR DETERMINATION! WE HAVE NOT SAILED HALFWAY AROUND THE WORLD TO MEET OUR END IN SOME ORIENTAL BACKWATER! WE SHALL BULL OUR WAY THROUGH THEIR PITIFUL BLOCKADE AND SHOW THEM WHAT ENGLISHMEN CAN DO!"

Sir Edmund was at her side, once more proud and upright (his wife's chest was magnificent). He had finally left his duel to settle into obscurity, the present danger more than enough to keep him occupied. Even the scorched circle of decking on the captain's quarterdeck was an event from the distant past. (His first rocket experiment a disaster.)

Constance Daphne turned to him as she finished her last sentence and added, "WOE BE TO THE MAN WHO UNDERESTIMATES THE STRENGTH ABOARD THIS SHIP!" She smiled grimly. "THERE ONCE WAS A MAN NAMED AL SMITHERS! (the Bacis smiled knowingly) WHOSE BAD MANNERS WOULD GIVE ONE THE SHIVVERS! BUT HE PICKED THE WRONG MAN! JUST AFTER JAPAN! NOW FRESH WORMS' MEAT IS ALL HE DELIVERS!"

So raucous was the crew after that rhyme; though she was loath to do it, Captain Constance Daphne had to hush them. "WE SHALL HAVE OUR TIME TO LAUGH SOON ENOUGH, MY BRAVE MEN! TO YOUR GUNS NOW. OUR ENEMY AWAITS! She turned to Sir Edmund who was mildly entertained by her performance, it putting the final cap on his remorse for the departed American.

The naturalist had one final detail to add to the captain's plan. "BOSON! YOU AND FIVE GOOD MEN ROLL OUR SIGNAL CANNON TO THE BOW AND PREPARE TO FIRE. WE'LL LET THOSE CHINAMEN THINK THEY'RE FACING A POP-GUN!"

Once the little cannon was in place between the two massive carronades all was ready. The war junks were almost upon them, their gunnels crammed with angry, greedy Orientals bent on boarding the little unarmed Baci. So certain were they of their victory over the plodding merchantman that they did not so much as fire their first cannon.

Sir Edmund hissed forward to the crew of the signal cannon, "Fire a few shots, there, men. Be sure your aim is terrible and your speed at reloading something like a Frenchman's!" With that the signal gun was fired, its sad little pop and tiny poof of smoke barely enough to be noticed.

But it was.

The pirates lining the rails of all four junks pointed and laughed and fairly licked their lips at the pathetic show of force by the oncoming ship. Then, barely a hundred yards from certain death should their plan go awry, Captain Constance Daphne had the ship's boy, Little Jimmy, begin to lower the Union Jack as a show of impending surrender. "Slowly, lad!" she hissed. "Back the royals!" she continued to those aloft and alow. "Helmsman, come up a point. Luff the mainsail!" She turned then to the men crouched beside the ropes hung off the stern and dragging. "Ready to cut those lines, there!"

The two largest junks had nearly lost weigh and were about to scrape alongside the Baci, having preformed the neatest bit of 'coming about' any sailor could ever wish to see. Hoards of jostling Chinese pirates (a fearsome sight; all of them dark haired and mustachioed, with angry slanting eyes and compact stature) now climbed to the rails of their ships in preparation to jump aboard the hapless English vessel.

The two smaller junks also backed their sails and were nearly dead in the water, now awaiting the signal to raft-up with their larger cousins.

Then all hell broke loose.

"AWAY THOSE LINES! BRING UP THAT HELM! FIRE AS YOU BEAR, BRAVE BACIS! LET US GIVE THOSE YELLOW DOGS A TASTE OF ENGLISH IRON FOR BREAKFAST!"

And with that gun ports flew open and belligerent snouts poked forth and began to blast heavy iron into the startled faces of those preparing to board the good Baci. Thunderous roars barked again and again. Even Gnarly Dan's great 'smashers' sent forth their mayhem of swarming grape shot, bits of chain and old bent nails. Guns were sponged out as quickly as the trained Bacis could manage. Fresh powder bags were rammed home, balls rolled in and tamped and crews stepped away as the Baci bit again and again, the devastation on the decks of the two larger junks instantly appalling. The decks ran red with blood as limbs and half-bodies blew through the air. Two masts came down like tree trunks and already a pitiful symphony of high squeals and screams rent the air. The Bacis stayed bent to their guns, sending forth their fearful anger as their ship responded to the new power of her trimmed sails and the loss of her dragging tail. Marksmen in her tops fired muskets and rifles into the writhing mass of humanity on the two nearest junks.

At last the smaller pirate vessels came to life, first with small arms as they maneuvered to bring their cannons to bear.

"GUNNERS!" Captain Constance Daphne Fitzwillie shouted, "FIRE ON THE OUTLYING JUNKS; THEIR LARGER BRETHERN ARE DONE FOR! CRIPPLE THOSE DOGS SO WE MIGHT LIVE TO FIGHT ANOTHER DAY!"

And once more the Bacis' withering fire was directed at her enemies. The smaller junks at last began to use their artillery and the good Baci suffered. The starboard junk lost a mast and veered off. The port junk kept up a heated exchange, but the Baci's gun crews aimed well and often, their iron punishing the wooden ship constantly.

Sir Edmund had left the cannons to their crews, they being entirely capable and proficient. He had his Boxer-Henry pre-proto-prototypical rifle out and in lethal action, singling out pirate after pirate and sending him in pursuit of his own vision of heaven. Twice the apparent captains of various junks appeared at the stems of their vessels shouting angry orders and pointing to the departing Baci and as many times Sir Edmund drew a cold bead and eliminated the man.

"Most impolite to point," he muttered each time.

Captain Constance Daphne Fitzwillie stood on her quarterdeck clutching her former husband's bulky Naval Service pistol in one hand and his Naval Service sword in the other. There was little doubt she was prepared to battle any foreigner who sullied her deck, scorched circle or no.

At last the fighting slackened and then died altogether, the enemy astern and in no mood to continue. One of the larger pirate junks began to smolder and then burn as flames licked up her foremast and onto the sail. Pirates could be seen hastily fighting the fire and then giving up as the flames gained and spread. Swarms of men dove from the ship's sides while several Oriental pirates could be seen in the distance attempting to beat the crew into remaining and fighting the blaze.

But the fire continued to gain until it reached the powder magazine. There was a tremendous explosion as the huge junk buckled in the middle and both ends blew high into the air, the bow tumbling slowly. Bodies arced like fireworks and splashed with the falling timbers into the surrounding water. A huge cannon landed on one of the smaller junks, nearly capsizing it.

When even more junks were sighted the H.M.S. Baci crammed on more sails; studdingsails and then topgallants loosed and sheeted home. The little ship picked up additional speed, her bluff bow smashing through the Pacific swells, cleansing her sides and washing the smell of gunpowder and death from her decks. Rigging and sails were mended, comrades were located and congratulated and those supremely unfortunate were gently stacked at the base of the foremast.

Captain Constance Daphne and Sir Edmund now stood side by side. Gnarly Dan came back to them and waited in the naturalist's shadow, the three exhausted but sadly pleased with their day's work.

Sir Edmund was the first to speak. "Rather a nasty dust-up. It appears our friend Naughty Nat is not the only soul bent on our destruction. It would appear we must return to our little island another day." He examined a long rent in the sleeve of his jacket and noted, "A rather determined lot; I believe they had us outnumbered, outgunned, and for a moment there, more or less under their thumb. Amazing what surprise and determination can overcome."

Gnarly Dan snuffled loudly. When the captain and naturalist turned back to him he said quietly, "Yer Bacis'll do more than ya ever dreamed. They's good men and brave men. Yer common gob'd be the most unappreciated soul afloat. Warn't a man on this here ship what wouldn't lay down his life fer either of ya." He stopped then and examined the buckle on his right shoe. It was bent nearly double.

Captain Constance Daphne Fitzwillie cleared her throat softly and swabbed a tear from her cheek. She looked long at the old salt and then to the men behind her on deck and in the rigging. At last she turned to the bodies lying at the base of the foremast. Without a word she left Gnarly Dan and Sir Edmund and went below decks. The naturalist and the old salt thought she was retiring to her cabin to regain her composure when in point of fact she had descended to the orlop deck, there helping the surgeon and his assistants with the plethora of ragged wounds the good Bacis brought to their attention.

The weather cleared and the H.M.S. Baci encountered no more pirates near the mainland of China. They sailed on, repairing as they advanced, the good ship once more whole and hearty (excepting of course her rotted timbers near the keel, the row of wounded knees on her starboard side where Mr. Whale had registered his discontent, and the recently appearing crack in the mainmast, it having been sprung in one of the multitude of storms they had endured).

Through the Sulu Sea they passed, twice sailing out of range of a new group of pirates in pursuit. Then near Mindanao where they were ill advised to attempt to water the ship, they were set upon by Ilanum pirates, a fearsome lot that burst from the underbrush with spears and curved swords. The Bacis quickly formed a rather loose version of the British fighting square and under Sir Edmund's direction, reduced the hoard to jungle fodder forthwith. Unfortunately the Bacis did not linger to complete filling their water kegs so by the time they reached the island of Borneo, they were a pretty thirsty lot. Again a heavily armed party was sent to shore with water casks, and this time the attack came from the sea. A throng of Dayak pirates raced into the bay in their little prahus, bent on overwhelming the good ship before an adequate response could be mounted (a fine theory ordinarily). Unfortunately, the Baci was primed and alert, all her armament loaded with grapeshot, her boarding nets rigged and lookouts in each top. No sooner did the fierce headhunters round their cape when masthead hails declared their presence. A terrible storm of cannon grapeshot found the light boats immediately, and before they were within musket range, the party had been devastated.

Those on shore were able to complete filling half of the water casks and return hastily to the ship, the bay afloat with debris, bodies and churning sharks.

Once more the H.M.S. Baci resumed her journey, at last achieving New Guinea. The first order of business was completing their acquisition of drinking water. Once more several boats were lowered; each towing a raft of empty casks in their wake. Gnarly Dan and Sir Edmund Roberts were in the first cutter. Leading those in the second was an Australian chap by the name of

Earnest Erwin, a likeable fellow with an endless chatter, a love for animals and a keen sense of adventure. "By cracky, otta be some huge crocs in these swamps!" he advised his boat mates. He pointed to the inlet the other boat was approaching. "A bloke'll be sure ta find some big 'uns up that stream an' they're sure ta be grumpy with our splashin' about! How I'd love ta get up close ta one of those beauties!"

For all of his personable characteristics, those Bacis who shared his boat thought he was patently insane (in all likelihood the lion marmoset skeleton found in Sir Edmund's Bermuda chest was from one of Erwin's pets). With the possible exception of kittens and puppys, all forms of animal life were best appreciated by the Bacis at mealtime. Rats, weevils, fish and fowl were all truly fair game. The Australian at the bow of their craft was obviously sadly misinformed and headed for trouble.

Which he found.

Later that day, far up a narrowing stream where a spring of fresh water allowed the men to fill cask after cask, a mammoth crocodile warily observed them from a muddy bank. Four men armed with muskets kept constant vigil while Sir Edmund hastily sketched the beast and Gnarly Dan fretted about like an old hen. Earnest Erwin however couldn't get enough of the crocodile. Closer and closer he crept, constantly stopping and calling back some bit of obscurata to those who stared in disbelief. "It's a she-croc, mates! And what a beauty she is! Just take a look at the size a' her head! Her jaws alone are half the length of me body! And look at those teeth! Huge!"

On and on he prattled, moving with more caution as he approached the watching crocodile. At last he was impossibly close to the giant beast, sharing the same muddy bank and no less than a body length away. Ernest Erwin turned a last time to the astonished crew and softly called out, "See, mates! She's content ta just lay in her muddy nest and watch! By cracky she's a big one! Don't I love her! And she knows it!"

With that remark the huge crocodile decided she did love Ernest Erwin; so much so that she burst from her lair with unbelievable speed, opened her mouth wide and scooped up the sailor as she advanced, thrashing her head about twice before she swallowed him whole.

Not a man moved. Not a shot was fired. Even Sir Edmund stood with his own mouth agape.

The crocodile then slid down the bank and into the dark stream where she submerged and apparently moved farther upstream, leaving a long trail of silently bursting bubbles and the memory of the game little Australian who had nothing more to teach the good Bacis.

They returned to the ship, more shaken than anything, the casks in tow and bobbing heavily behind. Sir Edmund sat at the stern of his cutter and stared back at the jungle. He thought once more of the little Australian, shook his head and commented, "Stout fellow. Could have done well with a bit more in the common sense department."

They plied the waters of New Guinea for more than two weeks, Sir Edmund's quest for sea maidens unanswered until near the end of the third week. While submerged in Halley's patented diving apparatus with Gnary Dan and Captain Constance Daphne Fitzwillie, a remarkable pair wrestled into view. For all the world they seemed to be involved in a slow-motion dance or contest of sorts, grips changing with glacial speed. Constance Daphne was the first to voice the obvious. "Why they are both men!"

Neither Sir Edmund nor the old salt, Gnarly Dan cared to comment.

"Lord, they are a handsome lot!" the captain continued, at once back with her sea master and their incredible journey. She could not stop looking at the two approaching sea masters and making her comparisons. They were both well muscled and pleasing to the eye. Both had long dark hair and an intelligent, yet sensitive edge to their demeanor. The captain could not help but imagine being taken to sea by the pair of them.

Sir Edmund noticed the change in Constance Daphne. "We would gladly leave you to be alone with our new friends, my dear; but we don't appear to have a convenient door available." Little did he know his wife was at that second restraining herself from slipping out the bell's open bottom and swimming to the pair. She neither answered nor turned to Sir Edmund.

At last Gnarly Dan piped in. "Gotta say, they's a handsome lot. Me second wife's brother'd be 'bout that well found. Girls couldn't get enough a' him. Didn't seem ta notice, though. Preferred gents, it seemed, though I ain't sure."

The two sea masters tussled by, it never being clear if they were asleep and dreaming or involved in a ritual of sorts. All that was certain was Captain Constance Daphne's shortness of breath and remarkable accumulation of perspiration, her white blouse once more transparent, Gnarly Dan and Sir Edmund appreciative but jealous.

Sir Edmund's notebook was offhand and brief:

Lost a crew member to a rather dramatic crocodile, the latter fully the length of three men. Two further encounters with pirates. Marital bliss is that. Sighted two sea masters off the coast of New Guinea.

Maximus maximus
Handsome. Muscular. Long hair
Maximus minimus
Handsome. Muscular. Long hair.
September 7, 1835
Coast of New Guinea

SIGHTING FORTY-SEVEN

On to the New Holland (Australian) coast the good Bacis sailed, making a nice landfall after pleasant sailing. They anchored in Sydney Cove and were pleased to be back under the protective arm of the British Empire. The town was clean, the warehouses full, offering the naturalist plenty of opportunities to explore and attempt to find new contraptions for his quest. In the week that followed he pursued cockatoos and the great jumping beast, the kangaroo, and in neither was he disappointed. Additionally, Captain Fitzwillie and Gnarly Dan were astounded and beguiled by both, the old salt slapping his knee and laughing raucously with each long bound of the kangaroo while Captain Constance Daphne was much taken with the baby they spied tucked in her mother's pouch.

Sir Edmund explored the waters inside the great surrounding reef, gravely disappointed that the sea was not teeming with sea maidens as Gnarly Dan had predicted. "Used ta be they was pools of 'em in ever' far off patch a' sea," he lamented. "They's disappearin' afore our very eyes. Won't be long an' all them young gobs'll have is our stories an' His Honor's painted pictures. See if they don' start sayin' we made 'em up!"

"Fear not," the naturalist assured him, "they are documented, described and illustrated; there breathes not a learned man who would have the audacity to doubt our discoveries! Your sea maiden is as firmly established in the annals of science as the vaunted dodo and America's famed passenger pigeon. Mankind is powerful but we are incapable of obliterating an entire species! Poppycock to think so!"

But it was obvious the old salt was not convinced. He looked at the empty water and then back to his companion. "And you'd have a reason we ain't seen none, Squire?"

As luck would have it, a sea master swam below them as Gnarly Dan was finishing his sentence. "One bird don' make a season," the old salt mumbled while Sir Edmund began rapidly sketching the sea master, he having returned and begun circling Halley's patented diving apparatus.

Sir Edmund's journal was again brief:

Wonderful island! Saw kangaroo and cockatoo (appears to be a penchant for 'oo's on the island!). Also spied a sea master. Our 14th male. Pity Captain Constance Daphne was not with us. She no doubt would have added another "OO!"
Magnus solo
Handsome. Well developed. Curious. Long hair. Green/blue tail.
October 17th, 1835

Sydney Cove, New Holland

Editor's note: While there is no mention of it at this stage of their journey, apparently a remarkably large black or brown mamba found its way onto the H.M.S. Baci during her stay in Australia. The snake's reign of terror began approximately one week after the ship departed the Great Barrier Reef.

SIGHTING FORTY-EIGHT

Still unaware of their serpentine stowaway, the Bacis set a course for New Zealand, the only hint of their new passenger being the dramatic decline in the number of rats spied in the ship's hold. Then, six days out, Quakey Al went deep below decks with Sir Edmund, Gnarly Dan and Chips, the carpenter, to investigate the state of the old ship's timbers. Gnarly Dan was the first to remark the complete absence of rodents dodging in and out of the shadows.

"She seems a bit on the still side," he commented to Chips. "Ain't no little 'friends' scurryin' about. I know we din't eat 'em all."

Quakey Al was instantly nervous. The old salt indicating things were out of the ordinary was upsetting, and while he had absolutely no fondness for rats; excepting possibly stewed with vegetables and fat, he was less than comfortable with any indication of unusual circumstances.

He turned and addressed a question to Chips who was at that moment testing a timber with a sharp knife, "Think we's sinkin' an' they done gone?"

Chips did not look up as he answered, "If ya gotta know, mate, from the looks a' these punky rails, we shoulda done that years ago. The ole' girl's holdin' herself tagether wif hope an' prayer."

"Once had a aunt what was like that;" Gnarly Dan interjected, "over a hunnert an' couldna weighed more'n a dead cat."

At that instant Quakey Al caught a glimpse of a large, long shadow pass between his feet. He jumped onto the nearest cask. "There! There!" he shouted and pointed. "It'd be a snake, an' a bloody big un, too!"

"Saw nothin', Chips answered.

Gnarly Dan had. "Lord above," he gasped, "he'd be big enough ta worry Adam, Eve, an' a whole boatload a' t'others!" He had seen less than half of the snake's length as it passed into a dark cove, but it was substantial enough that what he saw was nearly as long as he.

"D. angusticeps," the naturalist proclaimed with concerned finality. "A mature specimen. We should inform the captain; it is deadly."

Quakey Al nearly fell from his perch. "Deadly sir?" he asked, hoping he had misunderstood. "You'd be meanin' 'scarey', wouldn't ya, sir?"

Sir Edmund's smile was grim. "Deadly. A beast of that size could, no doubt terminate a bull. Apparently it has spent some time dining on our rodents. I fear it will soon be searching for other nourishment."

It sounded equally horrible in the light of day above decks. Captain Constance Daphne Fitzwillie thought long before she spoke. "And if we organize a hunt with all hands, is it possible we can corner and annihilate the beast?" she asked the naturalist.

Sir Edmund allowed that it could happen but he was not hopeful. Regardless, the search was organized and accomplished not once, but three times and all that happened was that every man-jack aboard was now aware and duly frightened. For the first time, those on watch in the dark hours were envied, every bulging hammock inspected with trepidation. In the middle of the first night following the snake's discovery, there were no snores below decks. Men whispered back and forth. "What was that?" was hissed more than once. Poor Jack Scratch, fully reformed and penitent, had begun to wear his kitten and puppy, Connie and Danny, in a sling about his body. He was nearly paralyzed with the fear they would be the serpent's next meal. That night he lay in his hammock, his arms snuggly around his two pets, his eyes wide as cannonballs. "Ain't right," he muttered again and again. "They's just little things. Woun't hurt nary a soul."

As feared, in the darkest hours the beast slithered up from the hold; thick as a big man's forearm, wary and hungry, its tongue testing the foul, close air below decks. The scent was densely fragrant to the monster. It smelled of men and filth and dampness and mold and it smelled of small mammals. It smelled of a fluffy kitten and a soft puppy. Silently it slid beneath the listening men, under Quakey Al, and Big Bill, and Little Tim; beside Gimpy, Itchy Ben, Sloshy George and Fretting Willie, all of whom lay on their backs with their eyes wide open. It passed near them all and then hesitated beneath the hammock of Jack Scratch. It paused and listened and tested the air carefully and then raised its head higher and higher, honing in on small mammals nearby. Closer and closer it stretched, the hammock still out of reach but only just. It was within a hand's length of the now-alert animals when Gimpy made out the outline of the back of the snake rising before his own eyes.

In a motion he yelled out, struck the back of the beast's head and flew from his hammock. There was a flurry of exploding bodies as nearly fifty men leaped to their feet yelling and calling out in panic as they scrambled for the ladders to the deck above. Four men stepped on the snake as it retreated to a corner, and four men were struck by its wild attacks. Twenty Bacis were certain they had been bitten, tearing off their pants once on deck and pawing frantically over every inch of their legs in search of telltale marks. Jack Scratch crooned to his charges, he and they unscathed. Of those sailors actually bitten, death came quickly, as requested.

After that not a man would venture below decks until morning. The ship's officers also deserted their cabins. With the exception of those managing the ship, every man spent that day searching for the monster, they being armed with knives and clubs and pikes and pistols but to no avail. That evening everyone made arrangements to sleep on deck, midnight finding them in the rigging and moving higher with each advancing hour. By dawn the good Baci looked remarkably top heavy. Captain Constance Daphne spent the night pacing her quarterdeck with Sir Edmund at her side, each of them with one of the naturalist's dueling pistols tucked in their pants.

The madness went on for three more days and nights until the captain would have no more of it. She announced she would be returning her cabin, "below decks!" she emphasized. Not to be outdone, the naturalist allowed that he would be in his study if required. While they were fine examples, there were no other takers. Midnight found the rigging full, Constance Daphne at her desk with an oil lamp flickering, and Sir Edmund bent over a Chinese blowgun examining the poisonous darts he had arranged in a neat row before him, his dueling pistol primed and charged and within reach.

The captain started when she thought something was moving about with her, at last attributing the perceived motion to Sir Edmund at his augured hole. "Silly man," she whispered and smiled to herself. But when the big snake rose before her eyes she was unable to speak. It swayed slightly, testing the air with its evil tongue. Slowly it drew back, muscles tensed, eyes intent.

Sir Edmund's journal relates that he had indeed been at "a point of secret vantage', when he spied the serpent. Because of the relative positions of captain and beast he instantly knew his pistol to be the wrong weapon.

He was armed in a trice. A little dart blew through the augured hole, the naturalist trusting past practice and a developed sense of coordination to guide the little missile. The snake spun around as if stung, struck randomly behind itself and then transitioned into a writhing, angry mass before dropping dead as a marlinspike.

Hung from the spanker yard the next morning it was awesome; thick, at least twelve feet long and a glistening green-black. Once more the naturalist was hailed; man, boy, captain and even little kitten and boisterous puppy safe at last. Sir Edmund thought Jack Scratch was on the verge of renaming his puppy in his honor, but it was not to be.

"Oh, the deferred rewards of fleeting fame," Sir Edmund lamented to the captain.

"Your reward, sir, may be deferred, but it will not be fleeting," she teased within earshot of several members of the crew.

Snakeless they resumed their voyage, the serpent relegated with a heave to the fishes and sharks. Sir Edmund did get his reward one moonlit night, the stern windows open in the captain's cabin, she bathed and fragrant, a translucent silk robe alternately teasing and then opening to the sea breeze as she walked to the naturalist. "You sir, are my hero," she cooed and pulled him gently to her.

"They's kissin'!" passed from those in the rigging above her skylight. "An' ain't our Cap all decked out an' fit fer a sail!" another added. "Ole Sir Eddy's 'bout ta make a discovery 'er two hisself!" was bandied between spanker boom and mizzen tree.

And what a night it was.

The appreciative, loving gentleness of a woman was visited upon Sir Edmund, every preconceived notion of sexuality and bliss dashed, overwhelmed, outstripped and absolutely smothered in a night of wild abandon alternated with caressing escape.

The sun rose on a contented ship, the captain's lesson in love firmly entrenched in the minds of the crew and the heart of the naturalist. The good ship's sails bellied forth; her full complement spread and drawing well, her wake creamy and arrow straight. And so it was for days and then weeks, until at last New Zealand hove into view. Sir Edmund roused out Halley's patented diving apparatus and descended, the captain and the old salt, Gnarly Dan, accompanying him, the fates, gods and minor deities poised to tease at least two of the three.

When at last a sea maiden drifted into view in the arms of a sea master, she was a mimic of the fair captain; beautiful, content and very pregnant. Gnarly Dan was the first to comment. "Ain't she precious as gold dust an' more special than yer doubloon," he whispered. Constance Daphne put her hand full to her tummy, rubbed idly and smiled to herself.

Sir Edmund looked long at the sea maiden's shape and found himself thinking not of her, but of his ancestral home, of the fields and moors and forests of his youth and the joy he knew he had been denied these many years. A child. He had come to long for a child much as he had previously longed for recognition and fame. A child. A little 'Sir Edmund' of Constance Daphne that he might lift gently from its cradle and actually hold to his own chest. A tiny child. A tiny heart. A tiny mind. A future that he might help to guide. His own legacy; his staggering wealth for once had meaning. There was, for the first time in the naturalist's long and full life, an actual future beyond his own existence. That which he had sought through fame and recognition he discovered late in life as available through perpetuity; through love and sharing and creating. The sea maiden before him, aswim in the waters of the world, bathed in the salty depths, carried her child with a resolve as ancient as the world. Sir Edmund longed for such a thing to enter his own life. He looked secretly to his love, Constance Daphne Fitzwillie.

She looked back to him. Studying him at first, full of a mother's trepidations regarding the depth of her husband's heart—her child's father. This man before her, cloistered in the cramped odorous diving bell was the partner of her first child. Had it been a mistake? Was he the fool? The opportunist? The invader of her sanctity? She saw that he was looking to her; that he appeared to be similarly moved.

"Yes," she mouthed after Gnarly Dan looked away from the involved two and pressed is nose to the glass and stared at the sea maiden.

"Yes?" Sir Edmund whispered.

"It is so," she replied and smiled.

His journal reads:

The coast of New Zealand! Its magnificence awaits us. . . .yet it has already offered up a wondrous secret and a sea couple; she pregnant.
Maidenus blissfulus
"Nancy"
Long hair. Content. Very pregnant.
Magnus blissfulnus
Handsome. Attentive.
Sighted off the coast of New Zealand. Resolution Island.
November 2, 1835

SIGHTING FORTY–NINE

New Zealand was explored, prodded and prompted and yet she yielded up not another sea maiden or master. So off to the Maldives the good Baci sailed, her crew happy, the naturalist expectant and the beautiful captain with a bounteous chest abloom with anticipation, a vast, vast stretch of ocean before them. While the crew crowded on sail, Sir Edmund expanded his experiments with Congreve's rockets; various assistants helping to fashion copper troughs and tunnels through which the pyrotechnics could depart the ship without leaving a flaming Baci in their wake. Further, Sir Edmund, after looking long at Halley's patented diving apparatus, turned another facet of his attention to underwater craft.

"Halley was wise, but hardly prescient," he lectured the captain. "Why, Leonardo da Vinci was years and years ahead of him, though peaceful in intent," Sir Edmund confided.

Captain Constance Daphne stifled a yawn. "You don't say, sir," she added, hoping her amour would at least be quick with his exposition.

"Good Leonardo spoke of 'wickedness in the hearts of men' and therefore attempted to conceal his theories regarding under sea machinery."

"Indeed," Constance Daphne responded, all the while staring out the stern windows of her cabin at an albatross that had dogged them for some weeks.

"He feared mankind would 'sow murder in the depths of the sea'; " Sir Edmund continued, "a capital idea when one considers that cur, Naughty Nat! Surely Mister DaVinci would have had his peaceful leanings sorely tested had he met that despicable pirate. No doubt the villain is at this moment seeking us, a vast armada in tow." He waited for a response and when he got none, went on, "Now, Bushnell had sound scientific principals and Fulton expanded on those. I believe we can forge an underwater vehicle to facilitate our sea maiden quest while allowing itself to be of use in an assault on the wretched pirate, should the opportunity present itself."

Again the naturalist looked to his captain. Impatient for her response he bulled onward, frustration tempering his excitement. "Think of it, my lovely captain; ballast, pumps, rudders both horizontal and vertical, and wonder of wonders, dearest; a screw propeller!"

At last he had her attention. "A what, sir? What was that you mentioned?"

"Archimede's screw! A machine to propel our cunning submarine whilst underwater. Imagine!"

Captain Constance Daphne may have imagined. And then again, she may not have. She makes no mention of it in her log, her diary or her occasional letters to her sister Agnes. Regardless, Sir Edmund proceeded, first with elaborate plans and drawings and then with various hull models he pulled behind the good Baci, all the while measuring drag, stability and controllability. At last satisfied, he and several of the ship's craftsmen began work on the submarine.

Sir Edmund was up to his elbows with them in the hold, explaining as they fashioned wood, copper and iron, "Gentleman, it will be sufficient to carry six aquanauts: four employed in propulsion, one mastering the craft and one designated as an aquatic explorer; he observing through one of the viewing windows. No longer shall we be required to sit idly by hoping for a chance sea maiden encounter! Why, we can seek the dears out! Find their homes! Follow their travels!"

The naturalist waxed on for hours and then days and weeks as the little craft took shape. There was a steady stream of visitors, the good Bacis equal parts curious and disdainful. Even Captain Constance Daphne Fitzwillie remained unconvinced, she being the best able to voice the common sailor's trepidations.

"Suppose it goes down and refuses to return to the surface? Suppose the air turns to poison and the entire crew perishes! Suppose it crashes into a submerged rock or reef. I'm telling you, Sir Edmund, you have stretched your luck far enough with Mr. Halley's diving bell; this project smacks of madness!"

Unfortunately, for all of her attributes, the captain did have a weakness or two. She was absolutely incapable of reframing from further comment.

"You do remember your infamous kite, do you not?"

Sir Edmund was dashed. "And you, my fair captain, remember our departed American friend, Mr. Smithers?" he countered.

Apparently, the naturalist's remorse had been assuaged.

With that, the subject was dropped and the work went on as the Baci sailed ahead. The Maldives were next, tropical and lush and yielding up another success for Mr. Halley's patented and patently simple diving apparatus. Sir Edmund and Gnarly Dan had descended as the H.M.S. Baci lay at anchor. Quietly and unnoticed for some time a sea couple drifted into view, they embracing and seemingly asleep. At last Gnarly Dan spied their approach.

"Ain't we about ta have company," he announced. "They'd be right pleased ta be ta gether!" he added. "Yer sea maiden always chooses right. She won' make the kinda stupid mistake us gobs is capable of; why they ain't been a sea maiden yet what ain't chose well when it comes ta her mate. They knows ta the bottom of they heart when it'd be a proper match-up"

Sir Edmund was unconvinced "And how, my good Mr. Dan, is it that a sea maiden can choose better than we? What can our undersea friends know that escapes us so often and so easily?" he queried.

"If that ain't the stupidest question what a gob ever uttered," Gnarly Dan countered. "If I'd a know'd that then I'd still have all me wives, now wouldn't I?"

It was the naturalist's turn at incredulity. "Good lord, man, you never tire of telling me you currently enjoy three wives; surely, you are not intimating there were previous (and oh so lucky!) Mrs. Dans?"

"They been an even dozen by my count. Now, what say we belay proddin' me life an' pay a bit more 'tention at what'd be outside this here bell."

Which they did. Sir Edmund's journal reads:

Have begun work on an undersea machine. Accomplished the Maldives and spied our 10th sea maiden and sea master couple. Am informed they mate for life and enjoy 'marital' bliss for the duration.

Maximus fortunatus
Strong body. Healthy.
Maidenus prescientus   *"Ophelia"*
Sighted off the Maldives
December 18, 1835

Off to further adventure the H.M.S. Baci sailed, Sir Edmund helping the ship's carpenter work on the underwater machine. "We are embarking on a whole new area of scientific exploration," he explained to the dull-eyed craftsman. "While we know the best shape for a ship such as ours to part the turbulent seas, we are at a loss regarding what configurations best move beneath the water; though the multitude of fishes must be trusted to have been well modified for their environment."

And so while his first models were certainly fish-like; thin, tapered at both ends and rather more tall than wide, he was finally satisfied with a rather blunt cigar-shaped design. Sir Edmund first considered human propulsion but found himself longing for a method that did not involve sweaty, smelly sailors in close quarters with himself.

Sir Edmund's rocket experiments also progressed until the naturalist settled for fully enclosed copper tubes through which the rockets would roar as they traversed half the length of the good ship Baci. He moved the long (16 foot) guidance stick from the side of the rocket to its center, using carefully drilled porcelain dinner plates as exhaust vents surrounding the centered stick. It was actually old Gnarly Dan who moved the naturalist to try tail fins.

"It'd be yer feathers on a' arrow what keeps it true, Squire. Seems some well-placed feathers could steer yer course better than them ramrods what you got hangin' off the stern of yer fireworks."

Sir Edmund did not laugh at the idea of feathers adjacent to the fiery exhaust, so taken was he with the concept of fins or guidance vanes on his missiles. Copper 'feathers' were fashioned and attached, the first fully too small to do their work, those rockets whirling crazily through the air, reminding every onlooker of Sir Edmund's ill-fated kite experiments (although no one mentioned them) but the second and third tries with expanded versions worked extraordinarily well, the rockets rattling noisily through the length of angled copped tube before they roared off into straight flight, delighting and impressing most.

Captain Constance Daphne Fitzwillie stood at her quarterdeck and watched with concern until the copper piping was finally disassembled and removed from between the myriad of rigging, sails and masts.

Sir Edmund noticed his captain's anxious looks. "Larger rockets will require longer and more substantial copper pipes to sully your fine ship, my captain, but I believe they will carry explosive and incendiary devices sufficient to give that cur Naughty Nat pause. I trust you find it within you to tolerate the inconvenience."

"How powerful?" she asked simply. "More than our current array of cannons?"

Sir Edmund thought carefully before he answered. "My dearest friend, Congreve himself hurled bombs in excess of hundreds of pounds over greater distances. As you well know, the good Baci's largest cannons throw six pound iron balls. Further, we can design our new, larger missiles to burst into devastating storms of fire upon impact."

So ended their discussion, the captain interested if not mollified, Sir Edmund determined to requite himself in his wife's eyes. He continued his experiments, increasing the size and accuracy of his rockets, daily transforming the Baci's deck into his proving ground, the crew delighted with the noise and sparks and fiery contrail. The major weakness was the rockets' flight in cross winds. At such times they curved off gently, landing in the distant ocean with a splash far from their intended mark. Meanwhile, Sir Edmund was working on an apparatus to make the long tube unaffected by the ship's pitching and rolling by mounting it on a self-leveling watery device.

And while the H.M.S. Baci sailed toward Arabia, the mysterious land of harems and sand and camels, Sir Edmund envisioned his own version of a thousand nights. Captain Constance Daphne Fitzwillie now more pregnant and uncomfortable longed for a handsome bare-chested Malamuke to massage her aching body and anoint her with exotic oils.

They achieved the port city of Madina ash Sha'b at last and were denied entry. Afloat in the hot bay, the dry, arid wind baking tempers, Sir Edmund had Halley's patented diving apparatus roused out of the hold and lowered into the steaming ocean. Gnarly Dan accompanied the naturalist, Captain Constance Daphne in no mood to be any more constricted or inconvenienced than she already was. So while the two adventurers were lowered into the deep she leaned on the rail of her quarterdeck and dreamed of iced sherbets and cool winds and large, soft comfortable beds.

Sub-aqua, the naturalist and his companion immediately began to think better of their decision until at last a pregnant sea maiden drifted into view, she at once beautiful, content, and at absolute peace with her condition. As Sir Edmund wished silently that his fair wife, the captain, could attain such gravid bliss, the old salt, Gnarly Dan launched hesitantly into his 'pregnant sea maiden' lecture.

"As ya may remember, yer honor, they hair turns white . . ."

As feared, the naturalist cut him short. "Her hair turns white once impregnated—remains white through the gestation period. Reverts to natural color thereafter. Most happy. Most beautiful. My lord, man, must you repeat everything you tell me, ad nausem?"

Both gentleman were drenched in sweat and bordering on misery. Sir Edmund was piqued and Gnarly Dan was hurt by the diatribe.

"Ain't you an' our cap both in fine moods," he muttered. "Though you'd not be curious 'er polite enough ta ask, that sea maiden be thinkin' a her young 'un. They does a lot a that whilst carryin'. Like our own mums, a sea maiden with a baby inna hold carries the world's most precious cargo an' they don' take it lightly. Ya might consider that afore castin' ugly waves on our Cap's bow."

Sir Edmund's journal reads:

Unwelcomed arrival in Arabia. Denied access to shore. Captain Fitzwillie is less than brilliant company. Sighted our 42nd sea maiden, she quite pregnant.

Maidenus contentus
"Peggy"
Remarkably pregnant. Content. Preoccupied. Long white hair. Blue
tail.
Sighted off shore of Arabia
January 30, 1836

SIGHTING FIFTY-ONE

Fleeing the lack of Arabian hospitality the good ship Baci made for the southern island of Madagascar. Sir Edmund continued his underwater machine project, the shape decided upon and vessel slowly taking shape in an open area of the hold at the hands of Chips and a talented crew of assistants. Sir Edmund was now positively adamant that it would not be propelled by sweaty, odorous sailors, his recent confinement in Halley's patented diving apparatus with Gnarly Dan sufficient to temper his tolerance for the musk of mankind at work.

"I have no clue as to how we will propel the machine," he informed Chips, "but I shall turn all of my considerable talents to the task and I believe I shall prevail."

Had he actually been listening, Chips may have been mildly interested, but he had suffered the naturalist's theories and lengthly explanations far too often.

A nice landfall on the coast of Madagascar occurred one calm evening. The Baci anchored within earshot of the jungle sounds and heady smells; the booming of the island's flightless parrot unnerving more than a few of the sailors.

"Think of the flora and fauna across that narrow stretch of water!" Sir Edmund enthused to Gnarly Dan.

"Any land what ain't got a port an' a town ain't worth an honest sailor's attention," the old salt moaned. "Has the gentleman any idea how long yer common gob suffers without a lass?"

Sir Edmund did not answer, but Captain Constance Daphne Fitzwillie, her back aching, the internalized youngster kicking at her stomach until she believed she would soon step once more to the rail and lose the remainder of her dinner, heard parts of the exchange and misunderstood the old salt's last word.

"Breathes there a man who does not spend his days complaining and his nights pursuing the company of strong spirits or women?"

It was the old salt's turn to hear incorrectly.

"Right you are, Cap'n Constance, ever' man loves a 'strong spirited woman'!"

It was not the right thing at the right time. The very pregnant, very nauseated, very tired and very sore Captain Constance Daphne Fitzwillie turned on the unsuspecting old salt. "You, Mr. Dan, have earned yourself the right to inspect and then paint the foremast, mainmast, and mizzen mast poles. Bright white, sir. And if one drop of paint sullies this ship's decks, you sir, Mr. Dan, shall be seized over our warmest cannon to meet the gunner's daughter (read: be flogged senseless)."

And so the old salt departed their immediate company. Sir Edmund was about to speak in Gnarly Dan's defense when he spied his wife's withering stare and remembered some remarkably important matters that needed attention in his study. "Must go below," was all he left in his hasty wake.

The following morning Sir Edmund and Gnarly Dan escaped the Baci and explored the fecund island, delighting in its lemurs. They found a sheltered inlet and there spied the 43rd sea maiden, she lying and contemplating the state of the universe.

Sir Edmund surprised his companion by exclaiming, "By jove it has been far too long since I have allowed myself the pleasure of bestowing a maiden's common name. This fine specimen is tranquil indeed, so 'Quiterie' she shall be! From the French; connotes tranquility! Ha!"

Gnarly Dan looked to his naturalist friend. "As ya' wish, Squire. Lord knows she'd be 'tranquil'. Been awhile since we's been inna company of a 'tranquil' woman. When did ya say our Cap is due ta have her stowaway toss out a grapple an' board our ship?"

The familiar tone rankled Sir Edmund. "Our Captain? My wife! Captain Constance Daphne Fitzwillie-Roberts! One in the same and due sometime in the future. A concern, I assure you, that is absolutely, irrefutably, none of yours!"

Sir Edmund's journal reads:

Wonderful landfall! Wonderful news! Our 43rd sea maiden sighted on the shore of Madagascar, that most unusual of islands!

Maidenus preoccupadus
"Quiterie"(!)
Supine. In reverie. Long hair. Average weight. Beautiful. Gloriously not pregnant.
Bay d'Antongila, Madagascar
February 16, 1836

Darkest Africa beckoned the H.M.S. Baci. Land of antiquarian civilizations and home of Cleopatra, her barge and her asp. With wondrous anticipation Sir Edmund Roberts, gentleman naturalist, sea maiden questor, only recently married, and father-to-be, looked to the distant shore of that great continent. All the while, his underwater machine progressed, its cigar-like shape nearing completion, the naturalist; concerned as he had not yet arrived at a solution to the problem of its propulsion whilst submerged.

"It will occur to me," he muttered again and again, his carpenter, Chips lamenting that it was far more reasonable to build the craft around an idea instead of the other way around.

"We'd be movin' arsey-varsey," Chips complained. "No good never comes a' such a thing!"

"Double negative," was the naturalist's curt response.

They left Madagascar in the face of the monsoons; the rain and wind a constant nuisance, the captain miserable beyond words. Sir Edmund continued his experiments with rocketry, the missiles' warheads now in excess of one hundred pounds. Daily he rigged the long copper firing tubes inclined and positioned to fire off the stern of the good Baci, his logic being that they were most likely to be the mouse and not the cat when the despicable rogue, Naughty Nat made his next appearance.

One relatively calm afternoon a large dhow sailed out of a rain squall, her crew obviously surprised to confront an English vessel. It was not noteworthy until the Bacis found themselves downwind, whereupon the smell of fettered humanity drifted across the deck.

"That'd be a slaver," Gnarly Dan informed Sir Edmund and the captain. "Chock-o-block full a' Africans bound ta spend they life in misery. Ne'er mind a bad marriage, slavery'd be the worst state a man can find hisself in!"

Captain Constance Daphne was instantly aghast. "That vessel is transporting shackled human beings?" she inquired, her eyes narrow. "Chained cargo to be sold?"

"That'd be so," the old salt averred. "An' no members a' our Royal Squadron in sight ta set things right!"

"Then it is for us to do!" Captain Constance Daphne proclaimed. "PREPARE TO BRING THIS GOOD SHIP ABOUT!" she shouted to the first mate, Dusty Dennison.

Sir Edmund had come from his rocketry preparations just abaft the main mast. He stepped to his captain and advised, "I am informed that weatherly little vessel with her triangular sails will show us her heels in no time. Perhaps a brief exhibition of our fireworks will suggest to her that her best interest would be served if she 'hove to'. We are currently in a handy position to give some of Mr. Congreve's rockets a test or two."

The crew on the dhow was animated as they hurried to bring their vessel to its best point of sailing. Captain Constance Daphne Fitzwillie watched their progress and then turned to her first mate. "BELAY THAT, MR. DENNISON; WE SHALL BE ANSWERING SIR EDMUND'S INSTRUCTIONS IN A MOMENT. MR. JAKE, LOOK LIVELY! ALERT THERE IN THE RIGGING, IF YOU PLEASE!"

Sir Edmund now called out to his assistants, "BRING UP TWO ROCKETS! INSTALL ONE POST HASTE!"

The rockets were brought up from the hold, the first one slid into the copper tube and prepared to be launched. The naturalist directed the helmsman, turning the good Baci's stern to the fleeing dhow, all the while adjusting the angle of the copper launching tube by a series of blocks and tackles. At last satisfied he took the recently lighted cigar from his mouth, timed the Baci's reaction to a subtle breeze and fired the fuse on the first rocket.

"ROCKET ONE IS ALIGHT!" he called out as he stepped far to the starboard of the now hissing fuse and the base of the launching tube, it poised above a large, shallow water-filled tub to protect the deck. Crew members covered their ears and smiled to one another as they stole glances at the blissfully fleeing dhow.

"Our naturalist gent's got a surprise for that one!" they joked to one another.

Then with a significant roar the rocket motor ignited and the missile whooshed and rattled and banged through the long copper tube. Once departed it streaked through the African air, quickly closing on the now-startled crew of the dhow.

As the rocket approached, the slaver's crew jumped about and pointed, then ran to the bow of their ship as if they would find safety there. The rocket roared forth leaving its trail of sparks and rolling smoke. It appeared at first that it was dead-on target, but a last minute puff of wind made in veer to the port just enough to miss the dhow.

"LOAD THE SECOND ROCKET!" Sir Edmund ordered just as the first rocket exploded some distance ahead of the dhow.

The second missile was gingerly hoisted into the still-smoking launching tube. Sir Edmund made further adjustments to its angle (not only was the dhow hastily departing, the good Baci was slowly sailing away from it).

Again, he took the distant ship's measure and again he touched his glowing cigar to the fuse, calling, "ROCKET TWO IS ALIGHT!"

It roared forth, pleasing the crew once more and increasing the consternation and panic of those manning the distant dhow. As it closed the distance, this time veering neither right nor left, the dhow's crew to a man threw their arms over their heads and dove into the water, thrashing mightily as the missile raced just above the dhow's twin masts.

A third rocket, though brought up, proved unnecessary. The Baci came about and sailed back to the bobbing dhow. The two lateen sails slapped idly as the Bacis boarded the ship and set about freeing its cargo; no small feat since, though small, the dhow was carrying nearly two hundred shackled Africans. A skeleton crew from the Baci agreed to sail the captured vessel around the Cape of Good Hope to Freetown in Liberia if need be, while their main hope was to intercept a ship of the British West African Squadron and thusly relieve themselves of the dhow and its awesome responsibility. Some twenty-six of the slaves let it be known they wished to transfer to the Baci, they having willing hands and a great desire to join such an apparently healthy enterprise. Captain Constance Daphne agreed, her own crew suffering from years of attrition.

So the dhow sailed south ahead of the H.M.S. Baci while Sir Edmund petitioned the captain to allow exploration of several bays for sea maiden fauna. The second week of such activity yielded the naturalist's fifty-second sighting; a sea maiden and sea master. "Pleasure to see one couple that is not at odds," the naturalist said.

Gnarly Dan shook his head slowly. "Won't never see yer sea maiden an' master at odds. Can't be no squalls under the sea."

"Oh please!" Sir Edmund protested.

"True enough, Squire; she captains their ship an' he does what he's tole!"

"Sounds unhealthy," the naturalist responded.

"An' you'd be the picture a happiness!" Gnarly Dan laughed

Sir Edmund's journal reads:

Glory to the Right of Search! England expects that every man will do his duty, and we have. Liberated some ten-score of slaves, saw much of the African coast and sighted a sea couple!

Maidenous commandus
"Rosey"
Beautiful. Commanding. Long hair. Strong body. Comely chest.
Magnus lesser
Stout physique. Long hair. Content.
April 21, 1836
Sighted near Madagascar.

220

SIGHTING FIFTY-THREE

The H.M.S. Baci made a stormy final passage down the African coast to Cape Town, Sir Edmund Roberts, gentleman naturalist and sea maiden questor, further refining his knowledge of rocket technology and also supervising the construction of his underwater machine; the germ of an idea regarding its propulsion at last festering in his quite busy mind.

Meanwhile, far to the north events were unfolding that would profoundly impact the voyage of the H.M.S. Baci. The pride of the United States Navy, the U.S.S. Constitution sailed into Zanzibar on a mission of goodwill. Her captain and various ambassadors were to meet with the Sultan in an attempt to fortify his support of the slave trade. Further, they were seeking information regarding a British subject who had terminated one American, a Captain Smithers, the brother of a very influential Congressman.

A grand dinner was planned, preceded by a parade of the Constitution's crew in an attempt to impress the vizier with a show of American pomp. All went well, a spectacular and prolonged dinner and then party of sorts followed, the festivities extending late into the night, vast quantities of alcoholic beverage consumed. The only damper on the Americans' spirits occurred when they rowed in their various boats to where they had left their ship.

It was gone.

The only hint to its whereabouts came weeks later when the British Squadron sailed into Zanzibar with the news they had seen the great ship sailing south in the company of what they thought to be a prize, later described as a pirate vessel with a black circle on her foresail.

There was better news on the Baci. Captain Constance Daphne Fitzwillie was no longer the victim of morning sickness, though her expanding girth took its toll on her humor. She was predictably anxious to achieve English waters and put an end to their life afloat, and while Sir Edmund Roberts commiserated, he had no intention of abbreviating their voyage.

The tension between the two increased until it graduated to full-blown arguments that would have been quite entertaining for the rest of the crew were they not also victims of the captain's wrath. Where she had previously (according to her letters to her sister Agnes) considered herself quite fortunate to be in the company of a shipload of men, she now detested them all.

"One sensitive human being with whom I could converse would be a blessing," she complained without end. The Bacis gave her wide birth, at first trying to win her favor by hauling the naturalist's ridiculous over-stuffed and quite comfortable chair to her quarterdeck.

"Is this some kind of attempt at humor?" she inquired when she first spied it, only slightly mollified when she sank onto it to the immense relief of her lower back and legs.

"I'll have it returned immediately to my quarters, dearest," Sir Edmund suggested in an attempt to calm his wife.

"You sir, will do no such thing!" Constance Daphne replied, all the while pouring her blame for her discomfort into her stare.

"Indeed," the naturalist whispered and slunk away.

They sailed to Cape Town on pins and needles, every noise and every movement of the good Baci an irritation to the captain. At an adjacent uninhabited bay and in great secrecy Sir Edmund had a forge set up on shore where he directed the casting of his submarine's propellors and huge drive shafts. As they cooled he attempted once more to explain their function to the mystified ship's carpenter.

"Of course they are huge, my good man; their mass will be used to store energy. The craft will be towed behind the Baci. The drag on the screw propellors will slowly translate itself into increasing revolutions. Much time will pass; perhaps days, the shafts revolving with increasing speed until they achieve movement coincidental with the forward progress of our ship. So heavy is each shaft that it will act as a flywheel. Those onboard the underwater machine will at that time cast loose from the Baci and be free to explore at their leisure. By my calculations the shafts will probably take at least a day to shed their stored energy!"

Chips was in a total fog. "How would the good gentleman stop such a thing?"

Sir Edmund shook his head in disgust. "Why would we need to do that? It is designed to traverse the sea's depths, not spend its time at a dock. We have Halley's patented diving apparatus for static observation."

The old salt shook his head and walked away muttering, "Heard sim'lar great plans concernin' a kite."

Sir Edmund thought better of killing the carpenter. Had he been on more cordial terms with his very pregnant, miserable wife he would have given more serious thought to the matter.

Once back on the Baci, the diving bell was indeed lowered to the cold water where Sir Edmund and Gnarly Dan spied their forty-fifth sea maiden, she aswim to the delight of Gnarly Dan and Sir Edmund. She appeared to be performing a dance of sorts, replete with the most graceful movements.

Gnarly Dan was enraptured. "Though his honor may not be of the same mind, yer dancin' woman would be the most pleasing thing what a gob could see. 'Tis the base difference 'tween man an' woman: what we is all clumsly an' bangin' inta every day, while yer woman seems ta glide through 'er all." He looked to Sir Edmund for comprehension, and seeing none, concluded with, "It'd be like life's a dance an' we men comes to her all elbows an' knees."

"Hmmph," was the naturalist's contribution.

His notebook reads:

The underwater machine progresses! Our voyage is nearly complete and our fair captain, though beautiful is not fit company. Yesterday she actually knocked me on the head for suggesting she complain a bit less. Sighted another sea maiden.

Maidenus dancus
"Scarlet"
Graceful. Beautiful. Long hair. Lithe body. Languorous chest.
April 28, 1836
Sighted off Cape Town, southern Africa.

SIGHTING FIFTY-FOUR

The worst argument of the entire voyage occurred when Sir Edmund suggested a trip to the southern pole would be a capital idea. "The cooler weather might help your disposition, dearest," was the lighted fuse.

"Having no back ache would help my disposition, you imbecile. Food that would remain in my stomach would help my disposition, you idiot. Fewer kicks and prods from my interior would help my disposition, you unthinking dolt. The company of an intelligent woman would help my disposition, you ham-handed, ignorant boor; or at least the presence of one sensitive man would help my disposition, you foolish nincompoop. Unmoving land beneath my feet would help my disposition. And, if you must know, a feather bed with comforters and soft pillows would definitely help my disposition; though *you* would rather think of submarines and other women. And truth be known, a land with absolutely no men would probably allow my disposition to soar to heights unimagined, sir. If you know of such a place, please direct our helmsman!"

She was still speaking as Sir Edmund backed away to the sanctity of the hold where he could supervise the finishing touches on his underwater machine. Gnarly Dan accompanied him, whispering as they walked, "This'd be a time ta be a bit more quiet, Yer Honor; our Cap is close ta mutiny if ya ain't noticed."

Once below decks both men heard the helmsman alerted and then sails altered as the good H.M.S. Baci turned her course southward and toward the land of ice. Sir Edmund and Gnarly Dan exchanged glances without commenting.

The weather became predictably colder as they sailed toward the ice islands. Sir Edmund's underwater machine was lowered over the side several times, further ballasted and then put through various sea trials, all of which she passed wonderfully. The only problem was the frigidity of the water through which they traveled. Although the entry port on the submarine was designed to allow the magnificently pregnant Captain Constance Daphne Fitzwillie access, men encumbered by layer upon layer of clothing found it nigh impossible to accomplish.

The underwater vessel was at last stowed in the hold to await their return to warmer waters. Ever colder air greeted them as they progressed, the men not at all pleased as they passed ice islands of increasing size, some of them dwarfing the good Baci. Still air, fog and icy mists dogged them with its haunting presence, Captain Constance Daphne stoic but concerned for her child. It was on just such a night, the moon full and setting the fog aglow, the good H.M.S. Baci nearly becalmed in a sea of pack ice, that an event occurred that was debated for some time. At least half of the crew was awake and at the rails or in the rigging on the lookout for ice flows that could threaten their ship. Just past midnight an eery creeking and crackling and moaning wafted across the water, cutting through the dense fog and chilling the men to the bone. Even the captain struggled from rail to rail on her quarterdeck attempting to locate the direction of the sound.

"WHERE AWAY?" Deadeye Dick called again and again from the mainmast trees. The foghorn was pumped, released and then silenced as the crew strained to hear a reply.

Nothing.

Then a shrouded, distant shape appeared off the larboard bow. Bacis ran to their ship's rail to get a better look.

"THAT SHIP!" Deadeye Dick hailed.

"THE H.M.S. BACI REQUESTS YOU IDENTIFY YOURSELF!" Captain Constance Daphne shouted through her speaking horn.

And then like a giant nauseus wave the same thought reached out to everyone: NAUGHTY NAT!

Constance Daphne was the first to give voice to their fear. "RIG THE BOARDING NETS! LARBOARD GUNNERS, CAST LOOSE YOUR CANNONS! PRIME AND RUN THEM OUT! ARMORER, ISSUE SMALL ARMS! MR. JAKES, ON YOUR TOES, THERE!"

Sailors ran to their stations. Boarding axes, pikes, musketoons and pistols were hastily grabbed.

But the other ship was still. Her shape was beginning to materialize and something was dreadfully wrong with her appearance. She was the wrong shape and her masts and rigging positively glowed.

It was Jack Scratch who identified the problem. "SHE'D BE ICE-BOUND MATES! COVERED FROM KEEL TA TRUCKS WITH ICE! AND AIN'T SHE AN OLE SPANISH GALLEON!"

"She'd be a caravel," Gnarly Dan offered to Sir Edmund. "Nigh on the 1500's. What she'd be a ghost ship," he added with quiet respect.

There was not enough wind to maneuver the Baci. Captain Constance Daphne, though she would have liked to go herself, ordered a launch lowered and sent across the ice-choked water.

Sir Edmund, Gnarly Dan, and a rowing crew went, every man looking over his shoulder as the ghost ship became closer and more clearly defined. Her foremast was gone, her mizzen little more than a stump and her remaining rigging, though glistening with ice, was tangled and ruined. She had the old-style high forecastle and sterncastle, they making her look as if from an old picture book.

The launch bumped through the icy water, at least reaching the ship's tall side. The ship was grappled and the naturalist and the old salt scrambled gingerly up her icy planks. They made their way immediately to the captain's cabin, struggling past blocks of ice and frozen bodies as they went. It was as they threw their shoulders against the door that a deep jolt was heard from the bow and a low whistling started in the mess that was her rigging.

Those still in the launch called out, "SIR EDMUND, SIR! THE WIND'S PICKED UP AN' SHE'S UNDER WEIGH; WE'S HAVIN' A DEUCE OF A TIME WITH THE ICE!"

At the same time the fog impossibly thickened, obscuring the distant Baci. Cold thoughts ran through the men on both ships. Captain Constance Daphne had the foghorn sounded and then ordered a cannon shot. "COME BACK, YOU FOOLS," she called, "YOU'LL BE LOST TO US! RETURN TO YOUR SHIP!"

Several large ice flows banged against the Baci. Men with long poles were sent to the bow to try to fend them off. The wind quickened further.

On the ghost ship Gnarly Dan and Sir Edmund worked by the light of their lanterns. They had found and gained what was at least a captain's cabin, "More like yer admiral's" the old salt ascertained correctly. Above them the ship's icy rigging began to work as the wind increased. The Baci's warning shot interrupted Sir Edmund's prying at the drawers of a large desk.

"Lord above, will that woman give us a little peace!" he moaned as more ice floes thumped into their ship and the launch's crew again called out.

"OUR LINE'S GONNA PART, MATES! LEST YA WANTS TA BE LEFT, YA'D BETTER SHAKE A LEG IN THERE!"

Gnarly Dan had no intention of making any of his three wives into widows. He pulled at the naturalist's sleeve. "Squire, things is gettin' a bit ripe. We'd best get back to our Cap an' return when things calms down a bit!"

Sir Edmund grudgingly grabbed what he thought was either a journal or the ship's log and a paperweight and hastened with Gnarly Dan back to the launch. The naturalist was dashed cruelly when the launch swayed from the side of the ghost ship and then slammed into his leg. A secondary cracking could be heard. Sir Edmund fell into the launch as Gnarly Dan reached the outstretched arms of his mates and stepped across the seats to the bow. The grapnel was released and they rowed like heroes back through the fog toward the horn and the successive cannons being fired.

"You, sir, are a fool," the captain greeted Sir Edmund as he was hauled back onto the Baci, his right leg bent awkwardly. So seeing, Constance Daphne dissolved to incredible tears and had her husband carried below.

The wind increased, the fog thickened and then disappeared altogether. Morning found Sir Edmund hobbling about in a haze of pain-relieving opium while the crew scanned the ice-choked waters for a trace of the previous night's apparition.

No ship.

When the naturalist regained his faculties he pored over the manuscript he had recovered, each entry further astounding him. At last he reported to their captain, "It would seen the good ship we boarded was lost in a hurricane of the year 1502, transporting Admiral Antonio de Torres, Governor Bobadilla of Hispaniola and untold riches in the company of 31 other ships, all treasure-laden and presumably also lost. The trinket I grabbed for you in answer to your insistent beckoning—solid gold. The grand table on which it sat—if we can believe the governor's accounting—solid gold. You might find it worth your while to cast about a bit in search of our lost ship, though it is neither here nor there to me. She was the fabulous El Dorado."

Cast about they did, the crew's courage enhanced by the golden dagger Gnarly Dan happened to lift as he hurried Sir Edmund to the launch. But it was to no avail. The vast floating ice and drifting fogs had swallowed up the galleon once more. All they found before they departed the icy chill was a large ice island peopled by a crowd of sea babies and a brace of penguins.

As the good ship Baci drifted by, Gnarly Dan explained, "They's just makin' friends with the locals. Yer sea baby'd be as open an' friendly as a gob could wish. They mum's is proba'ly around somewheres. Hobknobbin' like they does. Any sea masters'd likely be wrestlin' sea lions or some such sport."

Sport indeed, but unobserved.

Sir Edmund Roberts' journal reads:

Phantom ships and frolicking sea babies. Ice birds (penguins?) and ice islands. I believe it is time we steered the good ship Baci to home waters. Our nemesis, the heinous pirate, Naughty Nat is apparently but a memory and my new bride is full with the bloom of life, though a bit piquant for my taste (this dangerous comment confided to the obscurity of my journal).

Sea Babies 18 and 19
Sex indeterminate
Quite healthy. Apparently happy. Beautiful coloration.
Sea babies sighted in the company of local fauna.
May 5, 1836
Queen Mauds Land

SIGHTING FIFTY-FIVE

Grudgingly the good H.M.S. Baci left the ice fields in her sparkling, frosty wake, all dreams of further riches dashed as the temperature fell and cases of frostbitten fingers and toes increased beyond endurance. Young Shackelton vowed he would return, as did the ship's other boys, Larsen and Norenskjold (Crazy Otto), to the amusement of the crew; vows to do this and that common fare on a ship on an extended voyage. Further, the captain had taken to going into false labor from time to time, sending the staid crew into apoplexy, enough water boiled each time sufficient to scald a whale to bare bones.

So, homeward bound at last, St. Helena Island and the Cape Verde Islands (once more) the last planned explorations.

Meanwhile, Sir Edmund Roberts continued a set of dazzlingly successful trials of his underwater machine. (He'd named it Baci Secreto, for it was his 'secret kiss'. In a rare moment of intimacy, Captain Constance Daphne Fitzwillie had smiled knowingly upon learning the submarine's name.) By towing the vessel astern the Baci, the passage of the water through its propellers started them turning ever faster, the obscenely heavy axles on which they were mounted grudging revolving and storing energy. Each time Sir Edmund and Gnarly Dan cast loose from the mother ship (not in reference to its captain), they found their little craft maneuverable and eminently sea worthy. And when they closed the hatches and rotated the vessile's diving planes they slid beneath the ocean effortlessly, fairly taking away old Gnarly Dan's breath.

"Lord above," he exclaimed again and again as they dove beneath the waves, the craft immediately more stable and quiet, the weighty drive shafts revolving silently under their feet (Sir Edmund had anticipated the tremendous torque and so designed counter-rotating shafts and propellers). As Sir Edmund had predicted (hoped) the heavy shafts revolved for hours on end, their engaging a lower gear to the propellers allowing the submarine to slowly explore the ocean's depths, husbanding its time submerged and allowing its occupants glorious undersea vistas.

Sir Edmund also continued his experiments with rockets, increasing their size and enhancing the pryrotechnics of those designed to spread flames on impact.

Equally busy was the cur, Naughty Nat, afloat in the U.S.S Constitution and fairly reveling in the awesome firepower underfoot. "We'll find those cowardly dogs and blast 'em ta' matchwood," he proclaimed to all who would listen. Gunnery drills and sail handling practice had gone on at an unprecedented rate, the pirate crowd beginning to grumble a bit about the new discipline. Unfortunately, Big Boils Ben protested a hint too loudly. "We'd be workin' like lubbers!" he whined.

"An' you'd like a nice rest!" Naughty Nat suggested, leering.

Big Boils Ben's eyes widened as the pirate captain pulled out his musketoon and blasted the complaining rat.

The last bits of the unfortunate pirate were fed to the sharks the following morning.

"Them lousy Brits has dashed us ten times!" (exaggeration was his strong point) Naughty Nat regaled his pirate crew as he tossed pieces of BBB over the side to the frenzied fishes. "We've got men enough, cannon enough, and iron balls enough ta make our point. That blasphemous wet belch of ship, the Baci, has made ever' one a' us look like a girly-man to the world. You'd not be brave pirates no more. You'd not be strong men. Why, you're less than maggots ta' everybody who hears of how them weaklings stuck their thumbs in our face!" Then Naughty Nat once more welded his men to his side. "That pea shell of a ship is loaded to the gunnels with gold. Our gold. Your gold! Now I asks ya mates; does ya want ta get yer gold back?" (Though educated and intelligent, Naughty Nat often reverted to the pirate vernacular when conversing with his scum.) "Arrrgh!" he growled and answered for them. "A' course ya does!" he exclaimed at last, pulling out one of his four pistols and discharging it in the face of Slow Al, a pirate who moments before had tentatively raised his hand to ask a question.

"I asks ya again, mates; are ya ready ta' reclaim our booty?" To which the newly enthused hoard shouted and cheered.

Of a more civilized bent (though only marginally so) the long arms of the United States Navy were casting about to find their lost ship (the U.S.S. Constitiution) and the man who had dispatched their illustrious Captain Smithers. (With time and across great distance, lines were blurred and it was surmised in some influencial circles that perhaps Sir Edmund Roberts was somehow obliquely responsible for the loss of their warship.) Ships were at sea with the intent of bringing the naturalist to justice and locating "Old Ironsides".

Blissfully unaware, the H.M.S. Baci closed on St. Helena Island.

"LAND HO!" came from the masthead.

"Will I never have this baby?" came from the captain's quarters.

"Cast us loose," Sir Edmund Robers directed Gnarly Dan as the ship began to take in her sails. The old salt did so, took a last look at the surrounding waves and the little island and then descended, closing the submarine's hatch over his head.

"She's as tight as—"

"Very good, my man," Sir Edmund interrupted, desperate to arrest the old salt's allusion.

He spun the wheel regulating the little craft's diving planes, kicked the rudder to starboard and breathed deeply as his invention slid beneath the waves, bubbles dancing past the observation ports.

"I shall patent this wonder once we have returned to civilization," he informed Gnarly Dan for the hundredth time.

"Like ta see me English childrens," the old salt countered.

Soon thereafter a sea maiden and sea master were spied in the distant watery haze swimming together. "We shall pursue," the naturalist responded to Gnarly Dan's indication of the two.

Pursue they did, and eventually catch up with.

"Ain't she a beauty," the old salt whispered as he and the naturalist followed the gracefully swimming pair. "He'd be han'some enough; though they'd always be such;" he concluded, "it's like the undersea life agrees with 'em."

And so they chatted until much later when distant thunder interrupted their reverie. "Sounds like our Cap has needs," Gnarly Dan commented, certain Captain Constance Daphne Fitzwillie was in the throes of false labor once more. They gently turned the little undersea craft about, all the while ascending. Once on a par with the rolling waves Sir Edmund opened the forward hatch, breathed in the fresh sea air and looked about for the Baci, her topmasts instantly visible in the distance.

By the time they came alongside the good ship the underwater craft's propellers were almost still. Lines were lowered and secured, the submarine raised and Sir Edmund went to his wife, she once more at ease but still a bit too testy for banter. The naturalist kissed her forehead deftly, patted her swollen tummy and hastily departed, saying over his shoulder, "All will be well, dearest. We are nearly home."

He did not hear her response, although, "Sod you, you insensitive man," was not the parting remark for which he would have hoped.

They stayed but briefly in St. Helena's waters, the naturalist unsuccessful at spying another sea maiden or master, the crew spitting hourly in the placid waters and cursing the departed little dictator's name and memory, all of them in some way affected by his scourge of Europe and threat to the British Isles.

Sir Edmund's journal reads:

Another sea couple sighted and we nearing home! Our good and much-maligned Baci has served us well.

Maidenus enthrallus
"Tina"
Long hair. Beautiful body. Strong swimmer.
Maximus enthallus
Hale. Long hair. Muscular. Strong swimmer.
Sighted off St. Helena's Island
June 12, 1836

230

SIGHTING FIFTY-SIX

The last leg; Cape Verde and then home once more! (It should be noted that the events surrounding the H.M.S. Baci's stay in the waters off Cape Verde, though reported by many, are still clouded in mystery. The following account is an attempt to pull together a remarkably divergent amount of source material.)

The despicable cur, Naughty Nat rounded Cape Horn in the U.S.S. Constitution, his crew as excited as pirates can be to even a score and enhance their net worth. By all accounts the heavy American frigate was handled well, her armament in fighting trim, her hull sound. Twice she hailed passing vessels and learned the Baci had only recently been sighted. At St. Helena a party of Mr. Nat's scoundrels further verified the proximity of their prey.

Sadly, the fair H.M.S. Baci was not only small but well past her prime, and even now carrying comparatively light armament. The Constitution threw nearly 1200 pounds of iron with great violence when she discharged her cannons; the little Baci could spit out about a hundred pounds on a good day, and even then her timbers would protest mightily. Never in her builder's wildest dreams was she conceived as a warship, Captain Constance Daphne Fitzwillie's needs notwithstanding. The good ship was launched as a transport, her hold and timbers laid out with a cargo of coal in mind. To a degree Sir Edmund Roberts dared not imagine, her future depended on his hastily assembled rocketry and at least one more stroke of extraordinarily good luck.

Meanwhile, Captain Constance Daphne was so close to the end of her pregnancy that it was only with tremendous effort that she was able to perform her duties. Though loved and even adored by her crew, and respected and also loved by her recent husband, everyone knew the best thing for her now was rest, comfort and a decent midwife.

So northward through the South Atlantic waters they plowed; man, captain and boy ready to be home again. Even the slaves the Bacis had liberated looked forward to the freedom England offered, if only to ship out again as legitimate seamen.

Cape Verde was raised at last, and the same island (Fogo Island) that had offered up Sir Edmund Robert's first sea maiden sighting so many years ago, signaled the approach of the end of their long voyage. The naturalist's underwater craft had developed several stubborn leaks, her interior now a moldy cave more fit for mushrooms and albino rats than the naturalist and his companion, Gnarly Dan. Jack Scratch had taken it upon himself to remedy the submarine's propensity to ship water from her various seams but his biggest success had been in convincing his cat, Connie, and his dog, Danny, to accompany him into the vessel's damp interior.

Further, Halley's patented diving apparatus had been badly stoved during some recent rough weather. Impatient to deliver his wife to his ancestral home at Edmundshire Castle, Sir Edmund opted for a last seaside exploration of the island in the same vicinity as his very first sighting. Once more a watering party preceded him and once more the naturalist spied a sea maiden on the beach. Numbering that sighting is dependent upon whether she was a twin and therefore sea maiden sighting forty-seven, or possibly the self-same sea maiden the naturalist had observed years previously, making her sighting number one (once more).

Sir Edmund's journal reads:

Oh scientific quandary! I cannot ascertain if the comely sea maiden is a new discovery or merely my first revisited! Regardless, she is (still?) beautiful!

Maidenus mysterus
"Uma Amelia"
Healthy. Long blonde hair. Tidy chest. Green tail coloration.
Sighted on the beach at the Cape Verde Islands.
July 27, 1836

SIGHTING THE U.S.S. CONSTITUTION

Nostalgia gripped the crew of the H.M.S. Baci as they departed the Cape Verde Islands. For all intents their voyage was over, the last leg a formality. There was not a soul aboard the good Baci who dreamed their old nemesis was just over the horizon, fairly drooling to close with the little ship before another sea mile passed.

Captain Constance Daphne Fitzwillie embraced her final month of pregnancy, resigned that she would deliver her baby either on the H.M.S. Baci or in the comfort of her husband's manor. Either way it would be done soon.

Sir Edmund spent days and evenings in his study, organizing his research, touching up his paintings and practicing his speech to the Society for the Diffusion of Useful Knowledge. His companion, Gnarly Dan, had at last become a valet of sorts, pleased to fuss over the naturalist's affairs, ever verbal and in the way. In the old salt's periphery was Jack Scratch, helpful and anxious to please, his life at last pleasant, his gratitude directed to Sir Edmund and the old salt. Danny and Connie seemed similarly moved, they taken to sleeping in the naturalist's sea chest.

Barely three days after sinking Cape Verde, the wind strong and irregular off the good ship's quarter the old Baci's last series of masthead hails began.

"STRANGE SAIL ASTERN! AMERICAN NAVY BY THE CUT A' HER JIB! I'D MAKE HER A HEAVY FRIGATE."

Ominously bothered by memories of Captain Smithers, the naturalist left his work and joined his captain on her quarterdeck. It was as they stood at the stern of the Baci, passing Constance Daphne's glass back and forth, that Gnarly Dan climbed the mizzen ratlines and was the first to see the distant ship shake loose her fore topsail. What the old salt saw he could not command his voice to shout. "There'd be the black ball," was all he said and it was instantly relayed throughout.

There was no mad running around the ship and no shouted orders for boarding nets, or guns to be run out or the deck cleared for action. Sand was cast under foot to absorb the inevitable blood, and buckets were filled with water. Partitions were struck and guns were cast loose, tompions removed from cannon mouths and powder monkeys sent to the bowels of the little ship to begin ferrying charges to the guns, the men moving as in a dream, the distant ship growing in size and menace with each passing hour.

Efficiently and with no fuss Sir Edmund's rocket tube was rigged at the stern of the vessel as large missiles were gingerly placed in a long row near the ship's waist. Captain Constance Daphne Fitzwillie excused herself as she went to her quarters, struggled into her first husband's Royal Navy coat, wanly patted her tummy and returned to be with her men. It was as she exited her room that the strangest of feelings washed over her. At first she thought she was about to enter another bout of false labor, but that wasn't quite it. Then she wondered if it weren't relative to the ominously oversized ship about to do battle with them, and while she recognized the magnitude of that threat, she dismissed it as the source of her sense of foreboding. Sir Edmund had his rockets. He was the master of their fate and had requited himself well time and again. She looked to her tummy. It was lower. Much lower. There was not a chance in the world she would call things normal.

No sooner did she reach her quarterdeck when cheer after cheer echoed across the Baci's decks. At first confused, Captain Constance Daphne looked about to see if perhaps a British Squadron had miraculously appeared. But when she understood her crew was celebrating her presence and saluting her courage, she felt, for the first time in her life, weak in the knees.

Sir Edmund came to her side and suggested she take his chair, allowing it would be some time before the pirate was within range. To her credit she answered, "Thank you, sir," turned to the overstuffed piece of furniture, dragged it noisily to the starboard rail and succeeded in heaving it over the side before anyone knew what she was about. Again, bold cheers rang round the Baci. Backs were slapped and sad smiles exchanged.

"That'd be our Cap," was their quiet hale.

A cold meal was served along with a double ration of rum. It would be some time before the Constitution closed the distance, though just the sight of her mass was the cold hand of death on every sailor's heart.

The only good news of the day was that Plunderer was not in sight. The battle would be ship to ship. One to one. Diminutive size notwithstanding, that fact was heartening. Jack Scratch first secured Connie and Danny deep in the hold but then thought better of it and ferried them in a makeshift bed to the naturalist's trailing invention. He baled briefly, tossing seawater up from the bilge and out through the open hatch at the top of the submarine's observation tower.

Again the wind freshened and veered, threatening to box the compass. Sir Edmund wet his finger and tested repeatedly, concern clearly achieving his countenance. He looked to the long tube through which his rockets would pass and then to the big ship closing on the Baci. "My good captain," he began, "we must have every possible advantage we can conjure, for it appears our Mr. Nat has outdone himself in the ship department. If it weren't so dreadfully dear to our survival there would be humor in it. Our current problem is the wind; we must not allow it to counteract our plans. A wind athwartships (across our side) is the worst possible scenario. With such a wind the likelihood of our rockets finding their mark is gravely diminished. Is it possible to position the old girl so we are moving with the wind either in our faces or at our backs?"

Captain Constance Daphne idly caressed her tummy as she called the master and first mate to her quarterdeck. Sir Edmund expressed his concerns. Before they answered the captain ordered a course correction that put the wind to the good ship's stern, allowing her to sail full and bye, but setting them on a nearly perpendicular course relative to the Constitution.

The huge frigate altered course also, its speed nearly unaffected.

"She'll be within range, soon enough, Captain;" the master said, rubbing his chin as he spoke, "an' then she'll repeatedly veer an' present her broadsides; she can afford the lost time 'cause she could outsail us in a bottle. We can't close with her or allow her to range alongside or we'll be pounded ta' matchwood. I'm sure ya' all knows the Baci's stern is her weakest point, Sir Edmund's rockets or no."

Things did not look promising.

At that moment the Constitution fired one of her long bow chasers, the puff of smoke visible, followed by a low boom and then a hole appearing in the Baci's spanker, main course and fore course.

Sir Edmund whistled in appreciation. "They are pointing well already," he mused and again studied his rocket tube. "Perhaps it is time to fire a slavo of our own."

"As you wish," Constance Daphne answered and then recoiled as if struck. "Not now, if you please," she commanded her tummy. "Not now." She looked about to see if anyone had noticed her condition. The crew of the good Baci was looking to the Constitution.

"LOAD ROCKET NUMBER ONE," Sir Edmund ordered.

The Bacis were quiet as Sir Edmund observed his first rocket loaded into the long tube. "LOADED, SIR!" came quickly. The naturalist looked to the Constitution which at that moment fired both her bow chasers. This time rigging suffered and the mizzentop yard was sent to splinters.

"Lord above," Gnarly Dan muttered from his carronade.

Sir Edmund called to the helmsman, "TWO POINTS TO LARBOARD, IF YOU PLEASE, AND HOLD THAT COURSE UNTIL THE ROCKET IS AWAY, SIR."

The little ship answered her helm and presented her stern full to the Constitution.

Sir Edmund tested the wind a last time, adjusted the angle of the firing tube and then lit the rocket's thick fuse. "ROCKET'S AWAY!" he called and stepped gingerly away from the hissing fuse. With a whoosh it ignited and roared and rumbled the length of the copper tube and arched into the air.

"LOAD ROCKET NUMBER TWO!"

Gnarly Dan saw the cat's paws to larboard as what started as a windy bluster built into a strong sidewind; catching the rocket mid-flight, sending it veering to starboard, wildly missing the frigate.

Sir Edmund narrowed his eyes and watched the rocket explode far from its target. The big ship fired another round from its bow chasers and then veered off from its pursuit of the Baci. Both of her last shots skipped ducks and drakes bracketing the Baci.

The little ship's sailors cheered madly, mistaking the Constitution's maneuver for an attempt to break off action.

"He is on to us," Sir Edmund informed his captain. "The rascal will now close at an oblique, denying us clear shots with our rockets. He is a remarkably quick learner, though still a wretched cur, our Naughty Nat. Our best option is to wait until he is closer-still to minimize the action of the cross wind. We must weather his iron if we are to survive."

While Sir Edmund's handsome uniform was back in the Japan Isles with Toshiro, he did take the opportunity to place that proud warrior's samurai helmet on his head, it's angry golden dragon astride the dome and ready to do battle. The naturalist's visage was fierce and beautiful all at once.

At that moment the big frigate fell off presenting a broadside. Sir Edmund stood tall and walked with a show of confidence to the rail facing the impending thunder. He placed his hands on his hips in defiance and said clearly in mock piety, "For what we are about to receive, we thank you."

The Bacis huddled behind cannons and bulwarks and exchanged giddy smiles. There lived no naturalist as brave as their own.

The Constitution's side disappeared in rolling smoke. Thunder raced across the open sea. A firestorm of iron cursed the little ship. A least ten of the frigate's heavy iron balls found the Baci. Men screamed, splinters flew and as quickly, the foretop went by the board. Baci's raced up the ratlines with hatchets and knives and cut until the topmast fell free.

The Constitution swung about and resumed her pursuit.

"Another rocket, sir?" Captain Constance Daphne called out to the naturalist, attempting to sound off-hand. She did not yet wish to admit how tenuous their position really was.

Sir Edmund tested the blustery wind and looked anxiously to the big frigate. He really believed it was too soon but he was feeling the edge of desperation.

"Perhaps," he answered and ordered the helmsman to swing the Baci's stern to the Constitution. In response the huge ship veered also, assuming a course that further increased the effect of the crosswind.

Sir Edmund made another correction and stepped to his missile. He adjusted the lines and lowered the top of the launching tube a trifle. He drew on his cigar, checked the Constitution and touched the fuse off. He did not step away as quickly or as far. Again, a magnificent whoosh and clatter as the copper fins banged through the length of copper pipe. The cross wind effected the rocket at once, but the naturalist had calculated as much. Slowly the missile arced through the air in a curve whose terminus, if unaffected, looked to be the big frigate. A few Bacis cheered in anticipation. And then the wind died briefly, the rocket's flight straightened, and then the wind picked up again. It would be another bad miss.

The Bacis groaned as one.

The Constitution, closer still, presented her side again for a broadside.

"COME ABOUT SMARTLY, MR. JAKE!" Constance Daphne called out to crew and helmsman in an attempt to present a smaller target. "LIVEY THERE!" Her last word was accented by the flame-laced cloud of smoke appearing along the side of the Constitution. The Baci spun on her heels, her profile diminished as a serving of 24 pound cannonballs smashed into the little ship's frail timbers.

A cannon was struck and upended. Half of a royal blew away. Knots and tangles of rigging fell to the deck, fouling lines and trapping gunners. Heavy blocks swung wildly. In a place where two balls had struck simultaneously a huge gap appeared in the Baci's bulwark.

Again Captain Constance Daphne winced visibly. Sir Edmund feared she had been hit and was strangely relieved when she caressed her swollen tummy with an open hand. "NOT NOW!" she commanded her smallest charge. Her mind was beginning to race back and forth between what her body was screaming out to her, and the big pirate vessel closing on them and threatening the survival of ship and crew.

"Perhaps we should give our brave crew something to occupy themselves," Sir Edmund suggested. "A broadside, perhaps?" Men were falling to the Constitution's barrages; it wouldn't do for them to have to wait for their own sad fate.

"Capital idea," the captain allowed. "MR. JAKE, PRESENT THE GOOD SHIP FOR A STARBOARD BROADSIDE, IF YOU WILL!" She wished desperately to sit down. No, she wished desperately to lower herself to the deck, to lie down, to draw her legs to her chest, impossible as that sounded, to close out all of the noise and smoke and confusion and concentrate on her own private battle. She felt a letdown of impossibly warm water. Her mouth dropped open. "God in heaven," she whispered.

Bacis raced from places of cover smiling grimly. Cannons were loosed from their moorings and aimed. All down the ship's side, gun captains gave orders. "Steady, there!" "Elevate!" "Prime and prepare to fire," rippled from gun to gun.

Coincidentally the Constitution was of the same mind. The Baci loosed her broadside first and it was followed by the Constitution's. Before the smoke cleared from the Baci's guns the big frigate's iron ripped into the ship.

Fretting Willie called down from the main top with disheartening clarity, "OUR SHOTS IS BOUNCIN' OFF 'ER SIDES LIKE BISCUITS!"

"That ain't good," Old Bubo said to the captain of the gun beside him, failing to notice the grave wound his friend had suffered.

"Another rocket, if you please, Sir Edmund," the captain then directed her husband, forcing the fight back to the front of her mind. "It cannot go on like this for long," she continued as both Baci and Constitution released another broadside. Constance Daphne loved the good little ship as she loved its crew, but they were becoming worlds away from her. Everyone seemed to be moving in slow motion. It was deathly silent. White pain struck the captain, unannounced this time. Iron balls blew by like scissors and thumbscrews, huge rents appearing in sails, sides and the men of the frail Baci. It did not appear the big frigate had so much as a line cut while the H.M.S. Baci had already taken the beating of her life with the fight just beginning.

"PRESENT OUR STERN, MR. JAKE!" Sir Edmund shouted to the helmsman, he nursing a sorely mutilated hand while attempting to throw his weight into the stiff wheel.

"RUDDER'S FOULED!" Runny Jake called in response. Men raced to the Baci's stern and leaned over to access the damage. There below them the naturalist's submarine had gained on the Baci. The rigging and spars and sails over the sides had slowed the Baci to the degree the underwater craft had outpaced it and nosed in beside the exposed rudder. Jack Scratch was in the submarine's open hatch and pushing against the Baci with an oar in an attempt to free the little craft. Levering the submarine's bow free at last he disappeared inside, kicked its rudder to larboard and allowed the submarine to slide from its wedged position.

'Bout time ta visit the sea bottom, he promised himself as he held his pets, Connie and Danny, to his chest, all the while trying to cover their ears to the mayhem above them.

"SHE'S FREE!" Runny Jake called to Sir Edmund as he muscled the wheel over and the Baci began her turn. Another broadside from the Constitution and he disappeared, leaving a nearly shattered wheel. MacMurphy stumbled back and took his friend's place.

The stern swung to the Constitution and Sir Edmund fiddled and fussed and finally ignited another missile. "ROCKET THREE IS ALIGHT!" he shouted and moved barely a foot from the base of the long copper tube. The rocket ignited, its exhaust roaring as it began its journey. It left the tube and clipped an errant tangle of rigging the naturalist had not noticed. The rocket cartweeled madly and then plunged into the ocean between the Baci and the Constitution.

"LOAD ROCKET NUMBER FOUR!"

"CLEAR THAT MESS FROM THE MIZZEN!" Captain Fitzwillie shouted and gripped her stomach, her knees nearly failing.

The Constitution was close enough that the pirates were now firing from her tops, the small arms fire enfilading the Baci's ruined deck. Chips and splinters flew up from around Captain Constance Daphne's feet. She felt herself sway with dizziness. Another personal attack was building like a horrible wave. *The Baci. The Baci. The Baci.* She chanted to herself both to take her mind from what was happening and at the same time force the fate of her ship back into her thoughts.

"WE HAVE HOW MANY ROCKETS?" she shouted desperately to her husband who instantly calculated and called back, "SIX MORE, CAPTAIN." His voice was distant. Pain built and wracked her body. She felt herself falling to the deck—lowering herself to sit on the deck—swooning to the deck—she didn't know which it had been. She didn't care. She was on the deck. The worst pain she had ever known gripped her; took her breath away and silently shook her whole body like a cloth doll.

No sooner did Sir Edmund answer his captain that the Baci loosed a weak broadside just prior to the frigate's thundering forth again. With it the rocket launching tube was reduced to twisted copper. The mizzenmast suffered so badly it appeared ready to snap barely ten feet above the quarterdeck. Flames came cascading down as the course that had been smoldering was finally alight and burning fiercely, half of its length draped over the rail and into the water below, the other half on the deck. Bacis raced to it with buckets of water. Flames reached the fourth rocket esconced in the tormented launcher. The missile ignited in a flurry of sparks and spun out of the tube and raced crazily about the deck. Hogshead Smith and Itchy Ben ran forward and attempted to smother the rocket's blast with armloads of wet sail. The rocket quickly incinerated the mound and then roared away and out number four gunport. Burned skin covered Itchy Ben's right arm. Most of Smith's pants were scorched away. No one had heard their captain's screams. The worst came with the firing of the Baci's cannons, the others mixing with shatterting wood and the resultant mayhem of the Constitution's broadside.

Sir Edmund looked to Constance Daphne. At first he did not see her for she was lying on the deck, her legs to her chest. He feared she was gone, struck by an unseen ball or splinter. He ran to her side and bent to her. To his initial relief she grabbed his ears and pulled his face to her.

"IT WILL NOT WAIT! IT WILL NOT WAIT!" she shouted again and again as she shook his head. Another contraction was building. She cursed it to go away. She cursed her husband to go away. She cursed the wounded little Baci, Naughty Nat, every pirate that who had ever sailed the seven seas, and then as she felt she would burst from agony she cursed every man who ever lived. And then the pain began to subside again.

Flames licked up the tarred rigging.

Sir Edmund attempted to lift his wife. Gnarly Dan was at their side. Together they carried her to the jolly boat and lowered her carefully into it. She was mercifully between contractions, though her head still swam from the memory of the last pain and the anticipaion of its inevitable return.

"GET HER OVER THE SIDE," the naturalist ordered and ran to the Baci's broken wheel. Another helmsman was down. What good sails the Baci still wore luffed in the spastic breeze.

The U.S.S. Constitution was turning to the Baci. She would be on them soon. Borders lined her rails, cutlasses and pikes and pistols brandished as they laughed and pointed and wet their lips. Hundreds of swarming pirates choked the ship's upper deck, confident they would have their revenge soon. As the frigate approached it wailed away with her bow chasers, further punishing the mortally wounded Baci.

The flames spread up the mizzen rigging into the top and then across to the tarred rigging and down. Burning canvas dripped onto the deck far below and still the Bacis manned those guns still serviceable. The good ship no longer answered her helm and as a result she was able to bring fewer guns to bear on the frigate that appeared to be preparing to ram them.

"DO WE STRIKE OUR COLORS?" Sir Edmund shouted to his men with quiet finality. "YOU HAVE FOUGHT LIKE CHAMPIONS; THERE WOULD BE NO SHAME!"

"WE'LL NOT STRIKE WHILE WE STILL HAS BREATH!" Hans Larsen answered for the crew.

"NAIL 'EM TO THE TRUCK!" Einbear yelled above the din to Slushy George who was firing down into the advancing Constitution, every shot finding a home on the frigate's crowded deck.

Sir Edmund saw Naughty Nat once more on the rail, his fists raised, his head thrown back in demented laughter. "MY RIFLE!" Sir Edmund shouted in the hopes it would miraculously appear.

The naturalist spied a diminutive figure high in the frigate's tops sporting a fore and aft hat and pointing madly and howling like a wolf.

Gnarly Dan nudged Sir Edmund roughly. "WHAT, IT'D BE HIS HONOR'S RIFLE," he allowed. "YA WAS PLANNIN' TA USE IT; WAS YA NOT?" The old salt smiled and winked wanly.

The Constitution began to turn for another broadside.

Sir Edmund nodded soberly to his friend, shouldered his weapon, drew a bead on Naughty Nat, and then said to Gnarly Dan from the corner of his mouth, "My good man, it has been a pleasure knowing you. You are a man among men."

One of the ship's boys bolted up from the Baci's companionway shouting, "THE FIRE'S BELOW DECKS AN' ALMOST TA THE POWDER; SHE'LL BLOW ANY MINUTE! JUMP MEN! JUMP FOR ALL YOU'RE WORTH! THE OLE GIRL'S HEADIN' TA' HELL!"

From this point on, everything is a bit confusing and incredibly sad. The British West African Squadron appeared on the scene. The American frigate Constellation also entered the mix. And the good, the fair little Baci exploded with a roar remembered by every gob and pirate within ten miles. Pieces of her splashed into the surrounding water, Bacis coming down like spring rain and some thrashing about until rescued.

Naughty Nat and the pirates were totally taken by surprise when one minute they were celebrating the Baci's demise, and the next they were surrounded by superior warships. They surrendered easily, daring not the first shot at either the Royal Navy or United States Navy; for they were still at base, despicable cowards.

Most records allow that Naughty Nat was hanged the following year. One tabloid speaks of two attempts to hang the cur, the rope breaking each time and a final transportation to the penal colony at Botany Bay.

Months later some contemporary American newspapers alluded to a United States Senator taking a Natalie Something-or-Other as his wife; she being a beautiful woman with the mystifying penchant for appearing in two places at once. The original Captain Fitzwillie by all accounts spent his last years in Bedlam.

The United States Navy struck all mention of the episode involving their flagship from its official records. The Royal Navy, at the insistence of Lord Frothingslosh, did the same regarding the H.M.S. Baci. She never existed. The H.M.S. Bounty was burned by the mutineers in Pitcairn Bay, years and years earlier.

The treasure aboard the Baci has never been recovered. The golden statue, the samurai armor, the doubloons, the pieces of eight, the silver, the bars of gold, the jewels; all lost. The Plunderer was never heard of again. The remainder of Naughty Nat's hoard could well be buried on Tortola, somewhere near Cane Garden Bay. Or he may have escaped from Botany Bay and spent it all.

Thus ended the forgotten voyage of the good, the fine, the wonderful little ship, H.M.S. Baci. Built as a collier she ended her days fighting bravely, crewed by some of the bravest sailors to ply the seven seas. Oh, that she could have reached England once more! It would have been a just reward for her and the men who gave so much of themselves in the years previous. Her final fight under the captaincy of Constance Daphne Fitzwillie was above criticism. She brought to the little ship in its last hours a brave heart indeed. Sir Edmund Roberts and Gnarly Dan also requited themselves well, their thoughts and actions always toward others and their fair ship.

If there were a marker (and there is not) to immortalize their bravery, it would say simply, "They were good souls, and they fought like heroes."

SIGHTING FIFTY-SEVEN

Once free of the Baci's rudderpost Jack Scratch had kept Sir Edmund's Secreto circling the Baci's lee side, using that bulk to shield him from the Constitution's ire. When Constance Daphne's boat was lowered he rendezvoused with it, and helped wrestle the captain through the hatch and into the submarine's dark interior. "Rest easy, Cap," he whispered as she lay doubled on the floor.

They were at the far side of their circuit when the Baci's powder magazine blew, spars and timbers narrowly missing the vessel. The explosion rocked the little submarine, throwing Jack Scratch to the floor.

Gnarly Dan and Sir Edmund tumbled quite handsomely through the air, the naturalist looking like an accomplished circus performer, the old salt Gnarly Dan windmilling nicely as he completed his arc. Both splashed into the salty brine near the undersea craft, Sir Edmund alert and swimming handily to its side, Gnarly Dan stunned but bobbing until retrieved.

Naturalist and old salt were greeted by their captain, she drenched in sweat, her hair matted and her face beginning to contort in advance of another contraction. In the shadowy depths of her mind she was relieved to see them. She attempted to say something of that nature. "I MIGHT HAVE KNOWN YOU TWO IMBECILES WOULD COME TO WATCH ME SUFFER!"

Sir Edmund was dashed. The contraction built and she added, pointing at him, "IT'S ALL YOUR FAULT!" Gnarly Dan leaned and whispered to his friend, "Don't pay her no mind, Squire, they does that just afore the little 'un ships out. She'll be all nice soon enough." The old salt began to move into position to do what he knew was left to him.

Constance Daphne grabbed Sir Edmund's arm and pulled him to her. Her grip was like iron. For the first time the naturalist saw pleading in her eyes. She was desperate for him to take the pain away, to deliver her mercifully from her unbelievable, unrelenting agony.

There was no boiled water. There was no midwife. Gnarly Dan's childhood on a farm and his experiences with his many wives and more children was all they had. And his sharp knife. The baby was born in spite of it all, and Captain Constance Daphne Fitzwillie stayed alert and healthy through the duration, though an unitiated observer such as her husband would say she knocked on death's door more than once.

"I say," Sir Edmund noted with relief once the child was in his wife's arms, comforted and quiet at last, "she would be rather loud, wouldn't you say?"

Gnarly Dan sat back against the submarine's wall and smiled to himself as he wiped his hands on his 'kerchief. "Never know'd a nipper ta be quiet fer long."

Jack Scratch hunched over the little ship's controls and headed the vessel toward the mainland of Africa, the propellers spinning well for nearly a day and a half. They surfaced, rigged a sail and reached the mainland, Constance Daphne's baby content with the ship's rocking, the captain's subsequent letter to her sister Agnes treating neither the childbirth nor her husband's vessel kindly.

Sir Edmund's notebooks (Jack Scratch had carried his cat and dog out in Sir Edmund's sea chest) have as a last entry some details concerning their week at sea. He mentions the baby fondly. *Handsome child, that! Female. Average height. Average weight. Healthy.* His wife. *She was brave throughout!* And Gnarly Dan, *Capital fellow, though by the second day I wished he were outside of my underwater craft!*

The last dialogue we can piece together was after the thick drive shafts had shed their momentum, the propellers at last still. The submarine became very quiet.

They were lamenting the brave Bacis, recounting stories and events when Gnarly Dan opined that it was a pity they had lost all of the treasure when the Baci went down. Constance Daphne half-heartedly agreed, her baby held to her chest, she all the while observing Sir Edmund lifting a section of flooring over the massive propeller shafts. He bent to one of them, produced a penknife and scraped a small section, carefully gathering the resultant shavings and handing them to his wife. Even in the vessel's gloom she saw them glisten.

"We had no other metal from which to cast our machinery, dearest. Our good crew kept my secret well. The propellers are golden also. I would guess 900 pounds total." He looked to Gnarly Dan. "You could have that tavern if you wish, sir. Support all of your wives; even have another child or two. Or wife."

Gnarly Dan smiled.

Jack Scratch cleared his throat noisily.

Sir Edmund chuckled quietly before he spoke. "A kennel, perhaps? Kittens and puppies?"

It has proved impossible to ascertain how many of the stout Bacis survived, as some were no doubt pressed into the American Navy, others into English ships. History seems to little note the common gob; his lot being to simply serve and and keep his head low.

Not a soul believed Sir Edmund's account of the voyage. There was by the time of his paper's publication no record of the H.M.S. Baci extant and apparently none of the crew had yet to find its way back to England. And so it was forgotten.

The naturalist settled into obscurity with his little family alternating its time between Edmundshire Castle and his estate, Edmundhurst. The castle was where they stopped first, and it was somewhere between what Constance Daphne hoped for and what she feared. Fully two-thirds of it was in ruins; crenels and odd stones tumbled from some of the walls, the moat stagnant and glazed with green. Leaking windows, collapsed roofs, cold drafty rooms with huge ineffectual fireplaces and long winding stone staircases did nothing for a woman with newly stoked maternal and nesting instincts. It was, of course, heaven to Sir Edmund for it had ancestral portraits and suits of armor in every dark corner, flagstone floors that allowed massive draught horses to drag in yule-sized logs, and centuries of dust and dirt, soot and grime that made thoughts of housekeeping a bad joke. But the grounds were romantic and magnificent all at once. They remained at the castle for several months and then packed up and headed farther inland to Edmundhurst.

Constance Daphne had no positive expectations after her stay at the castle and so what she found was not only a surprise, but also one of the finest wedding presents of which a bride could dream. What the Edmundshire Castle possessed in male-dominated mass and sturdiness, the manor had in style, elegance and charm. A huge Jacobean house, its gardens were a delight, the long, yew-lined entry stately beyond words, and the manor itself appointed to a fare-thee-well. Handsomely decorated and maintained by a staff that would have rivaled the Bacis in number, Constance Daphne could not have imagined such a home for Sir Edmund. The furniture was comfortable, classic and plentiful; the kitchen staff determined to make every meal a wonderful event, and the domestic army trained and attentive. Both formal and country gardens were everywhere, supplying fresh flowers that fairly cascaded from the tables of every room. The only wing that hinted of the naturalist was his library; the walls alternating with ceiling-high leaded windows and similarly soaring bookshelves. Leather volumes choked the shelves, and desk after desk was askew with Sir Edmund's writings, drawings or experiments. And most implausibly, the master bedroom was a dream; a huge, splendid, beautiful, floating escape from the world. From its windows Constance Daphne could look across the fields to the far horizon, much as she had done from her quarters in the little Baci.

When she asked her husband how he had accomplished such success in maintaining Edmundhurst he responded, "Dearest, as you know, these are the homes of my family. I have always left it to my staff to keep them as my parents would. More particularly; in the case of the manor, as Mother kept it; and relative to Edmundshire Castle, why, of course, as Father had done."

Upon reflection, Constance Daphne saw that it made perfect sense.

Gnarly Dan was in residence also, giving up the sea and attending his naturalist friend; his English family tucked in with him in a tidy cottage behind the manor. Jack Scratch saw to Sir Edmund's hounds and raised a few of his own, happily keeping the stables full of mewing kittens. He was the Pied Piper of pets; jumping and nipping fuzzy things following him everywhere he went.

A year did not pass that a former Baci failed to turn up, hat in hand, eyes lowered, and almost to the number they ended up staying; either working the outlying farms, tending the naturalist's various herds, or finding employment in the manor or the castle.

The Roberts family had five additional children, their total being one girl and five boys. Constance Daphne lived to a happy old age but she did predecease the naturalist.

There is one extraordinarily oblique reference to a subsequent voyage, and while some of the finest (and costliest) research organizations in England have yet to confirm such a thing, the possibility remains tantalizing.

The end.

Sir Edmund Roberts: The Early Years

Before HMS Baci set sail on its voyage to the far corners of the globe in search of sea maidens; and before Captain Constance Daphne Fitzwille subsequently entered Sir Edmund's life and commanded his heart; and absolutely years and years before old Gnarly Dan filled the quirky naturalist's mind with obscurata and homey advice, Sir Edmund Roberts traveled the world in search of faeries. In the company of the mysterious Lady S., he trekked deep onto the jungles of darkest Africa and the rain forests of the lower Americas. Together they braved vast deserts and broad savannahs, always studying, and ever seeking to increase their knowledge and catalogue their findings. At Mayan ruins and Egyptian burial chambers they sighted the elusive creatures, learning their habits (they revel in their lack of clothing) and deducing their histories (faeries invented ballet).

A collection of novelettes will soon be available (SIR EDMUND ROBERTS: THE EARLY YEARS; SIR EDMUND ROBERTS IN AFRICA; SIR EDMUND ROBERTS IN INDIA; etc.) documenting their adventures.

What follows are representative excerpts:

The Faerie Diaries

It was late in 1801 that the beautiful and mysterious "Lady S." came to her calling as a faerie aficionado. In the company of her paramour, Sir Edmund Roberts, the gentleman naturalist and cantankerous investigator of obscurata, she haunted the bogs, moors, forests and gardens of the British Isles in her search for the last of the elusive creatures. With time and recorded success the pair extended their quest to the continent and then the world at large. The candid travel diaries of the mysterious "Lady S." and the journals of Sir Edmund Roberts document nearly a decade of adventure and discovery. Both literary entities survived, complete with sketches, commentaries and watercolor illustrations. Sadly, the identity of "Lady S" did not. Blissful obscurity found and embraced her while Sir Edmund Roberts gained notoriety and then a level of derision that dogged him through his life.

This monogram presents the watercolor illustrations and relevant commentary of either the mysterious "Lady S." or Sir Edmund Roberts. Lady S. painted the first of the series, "Faerie Number One." Her diary entry follows:

December 11, 1801

Beautiful day in the country. Unseasonably warm.

I came upon this lovely creature while hiding from the mischievous Sir Edmund. A wren of sorts had just passed my cover when one of her flight feathers fell gently to the clearing to my left. No sooner did it light when I heard a faint stirring and saw a delightful little creature dash to it, lift the feather triumphantly and then haul it off in the direction from which she had appeared. After much searching I found a cunning little forest bed made of feathers and topped with down. While it did not appear to be a part of her permanent home it was obviously a retreat she used often. She was in the process of integrating her new find into the whole when Sir Edmund bumbled into our proximity and frightened the poor dear away. While I only observed her briefly, I did note that when walking she did so carefully and on her toes and her flight was much like that of the hummingbird; swift and erratic and accompanied by a cheerful humming sound. I am unsure, but believe she may have been singing to herself the entire time, even as she flew off.

Sir Edmund admires my watercolor picture but I believe he is unconvinced of her existence.

S.

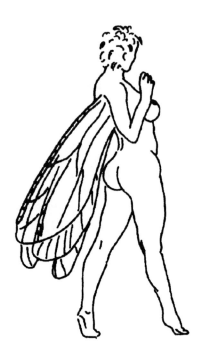

THE FAERIE NOTEBOOKS

Sir Edmund Roberts, Faerie aficionado and explorer, went in the company of the mysterious Lady S. to the coast of California, there disembarking and striking inland. It was a rather small party; bearers, servants and guides kept to a minimum. They trekked into the foothills, following streambeds, ever watchful for signs of faeries.

"Understand, Lady S.," Sir Edmund instructed, "there exists the possibility there are no native species of faeries hereabouts or if present they are as elusive as the red-skinned natives of whom we have heard but not seen." His remark was punctuated by an arrow pinning his hat to a nearby tree. "Thunder and damnation, we are under attack!" he exclaimed and pushed his companion to the ground. But no further hostilities were forthcoming. The two had faced wild animals and warring tribes previously and so, though surprised, neither was uncomfortable remaining in danger's presence.

"May I suggest, Sir," Lady S. later instructed, "it is entirely unnecessary to physically maul me when you wish for me to reduce my exposure. A word such as 'duck!' would be more than adequate. And dear friend," she continued, "it is considered bad form to grab a woman's bosoms as you push her to the ground."

"Hrumph!" was the best Sir Edmund could manage as a response.

They made camp on a clearing above the stream bed, a handful of large canvas tents, several trestle tables, a fire or two, the British flag on a makeshift pole and two incredibly comfortable chairs being their version of 'roughing it'. The following morning dawned early and chilled, Lady S.

remaining in her cot with various blankets pulled to her nose while Sir Edmund took his tea and wandered quietly down to the creek. Something immediately caught his eye, it being what he thought was a malachite butterfly alighted on a rock near the flowing water. But as the naturalist quietly shifted his position he realized it was indeed a faerie on her knees and apparently rather cold. Tiny goose bumps covered her exposed skin, her chest similarly affected.

"Siproeta Stelenes Bipagiata!"! he exclaimed mentally, "and alluringly perky; the truth be known!"

He was, unfortunately, a bit overbearing and smug when he relayed the news to his frowsy companion, she still abed. "'The early bird', and all that!" he taunted. "One cannot expect high adventure and great discoveries whilst asleep, my dear."

"I do not recall inviting you to my boudoir, sir," was her clipped response. "Surely your fabrication can wait until a more civilized hour. Good day," she concluded and rolled to the side, covering her head. And while she steadfastly refused to accept her companion's story, she did believe him. "Men are better kept off balance," she wrote in her diary. Later, Lady S. spied and retrieved huge nuggets of glistening gold from the same stream. Sadly, Indians subsequently attacked and drove the party out of the hills.

Sir Edmund's notebook reads:

Foolish woman; gold indeed! I sighted faerie nine at Sutter's Creek.
Faerie malachitis
Body of homo sapien sapien
Wings of Siproeta Stelenes Bipagiata
Faerie Nine

CPSIA information can be obtained at www.ICGtesting.com
Printed in the USA
LVOW12s1200191214

419399LV00002B/495/P